True Identity

....

Gisèle Bourgeois

True Identity
Copyright © 2018 by Gisèle Bourgeois

All rights reserved. No part of this publication may be reproduced, distributed, or transmitted in any form or by any means, including photocopying, recording, or other electronic or mechanical methods, without the prior written permission of the author, except in the case of brief quotations embodied in critical reviews and certain other non-commercial uses permitted by copyright law.

tellwell

Tellwell Talent
www.tellwell.ca

ISBN
978-1-77370-783-9 (Hardcover)
978-1-77370-782-2 (Paperback)
978-1-77370-781-5 (eBook)

For Victor

Part One

Who Is God?

Adrienne Blanchard was expected on January 2 but came into the world on December 30, 1962. It was an induced birth because her father, who was a friend and colleague of his wife's obstetrician, so wished. There were two advantages: first and most immediate was to avoid spending New Year's Eve in the hospital, and the second was so that his child would not lose a year of school. He was right to do this. Children born in December are always the slowest in the class, but Adrienne was more than ready to start school at five. By then, she could read in both official languages. French was her mother tongue, and she learned English by watching the follow-the-bouncing-ball cartoons, and turning pages of sheet music for her mother at the piano. Charlotte, Adrienne's mother, had a particular fondness for tropical tunes. She sang in a heavy Québécois accent, which she was sure she didn't have, imitating a Barbadian accent in English. An accent within an accent within an accent.

> *Will your lady friend leave the nest*
>
> *(turn page)*
>
> *again. That is very bad. Makes me feel so sad.*

After that, Dick, Jane, and Spot were easy. She grew up in the small, bilingual city of Moncton in Atlantic Canada in the province of New Brunswick. Speaking both languages was quite natural to her and to most of the francophone children in her neighborhood.

All the Blanchards were readers. Her father, Doctor Philippe Blanchard, was a member of the Book of the Month club, and received monthly news magazines and the city newspapers daily. Her grandfather, René Desmeules, owned a bookstore in Québec City. He sent his daughter's children a box of books by train three times a year. Adrienne, her brother René, and her sister Claude received their *Martines, Tintins, Spirous,* and *Sylvies* with great enthusiasm. They crowded around their mother as she ceremoniously opened the package. Being from a family of booksellers, Charlotte Desmeules always referred to a book by its author, editor, or collection. Never by its title.

"*Voyons ça...Trois Bibliothèques Roses, six Marabout Mademoiselles, le nouveau Tintin, et un beau Kessel!*"[1]

New authors were referred to slightly disparagingly as *"une nouveauté"*[2] until they sold a good deal of copies. There were no French language bookstores in Moncton although you could borrow books in French from the small public library in the old fire station on St. George Street. The French section was small and poorly stocked. The balance of the Anglo–Franco ratio inevitably falling heavily on the English side in all things. Bilingualism, paradoxically, was a one-sided phenomenon.

Moncton was an industrial town, its economy almost entirely dependent on the Canadian National Railway shops. They called it the hub of the Maritime provinces but it was a cultural desert for the French; for the English, barely less so.

This did not mean it was an unhappy or particularly boring place. There were festivals and parades, a morning and evening newspaper in both languages, baseball teams, political associations, a cathedral, a synagogue, pool halls, and even a masonic lodge. Adrienne was taught that she was lucky to be Canadian, lucky to be bilingual, and lucky to live in such a vital community. The Blanchards were members of several clubs and associations, and were avid curlers. They had a summer cottage at Crane Road in Shediac, a seaside community thirty miles from the city, which was paradise to them all. They lived in the security and prosperity of post–World War II Canada. This was a new and improved world. It was just a matter of time, her father told her, before all the countries in the world would be like Canada. It was no surprise that Adrienne grew up to be idealistic, optimistic, and Canadian to the bone.

---

1 Let's see. Three Bibliothèques Roses, six Marabout Mademoiselles, the new Tintin and a wonderful Kessel.

2 A new release.

True Identity

It followed then that Adrienne was upset when a child at school told her she wasn't really Acadian, that she was not pure. Her mother was from Québec, and wasn't her grandmother an anglophone? The Acadians were descendants of the French who had settled what is now Nova Scotia in the early seventeenth century.

Philippe chuckled to make Adrienne feel better, yet he didn't like what he had heard. The Acadians were an economically and socially disadvantaged minority. They were not in a position for internal division and the comparison of pedigrees.

"That's not true. Let me show you something," he said.

He pulled an old book bound in black leather from the bookcase, *History of the Acadians,*[3] and sat down in his favourite chair.

Each Acadian surname was traced to its original settler. There was a bookmark at "Blanchard, Louis." Little five-year-old Adrienne sat on the chair's armrest and looked over her father's shoulder as he explained the family tree. Her grandfather's name was at the bottom of the page. Below it, handwritten in faded ink, was her Aunt Jeanne, her father, Philippe Louis, and her uncle, Conrad Raymond. Beside Conrad's name were long words that Adrienne didn't understand, and Philippe did not explain.

Soldat. Mort au combat à 19 ans. Normandie, 1944

Medaille d'honneur du Commonwealth Britannique

Inhumé à Beny sur Mer, France.[4]

Philippe took a pen out of his breast pocket and drew three vertical lines below his name. He wrote "René Charles," "Marie Claude," and "Adrienne Lise," and their dates of birth. He laid the book down on the coffee table, gave Adrienne the pen and told her to write her initials carefully in the margin. She knelt on the floor by the side of the coffee table and did the best she could, but the letters were big and clumsy. A big wobbly "A" and a smaller "B." He asked her to read the first sentence at the top of the page.

---

3   Arsenault, Bona. *History of the Acadians*. Québec: Éditions Fides, 1994.

4   Infantry soldier. Died in combat at 19 years of age. Normandy, 1944. Medal of Honour of the British Commonwealth. Interred at Beny sur Mer, France.

"*Louis Blanchard arrivé à Port Royal à bord* Le don de Dieu *en 1623,*"[5] she read.

She hadn't yet learned to read dates, so her father helped.

"*Mille six cents vingt trois,*" he read. "*Tu vois, Louis Blanchard est dans chaque goutte de ton sang.*"[6]

Her doubts dissipated. Her place in the world defined. Adrienne Blanchard forever disregarded any other opinions as to her purity and her origins. She had signed. She was in The Book.

In Grade 1, she was introduced to a second book that would mark her life. She was given her first catechism, a small paperbound book titled *Qui est Dieu? Who Is God?* It was a powerful and poetic book for a child and would be profoundly disturbing to Adrienne.

The Blanchards' Catholicism was not an extremely committed one although the doctor liked to attend mass with his children and enjoy a traditional family meal afterwards. Behind closed doors, Charlotte stayed home from mass to prepare Sunday dinner, Philippe read *Lady Chatterley's Lover*, and Adrienne was never taught to pray. Not even a comforting nightime prayer.

"*Bonne nuit, chérie,*"[7] was all she ever got. Sometimes a tickle.

A certain nonconformity was a characteristic of the Blanchard family, but they were Catholic nonetheless. It was an intrinsic part of being French Canadian. Phillipe Blanchard was of the opinion that, although the politicians wore the medals, it was the Catholic Church that had been instrumental in the survival of the Acadian culture. English was the language of the Protestants, Jews, and atheists and therefore any contact other than what was strictly necessary was discouraged and frowned upon. The Church had created spiritual fences to keep out ideas, and the collateral effect had been to keep a language and a culture inside.

The only crucifix in the house was kept in a drawer. It was taken out when the Bishop came to visit. *Monseigneur*[8] would sit on the piano bench

---

[5] Louis Blanchard arrival in Port Royal aboard *Le don de Dieu* in 1623.

[6] Sixteen twenty-three. You see, Louis Blanchard is in every drop of your blood.

[7] Good night, sweetheart.

[8] Monsignor: Denomination for the rank of Bishop.

while the five Blanchards knelt on the living room floor to be blessed. Claude joined her hands prettily in prayer. René knelt but crossed his arms and looked out the window. Adrienne worried about the sign of the cross. She never remembered if it was from left to right or right to left. She ended up drawing a circle in the air.

Then the living room doors were closed, and the Bishop stayed to have a drink and a cigar with his friend Phil. They were from the same village in the north and had attended the same school. Philippe had flirted with the Bishop's sister as a young man before going to medical school in Québec City. There, he had fallen in love with the lovely and eccentric Charlotte who helped her father at the bookstore he frequented.

Roger Losier could relax with Phil who was the only person who knew his secret. His vocation was failing. The first time he had donned his purple Bishop's robes, an impostor had looked back at him from the mirror. His blood had frozen in his veins. The recognition had been unexpected and sudden. He prayed relentlessly, asking for God's help. He forced himself to be an excellent administrator, to study theology to the point of exhaustion, to write inspiring sermons, and to be an example to younger priests although he was young himself. He was barely forty years old when he had been ordained bishop. He had been the smartest in the class at the Sacred Heart, one of eleven children from a working class home. His future had been chosen for him. Roger had an unusual talent for mathematics and loved the outdoors. He would have loved to study engineering but being approached by the Church was such an honour that he had convinced himself that he felt the calling. It was a case of having been chosen and not of choosing. Passive versus active. A shaky foundation for building a life.

Philippe Blanchard, the practising non-believer, who already had enough on his mind as the Chief Medical Officer of the maximum security penitentiary, found himself trying to help his friend through a crisis of faith, and his youngest daughter through an existentialist dilemma.

Who Is God? was an illustrated catechism for children. It was printed on natural rustic paper with handcut edges. As you opened the book, the left-hand page held a black-and-white illustration. The opposite page held a short explanatory text in large block letters. It also served as a reader.

PAGE ONE

A young man and a young woman naked in Paradise. They are standing under a tree. The young woman is handing the young man an apple. Their faces are peaceful and in profile. They are looking at each other. There is a sparkling spring at their feet, and a small animal hidden in the foliage of the tree which they do not see, or they choose to ignore.

Eve is beautiful. Her body is perfectly white and smooth. Her long hair falls to her waist in beautiful waves. It covers her breasts and her left hand hides the space between her legs. He has beautiful hair as well. It falls to his shoulders. His body is narrower and stronger. Smooth and square. There is a leaf between his legs.

Adam and Eve are forever banished from Paradise.

Adrienne knew what was behind the leaf. She had walked into her parents' bedroom one day while her father was dressing. She had glimpsed a soft brown flower hanging under Papa's shirt. As for Paradise, she didn't really know what all the fuss was about. Paradise looked nice but there were a lot of trees and sparkling springs around home. The cottage at Crane Road looked something like Paradise. Maybe even nicer.

She loved this page and often took *Who Is God?* out of her desk and opened it on her knees while the Sister explained other things. The nun thought that the Blanchard girl might be a particularly devout child, but it was always the same page. It was Adam's face and Eve's hair she loved.

PAGE NINE

Adrienne couldn't quite understand why this page was supposed to be so tragic. It reminded her of the yearly trip to Québec City with Claude and her mother to visit her Aunt Madeleine.

A caravan in the desert. People, children, mules, carts, camels, are moving along the bottom of the page. A narrow road climbs up the middle margin to three small pyramids in the distance.

True Identity

Joseph and Mary must travel to Egypt for the first Great Census.

Aunt Madeleine was an artist and had never married. She let the girls stay up late, took them to restaurants, and gave them dark chocolate that she bought on her trips to Europe. Philippe and René meanwhile, would go up north to a cabin in the wilderness. They took rifles but never shot anything. The son chopped wood and made fires because it was so cold and there was no electricity. They wore Grandfather Blanchard's otter capes. Philippe opened cans of beans, which they heated on the wood burning stove. Poor René would have preferred to eat crêpes and hang around the bookstore in Québec City with his sisters.

The highlight of the trip to Québec City was the sleigh ride on the Plains of Abraham. This was the battlefield where French Canada had fallen to the English, and where General Montcalm had surrendered to General Wolfe. Charlotte, Madeleine, Claude, and Adrienne snuggled under bear skins in the sleigh. Her mother always cried when she saw the Château Frontenac shining on the cliff above the great white Saint Lawrence River. She called it *"Le Fleuve"*: "The Seaway," like a proper Québécoise should.

"Comme c'est beau!"[9]

Madeleine would reach over the fur blanket and take her sister's hand. Adrienne was jealous of the city. Her mother loved it so much.

As for the census, the year Adrienne had turned four, an army of nice ladies had knocked on every door in Canada. With her husband's approval, because these things were considered provocative francophone politics, her mother had requested a French-speaking canvasser. The census committee had graciously obliged. Charlotte was pleased and Phillippe was surprised. Maybe times were changing.

Adrienne remembered sitting on the sofa beside her mother while a very nice lady filled in a long questionnaire. Her mother had made a pot of tea. They had counted twenty million Canadians, and everyone had been very pleased. It had been a very civilized event.

---

9   It is so beautiful!

PAGE FOURTEEN

A giant is standing outside an old stone castle. He has long hair and a beard. He is brandishing a mace. His mouth is open to show his teeth, his face is wild with fury. He is wearing a very short dress tied by a string at the waist. He has long, powerful thighs. In the distance, men wearing turbans and carrying swords are chasing desperate women who are fleeing with babies in their arms.

King Herod is furious. He is jealous of the Messiah. He orders the death of all baby boys under the age of two.

This was a cruel tale like *The Pied Piper* or *Hansel and Gretel*. Adrienne quickly drew up a plan for how to save her baby boy from Herod. She would take a large Band-Aid and flatten his little tube, dress him like a girl, put ribbons in his hair and call him Sylvie. It would have to be the most secret of secrets. She wouldn't even tell her son he was a boy until he was older and out of danger. She also considered the idea of becoming Herod's friend. He would trust her and not suspect the deception.

Herod didn't impress Adrienne as much as one might think. Her father, to her mother's dismay, often talked about the men in the penitentiary. They were hard and dangerous men, often doomed to an underlife when they were freed. Every once in a while, an ex-convict came to their house in the city to ask the Doctor for a job, a sandwich or twenty-five dollars for the bus to Toronto. Charlotte would quickly send the girls upstairs.

Philippe was known to have the respect of the more dangerous inmates who, kept in solitary conditions, took any excuse to visit the infirmary. They liked to chat and brag about their exploits. Philippe liked to engage them in personal conversation.

"You're always bragging Jimmy, but if you're so smart, how come you got caught?"

He peered into Jimmy's ears. A murderer with terrible excema. A small vengeance. He came every day for his drops.

"A snitch, Doc. A snitch," said Jimmy.

"OK, a snitch, but bragging about what you did doesn't look good on your parole application. If you're smart, you'll keep it down."

Once, the Warden had called in the middle of the night for Philippe to go "talk somebody down." Adrienne had no idea what that meant, but Claude told her that their father had saved someone's life.

PAGE TWENTY-TWO

The last page. The grand finale. The page that would traumatize Adrienne.

The sea, calm and unending
A horizon to the infinite
Over the horizon, a triangle
Hangs in the sky
Inside the triangle
There is an eye
God sees all
God knows all
God is all

God was watching her. It didn't take long for Adrienne's overactive imagination to run away with her and turn this allegory into a full-fledged reality. She became silent. She used the bathroom and undressed with the lights off. She refused to take a bath and avoided eye contact. She covered her bedroom window with a towel. This lasted for three days.

Charlotte was worried that something unspeakable had happened to her daughter. She went upstairs to Adrienne's bedroom and sat on the edge of her bed. The five-year-old had pulled the blankets over her head. Charlotte feared the worst. Her hand was shaking. The ashes of her cigarette fell to the floor. Claude listened in the hall outside the door.

"Has something bad happened to you Adrienne?" her mother asked. "Has a bad person come near you? Tell Maman."

Adrienne was feeling absolutely wretched and wanted life to go back to where it was before she saw page twenty-two. She pulled her blankets down to her nose.

"I'm afraid," she said.

"Afraid of what?"

"Just afraid."

"There is no need to be afraid. You have your father and mother. You have a home. You are safe."

"Afraid of God. He is everywhere and he is watching me. It's in the catechism," Adrienne cried.

Charlotte simultaneously burst into a fit of anticlerical indignation and felt profound relief.

"Is that it? Oh, Adrienne! God is in heaven minding his own business! Those are just the silly nuns and their silly stories! Have they nothing better to do than to frighten our children?"

Philippe had come home and joined the procession to Adrienne's bedroom. He put his stethoscope around his neck because he knew she would respect it and let him remove the covers. He was not God, but he was her father and therefore commanded obedience. She was wearing a pair of pyjamas under her nightdress, socks and gloves.

He said nothing. He listened to her heart, removed his stethoscope and looked at her very seriously. Then he tickled and he tickled and he tickled until Adrienne was laughing so hard, she needed to pee.

"Papa! Stop! Stop! Please!" she screamed in laughter. "Maman! Tell Papa to stop! Help! Please!"

The laughter was music to Charlotte's ears. Adrienne relaxed, and tearfully described the triangle to her father. He told her to bring the book home the next day so he could have a look at it. He explained what he thought the triangle and the eye really meant. His guess, although they would see tomorrow, was that she had to behave herself at all times in public. The eye was out over the ocean and represented the outside world. However, it was important for her to know that in the bedroom and the bathroom she could do whatever she wanted.

"Anything?" she asked.

"Anything. Not a bad deal if you think about it," her father said. He laughed to himself. The sexual nuances were lost on a five-year-old.

She felt much better. The hysterical laughter had relieved her anxiety and what her father said had made sense to her five-year-old self. She took off the gloves, socks, and night dress, and stayed in her pyjamas. The following day, she spent more time than usual in her bedroom, but soon she forgot the big eye and skipped to school trying to decide whether to be an astronaut or a ballerina.

A Dubious Act of Charity

The late sixties and early seventies would change everything. Claude and Adrienne would be the last generation of little girls to wear hats and gloves to church, which implied the privilege of being the first generation not to do so. The triangle with the eye disappeared.

The Blanchard family was not untouched by those years of moon landings, birth control pills, bell-bottom pants, marijuana, and priests playing guitars. René, Claude, and Adrienne complied with all the rites of passage.

In the spring of 1973, René was eighteen and about to finish high school. He had chosen to attend the English school, Moncton High, rather than the seminary where francophone boys usually completed their schooling. He let his sandy hair grow long and anglicized his name to Wren. He expected total rejection by his parents. But René's or Wren's attempt at rebellion backfired because everyone was quite pleased. It was a rebellion without bloodshed. His father really didn't mind. René could never change his roots but, like his father, he could grow new branches if that was what he wanted. Surprisingly, Charlotte also preferred this Protestant school. There were lots of sports and less nonsense. She liked his new friends. They were handsome boys, confident and sure of themselves. Bob and Eddie.

They made charming attempts to speak French, which delighted Charlotte. When the weather was good, they ate their lunch with Wren/René at the picnic table on the back porch. Charlotte provided a pitcher of water, glasses, and often a good dessert. Eddie and Claude flirted through the kitchen window.

As for Wren's anglicization, it didn't last very long. His mother and father just ignored his new name. He had no choice but to answer to René. Not a word of English was ever spoken inside the Blanchard home. He waited until he finished high school and quietly began to introduce himself as

René again. He enrolled at the Université de Moncton to study French literature. It had been a momentary crisis of identity.

Claude was sixteen. Her nickname was Clo. Two years younger than René, she had had the opportunity to attend the first public French High School in Moncton. Like René, she had refused to go to the convent school. Her idol was Françoise Hardy, a winsome, ethereal Parisian singer. Like Françoise, she wore skinny turtleneck sweaters, bell-bottom pants, high heel boots, and pale lipstick. Clo memorized the lyrics to Françoise's songs, locked herself in her bedroom, and swayed stylishly to the Parisian sounds.

She dyed her hair golden blond and wore it long and straight. She was a beautiful girl, the kind of girl who turns heads and who men tell lies about. She was impulsive and impatient, but natural, agreeable, and she liked to please. But what best defined Claude was that she was feminine to the utmost degree and, as such, took it on herself to be her little sister's guide to femininity.

It was their moment. Claude would be in the bathroom preparing for a dance or a party with eleven-year-old Adrienne sitting on the edge of the tub watching and listening. Claude sat on the toilet seat and demonstrated the art of the garter belt and nylon stockings. She showed Adrienne how to pluck those terrible eyebrows they had inherited from their father, and how to put on a brassiere. Claude would bend down from the waist and catch her hanging breasts with the bra. What fascinated Adrienne most was how Claude applied perfume. She would spray a thick cloud of Chantilly Lace directly away from her and then walk into it waving her arms and rolling her head.

"I am going to tell Maman to buy you a bra," Clo said. "You need one right away. And you should get your teeth fixed before you start high school. Mine are perfect. I don't know why yours are like that."

"Clo, Papa says the orthodontist is a crook. He makes poor people think they need perfect teeth. He gets rich and they stay poor," Adrienne repeated her father's explanation for not getting braces for the rather generous gap between her two front teeth.

"Oh! That's Papa," Claude sighed. "He's so embarrassing sometimes. He says that, but I heard him and Maman talking about it. Well, maybe when you're older and you can pay for it, you can get them fixed. Just that gap. Really, it's not so bad. Eddie says you're cute you know!"

She thought Adrienne wasn't very interested in boys, but she was wrong. Adrienne was the heroine of every book she read. She read adult novels, which she found under René's bed, with a flashlight under her blankets. In her preadolescent fantasies, she knew there was a man from a far-away place who would need her. Their love would be difficult, unusual, and profound. She wasn't far off the mark.

Those would be the good old days because the last years of the Blanchard family in Moncton would be marked by death. Two.

Yvette Landry disappeared in May 1973. Her body wasn't found for several days. In fact, most people thought she had run away. It rained heavily which made a proper search impossible and the days passed. The spring thaw and the heavy rains swelled the rivers and streams.

While the population didn't seem very concerned about Yvette, Philippe was worried. She was a schoolmate of Claude's and a girl from the neighbourhood. He could never quite disengage from the nature of his environment. He was surrounded by violence past, present, and future. Phillipe had seen true evil only once in his life: in the eyes of a serial killer. It was a fact that a victim's resistance excited them. The more difficult the prey, the better. He needed to speak to his daughters.

"They are wild animals," he said. "They want you to know who they are, so don't look into their eyes. They want you to fight, so play dead. They want you to scream, so stay silent. This will give you a chance. They will lose their fury. Do these things because we will find you and we will cure you, but we can't bring you back from the dead."

Claude rolled her eyes at her father's dramatic monologue. Philippe had a tendency to pontificate.

"Papa! Yvette's run away to Montréal. She used to talk about it all the time. They say her father is very strict. And rough. She'll call home any day now. You'll see."

Young runaways plagued the streets of Toronto, Montréal and Vancouver in those days. This seemed to be the hypothesis of the police as well. Adrienne, who was now as tall as Claude, and equally vulnerable, put the information away in a mental drawer to be used at a later date if necessary. She always expected the truth from her father and was not disturbed by it. You had to know what to do, like in a fire or an earthquake.

Ten days after the disappearance, Philippe was alone in the living room reading the evening paper. René tapped on the door. He looked agitated as he approached his father.

"Could I speak to you?" he asked.

Philippe was surprised, worried, and pleased all at once. It had been a long time since René had sought him out. Since the Wren business four years earlier, his son had drifted away. He folded the newspaper carefully and paid full attention. Father and son spent the next three days coming and going in the car, talking softly, and nodding a lot. Charlotte chain-smoked.

Yvette's body had been found downstream near the abandoned skating rink, tangled in the brush under the thick red mud of the Moncton marshes. She had bad bruises, a big lump on her head, scratches, cuts, and signs of sexual intercourse.

Philippe found an excuse to see the body. He made an appointment at the Hotel Dieu hospital with the urologist. He had an inmate needing renal dialysis and was preparing an application for early medical release from prison. He needed a second diagnosis. After his meeting, he went down to the morgue to invite the pathologist to a Club Richelieu event. The Richelieu was a francophone businessmen's club, the French version of the Rotary. Philippe was secretary that year.

Dr. Bouchard was a Québécois who was laying low in Moncton after rumours of malpractice in Montréal. He had the arrogance to suggest that the Acadian community should thank him for wasting his life and his talent in this godforsaken place. Philippe asked to see the girl. He said he was curious. Bouchard didn't care.

"She's got three hickeys," Philippe said. "Rapists don't give hickeys."

"She probably got those another day," said Bouchard. "Not the most virginal kid in town." The expert pathologist puffed.

Philippe tried again to plant the seeds of doubt. He pointed to the bruises and inflammations.

"These are the result of a previous beating or a fall?" he asked.

As a penitentiary doctor, Philippe could recognize the marks and the sequences of a beating in his sleep, but Bouchard had no interest in the case of this young Acadian girl or in the truth. She had been raped, beaten, murdered, and thrown into the creek. Period.

"She was brutally beaten and then dragged," the coroner said, dismissing Philippe's suggestion.

Bouchard was an idiot and he stank of gin. There was evidence of violence, not from days before, but weeks, months, and even years before. Philippe was disgusted. He was left with only one course of action: he would have to cross the line.

Michel Bourgeois was the principal suspect.

An abandoned train track bordered Hall's Creek from downtown Moncton to the town of Berry Mills, seven miles inland on the old industrial railway that had fallen into disuse. The afternoon that Yvette had disappeared, two little girls playing in an abandoned railway car saw a young man running up the tracks. The next day, they had seen him again. He was looking down, walking fast, his pants wet from the knees down. They were sure it was the boy who worked at Bright's Fish and Chips. They had not told their parents, afraid they would be punished for playing near the tracks. The last time Yvette had been seen was with the Bourgeois boy on the swings at Hall's Creek playground near the tracks and the creek. She had never made it to her babysitting job.

Average height and very thin, Michel was a nice looking boy. He wore wire-rimmed glasses and had long hair he tied into a ponytail. He listened to heavy rock music and smoked a lot of pot. He had been arrested for possession the year before and had spent a month in a juvenile facility. He was a short-order cook with a record, who lived in an old trailer by the hockey stadium. It was not the résumé of an outstanding citizen.

Michel Bourgeois and his mother, Pauline, were not strangers to the Blanchards. Stygmatized by her teenage pregnancy, Pauline had come to Moncton from a small village in rural Kent County. She was a struggling single mother who sold Avon cosmetics door-to-door and did house cleaning for extra income. For years, she had worked at the Blanchards for two days a week. Her Michel was the same age as René and when he was little, she had no choice but to bring him along to work. Charlotte didn't mind. He was quiet and well-behaved. The boys played checkers and read comic books in René's room. Sometimes he waited outside on the steps, amusing himself with something or other. He liked colouring books. The doctor treated a succession of Michel's sore throats and eventually took out his tonsils. Pauline had always been very grateful.

Michel had never minded being the son of a single mother although he had to fend for himself from a very young age. They cuddled on the sofa, watched game shows on television, and ate macaroni and cheese dinner on Friday nights. On Saturdays, they took the bus to Kmart and had a hot chicken sandwich and an ice cream float sitting at the lunch counter. Life was comfortable and predictable. The apartment was poor, but it was bright and warm, and the neighbours were nice to them. He slept in a deep, soft sofa in front of the television set. He could hear his mother breathing softly in the next room.

Pauline was a pleasant and attractive young woman in her twenties, and she eventually married Ron McKay, a nice man who owned three taxi cabs. She and Michel moved from a tiny fourth floor apartment in a shabby building in the East End to a pretty brick bungalow on a tree-lined street in a middle-class area uptown. Pauline was a smart girl and ran the taxi dispatch radio from home.

To twelve-year-old Michel, this great improvement in their standard of living was the worst thing that could ever have happened to him. A well-intentioned stepfather had come too late. A new school. A huge, lonely bedroom in a cold basement. A crying baby. Another crying baby. The perpetual ringing of telephones. And worst of all, he never had his mother's full attention. The nice buzz of marijuana made him feel better.

Michel didn't like to study and especially not at this new school, but he did like to do things with his hands. He painted his mother's nails in psychedelic patterns with the old Avon samples. He made bizarre sculptures with things he found in the garbage. As soon as he could, he quit school and got a job at Bright's Fish and Chips Takeout Restaurant on Main Street. He became an excellent short-order cook. Michel was good at the job and at eighteen his boss left him in charge of the kitchen.

During his first year at the restaurant, he was seriously burned in an oil fire. He suffered in silence for three hours until the end of his shift and then, well into the night, he knocked on Doctor Blanchard's door in excruciating pain. Philippe took him to the hospital, and for the following two months Michel came to the Blanchards' house every evening for Philippe to change

True Identity

his dressings. He was left with bad scars on his wrist and lower right arm but fortunately his wrist mobility was not compromised.

When the police banged on his trailer door to pick him up for questioning related to the death of Yvette Landry, Michel was gone. He had just crossed the US border on a bus at Calais, Maine, with a false birth certificate and driver's licence. His new identity was Brian Gordon Ogilvy, born in New Glasgow, Nova Scotia, in 1956. This made him twenty-two and not eighteen.

His friend gave him three hundred dollars, a wallet containing several authentic pieces of identification, and a return ticket to Boston and dropped him off two blocks from the bus station in a Nova Scotia town. Michel boarded the bus directly. With another four hundred dollars, which he had been saving for a motorcycle, he had seven hundred dollars in his pocket. His plan was to volunteer for Vietnam. He had considered it even before all this happened. He had heard somewhere that Canadians were offered citizenship if they stayed two years. He opened the bus window and felt the fresh, cold air on his face. Despite everything, he couldn't help feeling excited.

At the Blanchard house, the girls were sleeping and would never know what happened on that night in May. The doorbell rang at two o'clock in the morning. Charlotte climbed the stairs very quietly and knocked softly on her son's door.

"Descends, chéri. Ton père a besoin de toi."[10]

Philippe and his son knelt on the floor by the piano. Charlotte watched through the French doors of the living room as Philippe's friend Roger Losier donned a purple stole to become a priest and thus became sworn to secrecy.

Philippe had told Michel to call in the early morning, any morning, between six and seven o'clock, but he never did. Brian Ogilvy was an American serviceman living in Okinawa, Japan. Most of the time, Brian forgot Michel had ever existed.

It wouldn't have mattered anyway because the phone would have rung in an empty house. There was no one there. Soon after, Philippe Blanchard died of a massive heart attack and Charlotte Desmeules returned to her true home with her youngest, who wasn't quite sure where her home was anymore.

---

10 Come downstairs, Sweetheart. Your father needs you.

Lean Into the Wind

Across an ocean, another boy ran for his life. His father had come to pick him up at school after hockey practice. They were only twenty feet from their car when the car parked next to theirs was blown to bits by a bomb. The fourteen-year-old reacted to the strange behaviour of two large men driving by fast on a small motorcycle just seconds before the blast. He grabbed his father by the sleeve of his jacket, ditched his hockey stick, and yelled, "Run, *Aita!*"

Aita means father in Basque.

Debris flew through the air. A fender. A briefcase. A hand. Father and son crouched, then ran through the smoke and fire. The father was overweight and he was a smoker. He was breathing too hard and dragging his left leg that had a bad knee.

Don't die. Please, don't die Aita! the boy begged in his mind.

There came a second blast which brought smoke and bits of burning metal and glass, bloody body parts, a military cap, a piece of windshield. They were a little farther away and were not hit. They took refuge behind a bus stop with three other people who avoided eye contact and said nothing. Acrid smoke. Coughing. Sudden deaf silence then whistling in the ears.

The faint sound of sirens got louder and louder. The father and son looked at each other and started to walk briskly away to distance themselves from the blast. The other people at the bus stop had already vanished. The father didn't have to tell the son that he hadn't seen the faces of the men on the motorcycle. They didn't get very far. A Civil Guard Land Rover screeched to a stop after they had taken only a few steps. A green-uniformed young man with the patent leather three-horned hat of the *Guardia Civil*[11] jumped

---

11 The Civil Guard. A federal police within the Spanish Armed Forces.

out of the vehicle. He blinked nervously as he pointed a machine gun first at the teenage boy and then at the breathless father.

"Identify yourselves!" he shouted.

"Iñaki Aramburu. From Getxo. The boy is my son, Francisco Xavier. We've just come from the Jesuits. My car is parked over there." He pointed to the burning Volvo.

It was an ugly conflict in a beautiful place. It had several names:

El País Vasco

Euskadi

Las Vascongadas

Le Pays Basque

Euskal Herria

What you called it depended on your point of view and your personal politics. The Basque Country is in the corner of northeastern Spain and southwestern France. The borders are amorphous and hypothetical as it has never existed on a political map of the world. Yet it is an old country with an old soul.

The Basques had witnessed the Roman garrisons, the invasion of the Moors, the hordes of the Goths, the Catholic kings, the Spanish Empire, the Carlist wars, the Second Spanish Republic, the Spanish Civil War, and the dictatorial regime of General Franco. They were an industrious people and had negotiated their alliances with their successive new administrators. Mostly they had insisted on collecting and distributing their own taxes and paid what could be considered an administration fee to the newcomer of the new crown. This was extraordinarily modern for one of the most ancient peoples on earth. The world's oldest Paleolithic cave paintings are found near, and their language resembles no other.

They were seamen, merchants, explorers, soldiers, shepherds, shipbuilders. They even boasted of a saint or two, but they were mostly seafaring men. Long before Columbus, in fact as early as the eleventh century, the Basques had reached the coasts of North America in search of cod and whales. Artifacts buried deep in the ground of Newfoundland and the Saint Lawrence River are proof of their journeys. They were fearless. They understood the stars and the skies and so became the pilots of the ships of the Castilian kings. They steered the vessels to safety in the storms and guided them home to deliver the bounty to the kings and queens.

From 1939 to 1975, it had been General Franco's turn to rule. Franco had been victorious over the Spanish Republic in a three-year-long bloody civil war and had ruled all of Spain for almost forty years. An iron fist. A false peace. In 1973, he was an old and dying man. The past had been grey and uneasy. The future was uncertain. There was hope, fear, courage, and wariness. Would Spain at last take its place in Europe? The clock was ticking and all over the country, everyone jockeyed for position.

The bomb Xavier and his father narrowly escaped killed a civil guard colonel and his adjutant who were parked next to their car. The bomb was detonated by ETA, a Basque separatist group whose objective was a communist workers' republic in an independent Basque homeland, the annexation of parts of France and the neighbouring province of Navarra. The method they employed was urban guerilla warfare.

Francisco Xavier Aramburu Quiroga was the son of a wealthy Basque family from the town of Getxo in the province of Vizcaya. Getxo was an affluent seaside township very near the capital of the province, the centre of Basque industry and economy, Bilbao. As all Spaniards do, he carried his father's and his mother's family name. The Aramburus were steel, the Quirogas were ship builders. It was a family of five. The *aita*, Iñaki, the *ama*,[12] Ana, the first-born, Begoña, and the only boy, whom they called Xavi.

When he was four and Begoña six, his mother came home from the hospital with his baby sister. Life did not go on as previously forecasted. Little Paloma had Down syndrome.

"God has sent us an angel," Ana told her children.

The angel spread her wings over the Aramburu family. Their gentle mother devoted her heart and soul to Paloma's care. Xavier and Begoña, who were strong and perfect, became two small figures in the background of an exquisite painting. Life revolved around Paloma who was pure and innocent.

---

12 *Ama:* Mother (Basque).

For the Aramburus, Paloma's integration was not an issue. She was never sent to special schools or signed up for any activities or programs. She was an extension of themselves. Ana took her everywhere, shopping, to tea with her friends, to afternoon concerts, for which she was often criticized by the fine ladies of Getxo and Bilbao. The child should be properly cared for, they said, which meant out of sight and not in an elegant café in mid afternoon. Oblivious to all of that, Ana doted on Paloma, groomed her like the little Bilbao princess that she was, and taught her many things including how to crochet with large hooks and thick wool.

Xavi sat with her quietly for hours while he read and she crocheted. He had lost his mother but gained an angel. He could understand that.

Like his father and grandfather, he studied at the Jesuit School of Nuestra Señora de Indautxu. The Jesuits, whose mission it is to educate the elite of society and the elite of mind, took an interest in the Aramburu boy. They recognized in Xavier a sharp analytical intelligence and a maturity beyond his years. He was eventually moved ahead one grade. As he grew older, he liked to provoke the priests with startling essays and uncomfortable debates. They didn't mind. He was encouraged to think for himself. Indeed, the greatest Jesuit of them all had been Saint Francis Xavier, their founder, who was a free-thinking Basque.

Because of his background, his personality, and his intelligence, the priests suspected he might play a part in the future of Euskadi. Xavier was not thinking so far ahead. He was a bright, strong kid who loved to sail. He felt the horizon pulling at him like a force of gravity. He would have been a pilot or maybe a whaler in the old days.

He was an expert sailor and a certified sailing instructor. He spent five summers at the National Sailing School in Santander, a pretty city on the Cantabrian coast only one hour west of Bilbao. His father would pick him up on Friday nights and drive him back to the school on Monday mornings. He signed up for successive two-week courses until he became a familiar figure around the school. He was Xavi, the rich, good-looking kid from Bilbao.

He had made it to Santander in a roundabout way. At age eight, he was sent to Ireland with a Catholic organization along with his sister and his cousin. He hated every minute of it. As he walked out the sliding doors at Bilbao airport, he immediately removed the group's yellow backpack. Like a businessman coming home from a particularly detestable journey, he said, "This is the last time you hang a yellow backpack on me."

So, the following summers, he was sent nearby to sailing school. Santander was a prestigious school with state-of-the-art equipment and world-class instructors. The children and teenagers trained alongside the Spanish National sailing team. For Xavier, sailing was second nature. It was about taking risks, controlling the elements, reaching for the unknown, and looking up instead of back. He basked in the wind and rain, in the cold and the heat.

He loved to lean into the wind, hold his body horizontal to the water on a bed of air, judge the correct force, assist the craft with his body and finally win the battle over the waves and the elements to carry him forward straight and fast. It was a pure and physical joy.

Unfortunately, Xavier didn't leave the school in the best of circumstances. It was all because he lost his virginity in a rather spectacular way.

He was just one month away from his fourteenth birthday. He was curious and desperate. He had spent the summer roaming, to the extent that a thirteen-year-old can roam, looking for an opportunity. Not just any opportunity, a good one.

By mid-August, somewhat pressured by the summer's end, he tried his luck at Bikini Beach. Bikini Beach was what the locals called the private beach at the Palacio de la Magdalena, a former royal summer residence reconverted to a small university specializing in Spanish language courses for foreigners. The beach was within walking distance of the sailing school. There were good-looking French and Danish girls that year, according to the older guys at the school.

"Wear your uniform," they told him, "if you want to get in."

The nice-looking adolescent had no trouble walking past the entrance in his official white jacket with the Spanish flag on the sleeve. He found his way to the beach and picked a good spot for observation. There were two girls reading and eating potato chips. He moved his towel closer for a better view.

Option one was tall and thin and very tanned. She had very short brown hair and wore large round sunglasses. She looked like a fashion model. Option two had long, curly, blond hair and freckles. She was a little chubby but had big, round breasts and a superb backside to match. He didn't know which one he liked best. Red bikini and black bikini. *At least they are nice to look at*, he thought. He was losing his nerve.

But then it happened. A gust of wind picked up the brunette's straw hat. Xavier was up like a dart chasing down the black-and-white *canotier*.[13] He caught up with it just before it rolled into the water. A hero. To make up for his crazy run, he walked slowly back to the girls, hat in hand, with a smile and an attempt at a swagger. The truth was that he looked adorable and absolutely harmless.

He nonchalantly dropped to his knees to give the brunette her hat.

"Tu sombrero, verdad?"[14] he asked.

In their hesitant Spanish they thanked him and offered him a potato chip.

"Would you like to sit with us?" the brunette suggested.

He was up like a dart again, got his towel and came back. Justine and Gabrielle did something quite extraordinary. They made a place for him between them. And that's how it started, how it happened, and how it ended.

The first night was a promise of what was to come. He took them to a café in the city centre famous for its ice cream cakes. As they walked back to their temporary summer homes, the frisky young Xavier put his arms around them both. The girls felt amused and comfortable with such a sweet and handsome young teenager.

It was a Spanish summer night. Hot, fragrant and long. He turned his head and spontaneously kissed Justine on the mouth, then with a giggle, he turned to Gabrielle. They walked all the way back to the Palacio that way. In alternation. The kisses got longer and wetter and deeper. Xavier found it difficult to wipe the smile off his face the next day. They would meet again at nine.

They went to El Sardinero, the public beach, where they resumed their kissing marathon in a secluded corner. Justine was a good kisser, but Gabrielle was more passionate. He still could not decide which of the two he preferred. Justine. Gabrielle. Gabrielle. Justine.

He could only nod when they took his hand and headed for the college residence. He was trembling with sexual anticipation. On tiptoe, they

---

13 Flat, straw, wide rimmed gondolier's hat.

14 Your hat, right?

snuck into the girls' room at the residence through an emergency door. The silence was broken only by their accelerated breathing and the scraping of cheap bedroom furniture on the floor. He stretched and twisted to feel it all and to feel them both. Xavier was swimming in a sea of female body parts. They were slippery wet and the boy knew the way into those warm, tight caves. It was easy, and it was wonderful.

That was the second night. On the third night, they weren't as quiet and he stayed until morning. On the fourth night, a third girl joined them but it was short-lived. They were interrupted by the residence director and a security officer who banged on the door and demanded to be let in.

Xavier was still in his jeans and threw himself out the first-floor window. They threw his shirt, jacket, and shoes after him, but all but one shoe landed behind an impenetrable rose bush. He limped into the school, barefoot and barechested, twenty minutes later.

Xavier Aramburu was expelled for unsuitable behaviour.

Driving home, his father glared at him.

"Watch the road, *Aita*. Please."

"I just can't believe it. I just can't believe it. You're thirteen. You're a snotty little kid who likes hockey and ice cream. Explain this to me!" The father's tone of voice gradually increased in intensity to just below a scream.

"Forget it, *Aita*, please. I have my certification anyway and I did all the courses, some of them twice," Xavier said. "I'll go to the US next year. Do some English. I don't see the problem."

"What are we going to tell the *ama*? Eh? I can't believe it."

"Well, believe it, *Aita*. It wasn't so terrible. OK?"

"Mother of God. Three! Did you count properly? You're sure they weren't four? *La gran hostia!*"[15]

Xavier exclaimed in exasperation. "I had the best fucking time of my life, *Aita*, okay?"

The bomb exploded the following spring. They told Xavier's mother that, by the time they had arrived, the fire was out and they had not been

---

15 The Great Host. (The communion wafer: the sacred symbol of the body of Christ. A sacrilegious but common swear word in Spain and the Basque Country. Equivalent to "Jesus!" or less emphatically "Shit!")

in danger at any time. That night, sleepless and shaken, Xavier looked out at the ocean.

    He was fourteen.
    He could sail a ship.
    He had carnal knowledge.
    He had witnessed an act of war.
    He knew the smell of massacred human bodies.
    There was no child left.

He considered where he came from, what he had, and what he was capable of doing. He reached the conclusion that fate had dealt him a hand with the greatest of privileges: the freedom of choice.

    Xavier Aramburu was gifted with superior intelligence, physical beauty, physical prowess, and an extraordinary sex drive. He would not sleepwalk through life.

Birth of a Foreign Combatant

As Michel's bus neared the American border at Calais, Maine, the exhilaration of the departure faded. It was a dangerous and fragile moment.

He was lucky. He got through. The mythical rock group Led Zeppelin was partly responsible for that. Michel had no idea about the concert. Three teenagers about his age boarded the bus in Saint John, a city two hours from the Maine border. The bus was only a third full. The three teenagers each occupied a seat for two, set their backpacks against the window and stretched their legs into the aisle. Michel watched them surreptitiously while they made themselves comfortable. He envied their carefree attitude and wondered if he would ever feel like that again.

Fifteen minutes had passed when one of them made his way to the back where Michel was sitting. This was the first person to approach him as Brian. He was suddenly terrified that his new name would not roll off his tongue.

"Are you going to the concert in Boston?" the boy asked.

"No. What concert?" Michel asked.

"Tonight. Well, tomorrow night, actually. Led Zeppelin. 'Stairway to Heaven,' man!"

"Led Zeppelin? Wow!" Michel was genuinely impressed.

Afraid that his accent would betray him, Michel spoke in short phrases and monosyllables. Someone named Brian Ogilvy would not have a French accent.

"I've got an extra ticket. One of our friends couldn't come. Girlfriend wouldn't let him, you know? You interested? It's legit."

"I don't know. Wasn't planning on it," Michel responded.

"Thirty-five bucks. The concert's sold out so I can always sell it at the door. In case you're interested, I'm sitting over there," the boy said.

True Identity

"Yeah, okay. Thanks, eh?" said Michel who was glad that the conversation was over.

The boy turned to go back to his seat.

"Wait. I'll take it," said Michel, latching on to the moment of normality.

Shortly later, they pulled in to US Customs and Border Protection.

"What is the purpose of your visit to the United States?" said the Immigration officer as he put his hand out for the documentation.

Michel was so scared he could hardly speak. The concert had been a sudden stroke of luck. It was a lot less complicated than saying he wanted to volunteer for Vietnam.

"Going to the Led Zeppelin concert in Boston," he said in a loud whisper. There was no air in his lungs.

The Immigration agent was tired. A lot of kids that were going to the concert had come through that day. Young Canadians tended to be a little disrespectful these days but this one was different. Maybe he was too respectful. He checked the ID, a Nova Scotia driver's licence and birth certificate. They were authentic. Brian also had a picture ID, a Pictou Institute of Technology student card. The officer turned the concert ticket over in his hand a couple of times. It had been bought months in advance.

"Your bus ticket?" the officer said.

Michel handed him his ticket. Whoever had bought it, had known that one-way tickets set off border police alarms everywhere in the world. They had also backtracked to Truro to take the Halifax to Boston bus. It had lengthened the trip by one and a half hours but it was a good idea. It matched the ID and they were expecting somebody coming from Moncton, not Halifax. A fugitive would not lengthen his journey.

The Immigration Officer did his job, which was to make a decision. This couldn't be the French kid from Moncton they were looking for. Besides, he had just heard that the culprit had been spotted in the Montréal Metro. This had been courtesy of one of inmate Jimmy's buddies.

The officer let him through.

"Make sure you're on this bus back home when the concert's over. You hear me kid?"

The bus arrived in the early morning. Michel wandered around the Boston South Station area and saw a Salvation Army sign. He remembered the Salvation Army in dark blue suits and funny military hats collecting for charity at Christmas on Main Street. They smiled a lot, sang Christmas carols, and played the tambourine. His mother had bought their TV tables at the Salvation Army surplus store.

He suddenly had a vivid memory of sitting on the sofa with his mother eating supper on those tables and watching *The Price Is Right* on TV. An American game show that consisted in bidding on a group of objects by guessing the combined price, it was his mother's favourite. She was very good at making the mental calculations. Once, she had hit it on the nose. To the penny! They had looked at each other, mouths wide in astonishment.

The Salvation Army hostel was full, but he was directed to a boarding house near the Post Office in Chinatown. At fifty dollars a week, breakfast included, he thought he should spend the money. He could live on one meal a day. He felt conspicuous and vulnerable on the street. Conspicuous and vulnerable were feelings he would have to get used to.

The Boston Police had no photograph of the suspect wanted for questioning in a small-town murder case up in Canada. Male, about eighteen years of age, five feet eight inches tall, light brown hair and eyes. Who were they kidding? There were twenty thousand of them in town for the concert and every drug dealer in the northeastern United States as well. They had no time for this. No one was assigned to the case.

Michel found his way to the concert at Fenway Park. Stoned, in the darkness, the music reverberating in his chest, he was okay.

Somehow he made it back to the boarding house and fell asleep for eighteen hours. He woke suddenly with a pounding heart and drenched in perspiration. He didn't remember who, what or where he was. He was drowning in an undertow, grasping at mental straws for clues to his existence. He struggled to come to the surface and finally his name emerged from the fog. And it was over.

Michel. Michel. Michel Bourgeois. The bus. Boston. Yvette.

When he came to himself, he was on his hands and knees on the bed. Stark naked. The facts of his life crept back. He put his hand on his heart and laid back on the small, narrow bed. The exhaustion and stress had come to a head. He calmed down slowly and remembered that he had a choice. He could end this now, take the bus home, and surrender to the police.

"You can come back at any time. Remember that." Those were the Doctor's last words to him.

Philippe Blanchard had told him that no matter what, he always had a choice. It was small consolation but at least it was a measure of freedom. He still had his return ticket. This was day five since he had gone to hide in the Blanchard's garage.

He looked around. It was a small, ugly room but the soft afternoon light came through the window and made it bright. He heard the comforting noise of city traffic in the distance. His things were in order, just as he had left them. He was surviving. Strangely enough, the terrible nightmare had cleared his mind.

He took a moment to take inventory of what René had stuffed into the bag. No underwear or socks. He made sure his money and papers were safe and opened the door of his room to have a better look at the house. Brian was coming to life.

He checked out the communal bathroom and showers and realized he would have to buy a towel and some toilet paper. He put his head under the tap in the sink and, with a sliver of a bar of soap that someone had left there, washed his hair and rubbed it dry on the dingy towel roll. The cold water on his head felt good. His new life would start by acquiring articles of basic hygiene. This gave him an objective. He was going forward.

It was supper time and he was hungry. He had missed breakfast and lunch. There was no time to do anything that day. He walked as quietly as he could past the manager of the boarding house who was watching television in the living room.

Michel looked for the war. He had thought it would be easy, but America was at war in Vietnam, not in Boston. There was no sign of it anywhere. He walked around greater downtown using a map he got from a tourist information kiosk. Still no war and no recruitment offices. In June of 1973, the Vietnam War was a tired and futile conflict.

He made a little life for himself in his room. It was satisfactory to Michel because he had grown up in a very similar place. He decided not to go back home but that he would not resist arrest. He would hide until they found him. He liked Boston.

Michel had never been anywhere except to his mother's small village in Kent County. He would have loved to have discovered Boston under other circumstances. He was fascinated by the bright lights and became relatively comfortable with his anonymity. The better he felt, however, the more terrified he became of being discovered.

He loved to hang around Faneuil Market and was drawn to it every day. He wandered around the large open space under the huge skylight. The food hall blew him away. He pretended he was choosing a menu and walked slowly past the oyster bar, the American diner, the health food café, the crêperie, the pizza place. The cooks worked behind glass windows ignoring and entertaining the passersby at the same time. He pictured himself making crêpes on the fabulous round grilling stone or throwing and twirling the pizza dough in the air. Michel liked to cook and smoke pot. Fast-food and drugs. The story of his life.

Pot was a blessing and a problem. It took the edge off, it helped him sleep, and it was his only friend. It was also expensive and not easy to find if you didn't know where to look. He was running out. In the unconsciousness of the first night, he had bought twenty joints before the Zeppelin concert at Fenway Park. They had charged him two hundred dollars but the stuff was fantastic. "Mexican Gold" the guy had said. Michel limited himself to just one a day but it had been crazy. He would run out of money much sooner and could be thrown into jail regardless of his fancy ID. Michel would not stand up to police scrutiny a second time.

He developed tools of invisibility. He walked at a slightly brisk pace as though he were going somewhere. He never held eye contact for more than two seconds, which was quite brilliant as science has proved that it takes at least three seconds to memorize a face. He felt safety in large groups and liked to do things at rush hours. It wasn't perfect, however. One evening he froze when he heard French spoken with a Moncton accent behind him.

"*Ah, non! J'ai oublié ma camera chez ma tante,*" said a female voice.

"*C'est trop tard asteure. Faudra que t'achètes des cartes postales.*"[16]

---

16   Oh no! I forgot my camera at my aunt's.
Well, it's too late now. You'll just have to buy some postcards.

The Moncton girl had forgotten her camera at her aunt's house. The sound and rhythm of his own language punched him in the stomach. He ran for blocks. Boston wasn't far enough away.

After two weeks, he had only two hundred and seven dollars, and two joints left. He went to the Yellow Pages and there it was: a recruitment centre in the Post Office just one block away from where he lived.

The recruiter was sitting behind a desk.

"Yes, can I help you?"

"Hi. I want to sign up."

"Why do you want to sign up?"

"To go to Vietnam."

"Right. Why?"

"I want to travel."

"That's not a reason. Why?"

"I don't have a job."

"Give me a reason," the recruiter pushed a little harder.

"I'm Canadian. I'd like to live here in the US someday."

"Now you're talking. Your name, please."

"Brian Gordon Ogilvy."

"Okay, Brian Gordon Ogilvy from Canada. Sit down. Fill in this form and we'll see what we can do."

A deep sigh escaped the Sergeant. In the land of the Boston Tea Party, Paul Revere, and war hero and President John Fitzgerald Kennedy, they were signing up foreign kids to die in a jungle fighting a war America detested. Give me your poor and your starving and we will send them to war. Now that the draft was abolished, how on earth was he going to fulfill a quota of ninety recruits a month?

Michel had been waiting outside the door for the office to open at nine o'clock in the morning. He was feeling strong, focused, and positive. He had realized that Boston was too close to home and that he could not survive forever on two hundred dollars. It was time to get going. The sooner he began, the sooner it would be over. He would live poorly, which he knew how to do, save his money and return to Boston or some other nice place and start a small food business. He had been inspired by the Faneuil Market.

It was true that the American military had a program welcoming foreigners who would fight a war under the American flag in exchange for citizenship. There was an information meeting for all interested parties every Wednesday night at six thirty. All of his questions would be answered at that time. It might be important for Brian to know that the next group was leaving for Basic Training in ten days.

"I'll be honest with you," said the Sergeant. "You have a ten percent chance of coming home in a body bag, a twenty percent chance of being seriously and permanently wounded, and you will see combat almost every day. It's not pretty. That's your first year. Now, if you stay in the military for at least three years, you have a very good chance of achieving American citizenship, which is what you want."

Joining the American military was a serious commitment. He would be subject to military law and conditions. In return, the military would take care of all his needs. It was a place to grow and prosper if he took advantage of the opportunities. He was given a small book entitled *Life in the Armed Forces* and told to read it carefully.

"Do you have a trade?" the Sergeant asked as an afterthought. Most of the kids were unskilled.

"I'm a cook," Michel said.

"Really?" the Sergeant's eyes lit up. "A good one?"

"Not bad."

"Specialty?"

"Fish and chips. Fried chicken. I'm good at pancakes. Breakfast stuff."

"Oh! Please please join us!" The Sergeant patted his generous paunch and flashed a jolly smile. "So, read that carefully," he said, pointing to the book. "And think about it. Maybe it's not for you. Maybe it is. So if there's something you don't understand, you live nearby, drop in any afternoon. The mornings are usually busier. If not, we'll see you Wednesday."

The Sergeant liked the quiet, earnest young man.

"I've heard a lot of good things about Canada," he said. "I want to go camping there someday with my kids. My paternal grandparents were from there."

Michel turned pale when he read the name tag on the green lapel: Paul Landry. He was a Landry, like Yvette.

A sunny day in May. A gusty, noisy wind. The sound of the rusty park swings was irritating. She was sitting on the swing, taking tiny steps in a counterclockwise direction to twist the chains above her head into a braid. When the chains were nice and tight and braided all the way up, she lifted her feet off the ground and crossed her ankles under the seat. The chains untwisted slowly and Yvette twirled around and around and around. She put her face up to the sun and enjoyed the dizzy feeling of the gentle spiral. It was the last small pleasure of a young girl with a good heart and a sad smile.

Michel leaned on the horizontal bar of the triangular swing structure watching her. Hall's Creek playground was empty. Her face was swollen. Her upper arms had big dark bruises.

"Did he beat you up?" Michel said as he pointed to the bruises.

"That was Tuesday," she said. "He's on a binge. It was bad today. He pushed me down the stairs. He heard I want to run away."

"Bastard."

"My mother didn't say anything."

"She's probably afraid she'll be next," Michel said. "Who's he going to beat up when you go?"

"I hit my head really hard on the corner of the radiator. Right here. I passed out for a second." She pointed to a spot directly behind her ear and under the crown of her head.

"Oh shit," Michel said. "That's a bad place. I can see a lump. It's swollen."

"I'm okay."

The swings squeaked on. The sharp, annoying noise of unhinged rusty doors.

"Sometimes I'm glad I never had a father." Michel said.

"Ron's your father."

"No. He's a nice guy but he's not my father. Did you start your period?"

"No, but it's coming I can tell. I have cramps."

"Really? Good. What time are you working?"

"Six."

"Same here. We've got two hours. Want to go to the rink?"

"OK."

There was an abandoned skating rink in the marshlands near the Hall's Creek railroad bridge. It was an old dilapidated stone structure that had the decadent air of a miniature Roman Colosseum. You had to walk a hundred and fifty yards through hip-high grasses and soggy terrain to get there. It was a good place to be alone. They would go there, smoke a joint, and neck; maybe go all the way if she felt like it.

They were tired when they reached their hiding place and lied down side by side in a spot inside the broken walls, shielded from the wind and out of sight. There were sheets of cardboard on the ground, some beer bottles, cigarette butts and a used condom. Michel lit up. They passed the joint back and forth. Yvette took a puff. Her hand was shaking. She missed her mouth. Michel made a face.

"You don't inhale the smoke long enough. It's a waste," he said.

Michel was an accomplished pothead. He had been toking since he was twelve.

"Everybody is always t-t-tell-telling me what what to do!" she stuttered. Michel blamed it on the joint.

"Come on. Don't be mad," he said.

He climbed on top of her, sucked at her neck, and squeezed her breasts. She stayed quiet and let him enjoy himself. She had learned to be passive. She looked up at the sky. She had never seen clouds move so fast. They looked like they were in a terrible hurry to go somewhere. Yvette felt strange, sleepy, numb. She was serious about running away to Montréal. Maybe she would get a job as a nanny for a millionaire widower like on that soap opera on television.

Michel was busy with his needs. He pulled her skirt up to rub his pelvis against her stomach. She wasn't wearing any panty hose. She didn't stop him.

He was pleased. Yvette was always afraid of getting pregnant and stopped him most of the time even if he always promised to pull out before anything happened. He unzipped his fly and pulled his pants down to his knees. No condom, but she was going to start her period anyway. They had done it tons of times and nothing had happened.

She was dry and her tight panties were in the way, just pushed to the side. It was difficult and uncomfortable for Michel but he didn't want to stop. He pushed in and out and it got better. He came fast.

He rolled over onto his back. He arched his body to raise his hips and pull up his jeans. He felt so relaxed. He brushed his hands over his face. This would make the busy weekend more bearable. He was working full-time now, and Monday was a holiday. It was Victoria Day for the English. *La fête de la Reine*[17] for the French. The bipolar society.

She was quiet. He shifted his weight to his side to look at her. He put his hand on her arm. He stroked the bad bruise with his thumb. He couldn't see her face. Her head had fallen to the other side. He jerked away violently when he saw a thread of blood leaking from her ear. He sat up. Her eyes were empty and staring at nothing.

He scampered backwards like a crab in a seated position. He was stopped by the wall.

"*Yvette! Réveille- toi! Arrête ça!*"[18]

With the tip of his foot, he touched her elbow to see if she reacted. He saw the lump on the back of her head. Her eyes were open. One side of her face was blue.

Yvette was gone.

Why did Michel do what he did?

As in every catastrophe, a chain of errors: youth's lack of judgement; a habitual drug user's lack of clarity; lack of a family structure and of social integration. And fear. Of death. Of punishment. Of incarceration. The certainty that he would be blamed. And soon it was too late to correct. The damage was done.

He hid her body then went to work. He visited her every day. He made sure she was there and then he kneeled a few feet away from her and rocked back and forth, his arms wound around his body. There was no peace. She lay there for days in the cold, wet mud.

This was the first murder of a child in the history of the city. Yvette Landry's funeral was held at Notre Dame de l'Assomption[19] cathedral and officiated by Bishop Roger Losier. The Mayor and the Member of Parliament were in attendance. She was carried up the stairs of the cathedral on the shoulders of six mounties in full regalia. She was buried in a shiny, white casket with gold handles. Her father and mother shrieked in grief.

---

17 The Queen's birthday.
18 Yvette! Wake up! Stop that!
19 Our Lady of the Assumption.

"That guy had better hide real far and real good because I'm going to kill him if I get my hands on him!" Yvette's father screamed as he walked away from the soft, brown grave.

There was a memorial ceremony at Aberdeen school because Yvette's younger brother was a student there. Adrienne Blanchard was chosen to read a poem. All the little girls trembled in fear when they thought that one day, Michel Bourgeois might cross their path.

My Name Is Koldo

No one expected Xavier's career choice. He loved the sea so much. At sixteen he left Bilbao for Madrid and the School of Mining Engineering. It was about the earth, about origins, about energy and survival. He wanted to know about these things.

He was the male portrait of his beautiful mother. He had dark shiny hair, bright brown eyes set wide apart, a distinguished nose, a square Basque jaw, and a gentle smile. He had sculpted cheek-bones and a wide forehead. A Roman bust. He was six feet tall and still had the lanky silhouette of an adolescent who had grown too fast. He was square-shouldered, narrow-hipped and had the strong, shapely legs and high, firm backside of a serious skater.

"*Ama*, I'm leaving!"

His mother came downstairs to say goodbye. His things were in the car where his father was waiting for him. The sun was shining down on him from the skylight above the door of the foyer. He was fussing with the collar of his jacket in the mirror, ready to go. She stopped at the foot of the stairs to contemplate this young man.

"My handsome son," she said. "I will miss you more than you know."

She looked up at him, took his face between her hands and kissed him on the forehead. He closed his eyes and inhaled her breath.

He arrived in Madrid in September of 1975, just two months before General Franco died. The following years would be called "The Spanish Transition." It was a period of change from an autocratic, confessional regime to a modern, secular democracy and a full member of the European Union. Madrid, the capital, was a city in spontaneous combustion.

The streets of the city were a laboratory of political and social change. The General was succeeded by the grandson of a king exiled sixty years before. The king appointed a man of the regime as prime minister. To the people's relief, disbelief, or indignation, he called democratic elections, opened prison doors, legalized the Communist Party, and prepared to write a new constitution. The country was redistributed into seventeen autonomous regions with a moderate to high degree of self government. Political parties. Regional parliaments. Elections. Unions. Civil marriage. Divorce. Pornography.

New vocabulary. New rules. New game.

Spain's Big Bang.

Xavier became more involved with the hockey team than with politics. The School of Mines team played in the highly competitive Spanish Roller Hockey League. Xavier had played at school since he was six and it was his game. He arrived late but the coach gave him a private try-out and he was in. He was the rookie and was welcomed into the team. They were a tightly-knit group ranging in age from the captain's twenty-four to Xavier's sixteen. Xavier was nicknamed *El Niño*.[20]

The young Xavier also had to learn to deal with his pronounced sexuality in the big city. He would become a master in the future, but he was not always successful in the beginning.

Her name was Angela. The egg she threw from the stands hit him full-on in the face. The referee stopped the game for the floor to be mopped up while Aramburu skated off the rink trying to get the yolk out of his eye and bits of eggshell from his ear. His teamates roared with laughter and slapped *El Niño* on the back in male camaraderie.

Fortunately, he soon discovered a treasure trove of lovely European and American students in Madrid studying Spanish on six-, eight- and twelve-week university programs. The courses lasted just long enough for Xavier to enter into a warm friendship and a physical relationship, before a tearful goodbye.

His engineering studies did not pose any special challenge. He got excellent results without much effort. He particularly enjoyed ancient metallurgy and geology. He lived in a college residence and spent his summers doing research for professors at the school, sailing and studying

---

20 The kid

English. He didn't worry a great deal about the future. The team occupied an important part of his life. He was playing tougher and faster hockey. He had improved with age and strength and made a difference on the rink. The team was at a sweet moment. The players were all in top shape and played well together. In his third year, they won the Spanish League and were invited to Rome for the World University Games.

They were excited to reach the semi-finals but were defeated by a superior Argentina. The team then faced a strong Brazil for the bronze medal. They pumped themselves up in the dressing room and charged onto the rink like unchained soldiers of the Empire. They won eight to seven in a loud, passionate, heart-stopping game, the game of his life. He marched with his teammates in the athlete's parade as proud and happy as could be, behind the Spanish flag.

The summer after third year he got a job at an iron mine in León in northwestern Spain where he learned something very important: he was not in the right place.

In his rented room at the one-star *pensión*,[21] he opened his eyes from a fitful sleep every morning at 4:05 a.m. and watched with dread as the fourth numeral of the digital display of his alarm clock radio rolled over. By a quarter past four, he was up and dressed, sitting on the edge of the bed watching the green numbers. He left the *pensión* very quietly to go for breakfast at a bar that opened early for miners.

He was always the first one there. He paced up and down the sidewalk under the street lights as the owner arrived in his old battered car and rolled up the steel door. For some reason, the clatter of the door made Xavier feel better. He had a *carajillo,* the miners' special: cognac and espresso flambéed by a Zippo lighter. It had a slight aftertaste of lighter fluid, but it helped.

"*Buenos días,*" said Xavier.

"*Buenos días,*"[22] said the bartender.

The bartender shook his head. He had been running the bar for over twenty years. Another junior engineer scared out of his wits. He knew the

---

21   Boarding house.

22   Good morning.

mine was hard. He had lost friends and family inside it. He was generous with the cognac.

Iron mines are deep and this one was one of the deepest in the world at nine hundred metres. Almost one kilometre straight down. Under a lake. Xavier calculated two hundred million tons of stone and water above his head. He gripped his clipboard with sweaty hands and jotted down numbers and calculations moving from one section to another. The days wouldn't die. The first time he heard the siren, he froze in panic. It was not the end of the world, just the end of the day. He learned to welcome the urgent, high-pitched quitting whistle. He made his way briskly to the shaft along the tunnels, head bent and shoulders round because of his height. The miners headed for the elevator in small groups in relaxed conversation, relieved that the day was over. Someone always sang a miner's song. Often, up to thirty miners jammed into an elevator with a capacity for twenty-two. Xavier didn't care, he just wanted to get out of there.

It took six very long minutes to reach the surface. Xavier stared at the back of the neck of the man in front of him. He didn't mind the smell, as he smelled the same. At one hundred metres, the sun teased them and at thirty metres it shone in their faces. It was summer. *Jesus*, thought Xavier, *in winter they never see the light.* He couldn't help himself: at ten metres he threw his head back, opened his mouth, and sucked in the air. When the sliding doors opened at the surface, someone behind him always patted him on the back.

He made it through his eight weeks. Mining was a profession of great dignity, but Xavier Aramburu could not do it.

He recognized his error and set about to correct it. Back in Madrid, he asked the Dean for permission to condense the last two years of his degree into one. He worked for ten months like an assembly line technician in a busy factory. He could do it, but it was a question of time. There was a lot of information to store, projects to do, papers to write. Most importantly, he needed a good thesis. He wanted his degree and needed excellent marks to get into Harvard.

He reluctantly gave up the team and took up running at dawn to keep in shape. As for sex, he hadn't the time or patience for the seduction of suitable young women. He flirted with the world of prostitution. It was not the place for a nineteen-year-old upper-class boy, but he felt moderately comfortable renting a room in an expensive hotel and tipping the concierge generously. It was an expensive and impersonal solution. Xavier liked the chase and the conquest, which prostitution annulled. Finally, he opted for some amount of self-denial.

His engineering degree might have been considered a mistake, but it was probably one of the best things he ever did. The last year of intense study of a scientific discipline fine-tuned his brain and taught him to think tridimensionally. He learned to understand and to resolve from the abstract to the concrete. But mostly, it taught him a lesson and put him in his place. Mistakes tend to do that. He also retained a serious case of claustrophobia.

He made it. He was accepted to Harvard Business School in September of '79. Xavier was able to relax. His last summer in Bilbao revolved around his family and the prenuptial events surrounding his sister's wedding. Begoña, who was twenty-two, was getting married on August fifteenth, the day of the Virgin of August, and the first day of *La Semana Grande*, "The Big Week," Bilbao's summer festival.

Xavier was happy. He would spend July and August as a sailing instructor in Getxo and take care of his Uncle Luis Aramburu's new catamaran. He was asked to help his fourteen-year-old cousin, Luis, prepare for his sailing certification and teach him to handle the new boat. Luis was a nice kid and the catamaran was a fourty-four foot beauty.

In a nationalist fervour, Cousin Luisito[23] had just changed his name legally from Luis to Koldo, its Basque form, which he considered to be his true name. Xavier was having to get used to this new Euskadi where suddenly everyone was changing their names and seeing a hero in the mirror. Four years in Madrid and summers away had separated him from the tide of events at home. Perhaps he was too detached: his identity did not rest on exterior factors. The new boat got its first dent because of this.

"Luisito, drop anchor." Xavier called the new "Koldo" Luisito out of habit.

"My name is Koldo," he said.

"Yes okay, drop anchor."

"Not until you call me Koldo."

---

23 "-ito," a suffix meaning small. It is often added to the names of children (and adults) as an affectionate form of address. "Little Luis."

They were driven off course by the wake of a large yacht docking beside them.

"I don't give a fuck what your name is! DROP ANCHOR *HOSTIA!*"[24] Luis, a.k.a. Koldo, didn't move. Xavier blocked the helm and the rudder then tried to reach the anchor, but it was too late. They crashed into the yacht portside. The damage was considerable. There was a long dent on the left hull. The brand new boat would be sent straight to dry dock. Xavier would have to file a report to port authorities. He looked at his adolescent cousin in disgust.

"Are you fucking crazy? You could have been hurt *hostia!* If the captain calls you sweetheart or if he calls you piece of shit, you obey," Xavier shouted. "He is in command. Do you understand the words 'in command'? KOLDO? Happy now?"

The boy had not expected these consequences. His face was a picture of mortification. He put his two hands on his head.

"Xavi! The *aita* is going to kill me," the boy moaned. He stood there in his huge swimming trunks which made his skinny body look even spindlier.

Unfortunately for Koldo, his father had been at the yacht club bar nursing a glass of white wine and watching his pride and joy sail into the harbour. From the large terrace windows, he had witnessed everything. He marched down to the jetty in righteous fury as they were mooring the boat.

"My fault!" said Koldo. He hoped that a prompt confession and his father's political affections would soften the intensity of the blow. "He called me Luisito. I was waiting until he called me Koldo."

Xavier had never heard anyone curse to that degree. Luis Aramburu left out no symbol of the Catholic church, no scatological reference, no insult known to mankind. Not even the Virgin Mary was spared. Xavier had to move aside and cover his face to hide his laughter. Koldo could see Xavier's shoulders shaking, felt comforted by this small act of solidarity, and giggled nervously. Luis looked from his son to his godson and then back again. The three of them had to sit down. They laughed so hard, their stomachs hurt.

"Call me Koldo," Xavier said as he tried to breathe, talk, and laugh at the same time. "What a brute!"

---

24 A common swear word in the Basque Country and Spain. In this context "Jesus," "Shit," "Goddamn it." It can also be an interjection of surprise or displeasure.

Koldo would never live it down but he wore the legend of his new name with dignity and humour. He had stood firm and he always would. Koldo, he was.

That last summer in Getxo, the family felt blessed to have Xavier at home. He worked hard at the port. He took his little sister into town for ice cream every night. He was the only brother of a demanding and nervous bride, but he came through for her. Begoña was smart as a whip, a clever young lawyer and entrepreneur who collected beautiful objects and sold them at small bazaars and Sunday morning flea markets. They made peace with their difficult relationship and mother-deprived childhood.

It was a bittersweet summer because it would be his last in Euskadi. He knew that he was leaving for good.

Begoña was married in a cloud of Balenciaga[25] gowns and Ecuatorian roses. The magnificent Xavier danced with the bride because of their father's bad knee. The groom almost went unnoticed.

Shortly after the wedding, Xavier was off to Harvard. His father, mother and Paloma accompanied him to Madrid to see him off. He was leaving on an afternoon flight to Boston. Father and son walked arm in arm in Madrid's Retiro Park in the hot August sunshine. Iñaki chose a secluded table at a quiet café. Xavier was expecting a comfortable conversation about plans for the coming year and the general state of the family businesses. His father enjoyed keeping him informed.

Instead, Iñaki pulled a letter from his pocket. He handed it to his son who recognized inmediately what it was: an extortion letter from ETA. It was a badly typed and smudged carbon copy with the image of a snake winding itself around an axe. It was carbon copied because it had probably been a group mailing. Iñaki's hands got dirty every time he touched it. Dirty letter. Dirty business. The Basque terrorist group had not disappeared with democracy. On the contrary, the violence had escalated. In just the first months of 1979, almost forty assassinations and several kidnappings of prominent Basque citizens had occurred.

---

25 Cristóbal Balenciaga. Renowned Basque couturier, based in San Sebastian and Paris.

If they didn't pay, the next letter could hold a bullet wrapped in tissue. The next threat might be a bull's eye painted on the fence of their house. Then a kidnapping or maybe a bomb at the factory. Unfortunately this was not unusual. Extortion was ETA's principal form of financing. They needed money to buy arms, to support their lives in exile, for public relations work among foreign journalists, to build bombs, to buy used cars, and print posters.

The Aramburu family had been singled out because they were wealthy but also because Xavier's mother was a Quiroga. The Quiroga family was staunchly Catholic and conservative. They had been on the wrong side during the Civil War and remained close to the regime. ETA did not forget the sins of the fathers. Both Ana's sisters had married within their social circle and had moved to Madrid.

Ana Quiroga had theoretically married beneath her when she had chosen Iñaki Aramburu. Iñaki came from generations of self-made men. The Aramburus played Basque sports, belonged to Basque gastronomical societies, and were known to hum Basque lullabies. They were uncomfortable Basques. Hardworking, patient, and rich.

Destiny would have it that one day at a picnic, sixteen-year-old Ana sprained her ankle and was carried four kilometres back to the bus on the shoulders of the biggest and strongest boy in the group. Iñaki Aramburu was a *pelota vasca*[26] champion and had a rugby player physique. He made her laugh until she forgot all about her ankle and, when he set her down carefully in her seat on the school bus, he told her matter of factly that he would have to get used to her weight because he was going to marry her.

"Oh really?" she said.

"Yes," he had answered simply.

They were married on the first Saturday after her eighteenth birthday because Ana warned her parents that she would not wait a minute longer. She would be a virgin on her wedding night and she would marry Iñaki. On that day, a Quiroga married an Aramburu. To ETA, Quiroga was trump.

The letter had to be dealt with one way or the other. It was not a surprise. It was a fact of life of the upper class in Euskadi.

---

26 Basque handball.

"Did you show it to Uncle Luis?" Xavier said.

"Yes, of course. He is more informed than I am about these things. ETA needs cash. There are hundreds of them living in France. Benito's boy, you know? He's not even Basque. Born in fucking Cordoba for Christ's sake! Anyway, Luis can make contact with someone who knows what to do. Can you believe it? He's going to try to negotiate payment in installments," his father said.

Iñaki lit a cigarette.

"*Hijos de puta.*[27] I think I should stay," said Xavier.

The summer heat, his imminent departure and the insinuation of personal violence to his family momentarily overwhelmed him.

"No. No. No," said Iñaki as he blew out the match. "Over my dead body. You are out of here. You are away from this shit. You are on that plane in four hours if it's the last thing I do."

Iñaki put his arm over Xavier's shoulders and gave him a comforting fatherly squeeze.

"Let's not be dramatic. This will be over soon," said Iñaki in his no-nonsense Basque way.

"I'm not so sure, Aita. It is ingrained and their ideal is impossible. A fatal combination," Xavier said.

Six years after running through the fire together, the father and son walked back to their hotel and talked about buying an apartment in Madrid. Ana missed her sisters. Paloma's cardiologist had moved to Madrid precisely for the same reasons. It was the logical thing to do. Iñaki didn't want to be a hero but he would shield his family to his last breath. There were plenty of business opportunities in Madrid. His brother could take care of things at home. It was only a four hour drive from Madrid to Bilbao. He really did believe that it would all soon be over.

The Aramburus would join a small but growing exodus of old Basque families leaving Bilbao for Madrid. Not barefoot. Not penniless. But an exodus nonetheless.

---

27 Sons of bitches (of common usage in Euskadi and the rest of Spain).

Part Two

Harvard Man

Xavier had to make a life for himself because he knew that Boston would not be temporary. It was first day of Harvard Business School. The professor was calling on his new students at random.

"Francisco Xavier Aramburu Quiroga?"

"Sir?" replied Xavier.

"Francisco or Xavier? Aramburu or Quiroga? Guide me here," the professor said.

"Xavier Aramburu."

"OK. An engineer. Mining. *Escuela de Minas, Universidad Politécnica de Madrid.*"[28] The professor's Spanish accent was perfect. Xavier raised his eyebrows in surprise.

"That's right," he said.

"Don't let your mechanical mind run away with you," the professor said.

"I'll try not to," Xavier replied.

"Basque, I surmise?"

"Yes. Bilbao."

"Interesting. Jesuit education, I see. Excellent."

"That was the idea," Xavier said.

"Do you have a mission, Mr. Aramburu?" the professor asked.

"Well, I'm looking for an apartment."

There was general laughter. Doctor Aboaf was enjoying the conversation.

"I'll have you know that my grandmother was buried in Constantinople, clutching the keys to the Aboaf home in Toledo, the capital of Castille," the professor said.

---

28 The School of Mines, The Madrid Institute of Technology.

He was Sephardim, a descendant of the Jews expelled from Spain in 1492. Wherever the diaspora had taken them, the Sephardim still spoke an ancient form of Castilian Spanish. The keys of the Spanish ancestral homes were passed down from generation to generation. After six hundred years, the professor's grandmother had taken the Aboaf keys with her to the grave.

"That's amazing," said Xavier.

"Yes. So, how are real estate prices in Toledo these days?" responded the professor.

Again laughter, and the doctor moved on. As the class was dispersing, the man who would be Xavier's lifelong friend approached him.

"Xavier? Hi! Charles Perry from Philadelphia," he said.

He shook Xavier's hand. He was the image of a privileged American. A towering six foot four, he was taller than Xavier and older as well. He was a handsome young man in his late twenties with blond hair, a steady blue-eyed gaze, and a firm handshake. He was impeccably dressed in bright, stiff cottons and well-ironed casual trousers.

"I've been to Spain a couple of times," he said. "My girlfriend is an artist and well, we went to Madrid, the Prado of course... Barcelona, Seville. Oh and Cuenca! I really loved Cuenca. We stayed in one of those hanging houses? Beautiful museum."

"OK. You've been around then," Xavier said.

"Pat studied art in Florence for two years, so we had fun meeting in different places. She'd love to meet you, I'm sure. She loves Spain."

"Of course. I'd love to. Really," Xavier said.

They walked to the library together for an orientation tour for first-year MBA students. Charles Perry volunteered information about himself and his fiancée Patricia Powell.

"We're both at school. Pat is starting her master's in fine arts at Tufts this year. I'm at a law firm in Boston. At the moment, only part-time while I get my MBA."

"You're a lawyer?" Xavier asked.

"Just recent. Last spring. Penn," Charles said.

Charles was from an extremely wealthy Philadelphia family dedicated to public service and philanthropy. The Philadephia aristocracy had always naturally assumed their heritage as the Founding Fathers of the United States of America. It was the birthplace of the Republic and of the Constitution.

Charles Perry was waiting for the right time and the right opportunity to run for public office. His grandfather was remembered as the best Senator in Pennsylvania history and Charles did not want to disappoint.

After the tour, they had lunch at the Cambridge Hotel. They hit it off. Charles was an inquisitive sponge and Xavier enjoyed the sharp conversation with an American. Charlie, the Democrat and the Protestant, believed in right and wrong. Xavi, the Basque and the engineer, believed in true or false. The relative versus the absolute. They were intrigued and amused by each other's arguments. On their second coffee, Xavier's eyes flickered to the back of the restaurant and said, "Weren't those two girls on the library tour?"

Charles turned and looked.

"Yes. I think I recognize the Asian one," he said.

"Let's go sit with them."

Charles was reluctant. For a moment, he wondered what he had gotten himself into with this sophisticated, good-looking Latin kid. They paid their bill and sauntered over to the girls' table. Young Xavier took the lead with the all-American behind. They made their classmates' acquaintance, Sherry and Mei. Mei, who looked like she was sixteen, was actually a thirty-year-old Japanese computer whiz and the conversation was lively and interesting. Xavier arranged to go out to dinner with both of them the next night.

"Did you say you were twenty years old? Where did you learn to pick up girls like that?" Charles later said, laughing. "Not one but two dates. Together," he said, chuckling with incredulity.

"I didn't pick anybody up. I just said hello," Xavier said.

"Right," said Charles in amusement.

Curious about Xavier, he asked, "Do you play Bridge by the way?"

"God no. Do you roller skate?"

"God no."

They shared a grin and a pat on the back. Charles invited him to dinner at his girlfriend's home in the city on Saturday night. Xavier agreed immediately. He appreciated the invitation. Charles was an interesting person of a complexity that was not evident superficially. Xavier waved goodbye and headed back to the dormitory. He thought about Friday night and how he needed to find an apartment soon. He wasn't allowed guests in his student residence room and that was going to be a problem.

Xavier's American life began. It was all up to him. He did not waste time in self-contemplation. To an important degree, the world he was living in was subject to his own will. He chose to climb inside it and make it move.

Xavier stepped back to appreciate the five large canvasses that were hanging from the rafters of the attic studio in Charlie's fiancée's large house on Beacon Hill. The Powell family lived in a federal style mansion in an affluent Boston neighbourhood.

"It's explosive and powerful," Xavier said to Pat. "And you are so tiny. Like a contradiction. It's fantastic."

Xavier's reaction was spontaneous. The paintings evoked the vibrant and violent forces of nature. Pat was a very small girl, with blond hair and big blue eyes. Her appearance was in direct opposition to the energy and passion of her art.

"Thank you so much! Charlie, did you hear that? Explosive, powerful and contradictory. From a Spaniard no less! What a wonderful thing to say!" she said.

"I knew you two would understand each other!" Charlie said. He was pleased with his guest. Pat went on.

"I knew a Javier Moreno in Florence, a sculptor from Madrid. He wrote his name with a 'J' and we called him Javi with an 'H' sound," she said. "Is your name pronounced the same way?"

"Not quite. Where I come from, it's written with an 'X' and pronounced like a soft 'Ch,' Shavy. Everybody calls me that at home."

"Good, it's Xavi then!"

Xavier had found a good bottle of Rioja at a Boston wine store. It was his father's favourite: Imperial from Bodegas Riojanas. Thankfully, they hadn't asked him for identification when he bought it. He was just one week from his twenty-first birthday, drinking age in Massachusetts.

Over a pasta dinner, they opened a second rare Rioja that they removed with some degree of mischief from the Judge's wine cellar. Pat was the daughter of Mackenzie Powell, a famous Massachusetts judge known for his liberal rulings, militancy in the Democratic party, his passion for his wine cellar, and his numerous wives. "Mac" to his family and friends, was at his Cape Cod home with his third wife, and twin daughters. Pat was the only daughter of his first wife who had died very young of cancer.

The excellent wine, common interests, and contrasting opinions made the conversation loud and passionate. The virtues of olive oil, graffiti art, Poland's Solidarity movement, Jimmy Carter, and the bizarre, according to Xavier, sport of baseball.

Pat's father, the judge, met Xavier at the tennis club soon after the dinner. He was delighted with his daughter and her fiancé's new friend. He had four daughters from three different wives. Charlie was the closest to a son that he had. To his chagrin, Charlie loved classical music, the game of Bridge, and the gentleman's game of tennis. Here was Xavier, a hockey player, a sailor, and a ladies' man. "My Basque" he called him. A man after his own heart.

To the Powells, Xavier became a sort of adopted cousin whose birthday was celebrated, who was picked up at the airport, who stayed overnight on important weekends, and who had a standing invitation to dinner.

Charles admired Xavier's frankness, clarity, detachment, and foresightedness. He was going to attempt a political career and he would go as far as he could. It was naïve to say or think that he could be president someday, but Charles allowed himself to contemplate the possibility. He knew that power and responsibility were lived in solitude, but he felt fortunate to have met Xavier. He was a friend and perhaps someday could be an advisor. Xavier treated them all with the gruff affection, comfortable familiarity, and lack of nonsense typical of the people of the place where he came from. Pat loved him. Mac loved him. Charlie loved him. Xavier had a family.

On his part, Xavier fell unconditionally in love with *Justine,* the other member of the Powell family. It was early October when he saw her for the first time at the Hyannis Port Yacht Club in Cape Cod. She was silver.

"There she is!" said Mac.

Xavier stopped in his tracks, put his hands on his hips, and swept his eyes over the sleek sixty-one foot Palmer Johnson sailboat. He stuck his tongue out and curled it over his upper lip. *Justine* had a lot of class. She was fast and beautiful, a voyager. She was named after a character in *The Alexandria Quartet.* Xavier remembered his first *Justine,* in Santander, many years before. This new *Justine* was just as sweet and exciting.

Mac smiled proudly. "So?"

"I want her," Xavier said.

"Well, you can't have her. She's mine," Mac said.

True Identity

Justine spent the summers at Cape Cod and the winters in Saint Croix in the US Virgin Islands. Mac employed a French couple from Antibes, from November to May. They sailed her down south and lived on her all winter then sailed her back up to Cape Cod for the summer. During the winter, Mac flew down to Saint Croix as often as he could. As for Xavier, *Justine* was his whenever he wanted her. During the five years he spent in Boston, he spent summer weekends in Cape Cod exploring the New England coast with Mac. He accompanied the French crew down to Saint Croix several times. He loved the trip down in the fall.

Mac's friendship was important to Xavier. He was sensitive and knowledgeable about the Basque issue. His knowledge of the problem was solid. The IRA[29] was close to ETA and Mac had handled some delicate extradition cases to Ireland. He was considered an expert in the matter. He knew exactly what he was talking about and this was comforting to Xavier.

In his second year, Xavier was contacted by the Spanish Consulate in Boston. He was asked to meet with a visiting assistant of the Secretary of State of the Department of the Interior. Carlos Martin was an affable *madrileño*[30] who arrived late for their appointment. Xavier counted seven shopping bags.

The Civil Guard anti-terrorist squad had busted an ETA hideout and discovered a good deal of information. Xavier's name was on a list but not to worry… It was not a hit list, just a list of influential Basques in the US. Xavier was somewhat offended by Martin's vaguely congratulatory tone.

It was not impossible, Martin told Xavier, that a Basque priest residing in New York might approach him, possibly asking for money. Upon this eventuality he was given a business card that read *"ABC Construcciones"*[31] with a phone number in Madrid. He was shown a photograph of the priest. And by the way, could Xavier help get his daughter into the Harvard MBA program?

Xavier walked out of the building, threw the phone number in the trash but committed the priest's face, name, and address to memory.

---

29 The Irish Republican Army.
30 Native of Madrid.
31 ABC Construction.

There were several members of ETA, who were protected by the IRA, in Boston working in Irish bars. They kept a low profile as they would never jeopardize their fragile legal status in the United States. Most of them returned to clandestinity in France or Spain but others secretly applied for green cards, married an American, and disappeared into one of the fifty states. They chose to burn their bridges, victims of their own war. They displaced themselves and future generations forever. Mac was conscious of the complexity and social drama of the Basque dilemma. For Xavier, it was just good to know that somebody knew where he was coming from.

The Druk and the Opera Singer

Life in Boston was fine. There was work. There were friends. There was *Justine*. Harvard did not have a roller hockey team but Xavier did locate a pick-up game in a Portuguese neighbourhood every Saturday morning, which he enjoyed. He had a comfortable apartment in Cambridge. There was a steady flow of women.

It was his master's thesis that made him semi-famous. In the early eighties, a common European currency was on the drawing board. Europe needed an instrument to compete with the American dollar. There were economists, political scientists, and philosophers all over Europe preparing the great change. The French called it the ECU, the initials for European Currency Unit, and the Germans called it the Euro. In the end, the Germans won the dialectic battle and it was baptized the Euro.

Xavier presented: The Druk, A Tribal Currency for the Twenty-First Century.

The Druk was a Bhutanese symbol of wealth. A dragon bearing jewels. Xavier proposed an alternative currency to live alongside the ECU or Euro. His Druk was a unit of barter for goods and services as in primitive societies. Instead of a fist of salt, the Druk would be the unit of exchange. Three Druks for an English class. One Druk for a coffee. The intention of the Druk was not to be profitable but to soften the blow of a powerful currency controlled by Brussels and Germany that would drag the weaker economies into a permanent game of catch-up with their rich partners. This was the heart of the essay. The consequences of the European Union, the widening of the gap between the wealthier and poorer states which would entail the widening of the social gap as well. The Druk could act as an emergency generator for small towns and communities. It was a unit of exchange for basic needs.

It was insightful, fun, premonitory, revolutionary, practical, disturbing, attacked, admired, and put away. Harvard proposed him as a speaker at the Davos Economic Forum Young Thinkers Seminar. The paper was featured in *Harvard Business Review*, a magazine read by Harvard alumni all over the world, including several heads of state. It was also mentioned in the leading economic press of the time.

The paper was uncomfortable to the Europeans and received condescendingly in Davos. But twenty years later, on January 1, 2000, a school teacher in Bilbao, a street cleaner in Milán, and a tour guide in Athens paid 30 percent more for a cup of coffee than on New Year's Eve. It was hard to swallow.

Thanks to the visibility he had achieved with the Druk paper, Xavier was offered a Doctoral Fellowship that prolonged his stay in Boston another three years. He liked the idea of a PhD and Charlie urged him to stay on. He was still so young, barely twenty-three. He enjoyed teaching and writing. His particular background as a Basque and an engineer gave his articles a slightly different edge. He contributed regularly to *Harvard Business Review* and his name became well-known among the Harvard intelligentsia.

He taught undergraduate macroeconomics and statistics. The students called him Buru, and he was popular for his foul language, clear explanations, and practical examples.

"Don't play me the fucking violin," Xavier would say. "Give me an answer."

There came an interruption in Xavier's smooth trajectory. He lost his head over an Israeli opera singer, Doctor Aboaf's niece. He met Naomi at a typical university dinner party at his professor's cluttered and tasteful home in Cambridge. Naomi had come from New York to perform a recital with the Boston Chamber Music Ensemble.

She had the lazy body language of an artist who is conceding you the privilege of her company. About thirty years old, she was a classical Middle Eastern beauty. Her thick, dark hair fell below her shoulders. She had olive skin, huge, dark eyes that bulged slightly, a prominent nose, and a generous mouth. She wore flowing black clothing that made it difficult to imagine her body.

Xavier was mesmerized as she sang an aria from *Madame Butterfly* at the professor's piano. Her powerful beauty, her exquisite voice, and the smooth theatricality of her movements took his breath away. She had long, slender hands that pleaded before her as she sang. He was seated beside her at the dinner table. She whispered unkind comments about her uncle, challenging Xavier's loyalty to his mentor and forcing him to share in her naughtiness. The wine was heady and the food exotic. He was aroused, and she knew it.

He was devastated when he was forced to leave. He had come by cab but would leave with Franklin, another grad student. The mine and the bomb had left their marks on Xavier. He detested elevators and parked cars, avoided high floors, drove a motorcycle, used cabs in the winter, and rented a car only when his father came to visit.

"You live at One-Eleven Soldiers Field, right?" Franklin said loudly. "I can drop you off."

One-Eleven Soldiers Field Road was a well-known Cambridge address where many older students lived. It was a large apartment complex on a busy road with direct access to the Business School campus from behind.

He was tongue-tied and overly conscious of his accent, but he managed to say, "You have a truly beautiful voice. I hope to see you perform someday."

"Yes. Nice to meet you." She smiled vaguely and looked away.

The doorbell rang at three o'clock in the morning. He jumped out of bed, knowing it was Naomi. One-Eleven Soldiers Field! The address had registered. The mailbox had his name on it. Mac was always giving him hell about that but now Xavier was glad. He looked through the peephole to make sure. Definitely not an *etarra*.[32]

"Naomi, just a minute," he said.

He rushed into the bedroom and threw the sheets and blankets into place. For a brief moment, he thought about opening the door naked but decided against it. He grabbed his jeans and a tee-shirt and dressed as he skipped on one foot on his way to the door.

"Hi," Naomi said.

"Hi," he said.

"Want to go out for coffee?"

---

[32] Member of ETA.

"Oh sure. But I don't think anything is open yet. I can make some. Come in."

"Oh. Later then," she said.

"Here. Give me your coat," he said.

He helped her remove her coat and threw it on the sofa. She had come to him in the middle of the night. His male confidence was reinforced. In situations such as those, Xavier didn't waste much time in conversation. He took it for granted that she had come to be with him.

"This is my place," he said.

She looked around the living room in approval as he gentlemanly placed his hand on her lower back. The apartment was contemporary, comfortable, masculine, and full of books in elegant professorial disorder. He had hung a very large black-and-white aerial photograph of the industrial section of Bilbao on the wall. It was a landscape of factories, smoking chimneys, parking lots, steel bridges, train tracks, and dead end streets. The guts of the real Bilbao, with the Aramburu Foundry in the foreground, rolling hills in the distance, and the river Nervión where the Quiroga Shipyards were situated, flowing through the centre.

"I like that," she said.

They were not children and he was not a gentleman. He pulled his tee-shirt over his head and unbuttoned her blouse. She did not stop him or even touch him. She remained impassive. Xavier felt a very strong desire for this hot-and-cold woman and leaned down to kiss her. He loved the sense of conquest and gratification of a first kiss.

Naomi moved her head violently from side to side. He had trouble catching up with the lateral movements. He kept losing her mouth. Her arms hung limply at her sides. He slammed his mouth on hers and, taking small steps, walked her backwards to the bedroom. His jeans fell to the floor. She seemed to be an observer rather than a participant in the act, but this just excited him more. He lowered her trousers and stopped on his way down to rub his face over her red lace panties. Her dark pubic hair was visible through the lace. He loved the musky smell. He sat on the side of the bed, removed the rest of her clothes, then leaned back and pulled her down above him. He was happy with her full, dark body.

She chose to dominate. She broke into loud lamentations and rolled around chaotically on his pelvis. Her hands grasped his and kept him away.

It wasn't good. There was no rhythm. He pushed up to try to make it better. She made a loud trumpet like sound and it looked like it was over. She stopped, got up and reached for her clothes. Xavier was in full erection.

She went into the living room and picked up the rest of her things. She looked into the bedroom as she was putting on her shoes. He was speechless, still in bed leaning up on his elbows, craning his neck to see her through the open door, his penis straining against the white sheets. Very matter-of-factly, she said, "Why don't you come to New York next weekend? You can stay with me. Friends of mine are giving a party for their gallery opening."

He was caught off guard but very flattered.

"OK. Where do you live?" he said with a cough.

She found a pen on his desk, wrote her address and phone number on the front page of a student's exam, and left. He heard the door slam and then went into the bathroom to take a shower. He pictured her naked in front of the piano in the professor's living room. She was playing with her dark brown nipples with her thumbs.

Xavier was hooked on a crazy diva.

She kept him waiting for more than an hour in the lobby of her building on the Upper East Side of Manhattan.

"Good," she said when she saw him. She didn't stop to greet him. He followed her to the elevators. He was just starting to perspire when it reached the twenty-second floor. Thank God, it was a fast elevator.

She apologized for being late. She was rehearsing a small role in an opera starring Kiri Te Kanawa. She would never have taken it on had it not been for the high visibility of performing for a moment opposite the world's biggest star.

"Kiri was a bit off today, I thought," she sniffed.

She pointed to his bag and said, "You can leave that here," so he dropped his bag in the middle of the hall. "Come here, darling, and help me relax. You did bring something nice to wear for tonight, didn't you?" she said, referring to his casual clothing.

Xavier turned into a subservient male slave. He obeyed her as she ran her bath. He lit scented candles as she stepped into the tub, dramatically dropping her bathrobe to the floor. He was permitted to see her low, round buttocks and column-like thighs. He would have liked to suck on them, but he sat on the toilet seat, massaged her neck and listened respectfully while she verbally dismembered all of her colleagues. He sat very still when she vocalized or sang a short snippet of her role. She liked the sound of her voice in the tiled, humid bathroom. Indeed, it was beautiful: like a nymph in a cave. But there was still no intimacy or affection until she saw him dressed to go out for the party.

He asked her for some time in the bathroom. He showered, shaved, and dressed, struggling to keep his duffel bag dry and neat on the bathroom floor. He had brought a white Mao shirt, grey pinstriped trousers with a matching vest, perfectly shined burgundy moccasins, and a Hermès belt, a birthday present courtesy of sister Begoña. His hair reached to his shoulders, as was the norm among young college professors. He was wearing a classical navy blue, double-breasted overcoat. A plaid cashmere scarf in burgundy, grey, and navy blue framed his perfect face.

When she saw her little toy all dressed up, she marked her territory. They made love on the foot of her bed. Naomi didn't bother to remove her red leather jacket with enormous shoulder pads. The spontaneous tryst was exciting and sophisticated. He felt better about having made the trip.

Xavier was not totally out of control nor surprised at the cold reception. Everything about Naomi was odd and unbalanced. Through all of this, he felt a dizzy excitement, a need of discovery, and a wish to escape the containment of his own history. He was twenty-five years old.

Anne and Karl Dubuisson had renovated the two upper floors of an old textile mill in Soho into forty thousand square feet of open space for their new art gallery.

Three Japanese chefs prepared sushi while a modern dancer interpreted a piece by Bach. A performance artist cried as she read the dictionary. On the upper floor, a photographer took flattering portraits of the guests in front of an authentic Basquiat graffiti background while a popular Brazilian group played bossa nova tunes. A camera crew moved through the spaces filming a documentary. The party was New York Soho of the eighties at its best.

Naomi was pleased. Anne Dubuisson had noticed the beautiful Xavier immediately, taken his arm, winked at Naomi, and made sure they were introduced to the right people. Xavier had an important social grace. He was poised and at ease wherever he was and whomever he was with. He looked directly into people's eyes. He was never in two places at once. His two feet were firmly planted in the immediate present.

A group of Wall Streeters recognized Xavier's name and challenged him to a lively debate. Had he called it Druk to rhyme with buck or fuck?

"Both," he said.

He shared stories about the Basque Country with Anne Dubuisson who had spent the summers of her childhood in Biarritz and he danced a very cool bossa nova. Naomi, who was an ice maiden in private but an exhibitionist in public, behaved like a woman in love. Xavier felt the satisfaction of a desired conquest.

Some of the party moved to a crowded disco on Fourteenth Street. Xavier was high on Naomi, on the party, on New York, on alcohol. The photographer arrived with his date, the young male model who had been at the party posing with guests. The model had a very handsome almost pretty face and a thick shock of blond hair, which turned out to be dark brown but expertly dyed. The sultry Scandinavian model was actually from Barakaldo, the blue-collar neighbourhood of Bilbao. He was a nervous and very social chatterbox who liked to please.

"Excuse me. Excuse me?" he said, trying to get Xavier's attention and make himself heard over the table and the loud music. "You're Spanish, right? Your name's Xavier?"

"Yes," Xavier said.

"I'm Ander. I'm from Bilbao."

"Hi. So am I," Xavier said.

Xavier was from Getxo and Ander from Barakaldo but these class differences were obviated in the interest of politeness, the neutrality of the territory, and the non-belligerent character of the two young men. They acknowledged each other with a nod across the table. Naomi got up to go somewhere and Ander rapidly occupied her space. He smiled and stared expectantly at Xavier like a puppy whose owner has just come home. Xavier felt obligated to small talk.

"So, what's your story? How did you end up here?" Xavier asked.

Ander was twenty-three years old. At eighteen he moved from Barakaldo to Madrid. *Not surprising*, Xavier thought. *A homosexual and particularly effeminate son would entail rejection and ostracism in many, if not most, Basque homes.* In Madrid, he had been studying dance and working in an expensive ladies' shoe store when an agent from New York came in to buy dress shoes in a hurry. She gave Ander her card the way she gave it to all the good-looking kids she came across in Europe. Ander took it seriously. He saved his money, bought a one-way ticket to New York, and planted himself at the agent's office door. He had been lucky. The agent was legitimate, thought he had a good face, liked his attitude, and decided to take him on for one year. Ander was a natural. He was graceful, intuitive, and immensely photogenic. It was working out.

"You're very handsome," Ander ventured in a clear attempt at seduction.
"OK. So what's that about?" Xavier asked.
"Just wondering..." Ander said. He lived his sexuality joyfully and openly.
"*Hostia, chaval. No,*"[33] Xavier said. He was direct but serene. He gave a commiserating shrug of the shoulders. He had been approached occasionally and was not particularly offended or disturbed.
"Okay, okay, sorry. Not a problem," Ander said, stepping back respectfully.

Xavier was not brutal. Ander was not upset. The sacrilegious "*Hostia*" and being called "*chaval,*" an affectionate form of the word "kid," made Ander feel quite at home. He instinctively felt comfortable and safe near Xavier.

Naomi came back with some coke and prepared four lines on the black glass table. She went first, then motioned to the photographer. Ander looked at Xavier, recognized his hesitation, and bent his head first to snort the powder. He very deliberately gave Xavier a private demonstration. Then he nodded to Xavier. It was an imperceptible nod. The nod of a compatriot meaning it's okay.

Xavier decided to let it happen. He had always been curious anyway. He imitated Ander and relaxed. The taste was disagreeable. He felt a numbness in the back of his throat. His big heart started to drum, and he felt like dancing. He danced with everyone and he danced alone. Life couldn't be better than New York at that precise instant in time.

She was sorry but she preferred to sleep alone. It was a question of viruses and vocal chords. Xavier was forced to crash on the uncomfortable sofa. She closed her bedroom door. He was left confused by the coke. He didn't know if he wanted more drugs or more sex. If that was the trade off, the choice was clear.

---

33 Jesus, kid. No.

On a pretext, he was left alone the next day. He walked around Columbia University, thought about Naomi, and about moving to New York. He was caught somewhere between frustration and anticipation.

That evening, Xavier arrived at Naomi's apartment early. He waited on the sofa, in the dark, looking out at Manhattan. Naomi arrived around six, claiming total exhaustion. He ran her bath again. She informed him that they were going to a dinner party. She revived in the warm and sudsy water, sat up in the tub and sang to the bathroom wall. From sweet and carefree to devious and harsh, the role had many variations in intensity. Xavier was in awe. When she got out of the bath, he laid his head on her stomach. He swept his tongue over the crease between her thigh and her abdomen. She pushed him away.

"Later, darling. I promise. I can't possibly now. I am in character."

It was an informal dinner with musicians with whom she had studied. These extraordinarily talented people were amusing themselves singing and playing Beatles tunes on the piano, cello and violin. Xavier sat on the floor of the small apartment and sipped a nice wine. He thought to himself that it was probably the best concert he had ever attended in his life.

Naomi sat at the piano and sang "The Long and Winding Road" in a sweet, quiet voice. She was wearing a strapless red top and tight, black leather jeans that accentuated her generous female curves. He leaned against the wall in the corner of the living room in the dim light.

Her beautiful hands danced over the keys as she sang directly to Xavier with a seductive smile. Her black hair caressed her naked shoulders. Each verse stabbed at his infatuated heart. The road ended here. He had found his destiny. Xavier Aramburu was sure he had been born to be the lover of this sublime and eternal artist.

When they left the dinner, he begged to go back to her apartment, but they went on to the disco and met up with the photographer and Ander again. She had taken a liking to the photographer and had commissioned a beauty shoot. Ander was excited and happy to see his new friend. Naomi, however, played the bored little girl role. Four fine lines. Four in the morning. Again the same.

The next morning she asked him to leave before noon, as a relative of hers was coming in from Tel Aviv. They hadn't made love. She said she had started her period. She ran out without a kiss or a nod. As she walked away, without turning back, she said, "Leave the keys in the ashtray."

Even a man in mad love gets the hint. Or maybe not.

Days passed and no news of Naomi. He lost his appetite and became distracted. Pat knew people who had been at the gallery opening and eventually found out what had happened. Xavier had outshone Naomi.

"Never outshine a diva," she said to Charles.

Meanwhile, Xavier couldn't help himself and dialed her number every day to hear her voice on the answering machine. Finally, three weeks later, there was a sign of life. Doctor Aboaf popped his head into Xavier's small office cubicle and said, "By the way Xavi, Naomi called the other day. Said to say 'hello.'"

"Oh really? How is she?" Xavier said. He was stricken.

"Very well. She's in Atlanta for a month. The critics have been very kind. They're on the road before they premiere at the Met."

It was clear now. She was away. That was why she wasn't answering his messages.

Say hello to Xavi. She wants to see me!

Charles drove him to the airport through the tail end of a hurricane. There was heavy traffic and a last minute detour due to flooding on the Logan Airport entrance ramp. Xavier was jumping out of his skin. Charlie didn't like to see Xavi so obsessed with a woman.

"Take it easy, Xavi," he said. "Plenty of fish in the sea."

Xavier wanted to throw himself out of the car. Charlie's strong point was not emotional intelligence.

In Atlanta, he took a taxi directly to the Civic Center, bought a ticket to the evening performance, located the artists' entrance, and waited. He would say he had come to see her perform. How could she forget that she had sung her entire role to him as he gently caressed her shoulders?

When she saw him standing by the artists' door, she exclaimed in disgust, "I can't believe you. Who invited you here?" Then she walked on.

He took a taxi back to the airport and spent the night sitting up on a hard bench waiting for a six a.m. flight to Boston. He walked into his apartment, went into the bathroom, took a razor, and shaved his head for being so vain and stupid. Then he went to bed.

The Gladiators

The bald head did not go unnoticed.

"That bad?" said Charles.

"Is there anything we can do to help?" said Pat.

"Oh dear," said Dr. Aboaf.

His students pounded on their desks and catcalled. His neighbours looked away, assuming he had cancer.

Three weeks later, he went to Madrid for Christmas.

"*Hostia,* why did you do that?" said his father.

"Grow it back. Now," said Begoña.

"Did somebody make you suffer, *hijo mío?*"[34] his mother asked as she caressed his bald head. She was standing behind him at the breakfast table.

"Yes. A little," Xavier answered quietly. He sat back, eyes closed, basking in the pleasure of his mother's hands on his head.

"Was she worth it?" she asked softly in his ear.

Xavier thought about it. "No," he said.

His mother paused and said, "Suffering is inevitable. But suffer only for someone who deserves it." She kissed the top of his head.

"*Ama,* thank you."

"Paloma, come here and touch your brother's head," she said.

The brother, the son: a place he understood. Ultimately, it was his role in the family that defined him. Paloma giggled as she explored her brother's skull with her hands. He reached up, took her hand and kissed her fingers. He would let his hair grow back now.

---

34 My son.

The events around the bald head were not an entirely negative thing. They precipitated the future. Xavier made the decision to move to New York. Despite Naomi's humiliation, he had felt at ease with the sophistication and the craziness of the city. Charles and Pat were getting married and leaving Boston for Philadelphia. He came into his own money as he and Begoña received an advance on their inheritance for the sale of the Quiroga shipyards to an English shipping line.

First, there were things to do. There was his dissertation to finish, a job to find, and an apartment in Manhattan to buy. He would need some time to leave Boston properly.

He also inherited the young Basque model. Ander called and asked if he could stay at Xavier's apartment overnight. He explained, honestly, that by staying at Xavier's, he could save the accommodation allowance the agency gave him. He was so polite and charming that Xavier found it impossible to say no. Ander was excited about a casting for a prestigious New England sportswear line. It was a very well-known Ivy league, all-American, traditional brand. He stayed for three nights, as he was asked to return for the second and then a third day of interviews and pictures.

He was a good guest. He left early with Xavier and returned only after Xavier came home. On the second night, he stopped by the local supermarket, bought groceries and prepared a delicious dinner. They polished off two bottles of wine as they reminisced about Basque food, Bilbao, the historic moment their country was living, and where they felt it would lead.

Ander described his early life in the bosom of a vehemently nationalist household where all that was strong and masculine and Basque was revered while he stole Italian and French fashion magazines from the hairdressing salon next door. His mother spoiled him, but he was an embarrassment to his father and was bullied at school. As a youth, he had searched other faces for a glimpse of recognition or just a hint that he was not alone. At the age of ten, he attempted to auto-correct to please his father. He developed a chimpanzee-style walk that he demonstrated to Xavier, who shook his head as he laughed. It was funny yet poignant.

It was curious that it was the gay son of a bartender from Barakaldo who would bring back the land of his childhood so intensely. The tastes, the pride, the traditions, and a painful hardness. It was a hardness Xavier knew he shared.

Ander got the job. His face was red with pride and satisfaction as he left Xavier's apartment with the contract in his pocket. His career was taking off. He would be earning over one hundred thousand dollars. Twenty percent went to the agency. The rest went to him.

"Will you help me manage my money, Xavi?" he asked politely.

"You know I can't do that," Xavier said. "But be smart, *hostia,* and don't dilapidate it. You're Basque but you're not stupid."

Xavier laughed and slapped Ander on the back knocking the breath out of the slender and willowy fashion model.

"I'll give you the name of a good financial advisor in New York. You can decide if you like him," Xavier said.

Ander nodded enthusiastically. "Oh yes, please!" he said. "I have plans for the future. I'm not foolish you know."

"I know. If you were foolish, you wouldn't be here. If you were foolish, you wouldn't have that contract in your pocket."

Ander hadn't thought of it that way. He smiled proudly. They said goodbye and sealed their friendship in Euskera, the Basque language.

"Agur, lagun!"

"Agur!"[35]

They gave themselves an embarrassed bear hug and Ander left. He disappeared for a time, but Xavier did see him again soon. On a Sunday morning in the spring as he was riding his motorcycle to the Cape, he pulled off the road in front of a huge billboard. He took off his helmet, looked up and smiled paternally. There was Ander. Blond streak hanging over his right eye, dressed in impeccable tennis whites, an American flag on his sweater, he was surrounded by four nubile blond beauties. An All-American boy, from Barakaldo, Vizcaya.

Xavier was soon ready to leave Boston. He read his thesis in January of 1985, one month before leaving for a junior vice president position at JP Morgan on Wall Street. The premise was unexpected, complex, and brilliant: The Economics of Catastrophe. In the triumphant era of the eighties, no one contemplated anything near a cataclysm. The panel sat with him for several hours discussing its implications. It was a skein of science, economics, and

---

35 Goodbye, friend. Goodbye.

enlightened future speculation. Simplify it and publish it, they said. Good luck out there but please come back to us. Summa cum laude.

Charles and Pat had married the summer before on the beach in Cape Cod. It was a beautiful Atlantic sunset when Pat and Mac walked down to the beach hand in hand to meet Charles. The guests were scattered on the beach, on the boat house, and on the dunes. Torches and small candles illuminated the path from the Dutch colonial home to the beach. Pat had designed her own gown, on which she had painted one large pale pink peony, her mother's favourite flower. There was a large, whimsical circus tent in the garden for the party and *Justine* was anchored close to shore and covered in pretty lights.

Xavier, dressed in a formal white dinner jacket and black linen Bermuda shorts, watched the ceremony from the bow of *Justine*. He looked on in friendly envy of their deep commitment and their blind trust in the future. He felt yearning and wariness in the same degree. For the moment, solitude was not loneliness, it was freedom.

He bought two apartments in Manhattan. Sister Begoña came to New York to organize the renovations and decor. She shook her head as she walked through them. How could her brother have bought the two ugliest apartments in New York City? Linoleum floors. The smell of boiled cabbage. The two apartments were side by side and took up the entire third floor of a small, nondescript prewar building on an uninteresting edge of the Upper East Side. He had terrible views on all four sides: a boring street, two brick walls and a depressing urban and industrial landscape of roof-tops, chimneys, and back alleys. Begoña rolled up her sleeves. She was excited about having a family pied-à-terre in New York City. She looked around and saw the apartments had high ceilings and lots of light. All a good decorator ever needs.

As it was a third floor, there was no need for an elevator. Nellie's, the best Korean grocery and deli in the neighbourhood was on the bottom floor. The subway was twenty feet away from the building's entrance. Central Park was five blocks away. Rosa, Bruno the janitor's wife, offered to do his housekeeping. He had everything a single man ever needs: food, transportation, a housekeeper, and recreation.

He gave himself one hot and wonderful month in the Carribean aboard *Justine*, and by March 1985, he was moving into his large loft that had a small guest suite apartment incorporated for visitors.

He walked into the JP Morgan building like an olympic athlete. He was tanned, rested, and hungry for new experiences and challenges. He did all of the things one must do on landing in a new city until one fine morning, he woke up feeling reasonably at home. He joined a health club, looked up old classmates, and found a café nearby frequented by fashion models. He was pleased with the apartment and his new life.

He was assigned an office on the sixtieth floor of JP Morgan's new building on Wall Street. The office had a fantastic view to the Brooklyn Bridge. Fortunately, it had a glass elevator and he could look out as he rose. From the marathon to the hundred metres: he had gone from the sober reflection of academia to the urgency and action of Wall Street.

The breakthrough came within the first weeks. These were the early days of the Swap markets where companies and institutions exchanged interest rates, currencies, cash flows, or securities to their mutual benefit. It was a deceptively simple financial instrument.

I'll pay your interests, you pay mine.

The large banks did the matchmaking and acted as brokers. The first swap took place between IBM and the World Bank in 1981, but in 1985 swaps were still new and very sophisticated instruments fresh out of the laboratories. JP Morgan rivalled with Chase Manhattan Bank to be King of the Swaps Mountain. There was a huge deal in the works at Morgan.

Xavier had a simple idea. He turned it over in his mind again and again. He threw rocks at it, and imagined every possible scenario of destruction or failure, but his technical adjustment just made the instrument better, safer, and hallelujah! more profitable. He let his engineer's mind run away with him and it worked. He was very excited. He knew it was brilliant.

He explained it to his boss, Wilbur Crawford III, who was a well-known Southern economist. Like Xavier, recruited and seduced from a university think tank. Crawford sat back in his chair and set out to destroy the idea. It was a tennis match and Xavier smashed the ball on every point. Like Xavier, Wilbur got excited. He organized a five-minute meeting with the Chief Financial Officer that same day. The CFO would receive them in the board room late, at five minutes to eight. They had to be brief, he had tickets to the opera.

Alone in the dark building with the exception of the cleaning crew, Xavier and his boss walked to the meeting with a slight spring in their step. Two smart men holding the secret of good invention.

"What did you say your name was?" said the CFO.

"Xavier Aramburu."

"You haven't been with us long have you?"

"Five weeks, sir," Xavier said.

"What have you got for me?"

Xavier explained the idea graphically on a whiteboard. The CFO listened with his elbows on the table, his hands clasped, and his index fingers pressed to his mouth.

"Crawford?" he raised his eyebrows and inquired with his voice.

"I'm excited about it," said Wilbur in his thick southern drawl. "It has to work."

This was Wall Street. The stakes were high and the players were shrewd. Hesitation was not the name of the game.

"Okay. Go for it. Total confidentiality. Forty-eight hours," he said. "I'll inform the president."

It was known as the Aramburu Innovation and became a technical mainstay of all future swap transactions in the eighties and nineties. Xavier was on the cover of *New York Banker* magazine with five other "New Gladiators." One of those gladiators was female.

> *Wall Street Women. Nineteen eighties. No dresses. No trousers. A serious suit. In shades of grey, blue, or brown. Pinstripes or textured, tweed-like fabrics. Single-breasted and slightly tailored jackets. Knee-length straight skirts with a six inch slit to one side. The shoes are very plain and have a round toe. They are called "business shoes." A two inch heel if they are tall and three inches if they are short. A cotton or silk blouse, with a collar, open to the second button. Never three. Three is a mistake. It is said that a plunging neckline and spike heels will get you to the boardroom table on your back looking up at the ceiling.*

A single string of small pearls at the neck. A leather or metallic hair band holds back very shiny, very healthy hair. They do not permit themselves the feminine gesture of pushing back their hair behind their ears lest someone remember they are women and hence should really be somewhere else. Some use two different methods of birth control to make sure. They are obsessed with body hair and carry a razor and tweezers in their large bags. A colourful silk scarf carelessly knotted around the shoulders completes the look. This is equivalent to the man's bright tie. Indeed, their goal is equivalence. Power will follow. They are pioneers.

Such was Alexa Howard. She was thirty-five years old, hardworking, ambitious, competitive, relentless, and single. She did not like Europeans. She did not like JP Morgan. She especially did not like the way Aramburu, the new Spaniard at Morgan, stared at her.

Xavier thought Alexa was funny, brilliant, attractive, and had a body he would definitely like to experience. She was not particularly beautiful, but she had a fresh, pleasant face. She was a brunette with shiny, dark brown eyes, a small nose with just a sprinkle of freckles, good cheek-bones, and short hair. Her body, however, was in a class of its own. In heels, she was as tall as he was, and very slender. Her nun-like business uniform did not fool him. He overheard her tell the journalist who was interviewing them that she was a volleyball player in college. *Of course*, he thought, *volleyball players have the best bodies.*

The magazine people had organized a photo shoot, a round table discussion, and a lunch in honour of their gladiator issue. Xavier nodded enthusiastically at everything Ms. Howard had to say and hovered around her during the photo session until the photographer told him to be still. He made the conscious decision to pursue this bright woman of the perfect body who made him laugh.

She agreed to one business lunch with him but turned down two private invitations. Just as he was about to give up, it dawned on him: she was a lot like his sister. The same intensity, the same defensiveness, the same sense of humour. He changed tactics. He had the perfect pretext. Charles' sister was getting married and Xavier had been invited to the wedding.

"Hello, Alexa Howard please?"

"Hi," she said.

"It's me, Xavier."

"I know."

"How do you know?"

"How do I break this to you, little Swap King? You have something of an accent."

"Me?"

"Yeah. You. What is it?"

"Can you help me with something?"

"Depends."

"I'm invited to a wedding. My best friend's sister in Philadelphia."

"Yes. So?"

She thought he was going to ask her to the wedding. She cringed and prepared a refusal.

"What should I buy as a gift? How much should I spend? I really don't know how these things are done here," he said. "It's a prominent family. Sorry to bother you but I thought you might be able to help."

The fox gingerly approached the trap. Alexa was quite the socialite and, having grown up in nearby Connecticut, she knew the stores of New York like the palm of her hand. She loved to shop and she loved beautiful things. For the first time, she was friendly and helpful. She sent him to a fellow called William at Tiffany's on Fifth Avenue.

"Be sure to tell him that Georgina Howard has sent you," she said. "That's my mom. I would say buy something small and only moderately expensive. You're a single guy and you're young. But William will help you out. Call me from the store if you have any problem."

He did call to tell her what he had bought and to send regards to her mother on William's behalf. Alexa pretended to be very busy at the time of his call, but Xavier could tell she was pleased.

Next he wondered if she knew of a good summer camp for his nephews. He neglected to mention that they were only two and three years of age. They met at lunch and had Chinese takeout on a bench in Battery Park. She gave him an envelope full of pamphlets and registration forms and offered to call the exclusive camp she had attended as a child in Maine.

"Yes," he said, "I'll talk to my sister."

But it was the shelving that did the trick. By that time, Alexa had assumed her role as Aramburu's shopping guide. They were becoming friends.

"I need some shelving for storage, and I'm having a hard time finding what I want. Sorry to be such a pain, Alexa. It's for my storage room down in the basement. I don't want to pay a fortune."

"Right. Let me think. Well, there's a place out on Route 46 in New Jersey," she said. "They import all kinds of Scandinavian stuff. Good prices, do it yourself. But I don't know…you'll never find that on your own." She hesitated. "You know, I might like to go, too. I'm thinking of reorganizing my closets. You have a car right?" she said.

"Yes, something like that," he said.

She laughed, assuming he must have an old battered car.

"That's okay. Saturday morning, pick me up around nine thirty. I'll make an exception and take you somewhere," she said, laughing.

He waited for her on the sidewalk in front of her building sitting on his motorcycle, holding an extra helmet and smiling from ear to ear.

"I cannot believe I am going to New Jersey on a motorcycle, with a Latin guy in a black leather jacket," she said, shaking her head as she clambered onto the bike in her fashionable outfit.

"Ha!" he said. "Maybe you'll learn something, Howard!"

She sighed with feigned irritation as he forced her to lean on his back and pulled her hands around his waist under his jacket. Alexa wouldn't admit it but she had been getting very impatient between Aramburu phone calls. She was arrogant and independent but Alexa loved, more than anything else, to be needed. As for Xavier, although he didn't realize it, he needed to be cared for.

On Highway 46, on the way back from the shelving expedition, Alexa's hands slipped under his shirt. Xavier bit his lip and smiled in anticipation. When it was safe, he guided her hands with his. They rode in the whistling noise of the wind and the thundering turnpike traffic. Those driving past the black Honda motorcycle had no inkling of the sexual game that was being played.

She directed him to a parking lot and they made their way to her apartment. He was quiet and walked fast. His arm over her shoulder, he held her very tightly to make sure she didn't regret or ignore her very clear invitation. Alexa was scolding herself. He was too young and totally fickle. She knew. She had asked.

He pushed her gently against the bedroom wall. His breathing was very loud. He had waited five weeks for her. That would be Alexa's small triumph. His impulse was to immobilize her so as to stand face-to-face, to feel her long body at last on his. He groaned in the deepest satisfaction at the vertical and symetrical embrace. He spread his legs to hold her inside his little prison, pinning her to the wall with his hips. He took her head in his hands and enjoyed a long perfect kiss while she fondled his buttocks. He murmured through the soft exploration of her mouth.

"Are you okay? Can I stay?" he asked.

"Shut up, Aramburu. For God's sake," she said.

They undressed each other impatiently and Xavier at last saw what he had come for. She was nothing short of magnificent. She had the slender, harmonious body of a modern dancer and twice the strength of most women. Xavier was abducted by her body. Her long, softly sculpted legs, and arms like ropes that wound all around his body. She had a fine bottom that was the happy, smooth inflammation of her interminable thighs. Her navel was small and tight, her beautiful breasts just filled his hands. Her skin was so taut and flawless that it seemed like marble. Xavier was the fat cat who swallowed the bird.

It might have lasted an hour. Spent, he fell on his back and breathed out, exhausted.

"*Diós!*"[36] he exclaimed as he rolled over.

"That was fun, we can do that again," she chirped.

"Give me a minute," he said, laughing.

He looked at her bedside clock. It was half past four. It was a Saturday in early May, the days were getting longer.

"What are we doing tonight, Howard?"

"You want to do a movie and a pizza?" she asked.

And what began as a sexual itch became a very good relationship. Alexa Howard would be Xavier's first real girlfriend. Affectionate, helpful, and available, he was a very good boyfriend. He was even almost faithful. She

---

36 God!

kept him so busy and, frankly, so satisfied that he reserved his sexual adventures for out of town trips and occasional fits of desire. Alexa never gave up her sarcastic attitude, but no one doubted that she was deeply attached to the young Spaniard. She kept his favourite beer in her refrigerator. She bought flowers every time she went to his apartment. She included him in her life as if he had always been there.

Just as she dressed like a nun for work, she was stunning on formal occasions. She wore clinging dresses that were either very low cut or backless, red lipstick, and she combed her short hair straight back for a sophisticated, wet, French look. It was very difficult to look better than Alexa Howard in a sexy gown. They made an impressive couple. The age difference sometimes sparked unkind comments to which Xavier countered, "I'm just a lucky son of a bitch."

Alexa had a serious social life. Charitable organizations. Dinners. Galas. Openings. A respected, important, active woman, and dashing young star Xavier Aramburu on her arm. She was an up-and-coming female on Wall Street and perhaps the future CEO of a big house. This was not an insignificant feat.

The names Howard and Aramburu sounded like a law firm and, indeed, they fell into a New York professionals relationship. They didn't live together but went everywhere as a couple. At that time, it was not unusual for successful Manhattan couples to share a country house on weekends yet maintain their separate apartments in the city from Monday to Friday. It was comfortable, independent, civilized, aseptic.

Friends were introduced into the equation. Charles and Pat were not enthusiastic about the match, but Charles was glad that Xavier had settled down and was not roaming the streets searching for fleeting joy between the legs of anonymous women. As for Alexa, there was DeeDee, an interior decorator and realtor. Early on, they were invited to a dinner at his townhouse in Greenwich Village.

Alexa and Xavier went to the dinner directly from work. He leaned his head on her shoulder in the taxi while she looked at some papers. He called her Alex, she called him X.

"Thanks for coming, X. Hope you don't mind but this will be a primarily gay party. DeeDee is my mother's first cousin and like a brother to her. He was an only child like my mom. So Deedee is the closest to an aunt that

I have. He's dying to meet you. He doesn't believe you're as good looking as he's heard." Alexa chuckled. "I told him you weren't."

"Okay. I can live with that," he said. "But maybe we can leave early? Go to your place?" He bit at her neck.

"Sure. But I warn you, the food will be fabulous, DeeDee is a wonderful host, and you will love the house."

"Good."

Deedee welcomed them briefly in the foyer.

"Yes you are a beauty aren't you?" he said, taking Xavier's arm.

He was an elegant gay man with a penchant for theatricality.

"You don't think my nose is too big?" said Xavier.

It was an unexpected reaction. Deedee laughed heartily.

"Alexa darling, congratulations! Not only gorgeous but a sense of humour as well!"

He kissed her affectionately on the cheek and nodded to Xavier in approval. A crashing noise came from the kitchen. Deedee winced and said, "We'll talk later. I have you seated beside me! Have a drink and meet some people!" He rushed off to the kitchen.

Alexa had brought a change of clothes and went to freshen up in the guest room. Xavier removed his suit jacket and tie, and rolled up his sleeves. He explored the party. There were a dozen people having drinks in the living room, which opened onto a large candlelit garden with a long, exquisitely decorated table set for dinner.

It was June 23, summer solstice, *San Juan*.[37] All over Spain, people would be building bonfires on the beaches. Even the children were allowed to stay up to all hours. Jumping over fires. Making love. Xavier remembered that special night with a tinge of regret, but he brushed the thought away. The weather was perfect. The garden was a dream. He was served a gin and tonic. Xavier was glad he had come. He looked around at the guests.

Ander was there.

Xavier saw him first. He walked directly up to him and roared, "You! What are you doing here?"

---

37 The feast of Saint John.

"Xaviiii!" Ander yelled. Totally astounded, he put his glass down, shook his head, and stretched out his hands in welcome. "Where have you been? I called you a hundred times. No, two hundred times," he said.

"I live here now, man. I left Boston in January."

In the smooth hum of the sophisticated Manhattan garden party, they had a loud and happy reunion in their booming Basque manner. Big hugs, slaps on the back, and foul language.

Ander introduced him to his boyfriend, who looked lost and a little jealous.

"Jeremy, this is my friend Xavi, who I talk so much about."

"Nice to meet you. This poor guy has been looking for you!" Jeremy said, reproaching Xavi unfairly.

"I thought maybe you'd gone home," said Ander.

"Jesus, no. Your cousins haven't sent me my invitation yet!"

Ander's face turned red. In Boston, he had confessed to Xavi that two of his cousins were active in ETA and that his father's bar was a meeting place. In the spring of 1985, the violence in Euskadi was worse than ever. Returning was out of the question. Xavier hadn't meant to make Ander feel uncomfortable. He shrugged as if he couldn't care less and mussed Ander's hair. Something in Ander always wakened Xavier's paternal instincts. He seemed so vulnerable, yet his young life was an example of hard work, honesty, and courage.

"No, I'm doing fine here but maybe you should go back, Ander. To Madrid. It's amazing right now. You wouldn't believe it. Everything is booming, fashion as well!"

Xavier took advantage to give Ander some good advice. Madrid was the place to be in Europe. It was the pulsating heart in all things of the new Spanish democracy, while in New York, the gay community was suffering the tragedy of the AIDS epidemic.

"I know. I've heard," he said. "We're thinking about it. That's one of the things I wanted to talk to you about." He nodded and glanced pointedly at Jeremy.

It was the third time that Xavier Aramburu and Ander Etxebarria had crossed paths. Xavier had not sought Ander out for several reasons: they had different life-styles and the Basque connection was uncomfortable. They were both out of the loop, but nonetheless, difficult social repercussions were possible for both of them. One did not befriend an enemy.

However, the shared experiences had become a kind of joint history. First, crazy Naomi who had brought Xavier to New York. Then, the Boston casting that had launched Ander's modeling career, and now through Alexa, Ander was firmly in Xavier's extended social circle. It seemed juvenile to avoid friendship. Throughout the summer and fall, they saw each other often. Ander invited Alexa and Xavier to fashion events, Deedee had more dinners, Alexa in turn gave Ander and Jeremy tickets to ballets and concerts she couldn't attend. To Xavier and Alexa, they became "the boys."

The first time they came to Xavier's apartment for a drink, Ander lagged nonchalantly behind Jeremy, hands in his pockets, as if he had been there many times before. When Xavier showed them the guest suite, Ander sat on the bed and tested the mattress. With a mischievous grin on his face he said, "This is my room, isn't it Xavi? If you ever get lonely…"

Ander had never experienced having a significant amount of money and lived with the sensation that it could disappear into thin air at any moment. He had over two hundred and fifty thousand dollars in his account. He checked his balance every day. The money just sat there, making no interest. Xavier managed to convince him to put seventy-five thousand into treasury bills at three months, six months, and one year. Ander circled the dates of issuance on his kitchen calendar. He worried that he was being taken for a ride by Citibank, which definitely could not hold a candle to the mythical Banco de Bilbao.

He called home occasionally. Fortunately, his mother usually answered. She whispered that she loved him, that his father had asked about him, but to wait a while to visit. Three years had passed. He waited. He was afraid his grandparents would die. And secretly, he adopted Xavier as a brother.

They met for Sunday brunch in Chinatown shortly before Christmas. Xavier was in high spirits because he was going to Madrid for two weeks. Alexa was put out that he hadn't invited her, but she didn't let on. Jeremy was sulky. Ander was nervous. The subject of Spain came up again.

"Stop talking about it for Christ's sake and come at Christmas!" Xavier exclaimed impatiently to the boys. Alexa's eyes widened.

"Have a look! Move your asses! Talk to my sister," Xavier insisted.

Begoña had divorced, moved to Madrid with her two boys, and was living with her parents. She had given up her law practice in Bilbao and used her inheritance money to convert an old warehouse into a fabulous and eclectic furnishings store. She stocked furniture from Sweden, Provence, China, Vietnam, and Tibet, and carried textiles, ethnic jewellery, and tasteful objects from all over the world. In only three months it had become Madrid's most fashionable store and the stylish young Basque woman, Begoña Aramburu, a welcome addition to Madrid society. Begoña complained and moaned about her terrible fate but, in fact, she was in love with her store and her new profession. Madrid was good to her.

Jeremy was "in the business," so to speak. He had studied art history in Chicago and was an expert in antique mirrors and oriental porcelain. He worked for a high-profile antique dealer in Greenwich Village. Xavier mentioned that Begoña was having trouble finding sophisticated buyers and Jeremy perked up a little bit. Ander was excited, and tentative plans were made for a trip to Madrid over the holidays.

Xavier flew out of JFK on December 23, assuming that the boys had decided against the trip. He hadn't heard from Ander since that day.

Who Will Cry for Me When I Die?

Xavier rushed down the stairs at half past seven and ran into Nellie's to get his *Wall Street Journal* and cup of coffee before catching the Downtown Express. This was his morning routine. He had been back for a week. New York was cold as hell and there was a foot of snow on the ground. Madrid, in comparison, with its cool but dry and sunny climate was so much more pleasant. He missed the sunlight and the deep turquoise sky.

Soon after he moved to Boston, his parents bought a large penthouse in Madrid near the Wellington Hotel where they had always stayed. It was steps away from the beautiful Retiro Park in a busy and elegant shopping district. Xavier loved the noisy comings and goings of the large household, which now included his older sister and her two boys.

Days in Madrid were full. Morning, noon, evening, and night were clear and separate entities. There was time for everything. Leisurely walks with Paloma in the Retiro, lunches with his father, siestas, family dinners around the table, and sophisticated city nights. He had fun. It was not the same country he had left behind six years before. It was unrecognizable. He felt guilty that he hadn't invited Alexa, but he was having a great vacation. His home, the family cocoon, was now Madrid.

However, for the time being, home, his place of residence was New York. Holding the newspaper under his arm and the steaming hot Styrofoam cup in his hand, he headed for the subway looking down at the ground. The sidewalk was covered with a treacherous film of thin ice. It was a typical New York day: cars honking, city workers perforating the streets, columns of working people moving as a mass, white smoke seeping from the sewers. It was 7:35 a.m. and Manhattan was wide awake. Xavier joined the march. In the cacophony, he thought someone had called his name. He looked up. A tall figure in a knee-length, hooded coat was standing at the top of the subway stairs. Xavier tried to see who it was. The Nordic hood kept the identity of the wearer hidden inside a textile tube.

"*Xavi! Soy yo.*"[38] The voice was husky and muffled. Xavier squinted to see inside the hood.

"Ander, is that you? Jesus, what are you doing here at this hour?"

"*Estoy enfermo,*"[39] Ander said.

He was sick. Xavier saw his face. It had to be AIDS. Xavier spared Ander any condescending pretense.

"Don't fuck with me please," said Xavier.

"I'm not fucking with you," Ander said.

"*Hostia! La mierda,*"[40] said Xavier.

He took his friend's arm, looking for a place to talk and to get out of the way of impatient commuters. It was not Ander's intention to interrupt Xavier's work day.

"Xavi, I know you need to go to work," he said. "I know that I shouldn't have come. But I need one favour from you. Just one."

"Let's get off the street. Come up to my place," Xavier said.

Ander shook his head violently. His voice trembled as he talked, his eyes were frantic.

"Listen to me, please. It's important. Don't say no. I want you to come to my bank, to fill out the forms for a joint account," Ander said. He was close to panic, in a state beyond reason or logic. Xavier addressed his fears.

"You, listen to me! One: calm down, *Hostia*. Two: I will do what has to be done. Three: you're not going to die. You heard me? *Hostia* Ander!" he said.

Ander nodded with his entire body. He felt embraced by a wave of relief.

"Accompany me downtown. We'll decide what to do," Xavier said.

They took the stairs down to the trains, and on that morning at the end of January, Xavier Aramburu and Ander Etxebarria started a long and painful voyage.

---

38 It's me.

39 I'm sick.

40 Jesus! Shit.

The subway was crowded. There was no point in speaking. Xavier gave himself time to think. It was time to call the priest. He searched the back of his mind for the name and parish of the Basque priest that the Spanish diplomat at the Consulate in Boston had warned him about years earlier. Ander abandoned himself to the movement of the subway and the comforting sensation that he was not alone.

"Jeremy?" Xavier asked as they exited the subway car.

"He left."

Ander showed no emotion at the name. Xavier assumed correctly that Ander had been abandoned. Disloyalty to a Basque, unforgivable. The traitor undeserving of thought, memory, or feeling. Ander might be dying but Jeremy was dead and buried to them. They arranged to meet at two thirty for lunch. Xavier would take the rest of the afternoon off. They would talk things over calmly and decide what to do.

"OK?" Xavier said.

"OK."

"Swear it."

"I swear," Ander said.

Xavier went to work. This was not just another day. He could not leave Ander to live through this alone.

Ander was terrified. He spent his days walking compulsively and aimlessly through the city. It was as if the physical act of going somewhere, anywhere, would take him to a place where this beast inside his body could jump out and run away.

He crossed the streets chaotically, secretly hoping he would be run over. There were times he welcomed the idea of death. Many young men stricken with the disease were taking their lives. It would be a rest from the noise inside his head. The anger was better than the fear. He chewed at his knuckles. He had just turned twenty-five and wanted to live. The tears were of anger, not fear.

He worried about his money, his things, his dead body. Curiously enough, thinking about material things gave him a small measure of serenity. A little island of peace. He made lists of what he had to do: organize his accounts, buy gifts for his parents, clean his apartment, buy good cleaning products, leave it spotless. He was considering cremation but he wasn't sure if Catholics were allowed. He refused to spend money on a cemetery plot that no one would visit.

Ander had no hope. The probability of survival was zero. These were the mid-eighties, the Dark Ages of the AIDS epidemic. Despite the anger, fear, and regret, he preferred to face the inevitable.

At that point, he had one hundred eighty-two thousand dollars in his account as well as seventy-five thousand in treasury bills. It was a good sum. He was proud of that and glad he hadn't spent it. His father would have to be impressed. He'd love to see his mother and his sister in a pretty house somewhere. Maybe they could buy a place in the village of Bakio with a view of the ocean.

He needed Xavi now. It had been three weeks since he had received his results. He was ready to start on his list. If Xavi agreed to a joint account, he could take care of transferring the money to Ander's parents when he died.

Xavier shook his head. They were sitting in a booth at Morton's Steak House and he was trying to obligate Ander to eat a piece of key lime pie. The boy could hardly swallow. Xavier could not do what Ander wanted. He would be accused of unethical banking practice and barred from his profession. It was squarely tax evasion aided and abetted by a banker. Ander looked unconvinced.

"We're going to do things right, Ander. You will write a will and I will be your executor. You'll pay your taxes. That's the way it is. Listen to me, I have one condition: not one penny goes to Spain unless I say so. It is your money and you need it now more than ever. It could save you," Xavier said.

Ander nodded obediently.

"How much does a will cost?" Ander asked. "I heard three thousand dollars. I can't afford that! I'm not working!"

"Alexa has a friend who does wills pro bono. And listen Ander, you're not going to die. I called a friend in Harvard Med this morning. There is a drug coming out at anytime. I'm calling somebody tomorrow morning about getting you on a list. OK? Now tell me. Who is taking care of you? Give me the doctor's name. Do you have insurance?"

Fortunately, Ander had signed a new contract with his agency in October that included good medical insurance for one year. He had been assigned a doctor whom he liked.

Xavier paused and said very deliberately, "Ander, if you're not better by the summer, you're going home."

"Home? No way."

"Yes, Ander. The care will be the same and maybe even better. I'm serious. Personally, if it were me, I would be home already."

"You don't know what you're saying!"Ander exclaimed. "My parents would never live down the dishonour. Their son, not only a faggot but a leper. No!"

"Their fucking tough luck. You know what? If I have anything to do with it, you will go home even if you get better. Start thinking about what you're going to pack."

The idea made Ander very briefly just a little bit happy. Suddenly, he had a future, a horizon. The summer. Home. He touched Xavier's hand.

"Thank you," he said, choking up. "I love you very much."

"Hey let's not get sentimental about this, *hostia*. We've got a lot to do. We have to keep you healthy for the cure. Shit. Eat. *Hostia!*" said Xavier gruffly, pointing at the pie.

Xavier had made up his own list: the doctor, the dog, the priest.

"We have you on Ander's file as next of kin, Mr. Aramburu. Is that okay?" asked Dr. Andersen.

"That's fine. I'd like to accompany Ander to an appointment. I will be helping and I have some questions," Xavier said.

"Wonderful. I'm seeing Ander next Monday. Why don't you come with him? We'll go over all eventualities," Dr. Andersen said.

The doctor gave even the eventuality of death a tone of normality. Xavier wanted to know what to expect and what he had to do. Knowing the future was a terrifying but useful privilege.

Alexa was next.

"Alex, Ander came to see me. He has AIDS."

"I knew it! Oh God," she said. "I smelled it that day in Chinatown."

"Would your friend Melissa help him with a will?"

"Yes, of course. Oh not Ander, please. How is he?" she asked.

"Physically, not bad. Too thin. Too scared to eat," Xavier said.

"Jeremy?"

"Don't know. Don't care. Alexa, another thing. Can you find a small puppy for Ander? Something easy to take care of? Fast," asked Xavier.

"I will. Tomorrow," she said.

Xavier did not speak nor did he hang up. He was drained. What could he say that was not totally inadequate?

"Come over. Sleep here," she said.

"Thanks, Alex. I'll be right there."

He would visit the priest on Saturday.

Joaquín Múgica had been the archetypal young priest of the seventies. He played guitar, had long hair, and wore blue jeans under his cassock. One ear was pierced with a tiny gold crucifix. He was a priest the hierarchy tolerated because he filled the churches with young people enthusiastically singing "Oh Happy Day." The bishops nodded approvingly and congratulated themselves on their progressive church.

Joaquín had finally gotten into trouble. Like many Basques, he was good in the mountains; a trekker, a climber. In his parish near the French border, he had sheltered *etarras* on the run and guided them through the mountains to France at night. He had been followed, photographed, and identified. More than once.

What to do with this working-class hero? Joaquín became a political football between church and state. As a priest, he was not subject to civil law but to ecclesiastical law. In his inviolable presbitary, Joaquín awaited instructions from his bishop. He had no intention of fleeing to France. He could be useful in a prison.

The Basque Catholic hierarchy had a problem. They did not want the ambivalence towards ETA by a sector of their church to be pointed out. The central government was applying pressure to solve the problem quietly. They were not keen to persecute a young, long-haired, folk-singing priest. It would be terrible public relations for the struggling government that had far too many issues to juggle as it was. Atheist and communist ETA did not like to be identified with a tolerant priest moved by Christian love. Inner power struggles had ETA ruled by hardliners. They did not appreciate a martyr who was not one of them. Their political and legal apparatus did not pursue the Múgica case.

It became a church and government affair and it was settled quietly as the government wished. Joaquín Múgica was sent to the American Catholic church and placed in a Hispanic parish in Queens, New York. He was ordered to behave himself. Joaquín was given his freedom but banished.

However, nobody had forgotten him. Múgica became a liaison between exiles and families. He was watched by three governments and useful to everyone. Meanwhile, he adapted to his new parish, worked on a psychology degree at St. John's University on Long Island, and was secretly expecting his first child with his lovely Dominican housekeeper, Evelyn. He was thirty-seven years old. He had lost some of his combativeness.

It was a long subway ride, which Xavier spent reading medical journals and articles on AIDS. When he arrived at the small urban parish, he was glad to see that he had guessed right. There were confessions before seven o'clock mass. He sat in the pew opposite Joaquín Múgica's confessional. When it was his turn, he opened the small door of the tiny confessional but didn't go in. He bent his head and said, "*Padre*,[41] I will be waiting outside in the vestibule when you finish."

The crisp, continental Spanish accent in a big voice resonated in the empty church. The priest peered through the square-meshed window that separates the confessor from the sinner. *Padre* Joaquín knew exactly who it was. He made the sign of the cross and gave him a priestly nod. Xavier waited for him in the freezing cold stone vestibule.

"Son. You have come. Welcome," Múgica said.

Xavier did not introduce himself or acknowledge the greeting.

"It's about Ander Etxebarria. He is ill. AIDS. His parents need to know that. Tell them Ander wants to go home soon. Possibly for treatment."

The priest was well built and very youthful despite his bald head and small wire-framed glasses. He sat down on a cold stone bench that was built into the vestibule wall and pulled out a pack of Spanish Ducados cigarettes from the pocket of his cassock. He sighed deeply and lit up. Xavier couldn't help a slight gesture of recognition. The pungent smell of the natural black tobacco was unforgettable. His mother had forced his father to give them up for Marlboro. His father had complained that the Marlboro's cost triple and tasted like hay. Joaquín saw the light in Xavier's eyes at the pack of cigarettes.

---

41 Father.

"I smoke only three of these a day. I keep them like a treasure in my freezer," he said, taking a drag. "Ander Etxebarria. The model from Barakaldo?" he asked, exhaling.

"That's the one," said Xavier.

"What a pity. I will make the call." Joaquín paused, took a drag and continued. "You are Francisco Xavier. The smart kid, the rich kid from Getxo? Jesuit College?"

"Is that who I am?"

Joaquín nodded while exhaling the smoke. "We're all fucked up, son," he said. "There are a lot of boys here suffering, you know."

"I hope you'll understand that you are not breaking my heart," said Xavier.

The boys Joaquín was referring to, were ETA fugitives. The bomb makers, kidnappers, and snipers who were wanted for trial in Spain. The priest shrugged, stretched out his legs, and looked at his feet. Then, he leaned forward, his elbows on his knees.

"Etxebarria..." He paused again and looked at the tip of his cigarette. "I'm afraid he will not be very receptive."

"Ander won't be a financial responsibility. To the contrary," Xavier said. He could have kicked himself for saying that. He had intended to be discreet but for some reason this priest pulled at his tongue.

"No. I won't mention that. Not for the moment. You're not as smart as you think you are, *chaval*.[42] Not when it comes to the homeland." The priest had a laugh at Xavier's expense. It echoed against the stone walls.

"So give me your phone number because, frankly, I really don't remember if I have it anymore or where I put it," Joaquín said.

Xavier gave him an envelope containing the information and three one hundred dollar bills. "For the Church," said Xavier.

The priest took the envelope and looked inside. He shrugged and said that it would come in handy. It was freezing cold. Five minutes to seven. A January night. Joaquín had to celebrate Mass. He got up to leave, squashing his cigarette on the ground with his foot.

---

42 Kid. Affectionate and popular expression for young males.

"What I wouldn't give right now for a good *marmitako*[43] and a decent Rioja, eh?" he said. He put a comforting hand on Xavier's shoulder. "I'll call you next week. It's not going to be easy."

Xavier didn't know what to think. He liked the bastard.

Ander carried the tiny Yorkshire puppy in an African sling. A warm and loving creature on his chest was more therapeutic than any medication. Master and pet began to resemble each other. Ander slept much better and, quietly, his anger lost its edge. He weakened slowly with baby Lucas in his arms. He went to support groups, smoked a lot of marijuana with his doctor's consent, and generally took care of himself but Xavier was disturbed by his dwindling vitality. This was a question of time, a waiting game. Xavier had managed to get Ander on a waiting list for clinical trials with a promising drug at a Boston teaching hospital, but he needed to be alive when they called him. Xavier was worried. Young men were dropping like flies. It was a battle between life and death, and Ander wasn't fighting.

How to keep a person alive? Ander needed more than food, water, and high potency vitamins. Joaquín Múgica did the best he could. He contacted Ander's parents but was faced with a brick wall. The cousins were even more adamant. He tried the parish priest who did not want to get involved. Múgica was then contacted by a high ranking *etarra* who inquired about Ander's money and the Getxo banker who was robbing him. It was distasteful and indecent. Ander stopped asking.

Xavier assumed the role of caregiver. Like all siblings of a challenged person, he did not consider the task a burden. It was a question of acceptance, organization, and keeping drama to a minimum. He took the responsibility without batting an eye.

All was not tragedy. The best day was the day they wrote the will. Xavier and Ander met with Joaquín Múgica on a Saturday morning. At Xavier's insistence, Joaquín had agreed to witness the will. Ander left everything to his mother and named Xavier as his legal executor. The three Basques walked into an empty and dark Italian restaurant at one o'clock for something to eat and for Múgica to see Ander's financial statements and accounts.

---

43 Typical Basque dish. Fresh tuna and potato stew in a fragrant tomato broth.

They staggered out of the restaurant at five forty-five so that Joaquín, who was dead drunk, might make it to his seven o'clock mass.

It was odd to celebrate the writing of a will, but Ander was so relieved that he actually felt hungry. They ordered wine and a three-course meal. It so happened that Ander and Joaquín had a talent that Xavier did not have. As priest and model, they were professional performers of sorts and had the extraordinary ability of remembering every joke they had ever been told. Joaquín and Ander went head-to-head on the jokes while the dog peeked out of his sling looking puzzled. Three bottles of wine. Six whiskeys. Irrepressible and contagious laughter. Shoulders shaking, feet pounding, aching jaws, wet eyes. A release. The gift of laughter.

The disease waited for the spring to show its teeth. Ander's general state deteriorated seriously in April. He was weak, suffered sudden alarming weight loss, and developed terrible yeast infections. Doctor Andersen wanted him hospitalized. Xavier and Ander set their personal protocol into motion. Ander called Xavier, then called his medical ambulance service. Xavier called Joaquín, spoke to hospital administration, and called DeeDee who picked up Lucas and closed the apartment.

It was the first of three hospitalizations. With the doctor's help, Ander and Xavier had decided against a private hospital, opting for St. Vincent's in Lower Manhattan. Ander's savings would not be depleted but most importantly, St. Vincent's was the frontline of the battle and had a dedicated medical staff. It was also closer to Xavier's office. He visited twice a day bringing rich cappuccinos and cartons of ice cream. He was at the hospital at seven o'clock every morning before work began. He shaved Ander's beard every morning with an electric shaver.

"You're from Bilbao, for Christ's sake. You can't go around looking like a bum," he said.

"Do I look really bad?" Ander asked.

"You're a good-looking son of a bitch and you know it."

"I know. I'm better looking than you. Even Alexa says so," he said, giggling. Ander still had the strength to tease his macho friend.

The second hospitalization was due to pneumonia and lasted three weeks. It was long and difficult. They came face-to-face with the reality of the disease. When a patient died on the AIDS ward, volunteers walked swiftly down the corridor, gently closing the doors of all the rooms. It spared the living the sound of the tears and the sight of the body. Xavier was reminded of a sinister flock of birds. Ander suffered both physically and mentally.

"Who's going to cry for me when I die, Xavi?" he asked.

"Nobody's going to cry for you because you're not going to die. You are on a list, Ander. Looks like eighty percent remission. Any day now, I ship you to Bilbao with a big red bow on your head," Xavier said.

Xavier lowered his voice not to be heard. "None of these guys have eaten a decent piece of *bacalao*[44] in their fucking lives. *Hostia*," he said.

Xavier was appealing to Ander's pride at belonging to a tough and sturdy race of whalers, mountain men, and adventurers. But even the cerebral and scientific Xavier, not given to patriotic chest-beating, believed this was true. He was wrong. AIDS did not respect the Basque DNA or anybody else's for that matter.

July 5 was a Sunday. Xavier took his time getting to the hospital. He had slept at Alexa's and stopped by his apartment for a shower and a change of clothes. He was turning the situation over in his mind. Alexa feared the disease and therefore feared Ander. She had helped in her own way but she had kept away. She had been troubled in the beginning and Xavier respected that. He was tested and showed her the results.

After several months, the situation had become tedious to Alexa. This third hospitalization had come just as she was packing her bags to spend her summer holidays with Xavier in Cape Cod at Charles and Pat Perry's. She was understandably very upset.

Ander had experienced a slight relapse and had been admitted to avoid complications. They were pumping him with antibiotics and it would surely only be a question of a couple of days. Xavier thought of asking Joaquín to come into the city. He could stay at the apartment. Ander adored Joaquín. Joaquín wouldn't have to hide his pregnant girlfriend. They could enjoy the city together. It was only a month before Evelyn's due date. Xavier could take Alexa to the Cape.

He finally made it to St. Vincent's at around eleven in the morning. He climbed the stairs to Ander's floor carrying two iced cappuccinos, one in each hand. Joey, his favourite volunteer, was waiting for him.

---

44   Cod. A staple of Basque cuisine.

"Thank God you're here. He's taken a turn for the worse. We called but you weren't at home."

Xavier put the capuccinos down on the reception desk and ran to Ander's room. A nurse and a doctor were working intensely by his bed, monitoring machines and trying to make him comfortable.

"Ander!" Xavier shouted as he turned into Ander's room.

"*Aita*? *Aita*? Is that you?" Ander called.

Ander sat up despite all the tubes. His eyes were glassy and delirious. Xavier was at the foot of the bed. He put his hands on Ander's thin legs to keep him still for the doctor. It only occurred to him to say, "Yes, I'm here."

"Are we going home?" Ander said.

Xavier felt faint. He broke into a sweat. He perceived what was happening and said, "Yes."

"Oh, thank you, thank you, *Aita*. When are we leaving?"

"In a little while. Tomorrow. Get some rest now. Rest up for the trip."

"OK, OK. I'll try to sleep."

The nurse pulled Ander down to the bed. He strained to put his head up and struggled to speak.

"*Aita!* Did you talk to Xavi?" he asked.

"Yes. Don't worry. He's at home packing your stuff," Xavier said.

"Oh good. He'll come. He's very busy, you know, but he'll come."

"You rest now."

The Angel of Death had some pity in the end and allowed Ander to die thinking that he was not dying, but that his father had come to take him home.

The machine spat out a single steady beep. The doctor did not resuscitate. The volunteers moved quietly and swiftly down the hall, closing the doors of the living. Xavier cried like a baby. Ander's last thought had been for him.

Together under Rigel

Xavier

It was Saturday at half past five in the morning. Xavier was staring at the urn. He had placed it in the guest suite on a table in front of a window. He had chosen the rusty steel finish. He didn't know why. Xavier was drawn to the urn involuntarily. He found himself standing motionless in the room at least once an hour. He saw a handsome, healthy Ander sitting on the bed smiling seductively and saying, "This is my room, isn't it, Xavi?" He had not been joking. Xavier understands that passion and desire have no boundaries.

He would dispose of the ashes later in the day. Through Joaquín of course, Ander's father sent permission to him along with his bank account number. The settling of Ander's estate was in motion and everything was going well.

At dawn on a Saturday, the traffic was light. The ashes were in a knapsack on Xavier's back. It was still dark but the church was open. There was only a homeless man sitting at the back, very straight, afraid he would be asked to leave the warm and safe refuge. A handful of neighbourhood people trickled in.

Joaquín had prepared a small table for the urn between the communion pew and the altar. Xavier decided Ander would rather be beside him. He took the first pew and placed the urn carefully on the seat beside him. It was seven twenty-five. He sat and waited. This was Ander's mass.

From behind the altar, a door opened. Xavier came to his feet. Joaquín walked with purpose to the altar, opened the great missal by its bookmark, joined his hands in prayer, took a deep breath, and looked up ceremoniously at the congregation. He did not see the urn on the table and his eyes searched. When he saw Xavier, he began. He would celebrate the Mass in Spanish.

Xavier had never forgotten the Mass. He didn't need the booklet. There was no hesitation in his responses. He stood with his arms crossed over his chest and his head up. Joaquín matched his tone and intensity. An uneasy duel arose between the two accidental friends. They raised their voices, daring each other to falter or to speak without conviction. They were giving Ander a proper Mass in this place where none of them belonged.

When the Mass was over, Joaquín descended from the altar, gave Xavier a kiss on the forehead, then blessed the urn. Xavier made no move to leave.

"What's the problem?" the priest asked.

"The bells," Xavier said.

"What bells?"

"The bells of the dead."

"I can't ring them until nine o'clock, Xavier. It's Saturday. It's against city bylaws," the priest said.

"*Padre*.[45] Ring the bells for Ander. *Hostia*," said Xavier.

"I'm afraid not," Joaquín said. "And keep your language proper in the temple."

"I'll pay the fucking fine."

"Always the smart-ass from Getxo."

"Whatever. *Padre*, Ander gets his bells."

Joaquín conceded and returned to the sacristy where the bell tower mechanism was. Xavier stood still, holding the urn in the crook of his arm. When the bells began to toll, he genuflected and walked slowly out of the church. From the open door of the sacristy, Joaquín watched as the arrogant Bilbaíno[46] reached the end of the nave, turned to face the altar, genuflected again, and made the sign of the cross. *A proper Catholic boy, no doubt about it*, he thought. The bells of death are bells of sorrow and of warning. Xavier needed to mark Ander's death.

The bells tolled until Xavier and the urn turned into the street for the ride to Boston. Seven long hours later, he rode into the parking lot at Hyannis Port Yacht Club. He was expected. Charles came out to greet him.

"I'm so sorry, Xavi," Charlie says. "Pat's not feeling well, she can't be here. She sends you her love."

---

45 Father.

46 Native of Bilbao, Spain.

Xavier was still sitting on the bike. Charles put his arm around his shoulders. Xavier felt numbed by the long trip on the highway. The urn was heavy on his back. Exhausted, he removed his helmet and rubbed his eyes. No place had seemed correct to stop for coffee with your dead friend on your back.

"The coast guard lifts the weather advisory early this evening," Charlie said. "We'll leave at eight. Do it at night. Under the stars. That will be nice. Is that okay with you?"

They left at sunset. The miracle happened. A windy and grey North Atlantic day became another brilliant pink and yellow evening. They pushed out on *Justine*. It would take about two hours to reach twelve nautical miles at ten knots per hour. Twelve nautical miles is the limit of navigational international waters, which is where Xavier had decided Ander would rest.

"Xavi. Twelve," Charlie said.

"OK."

They slackened the sails and steadied the vessel. While Charles and Xavier were busy at the task, Mac got a bottle of whiskey and poured three drinks. They made quiet conversation for several minutes. The weather. The boat. There was no hurry, but the urn was there.

"Beautiful night. Beautiful," said Mac.

"Yes. It is," Charlie said. "Are you ready, Xavi?"

"Yes."

"Have you done this before, son?" Mac said.

Xavier shook his head. He needed help.

Mac veered the boat to face the current and Xavier stood at the stern. Mac told him that the urn was quite full and that the ashes were not dust but a soft, pale grey earth. He needed to lean away, turn the urn upside down, and pour them steadily and directly into the water. Xavier nodded obediently, twisted open the cap and, out of nervousness, threw it into the water. He looked up, horrified at what he had done.

"That's fine. Go on," said Mac, who was at the helm.

It seemed simple then. Xavier leaned carefully over the side, stretched out his arms and poured the ashes into the sea, a sea that seemed calm but was racing north. In the soft light, a grey smoke pervaded the wake. Xavier leaned down a little more to release the urn from the tips of his fingers into the water.

"Listen to me, *lagun*,"[47] he said softly, "Follow the whales home. *Agur.*"[48]

The smoke was in a rush to disappear. It didn't give Xavier any time to contemplate it. It was gone like a breath.

Charles, who was always so correct, was beside him.

"Xavi, would you like to say something?" he asked.

"No, it's not necessary." Xavier looked at Mac. "I'd like to take her in, Mac," he said.

"Sure, I'll go lie down. I've had a long day."

"I'll sit with you," said Charlie.

Charlie and Xavi had another drink in comfortable silence. Xavier had relaxed and was quite drunk. The Mass, the trip, the ashes. It was done. He lied down on his back on the deck and looked up at the stars. He thought he had never seen them shine so brightly. Maybe they were shining for Ander. With his left hand, he held his drink on his stomach. With his right hand, he reached up to touch a star. It was Rigel of the Orion constellation, his favourite. For some reason he smiled. He felt like being with a woman. He needed to rest his head on a pretty shoulder. Not Alexa's. Somebody different.

Charles cleared his throat and said softly and politely, "Xavi, this might not be a good time to tell you this, but Pat is pregnant. I'm going to be a dad."

Xavier raised his head from his supine position.

"It's the perfect time to tell me that!" he said.

Xavier sat up and grabbed Charlie's hand, swinging it back and forth. Charles was guiltily delighted to have his friend back.

"Charlie *Aita*! Son of a bitch!" They both laughed. "You're going to have to stop all that womanizing...."

Xavier enjoyed teasing Charlie, who was so very straitlaced and was always scolding Xavier about his sex life.

They were startled by a radio transmission. Xavier jumped up, steadied himself, and shook his head. He had to attend to *Justine* and the return to harbour. He saw a large cargo ship about a mile away. They had been too preoccupied to notice.

---

47   Friend (Basque).

48   Goodbye (Basque).

"This is HTR *Dutch Sea Transport*, IMO6498255. Rotterdam en route Halifax, Nova Scotia. Do you read me?"

"Affirmative. HTR, this is *Justine* IMO5329434. Providence en route Hyannis."

"OK, *Justine*. Your sails are down and you have been idle more than one hour. Do you need assistance of any kind?"

"Negative HTR, thank you. Just having a drink."

"Good then. Enjoy the party."

"Thank you. Safe voyage."

Xavier hung up and looked out at the horizon. The bright night had turned the sea to silver. Ander was now smoke in this ocean and a tattoo on Xavier's heart.

Adrienne

Five hundred miles up the coast, Adrienne Blanchard was spending July at the Crane Road cottage in New Brunswick with her mother. She had just returned to Canada after four years in Europe where she studied German and Spanish. An unhappy love affair precipitated her return. You might say she was jilted at the altar. Mother and daughter were playing Scrabble.

The handyman came to fix the fence. While her mother was outside, Adrienne decided to have a peek at the dictionary. She had difficult letters. The old *Larousse* was on the bottom shelf of the old and tilted bookcase. What word could begin with "J" and might have an "M"? She went to the letter J. "*Jambon*" or "*jambe*,"[49] of course. She was muddled by the jet lag. If only she had a "B." *They're such good letters,* she thought, *but you never seem to have one when you need it.* She decided to trust in luck and not use her "J" right away.

She pushed the dictionary back in the bookshelf but the large book wouldn't go back in its place because there was an object behind the row of books. It was her father's *Merck Manual* that was on its side and pushed into a corner. She didn't know it was there. She decided to have a look at it before she put it properly into place. It was beautifully published in navy blue leather and silver letters. It had over three thousand onion skin

---

49 Ham or leg.

pages and described every disease known to man, as well as its symptoms and treatments. It was updated every year and distributed to doctors by the Merck Pharmaceutical Corporation. Charlotte kept it as a memory of Philippe. He had been dead for more than ten years by then. They had all rebuilt their lives. Adrienne leafed through the pages. She tried to think of an interesting disease to look up. She was kneeling on the floor. Suddenly, she sat back on her heels in surprise. She found two letters tucked inside the book. She recognized her father's handwriting.

The first envelope said: *A l'attention de Michel Bourgeois*.[50]

The second was a brown envelope and had a formal greeting in English: *To whom this may concern.*

Adrienne was stunned. She knew exactly who Michel Bourgeois was. His mother worked for them on Temple Street when Adrienne was very young. Her father took care of him when he burned himself at the restaurant. She remembered the fresh white bandtages on his arm. He killed a girl and ran away but Adrienne had always felt uncomfortable about that. On Fridays, Maman would often send René to Bright's on his bicycle to buy fish and chips for supper. Michel always hid an extra piece of fish under the fries. They all knew it was for Papa. Many summers, Michel's mother, Pauline, would drop by to visit with Adrienne's mother.

Adrienne heard the handyman's pick up truck pulling out of the driveway and her mother's steps on the kitchen stairs. She tucked the letters into the manual and put it back where she found it. The letters were not sealed but she knew they were not for her eyes.

"You cheat when I'm not looking, Adrienne?" Charlotte said, chuckling. She was delighted with her daughter's visit.

"I tried but I couldn't find a word," said Adrienne, laughing, as she put the *Larousse* back into place.

That night, she read the letters after her mother went to bed. She was not surprised. She could understand what her father did. He knew the system. They would have locked up a boy like Michel in two minutes. She gathered from the letters, however, that Philippe had not intended for the secret to be kept for so long. Where on earth was Michel? He should come home. And why did her brother also choose to keep the secret?

---

50 For the attention of Michel Bourgeois.

All of that seemed so far away. In another lifetime. René was married and had two children. Michel was probably safe somewhere, otherwise she was sure he would come back home. She wrapped herself in a blanket, went out on the porch and sat on the old wicker rocking chair. She sighed and stretched her legs. She was leaving for Montréal soon. It was the eleventh, and she thought she should leave around the twentieth. She needed to look for a job. And for a life. She was twenty-four. She rested her head back on the hard wicker and looked up at the stars. You couldn't see them like that from Madrid. Even the Milky Way was visible that night. She thought she had never seen the stars shine so brightly. She took her arm out from under the blanket, pointed it at the sky and chose a particularly bright star to wish upon. It was Rigel but she didn't know that. She recalled a childhood rhyme.

Star light. Star bright. She couldn't think of what to wish. The blanket fell away from her naked shoulder. She smiled. She decided not to be greedy. She wished for a kiss. Just a kiss on her shoulder.

Michel

Michel replaced the receiver.

"Captain? Looks like some guys having a drink," he said.

The captain nodded. He was an amateur astronomer and was at his telescope. Rarely had he seen a sky like that.

"A lot of that around here this time of year," the captain said. "Rich people. Yachts. Summertime. But you never know. It's better to check. Did I ever tell you the story of the ghost yacht I discovered?"

"Several times!" said Michel. Michel permitted himself a little joke. Six years feeding the captain three times a day had inevitably made for a certain intimacy.

"Don't need a woman! You cook better and you don't nag." It was another joke that the captain repeated at least once a week. Michel liked him and trusted him.

"Cook. Come have a look. Incredible sky. Extraordinary. I can see Rigel perfectly!" the captain exclaimed.

He was Dutch and rolled his Rs in his throat like the Germans do. Michel was smoking his nightly joint. He took one last toke. He had smoked it to the very tip and had to drop the butt so as not to burn his fingers. He approached the telescope as he exhaled the sour smoke. The captain guided him by the shoulders and adjusted the lens to show him Rigel. It was the seventh most brilliant star. It shone blue. It could only be seen by the naked eye on exceptionally clear nights.

Through the telescope, Michel glimpsed the sleek and elegant *Justine*. They had hoisted the sails and were heading for the coast. Boston. *Rich guys having a party on a yacht. Must be nice*, he thought.

Michel admired Rigel but his heart was not in it. He had something on his mind. He had been even quieter than usual since the captain announced that he was taking a new route around Europe and the Mediterranean after many years on the Pacific coast of North and South America. For six years, Michel had sailed monthly from Fairbanks, Alaska, to Punta Arenas, Chile. Most of the crew chose to stay in Chile but Michel would not leave this floating home or the captain, who had become a father figure. It suited him. He even liked his capsule-like room. He was "Cook." Nobody knew his real name, which was not real anyway. At least "Cook" was true. And as cook, he got his own small cabin and bathroom.

Six years on the ocean. North Pole. South Pole. Up the coast one month. Down the coast the next. Michel became very comfortable in that life. His fear of exposure had all but disappeared. He liked to take long walks around the cities on their route. He did the shopping in large, exotic food markets. His favourites were Vancouver, San Diego, and Lima. At the end of the day, he returned to his small womb inside the big mother ship. He had not chosen that life, but he was thankful for it. He had found his place.

They transported everything from fruit to farming machinery. The captain refused to carry oil or "chemical shit" as he called it. It was his own ship. He paid a reasonable insurance and he could do what he wanted. He had a good, profitable, and safe route. He made a lot of money. But the captain was fifty-five years old and wanted to spend the next few years near his daughter in Holland. He wanted to enjoy his grandchildren while they were still young. Ultimately, he hoped to buy a house and a nice yacht in Mallorca. He might find a good Dutch woman to warm his bed. She could be Spanish too, it didn't matter. So long as she was not German like his first wife.

For Michel, the problem was not Europe. He was looking forward to new markets and new cities. He had become a curious traveller. The problem was Halifax. It was the last port of call before crossing the Atlantic. It was two hours by car from Moncton. They would be stopping for three days to unload mangoes and orchids from Cali, Colombia, and to load pulp and paper for Southampton. The British press used only Canadian paper. It was the perfect cargo and the Captain was delighted.

Michel had a recurring nightmare. In a large market, he saw his mother but she didn't see him. He lost her in the distance. He tried to call out to her but he was mute. He couldn't remember how to speak French. He looked for his words and couldn't find them. He had lost his tongue. His mother tongue. He woke in a sweat, making strangulated groans.

He was stuck between oceans, between lives, between English and French, between Michel and Brian. Michel was thirty-two. Brian was thirty-six. He wore large aviator glasses and had a long, drooping mustache, as was the fashion of the eighties. Since he found out they would be stopping in Halifax, he saw the young Michel in the mirror. His hand shook as he shaved.

The captain suspected something was bothering Cook. He had taken a liking to the quiet young man. He smoked a lot of pot, but he was serene and good-natured. He thought that perhaps Cook was worried about the move to Europe. He hadn't made the connection with Halifax. He had forgotten that Brian Ogilvy was an American citizen but Canadian-born. In any case, sea Captains never asked questions. They respected men with secrets.

When the Senegalese pilot came to take the helm for the graveyard shift, the captain turned in. Michel got a blanket and found a quiet spot leaning on a chimney near the bow. He was not looking at the starry sky. He was looking at the horizon. The next land he saw would be his own. Something called "home."

Taking a Walk on Main

There were no mounties waiting for him on the pier but the Canada immigration officer was smart and wide awake. He examined the passport carefully. Michel was the last to disembark having prepared a buffet for the day in port.

"So, you're a Nova Scotian! Born up here, were you?" said the officer.

Michel had been hoping it wouldn't be noticed. He'd been to Vancouver at least fifty times and no one had pointed it out. As a rule, Americans came and went.

"Yes."

"New Glasgow. Any relation to the Ogilvy brothers? The guys in the New Glasgow Mystics band?"

He looked frankly and directly into Michel's eyes. He was one of those immigration officers who was convinced he had the magic power of reading the truth in people's eyes.

"Don't really know," Michel said. "I've been gone since I was a kid. My parents never kept in touch very much." He shrugged and smiled regretfully. He was good at being Brian.

"Right. It happens. Okay then, you guys are here three days, right?"

"Yeah. Captain says maximum three."

The self-sufficient civil servant stamped the passport. He had seen the rest of the crew. This guy looked clean. An American citizen was not considered suspicious of illegal entry. Routine.

It was a soft landing. That morning, he walked around the downtown area. Although he had never been to Halifax, everything was familiar. It was mundane things, like the billboards and advertisements in shop windows, that really hit home.

Canadian Tire. Atlantic Lottery. Moosehead beer. PEI potatoes. The commercial landscape of his youth revived memories that had been buried for years. Michel's memory bank had switched off a long time before, not only because of the stress of his cirumstances, but also because of the physical and cultural distance from Asia and the Pacific Coast. He had been very young and it had definitely not been in his interest to look back. He had adapted to his surroundings and survived like a Darwinian creature. Michel Bourgeois, however, had not completely disappeared. In Halifax, he was close, very close, to home. Foolishly, he decided to go for a drive.

He requested a twenty-four-hour shore leave for the next day and by nine o'clock, he was driving a rented car on the Trans-Canada Highway to Moncton. A baseball cap, dark sunglasses, and his moustache were his only disguise. He was functioning on pure adrenaline. He passed an Atlantic Traveller Bus on the highway and remembered the last time he had been on a bus on that highway, and where it had led him.

Michel was a war veteran who had never heard a shot or fired a bullet in combat. After two months of basic training in Massachusetts, he had been shipped out to Vietnam via Okinawa, Japan, where his unit had been put on hold. They never made it to Vietnam. They did nothing but train and exercise and wait for months until finally they had been redeployed one by one.

The Vietnam War was on its last legs, but the US had more than fifty thousand military personnel in Japan. Michel worked in the kitchens of one of the largest messes in the world. He was allotted small but pleasant military quarters. He had his uniform, his sergeant, his drill session, and his job.

His new identity as Brian Ogilvy became second nature. In the beginning he was a base rat, which was usual for boys from small towns. They were culturally displaced and therefore uneasy about roaming around a huge Asian city. He avoided any close friendships which, in any case, had never been natural to him.

He spent a lot of his spare time at the recreation centre playing cards. Rummy and Canasta were another thing he had shared with his mother. He signed up for Bridge lessons. The conversation was impersonal. Card night was an organized activity. It added structure, routine, and a safe degree of socialization to his life.

True Identity

One day, the perfect girl showed up at the card table. Judy was pretty, she had a very full figure, and she was shy. She was an administrative worker who played cards extremely well and possessed an infectious laugh and a cute smile. Michel liked that she was so impeccably groomed. Her hair was shiny and smooth. Her nails were flawless. Her skin was smooth and white. She smelled pretty. Even her eyelashes were perfectly combed. Her colourful and well-ironed clothes fit her perfectly despite her generous bulges. He walked her home and kissed her because it felt right. Boy meets girl. Simple and good. His first girl since Yvette.

They began to timidly explore Japan together on bus tours organized by the base. They didn't talk very much. They never moved in together. They watched television, held hands, and made love with the lights off. He saved her large pieces of cake from the kitchen. She made sure he knew his rights and opportunities. She pampered his file and made sure he took advantage of every opportunity. She signed him up for programs and perks he didn't even know about. Then, after three years, Judy was redeployed stateside. They talked about meeting in Hawaii for their next vacation, but it never happened. It was too bad. In other circumstances, he might have married her. She gave him peace.

The seven years he spent in Japan were soon over. Discharged at twenty-five with his citizenship papers and, thanks to Judy, certification as a professionally licenced sous-chef, it was time to move on. It never occurred to him to go home and face the music. Perhaps the uniform and a good war record would have influenced his case in a positive way. But his former life was more and more remote. It was an old movie he replayed in his head from time to time. Sometimes it even slipped his mind.

He used the Military Placement Service to find a job in the States. He chose a well-kept vintage diner near the shipyards in Portland, Oregon. A working man's breakfast and lunch place. It was open Monday to Friday from 7:00 a.m. to 5:00 p.m. He liked the idea. Oregon sounded nice.

He was excited in the beginning and bought a second-hand car and rented a nice room. It was not easy. The unfriendly boss was demanding and the pay was terrible. It was part of the deal of hiring a vet. He had a job and a car. The room was large and comfortable and in a pretty house, yet he felt poor. His salary would barely help him hang on to what he had. He didn't see how he could one day buy a food truck or have a space of his own in an upscale market like Faneuil Hall. He made no friends. He took refuge in soft drugs and became passive and dark.

That was until the day the waitress poked her head in the service window that connected the kitchen to the counter dining area.

"Brian, there's a foreign guy out here who just bought the whole pot of chicken soup," she said. "Wants to know what soup you're going to make tomorrow."

"Ask him what kind he wants," Brian said.

"Minestrone?" she yelled at Brian from the cash register.

"Okay!" he said.

The client returned, loved the minestrone and, again, bought the whole pot to take away. He asked to greet the chef. They decided on French onion for the next day.

It was the Dutch captain who loved soups. His ship was in dry dock being repaired. He was alone in town with his mechanic, who slept aboard ship. He was picking up a new crew to leave in three weeks. Would Brian like to see the world?

Hell yes.

And here he was, happy with his choice. He was on his way to Europe after five years on the Pacific Ocean. He was thirty-one years old. Thirteen years since he had taken that bus.

He had less than an hour to go. Amherst. Sackville. Memramcook. Moncton would be next. He waited impatiently for the green highway sign, his finger poised on the car indicator. The familiar Moncton CKCW radio jingle crackled through the radio. It was the Top Ten and the same DJ: The Little General. He laughed nervously. He looked at himself in the mirror. He saw himself strutting down Main Street. He was feeling cocky and sure of himself.

He made a list in his head. He wasn't crazy, he had no intention of getting out of the car. He followed the speed limit religiously. He topped up the tank in Amherst on the Nova Scotia border to make absolutely sure he wouldn't have to stop at a gas station in New Brunswick. He would go by the Blanchards' house. Drive by Bright's and by the building he lived

True Identity

in when he was a kid. Then Aberdeen School. It would be safe to have lunch at at the A&W car drive-in, if it was still there. He looked forward to driving down Main Street to see if anything had changed. He would save his mother's house for last. He was a little worried about that. He would have to find a way to see her without her seeing him. He would deliver his letter if she was not there. He would mail it from a post box in Halifax if she was.

He was bobbing his head to the music when he took the Botsford Street exit into town. He was excited. He felt safe in the car and under his hat. He thought he'd drive by the apartment and the school first, but he got into the wrong lane and was forced to turn right on Mountain Road over the old railroad bridge to Temple Street. When he reached the corner of Temple, he saw the Blanchards' house in the corner of his eye, but he didn't look at it.

Something had happened as he was driving over the bridge. It was the sight of the tracks. His teeth were clenched. His heart was swollen. He was going there. Where it happened. Yvette was in the car. It was as if she had been waiting for him all that time on the bridge. He turned right again, drove down Temple, crossed the small bridge over the creek, and pulled over by the side of the road. He turned off the motor and lowered his head to pull the keys out of the ignition. Very slowly, his head still down, he looked right.

The old rink was still there, but its stone walls had broken down. They hadn't torn it down. It looked like an old European ruin, overrun with grass and hay. A sign said: *Private Property. Trespassers will be prosecuted.*

Involuntarily, his shoulders started to jerk up and down. He broke into uncontrollable dry sobs. He forced himself to look past the rink to the trees that hid the creek where he had dragged her body.

He laid his forehead on the steering wheel and said aloud, "*Yvette. J'ai eu peur. Pardonne moi.*"[51] The pain came in French. He hadn't spoken the language in thirteen years.

The uncontrollable weeping left him gasping like a tired dog. It took an almost inhuman effort to start the car and head back into town. His arms were lead. He drew strength from the thought of seeing his mother. He would drive by her house and then leave town.

---

51 Yvette. I was afraid. Forgive me.

But he was headed for a surprise. The Blanchards' house was on the way. He was shocked. It was July and he hadn't expected them to be there, but the big family house was now a dental clinic. He wiped his eyes to make sure. They were gone, and not just for the summer. He drove by at 10 miles an hour and stretched his neck to see into the backyard. He drove around the block again.

The garage where he had hidden in the tool room and in the back seat of Madame Blanchard's old Chevrolet Pony had been torn down. Why wasn't it there? Nobody's life had stopped. It seemed to Michel that his pain was of no consequence to anyone but him.

All three nights, the doctor had come into the garage with a bag of food, the pills, a newspaper, and a *National Geographic* magazine. He put the car radio on low and smoked a cigar. They talked very softly for an hour or so. It comforted Michel, who spent four long days in hiding.

Philippe wanted to hear every detail. Her pupils. Her breathing. Her skin colour. Her speech. He asked Michel to concentrate. Had she been sleepy? Had she complained of a headache? Could he describe her coordination? Had she responded to him sexually? Did she describe her fall? Did Michel know if she had been regularly abused? How was she abused? The doctor was looking for medical clues to the accident that had taken her life. On the second night, Philippe had proposed the escape.

"You have a decision to make, Michel," he said. "I can take you in to the cops right now. I'll tell them I found you in my garage. Perfectly logical. They know you know us. The good thing is that all this will be over. It means you go through the system and you accept the consequences. We'll get you a good lawyer and we have the truth on our side. OK?"

Michel tried to hide his panic, but Philippe saw it in his face.

"Or...you can take a bus to the States and try your luck." He said. "I've asked around and I can get you good identification papers. The reason I'm suggesting this is that it's been thirteen days now. I can't lie to you, Michel. Prison is a possibility. You should have come to me right away. I would have taken you right in. Maybe we could have controlled this circus."

"I have some money. Here, with me," Michel said.

"How much?"

"Four hundred. I took it out of the bank in case."

The doctor sighed.

"What would you do?" asked Michel.

Philippe had no doubt about what he thought Michel should do because he knew better than anyone else what prison would do to him. He was barely a child. He would spend a minimum of twenty-five years in jail and come out a forty-five-year-old man. Learn nothing, do nothing, for nothing. Michel was innocent. He was a sensitive and talented boy. Philippe was very fond of Michel and did not have a conventional spirit or a faint heart. Perhaps he shouldn't have said what he did. However, it was the truth.

"What would I do? Run, probably," Phillipe said. "You can always come back. Maybe this mess will get ironed out in the meantime. Let some time go by, then call me in the early morning in a few months, whenever you can."

About thirty-eight hours later, Michel was gone but not without one close call. He was in the back seat of the car when he heard Madame Blanchard shout nervously from the kitchen window.

"Adrienne! Where are you going?"

"To the garage. To get my skipping rope."

"Don't your friends have a skipping rope?"

He heard the tension in her voice. Michel threw himself down into the foot space of the Pony. Stupidly, he had just smoked a joint.

"Mine's longer. We want to play double."

The eleven-year-old with the swinging ponytail and long thin legs in extra wide shorts, marched into the garage and picked up her skipping rope, which was wound on a nail beside the hose. Luckily, it was just inside the garage door. She picked it up off the nail while she waved to her friends who were waiting for her on the sidewalk forty feet away. The Temple Street sidewalk was nice and wide. It was a good place for kids to play. She was in a hurry and ran off without looking inside the garage but then stopped suddenly, opposite the back porch. Adrienne shouted to her mother who was still in the window.

"Maman, something stinks in the garage."

"There's a skunk in the neighbourhood," her mother said. "Stay out of there."

"Yeah. It really, really stinks."

She ran down the driveway to the sidewalk to play. He heard the little girls singing. He still remembered the song. It was imprinted in his brain.

SALT

The wind, the wind, the wind blows high

Blowing Adrienne through the sky

He is handsome, she is pretty

He is the boy from New York City

Take her to the garden, sit her on your knee

Ask her the question: Will you marry me?

PEPPER

Yes, no, maybe so

Yes, no, maybe so

Yes, no, maybe so.

YES!

They sang it again for Paulette, for Suzanne, and for Giselle. It was Adrienne's favourite.

René drove him down to Truro, Nova Scotia, to catch the bus to Boston. Michel remembered the doctor's last words as he gave him the papers and the money: "You hid in here but we didn't see you. You found these papers in the bathroom of the restaurant a couple of years ago and you never turned them in. You kept them to get into bars. Good luck. Remember, you can always come back."

Michel nodded and accepted the deal.

Seeing the empty Blanchard house made Michel realize the folly of his journey. He was risking being apprehended on this hot, lazy July day when the city was asleep and unconcerned with his fate. His captain and shipmates were waiting for him for a lobster dinner in beautiful Peggy's Cove, Nova Scotia. He was risking life in jail for a ride on Main Street. He was still the same stupid idiot! But he couldn't leave without doing what he had come to do.

True Identity

He found his way to Carling Street and parked on the corner opposite his mother's house. He had a perfect, unobstructed view. Nobody was outside on this sleepy summer day. The street was deserted.

The neighbourhood had seemed high class to him when, at age nine, he had moved from a dingy building in the East End to this middle-class neighbourhood of small brick bungalows with window boxes and well-groomed front lawns. Life had taken him to the prosperous green cities of British Columbia, the youthful and glamourous lifestyle of the California coast, and the historical and colourful South American ports. Everything suddenly seemed small and humble.

His hope to catch a glimpse of his mother was dashed. Everything was locked down. The curtains were tightly closed and there was no car in the driveway. Ron had built a garage. Through the window, he could see two new white cars with "Ron's Taxi" printed on the roof light. Things must be going well. He was glad. They were surely spending July at the beach in Shediac. His stepfather's large family all kept trailers at the provincial park. Michel wished that he hadn't been so rebellious. Ron was a good guy. He always included Michel in everything.

He had been stopped for the time it took to smoke a cigarette. The neighbours had always been nosy. If he stayed longer he might attract attention. He tossed his cigarette out the window and took the large pink envelope out of the glove compartment. He had bought it years before on the base and never sent it. He got out of the car and walked briskly, head down, to the house. With one long step, he was on the landing. He opened the small wooden post box that read *P and R McKay* in Celtic letters carefully stencilled on the side. He smiled sadly. He placed the envelope inside and returned to the car. Ten seconds and he was gone.

Pauline found the pink envelope several days later. It was addressed to her. By then, Michel was in the Azores. She frowned. It had no stamp and no return address. She thought it was an invitation to a baby shower but couldn't think of anybody who was expecting. *For my sweet mother on her birthday.* She didn't understand at first. It was July, her birthday was in November. Then she put her hand over her mouth and sat down very slowly. He was never far from her thoughts. She opened the card. Her son smiled up at her in his uniform.

God had answered her prayers. She put the photo to her lips. Then put it to her heart. Then looked at it again. In wonder. He was so handsome. He looked so well. He was not lost.

Mon Michel.[52]

---

[52] My Michel.

Part Three

Bienvenue à Montréal Welcomes You

Xavier met Adrienne Blanchard six months later in Montréal. It was February 1987. He was visiting his cousin Koldo who was pursuing graduate studies in political science at Concordia University. As the taxi travelled the forty-five minutes between Mirabel Airport and Koldo's apartment, Xavier entertained himself looking out the window at this new country. It was night. Montréal was a luminous North American city. It was also a sea of neon.

Spécialités Chinoises et Canadiennes

Pharmacie Bons Prix

Danseuses nues

Stationnements mensuels

Bière Froide[53]

The language and the scenery didn't seem to match. Odd. Like a mirror that is not quite right. He had never been to Montréal. It had a reputation for hot women and good food. He was looking forward to the weekend away. The fall and Christmas had been intense.

Charles ran for office in the November elections and won. His best friend was now the youngest man in the United States senate. Xavier had been present at important events and formed part of a small group of private advisors. Meanwhile, he had been promoted at the bank. While life seemed

---

53 Chinese and Canadian dishes. Retail Drug Store. Exotic Dancers. Monthly parking. Cold beer.

True Identity

to be elevated to an important degree, his power over his own life appeared to be slipping away.

Then, the Aramburu family descended on New York at Christmas for a ten-day marathon of shopping, musicals, and sightseeing. The Aramburus met Alexa but didn't really know what to make of her. Alexa, who was a highly organized and disciplined individual, had trouble understanding their chaotic way of life, let alone understanding their basic English. Plans were continually changed, appointments and schedules were never met. The Aramburus were not a family, she concluded, they were a single organism. Moving slowly. The chemistry was not great.

The relationship between Xavier and Alexa hadn't changed. They shared an important social life, good sex, and good humour. If Alexa wanted more, she didn't let on, but as a couple they had not grown. While Ander was sick, Xavier had not had the time or the inclination for other women but since the summer he had had several flings. After Ander's death, Xavier had turned not to Alexa but to physical activity. He skated furiously around Central Park in the early morning until the snow came, and then became assiduous to the gym. He had never been in such good shape. He was leaving his tall, boyish body behind to become a bigger, wider man. At twenty-eight, with one incipient wrinkle on his forehead, he was more magnificent than ever.

Xavier was angry with Ander. Just after scattering the ashes, he had gone to the apartment with Rosa intending to clean up and pack Ander's things. He brought cleaning products, empty cardboard boxes, and masking tape. Joaquín would come later with a rented van to pick up the furniture and the boxes which he would distribute to the needy.

They walked into a perfectly spotless apartment. Empty of bric-a-brac. Not a book. Not an ashtray. It was empty of life, like a picture in a magazine. There were three large boxes on the dining table. They were labelled:

Mis padres[54]

Xavi

Joaquín

---

54 My parents.

There were dozens of cleaning products carefully ordered on the kitchen counter and nothing in the cupboards.

Xavier walked around the small apartment, hands on his hips, shaking his head. He went to the bedroom. Ander's clothing, bedding, and towels were neatly folded into large, sealed garbage bags. The tan suede coat Ander loved, the Italian tux he treasured, and a good dozen cashmere sweaters were neatly ordered in the closet. Each item was in its own plastic dry cleaners' bag. A note on the door read: *Xavi?* Out loud, as if Ander could hear him, Xavier said bitterly, "Son of a bitch. You let yourself die."

The mattress was stripped and leaning against the wall. Ander had done all of this in his weakened state. He had had no intention of returning to his apartment. He had let himself die. Xavier would always fear that Ander had shortened his life so that he could go on with his. Ander was gone now, leaving an unlikely orphan.

As the taxi cab neared the address Koldo had carefully spelled out over the phone, *3891 rue des Tilleuls*, the scenery changed again. It was a quiet neighbourhood lined with rows of charmingly identical townhouses, tall, stately trees, and old-fashioned street lights. Peaked rooves with snowy gables and window boxes gave the street a storybook air. There were long, winding staircases reaching up playfully to each and every door. The old mansions were divided into flats, each accessible from the outside. *Canadians must not like the dark*, he thought. There was a shining light in every window and above every door. The immaculate white snow sat like a powdery Buddha covering every roof, every branch, every step. *It looks like Christmas paper*, he thought.

He climbed up the icy and treacherous steps to the third and last floor carefully, suddenly overwhelmed by the bitter cold. *Boston was never this bad*, he decided. He felt a hardness inside his nose. His nasal mucus was freezing. He pulled his scarf over his ears and mouth and concentrated on reaching the top floor where he fervently hoped that cousin Koldo was waiting for him. Fortunately, the door opened before he made it to the top. Koldo was laughing.

"Look who's at my door!"

True Identity

Koldo was very pleased with his cousin's visit. As he climbed the last few steps, Xavier answered, "*Hostía, Primo.*[55] Couldn't you have enrolled at the University of Miami! God Almighty."

"No, no. Montréal is great. You'll see! Come in. Hurry! We're losing the heat."

Xavier scrambled into the warm and bright apartment and closed the door behind him. Before he took off his coat, he stretched his arms out wide to give his cousin a good hug.

The fact that Koldo was studying in Montréal, the largest city in the province of Québec, was not a coincidence or a whim. Québec was at the forefront of the peaceful political pursuit of independence from Canada. Because of this, Québec was on the world stage. Euskadi was watching carefully along with the rich and independently-minded regions of Scotland, Catalonia, and Corsica.

Koldo, like his father, was a member of the Partido Nacionalista Vasco, the Basque Nationalist Party. The PNV had ruled with a comfortable majority for the ten years since the new democracy was established. Not even the revered Socialist Party of Spain had been able to cut into its support. They were conservative, traditionalist, and clearly locked in on independence and protectionist policies. These were the men the Basques chose to lead them. They reflected their deep-rooted belief in themselves as an old and separate nation. ETA and Euskadi coexisted in these ebullient eighties like a beautiful woman with a limp. The Basque Country enjoyed a period of prosperity and growth. It was a time of self-affirmation of the Basque identity. It was a time to build landmarks, nurture their language and culture and, in this way, mark their territory. Euskadi was doing well.

Koldo was twenty-three years old. He felt lucky to be young and alive at that exact time in history. He had his law degree from Deusto University in Bilbao, and was specializing in constitutional studies at Concordia. He was preparing himself to have a part in the negotiation for Basque independence and the creation of a new European nation. His ambitions were not humble.

Xavier was twenty-eight years old. He was Basque the way he was male, the way he was his mother's son: unquestionably, inviolably, organically. It was his physical, historical, and cultural identity. He believed that borders

---

55 Jesus, Cousin.

could no longer be built around identities in the twenty-first century, which was five minutes away. Xavier belonged to the Basques who left and had washed up on other shores.

Koldo was determined to show his sophisticated cousin Xavier a good time. He called a taxi straight away and took him out to a trendy restaurant in downtown Montréal for dinner.

Physically, the younger cousin was one perfect size smaller than the older cousin. He was a little shorter, a little narrower, a little lighter. He had a pronounced Basque chin and the Aramburu eyes. Brilliantly dark, almond shaped, and set wide apart. He had a small mouth that turned up naturally at one corner in a permanently crooked smile. He was comfortable with himself. When he laughed, his face crinkled up, he threw his head back, and his body forward. He liked to hitch his thumbs in his belt loops and wear clothes one size too big. Koldo was irresistibly pleasant and approachable.

Xavier looked around. At first glance, the atmosphere was not very different from the young professional crowd in New York. However, there was a straightforwardness and a lack of modesty that he liked. The skirts were shorter, the lipstick darker, the necklines deeper, and the eyes more direct. Montréal was a little wild, self taught, and unashamed of itself. The city felt good.

He knew the history. This relatively small population of French Canadians had survived for centuries surrounded by an ocean of English-speaking power. They had resisted the magnetic omnipotence of the English language and had not been hypnotized by American popular culture. Koldo was bursting with enthusiasm at his Québécois experience and was dying to share it.

Xavier sat back and received his separatist education with philosophy and, thankfully, a really great beer. He was on vacation. Canada and Québec had the highest standard of living in the world. The beer was superior and the women looked fabulous. Besides the weather, what on earth could be wrong?

The story Koldo told was fascinating. It was about historical heritage, constitutional debate, and human migration. The people of Québec had elected, by majority, a political party with a separatist agenda. Constitutional talks to accommodate Québec had come to a stalemate. The Party had passed laws to protect its culture and language. These laws were designed

True Identity

to assimilate immigrants into the Québécois culture and to limit the use of the English language, thus marginalizing the anglophone population. Despite a widespread sympathy for their agenda, the separatists had recently lost a first referendum for independence. They blamed this partly on the "new Canadians."

Immigration was both a blessing and a curse for Québec separatists. The population of Québec was the first in the world to approach a birth rate of zero. The "*Québécois de souche*,"[56] as they liked to call themselves, would be outnumbered in four or five generations. Their own highly advanced society was threatening their survival. Immigrants were necessary. However, much too often, the Latin, Asian, and Middle Eastern immigrants drifted naturally towards integration in the anglophone community. There was a real risk of dilution of an identity that had never been totally secure. Underlining all of this was the fact that French Canadians were a founding nation of Canada. They had a rich and vibrant culture and a long and proud history. They were unique and strong, and wished to be masters of their own destiny.

Koldo was about to extrapolate to Euskadi, hoping to get Xavier's opinion. But the genius' eyes were wandering. Koldo smiled at his cousin with his crooked grin and joined in the flirtation of a group of girls at the next table. It was common knowledge in Bilbao: Francisco Xavier Aramburu Quiroga's only weak spot was a nice ass.

Koldo's apartment occupied the top floor of the building. It was the home of a fine arts professor who was on a long leave of absence. The furniture and décor was shabby, faded, authentic, and tasteful. A Spanish roomate was never there.

Early Saturday evening, Xavier soaked in soapy, hot water in the large, claw-footed bathtub. It had been a good day. Old Montréal had been an interesting surprise and a boat tour of the port through the ice floes of the Saint Lawrence had been a treat for his engineer's heart. Montréal boasted a cycling path over thirty kilometres long that was perfect for skating as well. He had made plans with Koldo to come back in the spring. The weekend had been more than just a parenthesis. He and Koldo had become good

---

56 Rooted Québécois. Descendants of the original French settlers who trace their ancestry to before the English conquest of 1763.

friends. Away from Wall Street and his Manhattan social life, Xavier felt refreshed, younger, optimistic.

At Christmas, his mother had urged him to pay Koldo a visit. Apparently, Koldo's parents were worried about him. This was untrue. Koldo was a fish in water in Québec. Ana had sensed that something was troubling Xavier and thought that perhaps his cousin Koldo might do him some good.

Xavier, oblivious to family manipulations, stretched out to his full height as he got out of the bathtub. He was ready for anything. Koldo had organized a party. He had invited everyone he knew and told them that his cousin Xavier was a Harvard professor and the best friend of a future president of the United States. These claims were both exaggerations, but Koldo was from Bilbao where exaggeration and pride came with the package. Even other Basques have trouble with the Bilbao swagger.

So, a good day, a hot bath, a shave, fresh clothes, condoms in his pocket. It was party time. He helped Koldo prepare a heavily spiked sangria. A Mexican friend had come early and brought all the makings for large platters of nachos and cheese. The boys had a beer and a chat in the kitchen before the guests arrived. Koldo was in his element. A born politician, he loved to entertain.

The group was completely heterogeneous. Anglos, Francos, Europeans, Africans, South Americans. The extreme cold had forged a brotherhood among the foreigners who swapped stories about stiff underwear on clotheslines and recipes for homemade frozen yogurt on window sills. Franco-Canadians suffered from the long and dark winters more than anyone else. You find us in this cold dark place, but we are warm, and we are different, they seemed to say. Anglo-Canadians seemed more at peace with their destiny. Many looked to Europe for inspiration and culture. The United States was a rich and irritating neighbour, but better on your side. Xavier was beginning to understand the geopolitical mindset of Canadians. He was definitely in a different place. The odd mirror of the first day began to adjust itself.

Xavier gladly escaped a particularly enthusiastic Swiss girl to go to the kitchen to help Koldo make an emergency batch of sangria. Enrique, the Mexican friend, ran out to an all-night liquor store for wine and vodka. The mood was high. The party was roaring. Xavier and Koldo chopped up the half-dozen apples left in the refrigerator into tiny pieces.

"You know how to throw a party, eh *primo?*"[57] Xavier said, chuckling.
"I love it!" said Koldo.

A classmate of Koldo's popped into the kitchen for a glass of water.

"Hey Koldo. Professor Blanchard just got here."

Koldo stepped away from the table where they were working and turned around to look at Xavier. He seemed at a loss for words. Finally, he said, "I have to introduce you, Xavi."

"That's okay. You go. I'll wait for Enrique and then I'll be right out. Don't worry," Xavier said, waving him away.

Xavier was restless. He would have to talk to this Blanchard guy. He was probably a pain-in-the-ass economist wanting to talk shop. Enrique rushed in with fresh provisions and together they poured the three bottles of wine, the Cointreau, two bottles of vodka, and the two large bottles of lemon-lime drink into the large plastic bucket. Xavier threw in the fruit. They were warmly applauded as they carried the heavy bucket out to the dining room table. It was a return to a happier and younger time for Xavier. He was delighted to be there.

He winked at a stylish brunette with a dramatic haircut, a very long body, and a low, round bottom. He had talked to her earlier. She was a PhD in political communication or something equally terrifying. He looked around for Koldo in order to get his chat with the professor out of the way, but he must have ditched the professor. He was talking to an undergrad. He couldn't see her face. Xavier recognized undergrads easily. He had taught freshman macroeconomics for three years and had had trouble keeping his distance.

He saw her from behind. She had very long, straight legs, and blond hair that fell to her waist. She was wearing a black leather miniskirt, a billowy white blouse, and black high heels with an ankle strap. She was holding her drink in both hands and standing in a funny way. Her legs wound around each other like a child who needs to go to the bathroom. Her thighs were squeezed tightly together. The economics professor slipped his mind.

Koldo saw him coming, caught his eye, and grinned impishly as if he knew what was about to happen.

---

57 Cousin.

"Xavi, this is my English professor, Adrienne Blanchard," he said. "She speaks Spanish perfectly, by the way. This is my cousin, Xavier Aramburu."

Adrienne looked up. A large and beautiful smile lit up her face. In perfect Spanish she said, "Hi Xavier, it is so nice to meet you. Koldo has told me a lot about you!"

She disintertwined her legs, stood up on her toes, held his arm for balance, and kissed him on both cheeks. She had a small gap between her two front teeth. He felt himself falling inside it.

"Adrienne? Are you sure you're a professor?" he asked. He had always been asked the same question.

"No, I am not a professor," she said, laughing. "I am an instructor of technical English and composition at the university. It's a non-credit evening course but is obligatory for international students. I got the job on a fluke. The professor quit two days before the semester started. He was a burnout or something. I walked in with my humble CV and suddenly I had fifty engineers, lawyers, and journalists from all over the world staring at me two nights a week. They have no choice. Really. It's quite frightening."

"Don't pay attention, *primo*. She's an absolutely great prof. The classes are really worthwhile," said Koldo.

Adrienne and Xavier's eyes travelled over each other's faces. Koldo coughed to remind them of his presence and said, "Xavi, there's a nice bottle of Rioja in the cupboard above the refrigerator. I mean, if you're interested."

He put his thumbs in his belt loops and shrugged. Xavier reached out to touch Adrienne's arm as she had touched his.

"Professor, a nice Rioja?" he asked.

"That would be very nice," she said, smiling and nodding.

He led her by the hand through the noisy crowd to the kitchen. He made small talk as he looked for the bottle of wine, the corkscrew, and two proper wine glasses. As he poured the wine, he frowned as if he had forgotten something.

"Don't move, please, don't move. I'll be right back."

He went back to the living room, and found Koldo in a heated discussion about self-determination, of course. He took his cousin's elbow and separated him slightly from the others.

"Listen," Xavier whispered in his ear, "Is there anything going on between you and her? Tell me. Now."

"Nothing. Really. No problem," Koldo said.

"Are you sure?"

"Absolutely sure! Look...Would I have told you where to find my best Rioja?"

It was a half-truth. On class nights, Koldo would nonchalantly time his exit from the classroom at the same time as Adrienne's to walk to the Métro with her. In fact, about a month before, they had begun to wait for each other. Adrienne liked him and enjoyed speaking Spanish. Koldo was more than interested, he had been preparing a move. However, something strange had happened. He had had a *coup de coeur*.[58] He saw how Xavier and Adrienne looked at each other. He adored his cousin. Koldo was a Basque with a noble heart, he let it go.

Xavier stared at Adrienne's face. Her eyes were pale, somewhere between grey and blue and green, like the colour of the Caribbean Sea in early morning. Her eyebrows were two thick, straight lines. Her nose was straight and rather flat with two tiny nostrils. Her mouth was wide and generous. Her upper and bottom lips were exactly the same size and shape. She had a face you would remember. She was very pretty but her eyebrows and mouth made her look serious, even angry. It was the pretty face of an angry child.

He loved her hair. It was unfashionably long. It fell to just above her waist. He could not think of a nicer colour. It was the colour of dark sand with lighter streaks that fell delicately over her face. She had a long neck and pronounced collar bones. Her blouse was generously open at the neck. He could see the promise of lovely breasts inside a lacy bra. Long, romantic musketeer sleeves hid her hands and revealed only the tip of her fingers. And those teeth. The gap. He couldn't remember ever kissing a girl who had a gap like that.

They talked for a long time in their invisible kitchen cocoon. They spoke of the beautiful places they came from and the places they would like to see. They talked about the things they liked to do and the books they were reading. And politics. Why he was not a separatist. Why she was not a separatist. Madrid. Koldo. The slow dance of mating.

Xavier liked everything about this girl to the point where he was feeling ridiculously adolescent. He made funny faces and teased her about

---

58 A feeling of premonition.

everything. Contradictory thoughts raced through his head. First, he had the urge to move on her that same night. If that worked. Or, he might return to Montreal sooner than later.

By midnight, she was sitting on his knees. There was only one chair left in the kitchen and they were tired of being on their feet. His hands circled her waist. Hungry, and giddy from the wine, they were greedily finishing a tray of crumbled nachos. Koldo came in, punched Xavier playfully on the arm and smiled meaningfully at Adrienne.

And then, she had to go. The Métro was closing. She had to work the next day. She was also a freelance translator with a Monday deadline. Xavier was unpleasantly surprised. The film he had come to see was no longer playing. The dish he had come to enjoy was no longer on the menu. Pavarotti was substituted by an understudy.

"Don't leave me here with all these separatists!" he said, pretending to be offended.

"Don't worry, they won't bite you! Koldo is a separatist!" Adrienne said, laughing.

"Believe me, I know that. Don't leave, please."

He put his chin on her shoulder. He made instant plans to see her again. He could swing it in a month.

In the midst of his discomfiture, she surprised him and asked Koldo if they all might have brunch the next day at a café near the McGill University library. She asked Koldo to keep it under his hat, but she was going to a job interview in New York at the end of the month and would really appreciate any advice Xavier might be able to give her. Xavier was amused, and reconciled himself to a non-erotic, civilized encounter. Koldo cleverly declined the invitation but promised he would deliver his cousin to the restaurant.

Xavier put his hand around her waist and accompanied her to the door. Adrienne took off her shoes while hanging on his arm. She fished her boots out of the pile of wet winter gear strewn all over the floor. They said goodbye, complied with the parting kisses, and searched for something in each other's eyes. Something had been left unfinished.

The party wasn't over. The weekend wasn't over. He was not pleased about being alone. Adrienne had whet his appetite. He looked around the room and saw the political communicator dancing alone. Xavier smiled and moved to join her. He put his mouth to her ear as if to say something but nibbled at her earlobe instead.

"Do you want to go someplace?" she said.

Bingo.

He locked the door of the bathroom. He leaned his back against it, crouched a little to be closer to her height, and spread his legs. He took her round hips in both hands and roughly pulled her to him so that she could feel his size and erection. She gave him a seductive little smile and whispered something in French that he didn't understand. She licked his neck in long steady strokes. He gave her a deep, wet kiss. She pulled his shirt out of his pants while he reached inside her panties. He was ready and his tastes were clear. He put his hand on her head, raised his eyebrows, and looked into her eyes. It was non-verbal political communication. She slid down and did him a very nice favour. While Xavier was looking up at the bathroom ceiling, Adrienne was looking at her grey reflection flash by in the dead light and dirty windows of the Montréal Métro.

The Café du Luxembourg was a European bistro in an old mansion near McGill University. The black-and-white damier floor, the long, red leather sofa bench, narrow marble tables, and traditional cane chairs created a European atmosphere. It was a sunny and bitterly cold day, which meant the sky was as blue as the air was icy. The sun streamed through the windows and made the café warm and inviting. Xavier arrived early and chose a table with a view to the street, picked up the *Montréal Gazette*, and enjoyed an excellent cup of espresso. There was a low hum of quiet and easy Sunday morning conversation. He wondered if he would regret making this date. He was curious about Adrienne. She was unfamiliar, like a foreign coin in his pocket.

He saw her coming and couldn't help smiling. She stopped at the corner to wait for the traffic light and cross the street. A Montréaler in winter, she was wrapped in a thick, shapeless coat, a sexless and formless barrel, with a pointy wool hat called a toque, and huge mittens. She was wearing her large handbag strapped across her body to keep her hands free for balance and to protect herself in case of a fall. She wore stylish sunglasses in a humble attempt to look attractive in spite of the mother bear outfit. She was carrying something in her right hand. It looked like a bottle of wine in a brown bag. Xavier hoped it wasn't a gift.

Like all Canadians do, she walked into the restaurant pounding her feet and shaking her head. It was an instinctive gesture to shake off the snow whether it was snowing or not. She flashed her devastating smile. He was pleased to see her.

She was in jeans and a very large, grey, heavy-knit man's cardigan over a black camisole. She wore her clothes well and was blessed with the expressionless mask of youth. Only her smile disturbed her perfect features like a stone thrown into a still pond. She was as fresh and lovely in the midday sunshine as in the soft pink light of an intimate dining room. She sat down, lifted her heavy mane of hair with one hand, leaned to the right, and laid it all carefully on one shoulder, dividing her face in two. Left side, frank and open. Right side, hidden and cautious.

"How are you?" he said.

"Good, and you?"

"Good. Very nice place, I like it."

"Yes it is, isn't it? Is that your luggage?"

"Yes, I'll take a taxi to the airport after lunch. My flight is at 6:55."

"No, no. I'll walk you to the bus station. It's not far. You'll save thirty-five dollars and it's direct. Just as fast. Really."

"Sure. Great."

"Thank you for coming," she said.

"It's a pleasure," he said, laughing. "But you must promise you'll pass my cousin!"

She laughed and said, "Koldo is my favourite! Of course he passes! The truth is, he just has to attend class to pass!" she said, laughing again.

She showed him the wine.

"Is it okay?" she said.

"California Chardonnay. Fine," he answered, still wondering if it was a gift. He touched her chin.

She handed the wine to the waiter who put it on ice. That was the answer to the bottle in the bag. You were allowed to bring your own wine to the restaurant. Montréal was just getting better and better.

Xavier stared at her face. For a brief moment, the sun was at an angle that illuminated her pale eyes, turning them into two shining liquid stones. Fairy eyes.

Adrienne was not a fairy, but she was living the privileged and equally terrifying moment when life is weightless. She was at the intersection of chance, free will, and opportunity, when each decision can have permanent consequences. When one's future waits in ambush. She was more personal than the night before as she explained with exactitude where she was in her life. Xavier had never heard anyone so precise and conscious as to their place in space and time. It was like geographical coordinates but in human terms.

Madrid was past tense. The summer before, she had come home with a master of Spanish degree in her pocket and professional experience that included teaching, translating, and interpreting for the Spanish Chamber of Commerce and the Real Madrid Athletic Club. Her return had been precipitated by the fact that her fiancé, a Real Madrid basketball player, had dropped her unexpectedly to marry his high school sweetheart. She had adored her cocky, lanky, big-nosed Julio. This had altered her trajectory. She had decided not to stay in Madrid. It was his place, not hers.

Her older brother owned two small second-hand bookstores in Ottawa. He had seen the UN call for interpreters in one of the multiple publications he received. He had thought of his sister who was coming home and, without telling her, had spontaneously written away to request the application package. She followed all the steps of the selection process religiously. She wrote a difficult multi-language test and took a psychological evaluation at the UN offices in Ottawa. Then she attended a telephone interview going over her curriculum vitae. She made a tape recording of her voice reading a text in English, French, Spanish, and German. Finally, she went through an exhaustive security check. They needed photographs, essays of intention, and letters of recommendation. It had been a challenge just to complete the application.

Finally, Adrienne Blanchard, age twenty-five, citizen of Canada, had been chosen. She had won the grand prize, which was an all-expense-paid trip to New York City for the three-day final selection process. Only ten of the sixty finalists would be offered a position. She felt lucky to get the invitation but was not confident that she would get the job.

Xavier was intrigued. That selection process was exhaustive. He wondered if, for some reason, somebody important wanted to see her. He did tell her that he thought she had a good chance. He insinuated that she was too young and inexperienced to be on that list by accident. Somehow, her application had stood out. It was his honest opinion that she was a serious candidate. She had to be alert and tight in New York because maybe the usual criteria of long experience and polished skills were not applicable here. He didn't know about the UN but in the financial world in New York, people appreciated quality in content, independence, presence of mind, decision-making ability, and ambition. A fancy résumé was not everything.

She liked what he told her. She was flattered and excited. Xavier's opinion of Adrienne did not change. He thought she was an unusual, interesting, lovely girl. Something about her intensified the present. He hung on to her smiles. He basked in her attention.

Berri-de-Montigny Bus Station was in the rush of imminent departure. Conductors tossed carefully prepared suitcases into wet and slushy luggage compartments. The noisy, poisonous gusts of exhaust fumes filled the air. The deafening announcements in both official languages were unintelligible. Adrienne and Xavier reached Berri just in time to catch the last possible bus to Mirabel Airport for him to make it to his evening flight.

Adrienne smiled and put her hands on her head to keep her green toque in place on the windy platform. Standing up on her toes, she leaned forward to kiss Xavier on the cheek to say goodbye. She found herself with his arms around her waist and her whole weight on his chest. Her hat fell off. She looked up in amused surrender. He rubbed his nose softly on hers and kissed her gently on the mouth. He paused and smiled down at her. She smiled back up. The second kiss lingered and tasted of curiosity, the curiosity escalated to full-fledged appetite. Her hands explored his head, feeling his soft, thick hair and the shape of his skull. A soft purr came from deep in her throat and he moaned quietly in answer. They were both abstracted from the immediate moment. Noises were distant, the cold negligible, the airport unimportant.

Thankfully, the Québécois have a great indulgence for love and sentimentality. The conductor waited respectfully, enduring the cold by his open door, but finally had no choice but to interrupt.

"*Bon! Les amoureux, qu'est-ce qu'on fait?*"[59] he asked.

They separated reluctantly. Xavier boarded and moved down the aisle of the bus, keeping an eye on Adrienne through the windows. Adrienne picked her hat up off the platform. It was wet and dirty, which brought her back to the reality of her life. She was in Montréal in February, working two jobs and living in a distant cousin's basement in exchange for babysitting. She watched the bus leaving the station and permitted herself a small fantasy of her and the perfect Xavier walking about Manhattan.

Xavier sat down in a narrow aisle seat of the airport bus and brushed his fingers through his hair. He was slightly shaken. *What had happened between Friday night and now?* he asked himself. He looked out the window at the city. What had seemed a bizarre nordic outpost on Friday, now felt busy, familiar, and welcoming.

---

59 Alright, lovebirds. So what are we doing?

What Is Happening Here?

During those twenty-one pre-Adrienne days, Xavier's enthusiasm with this new affair dwindled. His auto-defence mechanism went spontaneously into full drive.

He was particularly charming and attentive toward Alexa. They celebrated her thirty-seventh birthday with a formal dinner party at the Harvard Club. The new senator and his wife attended. It had made the society page of *Manhattan Life* magazine.

Alexa looked wonderful in a black, strapless Oscar de la Renta gown. Xavier had bought her a classic Cartier watch before going to Montréal. She drew in her breath in expectation when she saw the box. She opened it impatiently but then took a moment to look up. Her heart had fallen; she was hoping for a ring. Alexa could not ignore the fact that Xavier had never said "I love you." No matter how exquisite the dinner, how rewarding the love making, or how amusing the face she made.

The drums were beating for Adrienne. Every time he looked at his calendar, he saw the circle around the twenty-seventh. If he drove by the UN, he went over her curriculum in his head. When he shaved, he saw the space between her teeth inside her enormous mouth. When he showered, he pictured her long, wet hair sticking to her back. Would it reach down to her tight, youthful canal? He saw her silver eyes staring out from a wet and angry little face.

In the end, he did warn Alexa that he would be busy on the weekend of the twenty-seventh. He told her that Charles had asked him to go to Washington for some brainstorming with his staff. What the hell. Maybe he would take the pretty and peculiar Adrienne Blanchard out and enjoy himself a little.

True Identity

The day came. He missed the call. Her message was on his desk when he got back from lunch:

Adrienne Blanchard will be at the Wesley Terrace Hotel on 49th Street until Sunday morning. She has a package from Koldo Aramburu.

His message was waiting for her at the hotel reception at four o'clock. It was equally non-committal:

Xavier Aramburu will be in the hotel lobby at 6:30. Please call the office before 6:00 if this is inconvenient.

She was sitting on a black sofa staring intently at the front entrance. He had come in through a side door and stopped for a moment to look at her. She was wearing a white, knit dress that had long sleeves, a modest, round neckline, a wide black belt, and a full skirt that hit her legs at a nice angle between her knees and her ankles. Her beige hair was tied in a loose ponytail caught by a black satin bow. Xavier admired the curve of her leg between the ankle strap of her black high-heeled shoes and the hem of the dress.

"Adrienne, *guapa!*[60] Hello! Welcome to New York."

"Hello! Thank you for coming," she said. "I hope this is not too far out of your way." She jumped up in a state of nervous excitement.

"No, not at all," he said. "It's exactly halfway between the bank and my apartment and on my subway line. You look beautiful."

"Thank you. We have an official welcome cocktail and dinner later, at eight, here in the hotel."

That was the explanation for the dress. He had thought it was for him. He liked the fact that she had the courtesy not to expect him to take her out.

"Here is your package from Koldo," she said.

The pint of Canadian rye whisky was in a brown paper bag. He put it away in his briefcase. Xavier smiled. Koldo was matchmaking.

"Do you have time for a drink?" said Adrienne.

"Yes, of course. Love to."

That's it, he thought. *A drink and goodbye.* He didn't remove his coat and placed his briefcase on the table. In the soft light of the bar, her face was a smooth, pink gold. The day had been stimulating. She was a person on

---

60 Pretty girl. A frequent greeting for a girl or a woman in Spain.

the verge of change. The adventure had started with an extensive tour of UN headquarters. Her guide was a tall African man named Patrick.

"I'm afraid I asked a silly question, Xavier." She said with a self deprecating grin.

"It can't be that bad. What did you ask?"

"I asked to see the secret shelters for the delegates. You know, in case of a disaster."

"Jesus, Adrienne!" He shook his head and put his hand over his eyes. He laughed softly.

"I know. I don't know what got into me. Too many movies," she said, giggling with her mouth closed.

He tried to be positive. "That's okay. You learn more about people from the questions they ask than from the answers they give. I heard that somewhere."

"Oh good. So, now they think I'm a nosy catastrophist!"

"No, they'll think you want to save your ass. Which can be an important quality, I might add."

They burst out laughing. It was a nice white wine. Xavier was enjoying the conversation. He was again charmed by her unusual face. It had become blurred in his memory.

The next day would be decisive, she said. In a realistic scenario staged by UN staff, the candidates would occupy the interpreting booths in the General Assembly to translate four three-minute speeches. Then, on Friday she would be interviewed by a panel for one hour at two o'clock. They were also evaluated at discussion groups led by UN personnel.

The good news was that they had been told that fifteen people, and not ten, would be offered a post. Even better news was that four people had not shown up. Now she had a one-in-four chance, not one-in-six. He raised his eyebrows at this, and she nodded in agreement.

"Adrienne, those are interesting odds," he said.

It was almost seven-thirty and the bar was filling up with Adrienne's fellow candidates.

"You had better join your colleagues, Adrienne."

She observed the group of young men and women of several nationalities congregating around the bar, and agreed. She picked up her evening bag and looked up at him, suddenly conscious that he hadn't taken off his coat and that his briefcase sat on the table like the Berlin Wall. He must have forgotten the kiss. She felt a stab of disappointment.

"Are you free for dinner tomorrow?" said Xavier.

Somewhere between the curve of her leg and the secret shelters for the delegates, Xavier had changed his mind. Adrienne was pleased. Very pleased.

While he showered and changed, she sat very still in the living room. They had come all the way uptown to 95th Street and Lexington Avenue to go to an Italian restaurant in his neighbourhood. There wasn't a single Spanish restaurant in Manhattan worth shit, he told her. The best you could do was Portuguese in Hoboken, New Jersey. However, the distance between the restaurant and his bed might have been a better indicator for his choice of the neighbourhood Italian joint.

She looked around in awe. His apartment was spectacular. You would never expect such a space in this ordinary building. It was a large loft with Japanese panels from the ceiling as room dividers. Xavier had designed an ingenious rail system for these hanging panels, which were essentially moving walls and doors.

"It's a good location and it was a good deal," he said. "I thought I would be teaching at Columbia when I bought it." He shrugged.

She had nodded respectfully. At age twenty-eight, he owned his own apartment. She sat quietly, glued to the sofa. She took a self-conscious sip of her glass of water. She looked around. No sign of the girlfriend at all. Not a single pretty pillow or a scented candle. Adrienne hadn't had a very good day. The practical trial had not gone well. She had not recognized an acronym for a UN organization and had gone blank for three seconds. It had felt like an eternity.

The water noises from the shower stopped suddenly and were followed by the muted rolling sound of sliding doors. She took a deep breath. He was, she imagined, in his bedroom with a towel around his hips choosing what to wear. His wet hair was sticking to the back of his neck. Her heartbeat accelerated. She felt sure that within the next few hours, she would be making love. He was a beautiful man. It had been a year since Julio. She felt a surge of heat and an involuntary contraction deep inside her. Adrienne was surprised by her own sexual need.

She looked down at her legs and at her new red shoes. She bit her bottom lip and hoped that he would like her body.

"Excuse me, Adri. Five minutes," he said. "I need to make a phone call, OK? Sorry about this."

"OK, no problem. I'm fine."

She remained seated obediently on the sofa in a state of nervous expectation. He had called her Adri. She felt the warmth and familiarity of a nickname being used for the first time by a person you like. He made the call from the kitchen from where she could hear him but not see him. He was booking flights for a business trip to Frankfurt and a stopover in Madrid for the weekend. She tried not to listen but it was impossible.

He came into the living room looking so very handsome in a dark long-sleeved shirt tucked into perfectly fitting light-wool trousers. As she had guessed, his hair was still wet. She was wearing the black miniskirt that he remembered fondly from Montréal. A thin black sweater with a large boat neck fell off one of her shoulders, and she had red spike-heel shoes on. She was dressed for a man, there was no doubt about it. He didn't intend to pass. He leaned down, pecked her on the cheek, took her hand, and helped her up off the sofa.

"Come to the kitchen with me while I prepare an aperitif. It's still early to go to dinner, don't you think?"

"Yes, maybe. Whatever you prefer." She really didn't know what to say.

"Tell me about Koldo. How is he doing in that great Montréal apartment? I'm dying of envy. I had a great weekend. I really enjoyed Montréal."

She filled him in on the latest news while he opened a bottle of wine and a package of toasted almonds. Koldo had slipped on the icy sidewalk and sprained both wrists. He now had two Mexican girls doing all his typing, as well as packing and unpacking his rucksack at classes. Xavier laughed so hard he had to put the corkscrew down.

They went back to the living room, each carrying their own glass of wine. Xavier placed the plate of almonds on the coffee table. He chose the armchair, she returned to her place on the sofa. They toasted to the United Nations for luck, and took a sip of the wine. He reached out and popped an almond into her mouth. She smiled and wrinkled her nose at him. It was their fourth meeting. They had a past.

"So, who is Adrienne Blanchard?" he said.

"I don't really know. I thought I saw her one day, but it wasn't her," she said.

"Ah."

"Who is Xavier Aramburu?"

"Complicated guy. I'll introduce you."

"Please."

"Right now. Come here," he said.

"Where?"

"Here," he said, patting his thighs.

Here we go, thought Adrienne.

She sat sideways on his lap. She was only slightly more elevated than he was. He put his glass of wine down on the table and pulled her closer. He nuzzled at her ear and stroked her legs between her knees at the hem of her skirt with every intention of starting a fire. Like two young ponies, they grazed at each other's necks. They were barely touching. She still held her glass of wine. They were teasing each other and being slow. She whispered, "Excuse me," and stretched her arm out to put her glass down. As she bent sideways, he lifted her sweater and blew on her side.

He sat her down on his knees again. She was facing him this time, her legs apart. Her straight tube skirt was hiked up high on her thighs. The gentle, curious nuzzling became noisy and desperate. He pulled her head down and greedily kissed her mouth. She returned the kiss with the same intensity.

"Let me see you," he said impatiently, pulling off her sweater.

Adrienne helped. She was not turning back. She was perched above him, her hands on his shoulders, her breasts in his face. His hands surrounded her waist. His head moved around her pretty black bra, softly tracing its contours with his lips. She purred and rocked softly, her arms around his head. Her mane of hair covered them like a private tent.

Xavier sat back slowly. He took her arms from around his neck and held them down by her sides. He looked up at her young face. She was a doll in black leather and lace. Her pale, silky hair fell softly to her waist like a veil.

"We stay, Adri? Or we go? Whatever you want. It's okay with me."

Adrienne smiled, "We stay."

He pulled her gently by the hand to his bedroom. An opaque, light appliqué on the wall made everything look soft and pretty. They undressed very formally, standing by the bed, face-to-face. They were not touching. He caressed her hair and asked her nicely to keep the shoes on. She nodded. When she was naked, he lifted her onto the bed where she remained on her knees. She rested her hands on her thighs. She stared at his face, too shy to look down at his body.

She was just as he had imagined. Her tousled hair fell prettily over her face. Her sensuous mouth was slightly open. He could see the gap between her teeth. The red heels and black soles of the shoes pointed up hard and sharp to the ceiling. He recognized her lanky arms and long slender legs, and discovered a fit young body with generous and pretty round breasts that hung softly and naturally. The triangle of soft, pale hair between her legs seemed transparent. He felt the arching of his back and the familiar fire. He made her hold his gaze a little longer as he slowly took off his watch. Kneeling with her thighs slightly separated, she endured the scrutiny.

He reached into a drawer for a condom. She managed to find air somewhere in her lungs and said, "It's not necessary for me."

He felt he could trust. He left it on the table.

He knelt on the bed as well. Their bodies met gratefully from knees to shoulders. His hands moved to feel her skin in places that he hadn't yet touched. They let themselves fall onto their side. He wrapped her legs around his waist and pulled her close, holding her firmly. He rocked his hips to stroke her vagina with his erect penis and feel her desire. She was incredibly wet and warm. Her eyes were begging. Her sweet anguish aroused him. This girl did not want to play today.

"Please," she whispered.

He penetrated her deliberately and hard. Her head fell back and her chest pushed up against his face. Her full breasts were near his mouth. He sucked at her neck. They moaned together as he pushed inside her and hit the place that felt the need time after time. He watched her tremble and cry like women in ecstasy cry. At last, he emptied himself into a calm and pulsating Adrienne. She cradled his head and kissed his face as he came to his climax. When it was over, their eyes met with the knowledge that they were good together.

Later, he was standing in the dark, staring ahead at nothing, arms crossed, in front of the kitchen sink. He was giving her time to freshen up. He had put on the grey cotton yoga pants he always slept in. When she came to find him, she was wrapped in a towel and asked very politely if she could please have a glass of water. He reached for a glass, filled it with water and, with great tenderness, put one hand at the nape of her neck, put the glass to her mouth and made her drink.

"What is happening here, Adrienne Blanchard? Tell me," he said.

"Whatever we want, Xavier. That's what is happening," she said.

He stood behind her, holding her with both arms against his chest like he was guarding a treasure. She felt a warm, powerful wall at her back.

Xavier awakened in an empty bed. It was 6:00 a.m. Adrienne was sitting on his sofa, fully dressed with her coat on. She had hardly slept. It was the last day, the day of the big interview. She wanted to get back to her hotel early in case the interview schedule had been changed. He tried to convince her to wait for him for only twenty minutes, but she ran out of the apartment apologizing profusely. He would pick her up at six, he thought he had said.

It was not a good day. He was in the office by half past seven. In a foul mood, he decided to cancel his date with Adrienne. He would leave a message with an excuse at hotel reception. He regretted having been so tender and intimate. He convinced himself that this had been an insignificant event. Just a good lay. She was not his responsibility. Adrienne's trip to New York had been planned long before he had met her. After all, there was Alexa. It might not be too late to call and tell her the brainstorming had been called off. Xavier was relieved, yet spent the whole afternoon watching the clock. He was calculating Adrienne Blanchard's whereabouts.

He didn't understand that Adrienne was a free-falling meteor. He was in her trajectory and they had collided.

When Xavier looked at his watch at two, Adrienne was sitting up straight on a hard metal chair in a windowless room. An imposing panel of four members was studying her file in silence. She recognized Mary Bennett, a British lady who had given a fascinating talk on protocol on the first day.

Nobody had warned Adrienne about the anti-interview. She was shocked by their first words as they shuffled the papers. It was Mary who began.

"Ms. Blanchard, we must tell you that your results were not satisfactory and, frankly, you mustn't harbour much hope of being offered a position here at the United Nations," she said. "Of the fifty-six candidates, we are afraid you don't rank among the first thirty. Or even the first forty, for that matter."

Adrienne nodded regretfully but with an optimistic smile. Controlling her disappointment, she searched for something clever or intelligent to say.

"I see," was all she could come up with.

It was a bluff. Adrienne was one of six "maybes." Her practical tests had not been strong, probably due to her lack of experience, but she was agile and young. She had postgraduate studies, no significant past, and no political leanings other than the pragmatic and tolerant spirit of most Canadians. The psychological tests had drawn a serene, focused, and confident character. Adrienne hung on to her smile and her self-esteem, but her heart had fallen to her feet. No New York. No Xavier. No international career. No new life.

Then the interview really got started.

"We are curious, Ms. Blanchard, as to why you chose English as your source language. Is French not your mother tongue?"

Adrienne swallowed hard and determined to do the best she could. Maybe all was not lost. She had expected this question.

"Yes, French is my mother tongue. I was born into a French Canadian family and it is the language of my childhood, my family and my primary and secondary education. Why did I choose English? You know, I don't remember ever learning English? It came easily and naturally to me as I grew up in a bilingual city in Eastern Canada. Then, I studied here in the United States, at a small university in Vermont that has a prestigious language department."

"Middlebury College, correct?" one of the panelists interrupted as he looked up from the glasses on the tip of his nose. He was holding her resumé in his hand and nodding knowledgeably.

"Yes," Adrienne said and smiled proudly. Middlebury was probably one of the best places to study languages in the world. The school was known for its revolutionary methods and rigorous curriculum.

"Then, when I went to Europe to perfect my Spanish and German, I found it easy to find work as an English teacher and as a translator. So, English is very familiar to me in a professional manner while I have never worked extensively in French other than for an occasional freelance translation or interpreting job." Adrienne answered carefully.

"I see," said Mary, who still did not seem very convinced. In a slightly scolding tone she said, "We ask you this because choosing English as your source language narrowed your competitive potential considerably. You performed extremely well in French."

"It's nice to hear I did so well in French. It is definitely my mother tongue. Thank you very much. It is true that the competition is extraordinary. I may have made an unfortunate choice."

Adrienne conceded the point and then realizing that there was nothing much she could do, she smiled and said, "You know, the place I come from and the French I speak have quite an interesting history."

"Why don't you tell us something about that?" said the intellectual-looking older man who had mentioned Middlebury.

Adrienne relaxed and gave them a brief history of the Acadians. She explained how the language and customs had survived through centuries of isolation from France.

The panel listened with interest. She described the Acadian accent as, *"Le bruit de la mer,"*[61] and demonstrated a peculiar rolling of the "r." She recited a short poem to illustrate its musicality. The interviewers were delighted. The majority were linguists and she was introducing them to a small treasure. She crossed her legs, put her two hands around one knee and wagged her foot as if she were chatting with a group of friends.

"How did the Acadians survive the English conquest?" a panelist asked.

The Great Deportation of the Acadians and their subsequent return home was one of Adrienne's favourite subjects. It was a simple footnote to world history, but it was a tragedy to the Acadian people and important to understand their past and present.

France lost Atlantic Canada - known then as "Acadie" - to England in 1711. This was a full forty years before it lost Upper and Lower Canada, which is present-day Ontario and Québec. By that time, the Acadians had been living in the beautiful valleys of Nova Scotia for more than a century. Their lands were prosperous, the villages had churches and schools, the society was growing. Several generations knew of no other homeland.

The Acadians were told they could stay, but would have to live under English rule and law. What to do? Start again in Québec? Return to

---

61 The murmur of the sea.

European serfdom? They were self-sufficient in the New World. France was a fading memory. Acadie was their home. They negotiated for an exemption from military service - so as not to take up arms against their Québécois brothers - and freedom to practise the Catholic religion. A deal was struck. They stayed, but they shouldn't have trusted the Redcoats. Revolution was brewing in the rich thirteen colonies to the south. Nova Scotia was prime real estate. These were cleared and rich farmlands to distribute to those colonials and to those soldiers who would remain loyal to the King. The English quietly began to prepare for a negative outcome of the colonial unrest. A massive deportation of the Acadian population was planned and put into effect in August 1755. In a cruel and surprise military action, the English masters burned the homes, confiscated the lands, and herded the Acadian population onto ships with only the possessions that they could carry. Families were separated. Children were lost.

The population was deported to Louisiana and some, back to France. In an attempt at permanent dispersal, the British let small groups off the ships as they sailed down the Atlantic coast. They later became known as the Cajun people. The word 'Cajun' was a deformation of the word 'Acadian.'

The dispersed Acadians struggled to regroup. Their wish was to return to their homeland despite the Redcoats and the distance. And many did. On foot. They were reasonably successful but, generally speaking, it took seventy-five years. Some returned to Nova Scotia but most resettled in the woods and on the shores of New Brunswick. Two centuries later, they form a vibrant and healthy Francophone community in the midst of English Canada.

"I am a descendant of Louis Blanchard," Adrienne said. "In 1625, he arrived in Port Royal at fifteen years of age from Normandy. Louis' great-grandson, Philippe, who my father is named after, walked back home from New Orleans. It took him twenty-one years. So wait for me, I might be back!"

Adrienne concluded with a pinch of humour and a large smile. Mary slapped her hands together in amusement and satisfaction. The interview was over.

Adrienne left UN headquarters by the official public exit to hand in her documentation to Patrick Kyenge, who was twirling like a small boy on a swivel chair beside the receptionist. He was a charming man. He was her tour leader of the first day and she was friendly with him. He sat beside her at the welcome dinner and was the leader of her discussion group.

He was an impressive looking man, over six feet tall, and perhaps in his early forties. The body under his elegant suit was lean and triangular as an arrow. He had a beautiful African face with a kind expression, and premature grey hair cut near his head in very short, soft curls. He spoke a slow and beautiful English with a light French accent and a deep African tone. He was from the Democratic Republic of the Congo and had been mischievously nicknamed "Patrick of the Condo" by one of the English candidates. The women of her group had shared the naughty little joke.

Adrienne and Patrick, both children of Francophone colonies, spoke French together.

"*Ah! Mademoiselle la Canadienne,*[62] you are the last one! I was waiting for you. How did it go?"

"Oh! Thank you. I'm not sure, Patrick," she said. She didn't want to admit they had told her she had no chance at all.

"And why is that?"

"They were very nice and I had a good interview. But they were not very encouraging. The competition is extraordinary, I'm afraid." She shrugged her shoulders and smiled.

Patrick wagged his head from side-to-side in an "I wouldn't be so sure" motion.

"Are you going to the disco tonight?" he asked. "We had to call the Mayor to get you people into Studio 54!"

"Really? How great! No, I'm going out with a Spanish friend who lives here in New York."

"Have a good trip home then."

"Thank you, Patrick. For everything. Hope to see you again!" she said, smiling.

"I would not be surprised," said Patrick mysteriously.

Adrienne thought he was trying to make her feel better.

Patrick was an infiltrated CIA operative. He watched her leave the building on the television security monitors. She was wearing her hair

---

[62] Young lady from Canada.

up in a tight ponytail, and sported a tailored, dark pantsuit. She wrapped herself in a red shawl as she walked out of the building. She walked fast and straight, without hesitation, aware of her surroundings, head up, shoulders and hands relaxed. He had had three days to observe her. She knew exactly who, what, and where she was. He was impressed. He had a feeling and made up his mind that he had to talk to Mary.

Adrienne walked back to the hotel and tried not to think about the interview. She had prepared herself for disappointment, so despite what she considered a bad interview, she felt lucky. It had been a great experience. She might try again. Something in Mary Bennett's attitude made her suspect she might have a chance.

By then, Xavier had become a permanent presence in her head. She took pleasure in how breathless and excited she was feeling. It was half past three. She had two and a half hours to get ready. She smiled to herself and thanked the universe for leading her to Koldo's party that night. She even forgave her ex-boyfriend for dropping her. She suspected the forces of destiny might be involved.

But Xavier made her wait. He never called. He never showed up. Seven hours and no word. She sat, fully dressed, made-up and perfumed, on the foot of her hotel bed, alternately staring at the television set and leafing through a travel and hotel magazine. He was in his apartment, watching television in his pyjamas and fighting with himself. He got off the sofa at ten, went into the bathroom, threw water on his face, and had a good look in the mirror. Who was he kidding? Adrienne Blanchard was not an unwanted obligation or a good lay. He was fighting an unexpected and intense attraction. He wanted to know how she was. He wanted to know how her interview had gone. The thought of not seeing her again was not acceptable.

He could hide or he could act. Whatever he decided, it had to be at that moment. He chose to act.

She picked up the phone the moment it rang. It was almost eleven.

"I'm downstairs. Forgive me," he said.

"You're in the lobby?" she said.

"Yes."

"Just a minute."

He waited for her opposite the elevators. Her arms were crossed. She carried no coat or handbag. Just a key in her hand. She wasn't smiling. *Angry girl*, he thought.

"Did you have dinner?" he said.

"I could have made other plans," she said bluntly.

His face fell and she felt sorry for him. She wondered if he might have an explanation.

"Actually, I ordered room service at nine. I'm okay. So, did you want to tell me something? Like 'sorry' or something like that?" She grinned sarcastically.

"Let's have a drink in the bar," he said. "It's quiet. We can talk. You can give me hell in all the languages you speak. I deserve it."

She was too annoyed to laugh. They sat on stools at the bar. She looked straight ahead, he sat sideways and searched her profile.

"I have a girlfriend," he said immediately.

"I know. Koldo told me."

"What else did he tell you?"

"That you weren't in love."

He was hit. It was a sad thing to hear and it was coming from his family.

"I have no excuse. I acted like a scared son of a bitch. I felt, no, I feel, threatened by you. I was hiding." He touched her hand fleetingly but sensed the contact was unwanted and took it away.

She took a sip of her drink and turned her head to look into his eyes. She took a moment to consider his words. He held her gaze. Above all, Adrienne appreciated honesty.

"You know what?" she said. "That was honest. It's alright, Xavi, I'm not a child. I knew what I was doing. And as I said, I knew you were with someone. It makes sense. You don't want to mess up your life. You should have called, that's all. You know that."

Her smile was not cheerful, but it was sincere. Xavier was a bit offended that she didn't make more of a fuss. Not knowing what to say, he asked about her interview. She shook her head. The euphoria was gone. She had no false hopes.

"I seem to have confused my mother tongue," she said.

"What do they know?" he said.

She looked tired as she described the interview and the panel's attitude. Xavier saw that he had made a hard day even worse. He said he was sorry and put his arms around her in a friendly hug. He was ashamed of himself.

Adrienne pulled away and said, "Xavi, I'm tired. It's been a very long day. I think I'll go up now. Don't worry about it. Really. Maybe we'll see you in Montréal."

She shrugged as if it didn't really matter. It was obvious that she wanted to end the conversation and put the episode behind her, but Xavier had not finished.

"Adrienne, the reason I came is that I don't want this, whatever it is, to be over. Can I see you tomorrow?"

He said he would pick her up at nine, but he was there at eight-thirty. She was wearing a Basque beret, and her hair in braids. The plan was Ellis Island. They hung on to the central pole of the Downtown Express with their feet wide apart to keep their balance. By Fourteenth Street, they were kissing passionately and Xavier was wearing the beret.

The Ellis Island Ferry sailed very close to the Statue of Liberty. Adrienne leaned over the rusty railing, straining to see the statue in every detail. Xavier wrapped himself around her to keep her warm and to feel her body. He was frustrated that he had wasted one night. They wandered around the grounds holding hands and reading the explanations on the faded panels. They walked slowly, pointing and whispering.

As they waited for the ferry back to the city, Xavier turned and walked back a few steps to have another look at the building. He had never been to Ellis Island and the visit had fascinated him. He felt a deep respect for people fleeing the dogs of hunger, poverty, and persecution. They were burying the past, burying history, burning bridges, starting again. Maybe that was the right thing to do.

He took her to a restaurant near Central Park for lunch and then for a walk down Fifth Avenue to the Rockefeller Center skating rink. They were stopping to kiss every few steps. It was Adrienne who said, "When are you taking me home?"

He buzzed two long and four short, and then opened the door with his own keys. From the bedroom, he heard, "I'll be out in a minute."

"OK," he said, and got a cold beer, which she kept for him, from the refrigerator.

The apartment was feminine and cluttered, which was a bit of a contradiction for Alexa. He had been surprised the first time he had seen it.

Her pride and joy was a beautiful Dutch doll house for which she collected miniature objects from all over the world. Xavier had bought her all the pieces of a typical Andalusian wine cellar complete with wicker chairs, tiny wine rack stacked with miniature bottles, and Spanish guitars, which she loved. The house was enormous, perhaps five feet wide by four feet high, but the extraordinary thing about it lay in its details: miniature mirrors and jewels, tiny blankets on the beds, and lamps that worked. It was electrically wired. Alexa had minuscule Christmas ornaments for the house and put up a miniature Christmas tree every December. He had helped her string the tiny lights onto the tree just three months before.

Xavier had played with it secretly. He would switch the caps on the little boys' heads, turn down a bed, or hang a painting upside down. He looked around nostalgically, knowing he would probably not be back. He turned on the small television set in the kitchen to watch a news channel.

"Hi," she said. She was dressed in workout clothes and smelled of mint. "So, how was your weekend? Lots of brainstorming with the boys?" she asked.

He smiled, delaying the inevitable.

"Good. How are you? Good weekend? How are your parents?" he said.

No answer. She was supposed to have gone to visit her parents in Connecticut. She got a soft drink from the refrigerator and sat down opposite him. Xavier saw the cynical smirk on her face and knew immediately that she was onto him.

"Go on, X. Spit it out. You can do it," she said.

"Well, then why don't you tell me what I am going to say, Alexa. If you already know," he said. He didn't appreciate her tone of voice. Despite his dry answer, she did not desist in her sarcastic attitude.

"Is she French? She looks French. Bohemian waif type. Young! Did you check her age? You could get into trouble you know!" she said.

He realized that she must have seen them somewhere. Adrienne in jeans and braids looked very young.

"No, she's not French."

"Ah. So, Montréal then? I knew I should have gone."

I'm so glad you didn't, was what he wanted to respond, but this was not a lovers' quarrel. This was the official end of a relationship. He wanted to do it properly.

"You know about this for some reason," he said. "OK. I have met somebody and it changes things, Alexa."

"You kissed her eyes. You closed them with your fingers and then you kissed her eyes," she said. "And you fixed strands of her hair into that stupid Che Guevara beret."

Adrienne's last New York wish had been to see the skating rink at Rockefeller Center. Alexa had seen them. He felt like hell.

"Oh my god! Alexa, I am so sorry," he said.

He leaned back in surprise. He was genuinely upset. He remembered the precise moment. *There's something in my eye,* Adrienne had said. Alexa had been watching from somewhere nearby, maybe from a window table at a café.

"She's a friend of my cousin's from Montréal. An instructor at the university. She came for a job interview and stayed for the weekend," he said.

He identified Adrienne because he thought Alexa should know. Then, from across the table, she whacked him on the head. He saw it coming and ducked, but she made contact.

"Oww! Alexa May Howard! My head is not a goddamn volleyball!"

He was exagerrating but it relieved the tension. His good-natured, hard laughing and generous Alexa came back. Her expression became softer. She sat back on the hard kitchen chair and sighed.

"I'm sorry," she said.

"I'm sorry," responded Xavier. "For everything."

He hoped he wouldn't have to spend hours explaining himself and dissecting their relationship, but he should have known that Alexa wouldn't want that either.

"I had a wonderful year with you, Alexa. It was a gift."

"Twenty-two months," she clarified loudly.

She had been good to him and it had been a comfortable relationship, but he couldn't give in to guilt and conventionality. He was sure of what he was doing. Adrienne was where he was going, head first.

There was not much more to say. She walked him to the door. They carefully avoided touching each other in the narrow hallway.

"Get out of here, Little Swap King," she said with some irony, a pinch of humour and a good deal of fondness.

He nodded like a friend who knows what another is feeling, put one arm around her neck and kissed her on the cheek. Alexa didn't go back into the apartment right away but leaned on the door frame. She watched him walk briskly down the hall and then break into a soft run as he passed the elevators to the stairwell. As he pushed on the bar of the stairs door with his hip, he turned, caught her eye, and smiled apologetically. He disappeared behind the door.

There was a certain joy in the the rhythmic sound of his feet running down the stairs. That sound was more painful to Alexa than the kisses on Adrienne's eyes. She found his keys a few days later in the doll house.

Like a Plant in a Pot

Between Alexa and Adrienne, there was Madrid. The mother's house. It was a time for Xavier to collect his thoughts and enjoy the idea of change.

Who was Adrienne Blanchard? The woman of his life? A brief affair? An excuse to leave Alexa? He was following his instincts, which were usually wrong as far as women were concerned. However, the skepticism in his heart was outweighed by a healthy excitement. Xavier looked forward to Adrienne like a rare event or an exciting journey, like the passing of a comet or a safari in the Serengeti. He approached her with a healthy appetite and a flutter of the diaphragm.

He was in a hurry to get to Madrid to be with his mother on her birthday for the first time in years. It was a surprise visit. Only Begoña knew that he was coming for the weekend. There were so many women in his life: a new lover, a wounded ex-girlfriend, two needy sisters, and a loving mother. Xavi was the proud beagle trotting ahead of his pack.

He managed to get to Madrid on Thursday afternoon, a day early. It was March and it was warm. The Madrid sky was a brilliant blue and the first almond trees had bloomed in Retiro Park. He grinned happily as he rang the doorbell, holding his garment bag in one hand and his roller vskates in the other. Pilar, the Aramburu's maid, opened the door and smiled in surprise.

He put his finger to his lips and Pilar nodded in complicity. She took his things and motioned to the den where, at four-thirty, his mother would be resting after lunch while Paloma had her *siesta*.[63] He walked quietly down the hall and opened the glass doors carefully so as not to give her a fright. She was watching a nature show on television, a blanket on her lap.

---

63 Afternoon nap.

"*Ama.* Surprise!" he sang out cheerfully. His mother was startled out of her afternoon lethargy. She blinked in disbelief.

"Xavi! What are you doing here?"

"*Amita*,[64] happy birthday!"

Xavier didn't allow her to stand up. He put his arms around her as he bent down.

"Your father's having lunch with some people from Bilbao, Xavi."

He sat on the sofa next to her armchair, leaned over the armrest, took her arm, and laid his face in her hand.

"I'm here till Sunday. For you. Lots of time for the *aita*," he said.

"Tell me, my love. How are you? Are you happy?"

"I'm happy, *Ama*. Very happy. Don't worry about me."

All of the members of the family came home in the next hour as word spread of Xavier's surprise visit. His father was beside himself with this small joy. Paloma held his hand and didn't let it go. She went wherever he went except into the bathroom where she waited outside the door. Begoña was relieved to see him; she had worried that he might not be able to come. Pilar ran out to the market and returned with fish for dinner, which she prepared in three different ways. The boy needed to eat properly. Hake with clams in a parsley and white wine sauce, cod in its own gel, and grilled sea bream splashed with vinegar, garlic, and red peppers. He relished each bite of the meal and every sip of the excellent wine. Everyone laughed as he forgot his manners and broke into loud groans of satisfaction. The sense of taste is the ultimate guardian of memory.

He sat Jon and Iñaki on his knees and entertained them with tales of his trip to Montréal. He described twirling spiral staircases encased in ice ten storeys high, people skating on frozen lakes, and children playing hockey on city streets, oblivious to traffic. He gleefully told the story of cousin Koldo's sangria that got sixty Canadians drunk as skunks and of Koldo falling on his face and recruiting two pretty girls to do his work.

"He's going to be *Lehendakari*[65] one day!" Begoña exclaimed.

"It was so nice of you to go up there," said his mother. "Your godfather really appreciated it."

---

64 Mummy. Diminutive of Ama.

65 Leader in Basque. The official title of the President of the Autonomous Basque Region of Euskadi. One of Spain's 17 Autonomous Regional Governments.

"It was fun. I loved it. Koldo is a good kid. I'm going back next weekend, as a matter of fact."

This news startled everyone.

"Alexa too?" Begoña asked. She was suspicious of his soft expression and a new light in his eyes.

"I'm not going out with Alexa anymore. Nothing happened. I'm fine. She's fine. Koldo and I are going skiing."

His tone did not invite questions. His sister connected the dots. He had met someone in Montréal, she was sure. The rest of the family received the news with a measure of relief.

Late Saturday afternoon, two trucks waited on the street until Xavier's mother went to a beauty salon. She was sent on the pretense of a special birthday dinner at a favourite restaurant. Then, Begoña and her staff transformed the living room into a spring garden of hydrangeas and tulips. Caterers invaded the kitchen to prepare an exquisite meal. Xavier, Paloma, and the boys, on Begoña's instructions, folded thirty napkins into birds of paradise. Any similarity to Begoña's design was coincidental but they were delighted with their works of art. They placed them with care on the three large, round dining tables that now occupied the living room. The Quiroga family in Madrid and intimate friends would join the celebration later.

When their mother walked in, she was speechless. Her Begoña was a wizard. She scolded her daughter for making such a fuss over her birthday. Xavi's presence had been more than enough. She saw her three children and her two grandsons standing together, so happy with their surprise. They had made this place into a garden and into a home. Her heart was full, but she was too proud to cry.

The next morning, Xavier boarded the plane for New York, taking the steps two at a time.

Montréal again. The snow, the staircases, the lights. Xavier arrived at eight. Adrienne and Koldo greeted him at the door. Xavier's face shone with the serenity of being exactly where he wanted to be. Adrienne shone in the same light. Koldo witnessed the gentle re-encounter of these two extraordinary people he had brought together. He was a fiercely loyal and territorial man. Adrienne and Xavier were now a permanent part of his universe.

Adrienne and Xavier became reacquainted in the bedroom. They were excited to be together. It was their beginning. They laid down on the bed, not taking the time to undress. Their heads together and their legs intertwined. Whispering, kissing, exploring, until the moment came when finally, he held both her hands down firmly above her head and let his own rhythm come. It was the rocking of a ship, a tree's branch in a storm, the beating of a large bird's wing. Adrienne, eyes wide open, looked up at him and gave herself without reservation.

Koldo's apartment became the centre of their existence. Xavier came every weekend and Adrienne moved in with Koldo in April when his roomate returned to Spain. The hard winter at last gave way to the sweet northern spring and summer.

Montréal was a city hungry for light, for music, for art, for fun. Every window and door was open wide. The smallest window box was pampered and treasured. Bicycles took to the streets. Sidewalk cafés popped up like jack-in-the-boxes. Montréal was Sleeping Beauty waking up and dying to party knowing that she will have to go back to sleep again too soon. Festival followed festival. Montréal in the summer was the place to be young and happy.

Adrienne was offered a job at the UN, but as a tour guide not as an interpreter. Her rejection letter was followed by a phone call from Mary Bennett, the British lady on her interview panel. Adrienne had left such an excellent impression that they wondered if she might be interested in a twelve-month stint as a guide. Three of their guides would soon be on maternity leave. She would have all the perks and advantages of an international employee. She would be reconsidered for interpreter at the next opportunity. She didn't need to worry about papers. Arrangements could be made for accomodation. There was only one thing: could she work on her German in the meantime?

It was a difficult decision. She had no desire to be a tour guide. However, they had dangled the carrot of the interpreting position she wanted. It was a foot in the door. She worried that Xavier would feel that she was following him. But she wanted this. Like her father, Adrienne trusted and listened to herself. She accepted. She enrolled in intensive courses at the Goethe-Institut to freshen up her German. Her contract with Concordia was up, so she concentrated on her German and lived on her savings. She had four months to prepare.

As for Xavier, he enjoyed Montréal immensely. He reluctantly flew back to Manhattan on the dawn flight on Monday mornings.

"You go to New York, I'll stay here with Koldo," he would say to a sleepy Adrienne as he kissed her goodbye.

Montréal reminded him of home. He loved the port, the industry, the hearty Québécois personality, its pride in its difference, and nature at its doors. He loved to skate the cycling trail. He mapped out a twenty-kilometre route that took him through the industrial sections of the old port, through city neighbourhoods, along the railroad, and past the white-water rapids of the Lachine Canal. Roller skates had been replaced by rollerblades. They offered him a new speed and a wonderful, smooth ride. Alone in the early morning, he loved to pick up speed and give himself to the sense of flight. Montréal was good for him. Adrienne was good for him. He felt like a plant in a pot: good earth, fresh water, and light.

Xavier worried about his future with Adrienne. He was happy and wanted the relationship to last. He was aware that the slightest gust of wind could blow him off the tightrope he was walking between loving boyfriend and horny son of a bitch. He was afraid to hurt her. He needed to be honest. He confessed to his chronic infidelity and his taste for sexual adventure.

So Adrienne knew from the beginning that a relationship with Xavier would either be short-lived or unconventional. She wondered if accepting this was a desperate wish to hold on to him, or a true belief that love could be based on something other than a sexual monopoly. Sooner or later, the time would come when she would feel betrayed, hurt, and unloved, but cowardice and caution were not in Adrienne Blanchard's nature. She came to the conclusion that she needed her own place in Xavier's life. She would find unexplored territory that was hers, and go as far as she could.

They planned their first summer together. They would spend a week at the Blanchard cottage at Crane Road in New Brunswick and a week in Bilbao for Koldo's sister's wedding.

Adrienne had her own little secret. She soon admitted that she did not use any method of contraception. It was simple, she explained. There was really no need. At twenty, upon requesting a birth control method, she had been diagnosed with infertility, and she had made a decision. As it was almost a certainty that she faced a childless future, if a miracle should happen, she would welcome it. There would be no second chance. It was definitely not a priority at this time in her life, but every time she made love, Adrienne was hoping for a baby. It was only fair that he should know. He or any other eventual father would not be held responsible.

"There. I had to tell you," she said. "But don't worry, Xavi. The odds are approximately one in fifty thousand. My natural odds are actually better than the pill's. I'd rather not, but, if it makes you feel better, I'll take the pill."

Xavier was taken aback at such an unexpected revelation. He was surprised, curious, and strangely amused. Even incredulous. They had just soaked together in the huge bathtub and made love three times during the day. They were in a state of grace: young, beautiful, and satiated. They were in the kitchen having a glass of wine and about to prepare dinner, which had become their Saturday night tradition. Koldo was in Spain for the summer and they had the apartment to themselves. An embarrassed Adrienne smiled cheerfully and tried to change the subject.

"Should I grate the cheese?" she asked.

"Wait a minute," he said. "Slow down." He flailed his hands up and down like a policeman waving a car to a stop. "I'm in shock. One in fifty thousand?"

"More or less."

"*Hostia*. It's going to take me a couple of weeks."

It was the perfect thing to say. Adrienne laughed from the heart and playfully gave him a spank on the bottom. They talked for hours with open hearts and clear minds. They had fun thinking up extravagant names for an eventual accidental child. Xavier favoured *Cachivache*[66] for a boy, or *Pirueta*[67] for a girl. Adrienne suggested *Encyclopédie*[68] might be good for either. That night, sitting on the steps of the rue des Tilleuls, Xavier told Adrienne he loved her very much. They marched forward without fear.

---

66   Trinket.

67   Pirouette.

68   Encyclopedia.

The Secret of Crane Road

They arrived on a hot and windy July day. Xavier was *le nouveau chum*: the new boyfriend.

The Blanchard's cottage was a traditional one on a tree-lined dirt road near the beach. It was a dark green Cape Cod-style cabin that was worn with age, dangerously leaning to one side, and in need of a coat of paint. Crane Road bordered on a provincial park beach, which turned out to be the best of both worlds, as Adrienne's brother René explained to the newcomer. Xavier looked around and grinned at the centre of Adrienne's universe.

"Hello. Did you have a nice trip?" said Adrienne's mother.

"Hello. Yes, very nice," said Xavier as he bowed his head respectfully. They called her "Maman": the *ama*.

Claude was reading on a lounge chair in the back yard and waited to be introduced. She was not intimidated by men like Xavier. She worked in London, England, for one of the world's most important communications groups that specialized in awards ceremonies and mega sports events. Fresh out of university at her first job in Montréal, she had fallen deeply, passionately, and stupidly in love with her married boss, and followed him to London. Jean Pierre Dugas was enormously talented, creative, and ambitious. He was a handsome and youthful forty-five-year-old. He was married, with three small children, and was the Québécois wunderkind of special events.

The eager and beautiful twenty-one-year-old was a summer intern on his staff in Montréal. She revered the ground he walked on. She took hours to prepare her clothes and hair for work. At last, it was not a boy trying to impress her, but a man she wanted to impress. An amused Jean Pierre caught her eye frequently. Flustered, she would smile and look away. Claude was the prettiest rose in the garden. Incredibly and inexplicably, still a virgin.

There was not a great distance between infatuated girl, passionate and secret lover, and conventional mistress, which is what Claude had become. In the meantime, she had also become an excellent professional to the point where Jean Pierre feared losing his employee more than his mistress. They were together on Tuesday nights and for occasional short holidays. It was the usual scenario: a difficult child and a dependent, depressive wife were powerful impediments to his divorce.

"Patience, my darling," he would say. Too frequently. She loved Jean Pierre blindly, but she did not want the same for her sister.

Xavier gave her a big smile and a warm kiss on the cheek. Claude remained seated. Their father was gone, and René was focused on his young family, therefore Claude considered herself the head of the household. She received him with an artificial smile as she looked up over her stylish sunglasses.

"Oh yes. The Spaniard." she said. "You're not a basketball player or anything like that are you?"

Xavier recognized Claude right away. She was the lioness at the entrance to the lair. He was a male stray from another brood. He was there for the little one.

The sisters were not identical, but they did look very much alike. Claude was not as tall as Adrienne. Her face was rounder, which made her expression softer. She had tamed her eyebrows, her teeth were perfect, her hair was dyed platinum blond, and had been cut and styled by expert hands. Claude's antipathy did not last, however. She couldn't keep up her attitude for very long, as Xavier was a friendly and affectionate man. The rest of the family took to him like bees to honey. Two days later, he was calling her Clo and she was showing him all her finances. She wanted to buy a small flat in London and needed serious advice.

Shortly after they arrived, while everyone plied Adrienne with questions, Xavier slipped outside to look around. Catherine and Valerie, René and Jocelyne's two little girls, followed him silently and in single file.

"You talk funny," said the little one. Catherine was six and Valerie was four years of age, and they were already culturally aware. They were familiar with Franco and Anglo, but this boyfriend represented a new human group

Gisèle Bourgeois

to be compartmentalized in their little heads. He needed his own category. They were figuring him out.

"Is the beach far?" he asked. "Can you take me there?"

"*Il faut qu'on demande la permission,*"[69] said Catherine.

"Ok," Xavier said.

The girls were allowed to go down to the beach only if accompanied by an adult, but they didn't know if this strange guy who talked funny, qualified. They ran up the crooked stairs and Valerie screamed at the top of her lungs through the screen door.

"Maman, can we go down to the beach with Aunt Adrienne's new boyfriend?"

"Of course! But don't be long. We're going to the Upick in twenty minutes."

Jocelyne smiled and waved at Xavier through the screen door. Silently, they pointed to a path across the dusty road. They led the way carefully over the dunes. After barely one minute, the man and the two little girls came onto a large, wide beach on a quiet bay. The flat, sandy beach stretched a couple of miles to the east and to the west, at a shorter distance, there was another separate grouping of cottages on a cliff.

Xavier's Crane Road education had begun. Catherine and Valerie proceeded to teach him how to recognize live clam holes in the wet sand, and how, with a soft pressure of the foot beside the hole, the clam would pee straight up your leg. They then demonstrated the art of standing perfectly still in the shallow water so that the minnows would come and tickle your feet. Xavier was a willing student. He took off his shoes, rolled up his pants, and let the girls show him these things that to them, were essential to life.

An apologetic Adrienne, who had changed into shorts and a tee-shirt, came running over the dune and onto the beach to find him.

"We're going blueberry picking, Xavi! Just put on your bathing suit, a tee-shirt, and sneakers, and you'll be fine. "Come on girls! We're going to the UPick! Blueberrry pie tonight! Yummy! *Grandmaman*[70] is making my favourite!"

---

69 We have to ask permission.
70 Grandmother.

Xavier had done a lot of things in his life, but this was a new world. He had snorted cocaine with fashion models and opera singers at Studio 54. He had discussed econometrics in Davos. He had strong relationships with former terrorists. He went to power lunches on Wall Street. But blueberry picking in a group was certainly a first. He felt like a character in an incomprehensible Scandinavian movie.

And if he had the impression that being a tall, dark, and handsome big shot somehow afforded him special treatment, he was soon relieved of that misconception. He was given a straw hat, which was too small for his head, and a very large tin cup, and then relegated to the third row of René's family van with Catherine and Valerie for the ride to the blueberry patch. The two little girls stared at him unblinkingly as he tried to untangle a piece of caramel popcorn from the hair on the back of his right thigh.

Madame Blanchard was in a hurry to get to the UPick, afraid that word had gotten out that the blueberries were ripe on the Chemin de la Haute Rivière.[71] She really did not want to have to buy her berries at the supermarket where she suspected they were several days old and, worse yet, not local. Heaven forbid, they might even have come all the way from Ontario. It was a gamble, Adrienne explained. The blueberries might not be ripe that day, some expert pickers might have come before you, or it might not be a good year for that particular patch. They were optimistic, however, because they had gotten a good tip from a neighbour that morning.

"Xavi! Like the Stock Market!" René called out from the driver's seat.

They parked the car on the highway dangerously close to a ditch. Madame Blanchard counted the half-dozen parked cars, unhappily. They walked up to an uninteresting rectangular house at the end of a long, paved driveway. People were coming in and out through a side door at the top of four very unsafe and rudimentary stairs. The eternal screened aluminium door slapped shut with an enervating snap every four seconds. They waited in line in the kitchen while a pudgy ten-year-old boy in a bathing suit, whose face was smudged with jam, weighed the containers and annotated the weight on a sticker, which was then applied to the recipient. The JP Morgan vice president humbly surrendered his big tin cup to the boy: 1.3 ounces.

---

71 Upper River Road.

Everyone's recipient properly weighed and stickered, they were shown the field behind the house. There were perhaps a dozen people on the right side of the field but not to worry, there were a lot of berries on the left and in a clearing behind the birches. So, off they went: the eight Blanchards on the blueberry mission. He followed Adrienne, who found him a small patch and gave him a short blueberry picking lesson. One had to pull on the berry very delicately, separating it from the stem without squeezing the fruit. If the berry was ripe, it would be easy.

"Only the blue ones, absolutely no pink," she said. "And shake your cup like this once in a while to give them space. OK?" She demonstrated a gentle shaking of the cup.

"Did you expain? Blue not pink?" Madame Blanchard called out to Adrienne.

"Yes, he understands."

"You're sure he understands?"

"Yes. Don't worry."

Xavier picked the first one carefully and then ate the next one, just for a taste. He alternated like this for awhile. They were deliciously sweet and fragrant, but consequently the bottom of his cup was barely covered, and the small patch was bare. Adrienne worked in concentration further on to his left. He decided to explore the clearing on his own.

He found a big patch in the woods at the foot of a tree, brimming with what seemed like thousands of wild, fat, dark blue blueberries. Francisco Xavier Aramburu Quiroga of Bilbao knelt in the daisies and soft sunshine of the North Atlantic forest and triumphantly filled his big cup to the brim. He looked for Adrienne's mother and located her far off in the other field. He trudged off to show her his trophy. He was sure she would like to see his berries. Besides their brief greeting, it was the first time they would speak.

"Madame, there's a very good patch over there. I can show you where it is," he said.

He said this very softly so that no one could hear. It wasn't Wall Street, but he had grasped the serious competition around the patches. He uncovered his cup with his hand and smiled his best smile, showing her all the beautiful berries.

Back in the kitchen, the boy re-weighed his cup, subtracting 1.3 ounces, and charged him a fair price for the blueberries. Xavier loved the primitive and efficient economic principle in one of the world's most advanced economies. Thirty minutes later, his pickings went directly into the pie that was made with loving hands. Wild fruit, hand-picked in the forest, a privilege to eat. Madame Blanchard gave Xavier all the credit for the best and biggest blueberries she had ever seen. Everyone laughed condescendingly, claiming favouritism for the newcomer, but Xavier was truly delighted. Sometimes you can win someone's heart in the strangest way, like showing them your secret blueberry patch.

Crane Road was a community of nineteen cottages that had escaped serious public administration. The residents named the streets, were responsible for their own stretch of road, painted their own signs, set traps for raccoons, and pulled down their own trees. It was a children's bike-riding, hide-and-seek, clam-digging paradise. In New Brunswick, it was referred to as a "cottage community." Life at Crane Road was simple, without ceremony or pretention. He thought of his father, who would like this place. For some reason, he also thought of the other father, who was not there. He was the man who had formed this proud little family in this small corner of the planet. His roots were vigourous and deep.

On the third day, cousin Lilly arrived in an old, dilapidated Land Rover with a red kayak haphazardly tied to its roof. She drove down the dirt road beeping her car horn in happy spurts and waving from the window. She had a warm smile and a good word for everyone. She quickly set up her tent under the trees in the Blanchard's backyard.

She was Philippe's sister's youngest daughter, and Claude's best friend. There was a family resemblance, but Lilly had her own style. She wore her ash blond hair short with a long fringe to one side, and wore no make-up except for an impeccable thin line of black eyeliner. She had the body of a serious athlete. She was a kayak champion and a marathon runner. She was fibrous and strong. At only twenty-two years of age, her fiancé had died in a car accident two weeks before their wedding. From that moment on, Lilly had considered herself a widow and devoted herself to her law career as crown prosecutor. She had just moved to Moncton from Fredericton, New

Brunswick's small capital city. They needed a tough, bilingual prosecutor in Moncton and Lilly fit the bill.

Xavier had been told she was a unique, witty, and down-to-earth woman. Lillian was all of that and more. She was in the water at the crack of dawn every morning. She taught him the technique of the kayak and proposed a day trip into the province's interior for some serious white water kayaking. He was game. Lilly and Xavier left in the Land Rover at five in the morning.

He rented a kayak, and they paddled side by side for forty-two kilometres downriver through an uninhabited forest. The river was fast and swollen by a rainy spring. The summer day was windy and unsettled. The conditions for kayaking were challenging.

"Teach me to curse in Spanish!" she shouted over to him.

"Really?" he said.

"Of course!" Lilly answered. "You can't curse halfway!"

They battled the rapids, screaming *"hijo de puta,"* *"hostia,"* *"estoy hasta los huevos,"*[72] among other jewels of the Spanish language. Their laughter echoed in the northern wilderness.

Xavier capsized three times. A strong swimmer and a professional sailor, he could handle it, but in a kayak, he had only his upper body to do the work. He was not able to raise his arms over his head for three days, but he fell in love with white water rivers, kayaks, and cousin Lillian forever.

It had been a windy July but on Xavier and Adrienne's last night, the wind died down. The bonfire ban was lifted. Adrienne was happy because she loved fires on the beach.

Everybody except Madame Blanchard was on the beach. René, Jocelyne, Catherine, Valerie, Claude, Lilly, Adrienne, and Xavier gathered around the fire. There were only five portable lawn chairs for the group. Adrienne and Catherine sat on a driftwood log they pulled from the dune. Xavier sat on a plastic beach chair close to the ground. Valerie lay spread-eagled on his chest. She felt the warmth of the fire on her back, and on her chest, the soothing pumping motion of Xavier's lungs made her drowsy. She raised her head.

"What country do you come from?" she asked sleepily.

---

72 Son of a bitch. Jesus. I've had it up to my balls.

"It's not really a country. It's a place across the ocean. Part of a country called Spain," he said.

"Farther than Prince Edward Island?"

"A little farther. Over there."

Xavier knew exactly where his home was. He looked up at the stars and quickly located the exact position. He pointed.

"See those three stars that are in a row with a bigger star above them, just to the right of the moon? Right under there."

"Is it nice like here?"

"Yes, it's very nice. You would like it."

"I want to go there. Can I?"

"Yes. Aunt Adrienne and I will take you when you're older. OK?" He gently pushed her hair out of her face and gave her a little kiss on the tip of her nose.

"OK."

Little Valerie rested her head on his chest again. Xavier's chin was on her head. He smiled sadly to himself. The idea of country and home and roots were such a clear, warm, and natural feeling in this far away, rugged place. Little Valerie had made it come alive.

Tomorrow he would be in Euskadi for the first time in eight years. A bodyguard was meeting them at the airport. He watched the fire burn.

Xavier and Adrienne would be the first to leave the cottage. It was a reminder of summer's end, like the first tree that turns in early September or the first Christmas song you hear on the radio. Too early.

Adrienne got up to stir the embers when René sat up and said, "Shit! The bonfire patrol!"

Two firemen were patrolling the beach in their new uniforms. They were wearing black Bermuda shorts, and short sleeved shirts with fluorescent yellow stripes aross the chest. One was tall and thin, the other shorter and well built. They approached the Blanchard clan.

"Hi there, folks. Got that fire under control?" said the tall fireman in English.

"*Oui, merci,*"[73] answered Jocelyne in French.

---

73 Yes, thank you.

Jocelyne was making a point. She was an educator, a hometown girl, and a graduate of the Université de Moncton. She was vigilant and strict as to the public use of the language. The shorter and muscular fireman quickly switched to French.

"OK. *C'est bien. Mais, faîtes attention. Il faut bien l'éteindre avec beaucoup de sable. Le vent pourrait se lever plus tard.*"[74] He looked at seven-year-old Catherine and said, "*Comment tu t'appelles?*"

"Catherine," she said.

"OK, Catherine. *Peux tu faire ça pour moi?*"

"*Oui!*"[75] Catherine answered enthusiastically. She was flattered and proud to be given a job to do by a nice fireman.

The young man stole a look at Adrienne. It was admiration at first but then he recognized her.

"You're Adrienne Blanchard, right?" he said.

Like most Monctonians, he unconsciously reverted to English. His partner was Anglophone. It was a question of comfort added to the eternal dilemma between politeness and conviction. Politeness usually won.

"Yes, I'm sorry. I can't make out your face very well. The fire. Do I know you?"

Adrienne felt put on the spot. She was afraid not to recognize whoever it was. She had been gone for so long. She made an effort to see his face through the halo of the fire. He took a step up for her to see him more clearly.

"Aberdeen School!" he said insistently.

"Oh, hi Robert! You were a year ahead of me. Of course I remember," she said.

He was pleased that she recognized him but there was a reason she hadn't forgotten him.

"How are you?" she said.

"Good. You?"

"Good."

"So. What are you doing now?"

"I'm a translator and a language teacher," she said.

"In Montréal?"

---

74 OK, it looks fine. But be careful. Make sure you smother it with lots of sand. The wind may pick up later tonight.

75 What's your name? Catherine. OK, Catherine. Can you do that for me? Yes!

"Yes."

"Oh hey, cool. You like it there?"

"Yes, it's fine."

"Married? Kids?"

"No."

He nodded meaningfully. That ruled out the movie star looking guy in the white jeans with the kid on his chest. He remembered her perfectly. He had always thought she was pretty. She had moved away very young. It must have been just before high school, he remembered. Or maybe grade nine. Around then.

"Down for long?" he asked.

"I've been down for a week. Going back tomorrow," she said.

"Ah, too bad. Just when the weather is getting nice."

"Yeah. It's hard to leave."

"Okay, so next time you're down, maybe we'll see you around. Wednesday is Jazz night at the Cosmo. Everybody goes. You'd know a lot of people," he said.

"Right. I'll do that."

"Right."

The fireman remembered he was working and that this group was francophone.

"Okay, merci beaucoup," he said. *"Passez des belles vacances tout le monde. Catherine, n'oublie pas ta job!"*[76]

Lilly chuckled as the firemen walked away.

"Xavi. Looks like you've got some competition from a hunky local firefighter," she said.

"I saw that. Adri, do I need to worry?" he said.

Xavier spoke softly not to disturb Valerie and Adrienne didn't hear him. She was drawing lines in the sand with her foot. Claude was curious.

"Adrienne, who was that?" she asked.

"Robert Landry."

"Landry?"

"Yes, Yvette's brother," Adrienne said.

---

[76] OK. Thanks a lot. Enjoy your holidays everybody. Catherine, don't forget your job!

René stiffened. Lilly sat up.

"Yvette Landry? The girl who was raped and murdered in the early seventies?"

"It was never proved!" René blurted out. He immediately regretted opening his mouth.

"Of course it was never proved. The guy who did it skipped town! This is so wierd. I looked at the case just last week. I was at the archives having a look at the unsolved cases in the area. A guy called Michel Bourgeois is wanted for the murder of the girl. Oh, I would love to get my hands on him," Lilly said.

René and Adrienne kept their heads down. Claude, who obviously felt no connection at all to the tragic event, enthusiastically picked up on the topic of conversation.

"Yes. It was awful. I knew her. She was in my year at school," she said. "We all thought she had run away to Montréal. Then they found her body down by Hall's Creek. Michel Bourgeois' mother worked for us, you know? He came to the house a lot when he was little. Quiet. Too quiet."

Little Catherine piped up, "What does 'raped' mean?"

The adults were embarrassed and startled but Jocelyne reacted quickly. In a distractionary maneouver, she took Catherine's hand and skipped away with a plastic bucket.

"Let's go get some nice dry sand to snuff out the fire, sweetheart," she said.

Xavier listened to the violent story. It seemed so completely alien to the moment they were living and to the quiet community that he was getting to know.

"Lilly, what would happen if he, well, just showed up?" Adrienne dared to ask.

"Showed up how?" Lilly said.

"I don't know. Gave himself up," she said. "What if he said something like, 'Sorry I ran away because I was scared but I didn't do it' type thing. What would happen?"

René looked at Adrienne. He was in shock and wondered what she knew. She had been a little kid. His father had been so careful, but had she seen the letters? Every summer, he checked to see if they were still in their place in the *Merck Manual*. He thought of putting them away in a safety deposit box at a bank in town but never got around to it. He intentionally ignored them. They burned his hands. He hoped they would disappear and that Michel would never return. He would not search for Michel, yet he did not feel he had the authority to destroy the letters.

"My dear Adrienne!" said Lilly emphatically. "He would stand in a court of law to be tried and judged by his peers for a crime he has been accused of after a careful investigation. Following that, hopefully, he would be locked up at the penitentiary for a good many years. Whoever helped him get away, I might add, should march right into the pen beside him. A kid like that could not disappear without help. It's impossible. That's the conclusion I've come to. Somebody knows something."

Those two somebodies were sitting right beside her and her Uncle Phil had organized it all. The incriminating evidence sat two hundred feet away in a book beside the dictionary. René turned white in the red glare of the fire. Adrienne decided to trust her father. Philippe Blanchard had done the right thing regardless of the consequences.

Xavier left Crane Road with the good taste of blueberries, saltwater, and community in his mouth. Adrienne was excited. She was thrilled that Xavier had invited her to the wedding and to meet his family. She felt loved. She felt sure. The next morning, as they drove down the road on their way to the airport, Michel Bourgeois was the furthest thing from her mind.

Back in Bilbao

José Luis Pons met Xavier and Adrienne at the airport. He was a smart and cocky ex-cop from Valencia who had come to Bilbao five years earlier to work in the lucrative protection business. Thousands of non-separatist Basques were under threat by ETA. Armoured cars, private body guards, and security alarms were big business. José Luis was well prepared. Besides being a cop, he had a black belt in karate and had spent two years in the Spanish Foreign Legion in North Africa. He was a cop with a peculiar hobby: he was a student of military strategy. Know your enemy. He applied ancient Chinese military tactics to European terrorists and it worked.

Joaquín had urged Xavier to get protection. The family was in no particular danger and Ander's cousins were, according to Joaquín, mere peons. However, the cousins could act alone in a personal vendetta that would be disguised as a political act or they could have some influence within a Commando. Xavier hired José Luis's small firm to protect his family while they spent two weeks at the family house in Getxo.

José Luis put his two assistants on the parents and sisters, but he was not particularly worried. The Aramburus had moved to Madrid years before and, although they were no longer paying ETA, they were well connected to prominent nationalists. Rich and capitalists but nationalists.

Younger people were more complicated. They often disregarded the danger and did not heed instructions. He was confident that a girl like Adrienne wouldn't be touched. ETA was keeping a low profile after a massacre in a Barcelona supermarket parking lot only a month earlier. A pretty, foreign female victim would not do at that point in time.

On the surface there did not seem to be a great risk. José Luis did not know that the nature of Xavier's problem with ETA was not political but personal. He assumed that at some point, this high-class guy must have played with fire because he was at risk. However, political or not, a fast and brutal kidnapping of the sort that never hits the press, was a definite possibility.

He whooped with joy after hanging up on the phone call from New York. This Aramburu guy was going to pay him five million pesetas for two weeks. That was almost half a million a day. It was completely outrageous. He punched the air. He pictured his dream: a black Porsche. He suddenly had doubts between black or red.

José Luis set up surveillance on the empty house two weeks before they arrived. It was never too early. Those five million were not going to get away.

The Aramburus arrived in a home full of holes and empty spaces. There were holes in the rooms and empty spaces on the walls where furniture and paintings had been moved to Madrid. There was no garden furniture on the terrace and no bicycles in the garage. There was no water in the swimming pool. It was the family house of a troubling dream where you stretch out your hand and something is not there. You climb up the stairs and you are in a different place. The Aramburus couldn't fool themselves. The cut was deep. It was a house without a voice.

Begoña's boys were spending the summer with their father, who had refused to bring them up to Bilbao from Ibiza for the wedding. Begoña occupied herself by fussing over everyone. It had been a long time since the family had attended a social event in Bilbao. She was hoping for a happy return and a taste of normalcy.

Paloma was bedridden on the second floor, sick with a cold and a slight fever. Her mother stayed by her side and her father fluttered. They worried about Paloma. Her heart and lungs were weak. Their greatest fear was pneumonia and they took extreme care with her colds.

It was the first time Xavier had come home with a girl. This was a different Xavier. He was serene, connected, thankful. Adrienne offered no resistance to their kindness and affection. She stayed close to Xavier and made no demands. She had no borders or personal agenda.

Ana apologized to God. Many years before, with her newborn baby in her arms, she had watched from the window as her beautiful boy played outside alone. It was the first day home from the hospital. He was only four. He was scampering about on the lawn trying to catch a wounded bird. She remembered her conversation with God that day.

Father in heaven, you have given me Paloma and I offer my life to her with all my love. But I beg you: send my boy an angel some day. This is the deal I make with you. Do not fail me.

She was a Basque mother with the authority to negotiate with God.

If Xavier counted the years he spent in Madrid, he had been gone almost half his life. The extortion and the psychological abuse of his family by ETA had darkened his memories. However, he was no longer an impulsive twenty-year-old. He had shared things with Ander and Joaquín that could only come from common roots. Good roots. The rest had to be sorted out somewhere in his head. He would not let himself detest or fear his home. He would not give them that satisfaction.

He asked José Luis about renting a motorcycle. The security man didn't like the idea. It was a paper trail, a licence plate to follow. It was also too easy to force a motorcycle off the road in the event of a kidnapping or an arbitrary execution. Xavier insisted. José Luis knew of someone who would loan them a motorcycle privately for a price. It was a new BMW K100 and Xavier was happy. Euskadi, Adrienne and a BMW bike. It was like Christmas. José Luis parked the bike in a different place every day and never let Xavier take it home. He moved it around the city and then drove them to and from the bike, zigzagging around Bilbao until they were almost carsick. He forced them to put on their helmets before getting out of his car.

"Trust me," he said insistently. "I know what I'm doing."

Xavier rolled his eyes but because of Adrienne, he obeyed.

And so with José Luis on their heels, they watched the sun rise on the whimsical Chapel of San Juan de Gaztelugatxe. They swam and made love at the beach in Bakio. Xavier did some surfing in Mundaka. They even managed to lose José Luis a couple of times, which invariably brought on a fit of laughter and the desire to be physically closer.

They had a wonderful family lunch in Getaria, about eighty kilometres from Bilbao. A typical fishing town nestled on the Basque coast, the locals say it is renowned for being the birthplace of famous men, for its Gothic church, and for its natural beauty. The naked truth is that it is a fabulous place to eat. The fish comes straight off the colourful boats in the harbour at dawn. The meat comes from the black cows in the dark green valleys of Vizcaya.

In summer, a dozen restaurants cover the port area with their inviting striped awnings and simple aluminium tables and chairs. The grills are out in the open air and are worked by the men. The port of Getaria is a celebration of Basque gastronomy.

It was just the place for Luis Aramburu to host a casual and relaxed pre-wedding lunch for his family two days before his daughter's wedding. It was just the place to welcome his godson, Xavier, back home, and just the place to host his son's Canadian professor. Uncle Luis was excited. He had nineteen guests and had reserved several crates of Txakoli. Txacoli is Getaria's own wine, young and acidic, made with the grapes from the hills overlooking the town. For Luis Aramburu, there was not a chablis or a sauvignon blanc that could compare. He wanted this meal to be perfect.

The BMW motorcycle roared into the port of Getaria at about half past one on a beautiful sunny day. Koldo recognized Adrienne's long hair that flowed down her back from under the helmet. He had just come in from a week of sailing in Mallorca with some friends and hadn't seen them yet. His chestnut hair was long and streaked gold. He greeted them both with a good hug. She kissed his cheek and they touched foreheads as they exchanged a private look.

They did not sit down immediately. As guests of honour, Xavier and Adrienne walked around the table being introduced to the groom's family and to other close friends. Xavier was Arantxa's favourite cousin and she was so pleased that he had come. She had had a huge crush on him as a little girl and would never forget him dancing with Begoña at her wedding. There was a sense of occasion and of happy expectation. Adrienne was seated between Koldo and his father, Xavier between his aunt and uncle. Luis Aramburu was the very picture of satisfaction. Although he had been told Adrienne could speak Spanish, he had forgotten. He got to his feet for a formal welcome speech. He separated each syllable and spoke very loudly to make sure she understood. The way John Wayne speaks to the Cherokee in old Westerns.

Horrified, Koldo frantically waved his hands to stop his father.

"*Aita*! For the love of God! She speaks Spanish better than you do. *Hostia!*" he shouted in filial embarrassment.

The guests broke down with good-natured laughter. Luis looked sheepish and sat down in embarrassment. Xavier leaned back in his chair, stretched his legs, put both hands on his head and laughed from the pit of his stomach. It felt so good to be home.

The wedding was different. The intimacy of the lunch in Getaria was lost in the formality and etiquette of a bourgeois social affair. Xavier and Koldo looked heartbreakingly handsome in grey tails, ivory vests. and pale blue ties as they walked briskly down the aisle to take their place with the witnesses beside the altar. Adrienne sat with Paloma and Begoña. She had bought a vintage dress in Old Montréal. It was a twenties-era, low-waisted gown in a dark rose colour that reached to mid-calf. It had small glass incrustations and a draped back open to the waist. Her smooth, tanned back was visible between the folds of the fabric.

Begoña had arranged for a hairdresser to come to the house and do everyone's hair. She ran about straightening ties, flattening shoulder seams, removing lint, pushing back stray hairs. She wore a formal, strapless, amethyst-coloured gown with an enormous bow at the waist. She covered her shoulders with an exquisite hand-painted silk shawl. Paloma was dressed in a peach-coloured raw silk shift, a matching coat, a pretty little straw hat, gloves, and flat Mary Jane shoes.

Begoña supervised Adrienne's hair. She had the hairdresser make a romantic feathery braid that hung down her long, tanned back. At the top of the braid she placed a beautiful antique art deco hair pin she had found in her mother's things. Adrienne looked languid, beautiful, and different. Almost liquid.

José Luis outdid himself. At the exact moment of departure, three large, armoured black cars pulled up to the house at great speed. The family was embarrassed. It looked like a presidential motorcade. Xavier instantly evaluated the situation.

"Let us out four blocks from the church," he said.

The Aramburus arrived at the church of San Vicente Mártir de Abando on foot at a leisurely pace, enjoying their city's streets and the balmy summer evening. It was a fine moment for them all.

True Identity

Begoña was right. You can't please everyone and especially not in Bilbao. They were harder on Adrienne than on Xavier. Koldo had said she was beautiful but the general opinion was that she was rather bizarre looking. The rumour ran that she had had her eye on Koldo but then had met Xavier and thrown herself at the bigger fish. Someone said they thought they had seen her before with somebody from Real Madrid. Obviously, a fortune hunter. And what was that dress about? It was more proper for a costume ball than a wedding.

As for Xavier Aramburu, he hadn't changed. He was too handsome for his own good, too smart for his own good, too rich for his own good. The Aramburus were fine people but he definitely took after his mother's clan, the Quirogas. They were a pompous and arrogant bunch who had thankfully almost all moved to Madrid.

Nevertheless, the wedding was perfect. The bride and groom were young and beautiful. The choir sang, the bells rang, the rice was thrown, the pictures were taken, the banquet was abundant, and the cigars distributed. It was Adrienne's last night. As they danced to a romantic ballad, Xavier undid her braid and her abundant hair cascaded down her back. Koldo charmingly shuffled up to them with a bottle of champagne, which he gave to Adrienne, and the keys to his car, which he gave to Xavier.

The stunning couple ran hand in hand through the restaurant kitchens to escape José Luis and got into Koldo's small red car. They drove around Bilbao for an hour, then sat on the beach in Getxo, barefoot in their gala outfits, and drank the champagne from the bottle. She dozed with her head on his shoulder. He put his jacket over her shoulders and looked out at the Bay of Biscay.

The sand under his feet felt soft and warm and good. It was his beach. It was where he had learned to love the water, where Begoña built elaborate sandcastles, and where he constructed intricate canal networks. It was the place where he buried Paloma's legs in the sand and then, to her joyful, innocent laughter, tickled her toes. First best friend, first girl, first boat, first beer, first fight.

It was the beginning and the end of the planet. His point of departure, his point of reference, his own personal horizon.

Sisters, Cousins, and Sons

José Luis started to earn his pay when Adrienne left for Montréal to prepare her move to New York. Xavier was staying another week. He had asked José Luis to arrange a meeting with Joaquín's sister, Mentxu, through her best friend Maria. He had a message that no one could intercept. Not the church, not ETA, and not the government. He also had a couple of pictures in an envelope. Joaquín and Mentxu used this method very seldom. She would know it was important.

Mentxu was an activist and a familiar face on the front line of demonstrations demanding that incarcerated *etarras* be moved to prisons in or near the Basque Country. She refused a clandestine meeting. She could meet who she wanted, where she wanted. In direct opposition to a meeting in an empty house, José Luis decided on La Viña, a classical and popular bar in the downtown core known for its *pintxos*[77] and excellent wine to make it look like a chance encounter. Nobody would find it strange that Xavier Aramburu and Mentxu Múgica should be at the same place.

Xavier sat uncomfortably at a small, narrow table pretending to read a newspaper. José Luis hung around the door looking like a night club bouncer. His assistants were sipping a beer at the bar. Mentxu arrived five minutes late. They were two well-dressed forty-year-old women. Mentxu was an elementary school principal and her friend Maria was a high school science teacher. They headed directly to the table beside Xavier. It was a rustic tavern-type décor, and the chairs and tables were low, narrow, and very close together. There was a long bench against the wall where Xavier was seated. Maria sat on the bench beside Xavier, and Mentxu sat opposite.

---

[77] Tapas in the Basque country. Larger and more elaborate than in the rest of Spain.

Xavier was only slightly to her left in her field of vision, so conversation would be perfectly audible.

Mentxu Múgica seemed totally unperturbed by the situation. She was more interested in what she was going to eat than in any secret messages. She kept the waiter at the table for five minutes and made him run through all the pintxos one by one. At one point, as the waiter was blocking her view of Xavier, she leaned sideways and asked him if he wanted anything.

"Are you hungry? Would you like to eat something?"

Xavier was flustered. In a strangled whisper, he said, "No, thank you very much."

The waiter took the order. Mentxu crossed her legs in Xavier's direction and lit a cigarette. She smoked Ducados,[78] like her brother. He remembered he was supposed to buy a carton, or two, if he could manage it in his luggage.

"He told me to look for a good-looking high-class kid from Getxo. You're the best-looking guy in here so I guess that's you," she said.

She said it in such a direct and natural manner that Xavier immediately felt comfortable. He smiled and shrugged.

"How is he?" said Mentxu as she sipped her txacoli.

"Very well. Happy, I would say," Xavier said.

"Really? That is good news. I did receive a letter just last week. They're good for my mother."

"That's for you," Xavier said, looking down at an envelope he had placed on the empty space on the bench between the tables. Maria picked it up and gave it to Mentxu. Xavier was proud of his little ruse.

"I'm sorry. It's a little wrinkled," Xavier said, while looking in another direction in an attempt to conceal the fact that he was in conversation with the lady at the next table.

Mentxu opened it and slowly perused the two photos. She pursed her lips and smiled with her eyes. There was some irony in her expression.

"What is the child's name?" she asked.

"Estíbaliz."

"Like the *ama*."

"Yes, he told me. I'm her godfather," Xavier said.

"You're not serious."

---

78 A brand of cheap cigarettes. Natural, untreated black tobacco. Highly appreciated by heavy smokers.

"I'm afraid so."

Xavier let the news sink in. Mentxu's friend Maria raised her eyebrows in disbelief and surprise. Mentxu exhaled a long trail of smoke.

"So...an Aramburu Quiroga is my niece's godfather?" she asked.

"Yes."

"*Hostia*. That's a good one."

A half smile on her face, Mentxu shook her head but she was not upset. She raised one shoulder in relaxed and amused acceptance. She also had something to tell him.

"Did you know our father worked at the Aramburu Foundry?" she asked.

It was Xavier's turn to be shocked. Joaquín had never told him that.

"No, I didn't," he said.

"For thirty-five years. He retired there. We used to take the bus to the factory after school and wait for him in the car to go home to the village every night. He went without a lot of things to send us to a good private school in the city," she said. "We had our *bocadillo*[79] and did our homework in the car. We used to see you there skating in the parking lot behind the office building. You waited for your father, too, I suppose. You were a cute kid. Younger than us. You wore the Jesuit College hockey team uniform all the time. I went out with one of those guys for a while, believe it or not."

Mentxu pointed that out and laughed. Xavier was speechless. He would have been seven or eight and Joaquín fifteen or sixteen.

"My brother always said, 'I don't know if that kid is a fucking genius or a fucking idiot.'"

"He still says that." Xavier chuckled.

"One day..." Mentxu began.

Suddenly something clicked. Xavier remembered.

"I almost killed myself and he carried me to the office building to my father. I broke my nose and my left arm," he said.

Mentxu nodded and smiled, pleased that he remembered the brother who had flown out of the car to his rescue. Joaquín had worried about him and asked his father to inquire. Iñaki Aramburu had personally thanked

---

79 A large sandwich made of traditional bread filled with tuna, meats, pates, cheese, or chocolate spread. It is given to children after school because dinners are usually light and very late - only after homework and baths.

her father and told him that his son Xavier was an unconscious *gilipollas*: a fucking idiot. Xavier put his elbow on the table and his face in his hand.

"I used to like skating off the delivery ramps, ski jump style. That day, I fell on my stomach five centimetres from a long, rusty spike that was sticking up."

"Now you know who picked you up."

"I was in a daze, I don't know if I said thank you."

Xavier sat back and shook his head. He was feeling strangely happy about this connection to Joaquín. Joaquín was the reason he was there. He thought he should hurry with his most important message.

"He wants to get out," he said.

"Out of what?"

"Everything."

Mentxu looked down at the picture. Her smiling, well-built brother was a man, not a priest. He was wearing blue jeans and a tee-shirt, sitting at a kitchen table with a pretty mulatto baby on his lap: It was a most American domestic scene. She was fast with her answer.

"OK. I've been expecting this and I have been thinking about it," she said. "He has been hinting in his letters. Tell him I'm on it. Tell him to call Maria at her school in September. Let's say around the tenth. Tell him to say that he is Sara's father."

"I will see him next week. I have to buy him a carton of Ducados," he said, grinning.

Xavier paused. There wasn't much more to say. It was time to go.

"I have to go." He stood up and tried to act unconcerned with the two ladies beside him.

"Give me a kiss before you leave, *hombre!*"[80] Mentxu demanded.

Xavier was still unconsciously maintaining a distance in view of the situation. He hesitated.

"It doesn't make any difference. Relax. If they've seen us, they've seen us," she said.

Mentxu got to her feet. "So, Godfather eh?"

"That's right!" He nodded and hugged her close.

---

[80] Man!

Xavier was moved. Somewhere there was a place to meet. This would end one day.

In his inexperience with covert operations, he forgot to pay for his beer and Mentxu took the bill. In human terms, the meeting was a great success. In spy terms, it was a disaster. José Luis shook his head and counted the hours before Aramburu's departure.

When José Luis picked Xavier up to take him to the airport, he was surprised to see him in a suit and tie. Xavier paid him for his services before they left the house. He put the thick envelope away very carefully in a zippered back pocket. The job was almost over. He had an appointment at the Porsche dealership at one.

"I have to make one stop. I need to deliver a parcel." Xavier said.

Xavier gave him a slip of paper with the address of a bar in Barakaldo. José Luis frowned. It was a hangout for sympathizers and not the place for a guy in a Brooks Brothers suit.

"Listen, boss. It's none of my business, but why don't you let me deliver the package? I'll do it on my way back from the airport. No problem. Guaranteed. Two hundred percent," José Luis said.

"No. I want to do this," said Xavier.

"Okay. It's your show."

Xavier carried Ander's box into the car. José Luis opened the trunk to store Xavier's suitcases and took out a sports bag. He changed into a pair of plain black running shoes with velcro closures, a bulletproof vest, a dark windbreaker, and he put on navy blue workout pants over his ironed, beige trousers. He pulled a ski mask over his head and rolled it down around his neck. He flipped his licence plates over. They were now false. He looked at his car and sighed. He might have to have it painted again.

Once inside the car, he reached into the glove compartment for a pair of tinted glasses that he had bought in Austria. They reduced glare and had a slight magnifying effect. He cleaned them carefully. They were made specially for hunters. He was dressed for dirty work.

He carried two handguns. One, in a holster above his right ankle and the other around his chest, breast high. He kept a Swiss Army knife, a can of pepper spray, and a whistle in a camouflaged side pocket of his sweat pants. From under his seat, he pulled out a portable roof alarm light. It was a blue, flashing light like those used in official motorcades. He checked the batteries as he headed for the highway to Barakaldo. It was a fairly long drive. They reached a shabby nondescript bar on a corner. It was a good location. Some letters were missing from the sign.

"Okay, this is the place. I'm going to drive around the block. I want to check it out again." José Luis said.

"Do what you have to do. I'm delivering a box of personal effects," Xavier said.

Xavier's mouth was dry. He would come face-to-face with a man he despised but with Ander's mother as well. The box held Ander's professional book, his passport and personal papers, a very expensive camera, and three small boxes. Xavier guessed that they were watches for his father, his mother and his sister. There was also an envelope with a good amount of cash.

Fortunately, there was place to park directly in front of the entrance. José Luis pulled the car up partly onto the sidewalk. He turned to Xavier, who was sitting in the back seat. He spoke carefully and clearly.

"Pay attention please," he said. "Go. I'll stand outside the door. I'll go in if I see trouble. Let me act. I know the laws and the limits. Obey me if things get complicated. I don't suppose you want to have a long chat with these guys."

"I doubt it," Xavier said.

"Are they expecting you?"

"No."

"Good."

Xavier got out of the car and walked across the sidewalk to the entrance carrying the large box. José Luis pulled up his ski mask, left both the front and back doors of the car open, put his flashing light on the roof of the car, and stood outside the bar, blocking the entrance. His back was to the street. Xavier was inside. Nobody in their right mind in Barakaldo would even dream of walking into the place, not even the *Ertxainas,* the Basque cops.

José Luis checked out his battlefield. There was a fat, tired-looking man at the till behind the bar. His hands and forearms were red and swollen from forty years of washing dishes and wiping tables with ammonia. His eyes were small and bloodshot. There were two young men at a small table having coffee. Xavier thought they were probably the cousins. Ander had told him that they lived nearby and spent most of their time in the bar.

Two older men sat at a table in the far right corner by the window. Xavier walked up to the bar and put the box on the counter.

"*Buenos dias,*"[81] he said politely.

His presence was not acknowledged. The man chewed on a toothpick and stared blankly ahead. The young men stopped talking. Xavier was alone at the bar. He waited the customary minute or so to be served and then in the silence, spoke without being spoken to.

"*Un café solo, por favor,*"[82] he said.

The bartender looked up and spat on the counter. The cousins got to their feet and crossed their arms over their chests. The two old men looked away. José Luis recognized the act of intimidation. He went in, slammed the door behind him, and kept his back to the exit. He kept his right hand Napoleon-like inside his jacket, holding his gun. The old bartender was panting. He was in the early stages of emphysema. Xavier shouted in the direction of the kitchen.

"*Doña*[83] Matilde! I have a gift from Ander."

"Don't come out!" Ander's father commanded to his wife, who was out of sight.

Despite her husband's order, Matilde came slowly out of the kitchen, wiping her hands on her apron. She had circles under her eyes, her face was lined and pale, her hair was dull, but Xavier saw Ander's beautiful face. He suddenly felt guilty for this stupid cowboy showdown. Ander would not want this. Xavier quietly pushed the box in her direction. No one moved. There was silence. Matilde touched it gently. Her chin trembled.

"Doña Matilde. I am Xavier Aramburu, the executor of Ander's will. Among other things, in this box, there is an envelope with thirty-five thousand dollars cash. Ander had heard about a cure in Martinique and took money out of his account. Then he changed his mind. He was skeptical in the end. He figured it was a hoax, which it was. He never had time to redeposit the money. He was well taken care of in the hospital. His medical records are also in the box. Good doctors. Good people. He didn't die alone. He was very brave."

---

81   Good morning.

82   Black coffee, please.

83   The female form of Don before a proper name.

The cousins had looked at each other when he had mentioned the cash. Ander's father had given Xavier no choice but to say it publicly. Matilde delicately caressed the box and nodded, trying unsuccessfully to smile.

"OK. That's it. Let's go!" shouted José Luis in the tense silence. It was done.

But it was too late, the match was struck. The old man grunted, grabbed a bottle of liquor and broke it over the counter. The thud of the thick bottle on the bar and the broken glass on the floor reverberated in the tense silence. He looked pathetic but dangerous standing there with the broken bottle in his hand. His chest was heaving like a dying horse. The cousins swayed and separated.

"YOU! You and the priest, fucking fascists, you split his fortune and left us a tip," he shouted.

From intimidation to threat. José Luis took one step forward, pulled out his gun and aimed at the cousins. His arms travelled in an arc from one cousin to the other. The cousins were unarmed. The old man's face was red. The veins in his neck were thick purple ropes. He was convinced he had been robbed of a winning lottery ticket.

Xavier couldn't see José Luis, who was behind him. He remained calm. He had expected Ander's father to be brutal. He spoke directly to the mother.

"I don't need your son's money, *Señora*.[84] And the priest is a good man. Ander was my friend," he said.

Matilde didn't move. Xavier was ready to leave. The vision of Ander's mother had upset him. He had delivered the box that Ander had carefully packed over a year before. Xavier turned his back and headed for the door. José Luis was still standing with his legs apart, aiming his gun at the cousins. He moved up ahead of Xavier and motioned to him to go out first.

"*Maricon de mierda. Vete a tomar por culo! Maricones los dos! Tú y el cura!*"[85] the father shouted in disgust at Xavier's back.

---

84 Ma'am.

85 Disgusting faggot. Go get screwed up your ass. Queers both of you. You and the priest.

Xavier stopped in his tracks. He would not let it pass. The animal would have preferred an assassin as a son rather than a homosexual.

"Yes, a *maricon*," he screamed back gesticulating. "Like your son. Come here, old man. You want to give me a little kiss? I bet you do. Come on, old man!"

Xavier blew him a kiss. The cousins were concentrated on José Luis, who had cocked his gun and was shielding and restraining Xavier like a basketball defenceman. José Luis was taken by surprise by his client's fury.

"They're going for you. You are a dead man!" Ander's father hissed from the empty sacks of his lungs, the broken bottle still in his hands.

Only human decency and José Luis' back kept Xavier from throwing himself at Ander's father.

"Tell the bastards to come for me. I'm waiting. You are a disgusting animal. He died calling out for you!"

The cousins swayed. The younger of the two moved towards José Luis and Xavier while the older one said: "You know the shit. You won't shoot."

Not true. José Luis fired four times. He shot at the feet of cousin number one, at the feet of cousin number two, at the bottles of liquor behind the bar, and at the ceiling. The cousins flinched. Xavier looked for a weapon. The father was too old and sick to move. Matilde closed her eyes but never let go of the box as the bottles of liquor behind her crashed to the floor. She hoped for a second that her husband would die.

José Luis ended the chaos. Still aiming at the cousins with his right hand, he screamed, *"Fuera!"*[86]

With his left hand he grabbed Xavier by the collar of his suit. With his left foot, he gave the exit door a karate kick and literally threw Xavier out onto the street. Then he backed out with both hands on his gun. He stopped in the doorway, took aim, and fired two more shots at the ceiling.

It was over. Five minutes of hate.

They dove into the open car. José Luis couldn't risk even a traffic infraction. Any brush with ETA could land him in court or in a cemetery. A good percentage of ETA's victims were security people on active duty. He put on his indicator, checked his mirrors, and got out of there as fast as

---

86 Out!

he could without going over the speed limit. As he drove away, he rolled his window down and reached up for his blue light with his left hand. He grabbed it and threw it on the floor in front of the passenger seat. He kept the ski mask on until they were four blocks away.

He looked through the rearview mirror at Xavier, who had slouched and rested his head on the top of the back seat. He was looking up at the roof. Drops of perspiration on his forehead. José Luis said nothing. He was not a psychologist. There was something he had not grasped but he had stopped trying to figure out the motivations of these Basques a long time ago. To José Luis, they were all out of their minds. Their conflicts were none of his affair.

When they reached the airport, he helped Xavier with his luggage and accompanied him to Security.

"Would you mind telling me who gave you my name?" he said. José Luis was unable to refrain his curiosity.

"They did. They call you the '*Valenciano*[87] with the glasses.' You're right. You're good and they know it." he said. Xavier thanked him and shook his hand.

In that instant, José Luis realized he had to leave. Bilbao was over. He drove off the airport exit and took a left to Santander. It was the first large city out of the Basque Country. Five days later, he was in his new red Porsche on the highway to the Costa del Sol, planning his new career as a private investigator.

Xavier went directly to the gate but didn't take a seat. He went into the men's room and into a cubicle. He pulled up his trousers, knelt on the floor, and vomited. Then he rested his forehead on the cold, hard rim of the toilet bowl.

Whatever Mentxu did, whoever she talked to, whoever she was, Xavier was never threatened or contacted again.

---

[87] Native of the city or region of Valencia in southeastern Spain.

Part Four

The Whaler and the Pharaoh

Xavier had returned home but Joaquín and Ander had been denied the privilege. Euskadi was as beautiful as it was heartbreaking but not better or worse than any other place. Their personal trajectories were the consequences of a convulsive moment in Basque history that it had been their fortune, good or bad, to live through. Xavier's future was not there. It was with Adrienne. He invited her to live with him and she accepted.

Those who thought he would find it difficult to share his daily life were mistaken. He made a place for her in his life, which was what Adrienne needed to survive. He liked who he was and how he felt beside her. Of course, there was Adrienne and then there would be others. In his own mind, they were clearly separated.

There were changes in his career as well. Morgan offered him a partnership on the best team of venture capital bankers in the world. An engineer, a professor, and a sharp financier, he was a natural for the job. At age twenty-nine, he would earn one million dollars a year plus bonuses that could easily double his salary. In the eighties and nineties, JP Morgan measured their profits not in millions but in billions precisely because of their venture capital fund. Their funding accelerated progress in medicine, communications, and industry, and, of course, produced great profit for shareholders. The job was quite simple and divided into six main steps:

1. Discover the genius
2. Fund the project
3. Design the investment
4. Participate in the administration and growth
5. Become an object of desire
6. Sell

He particularly enjoyed the search for prototypes. It was like finding a buried treasure or stumbling on the future. It involved visiting university labs, small industrial parks, and even neighbourhood garages. It took him closer to the world of science and experimentation.

Xavier and Adrienne lived within these new parameters with the clear intention to survive as a couple. The decision to live together had been right. They shared an important quality: they were both generous people and generosity feeds love.

The wind was at Adrienne's back. This was the place. This was the man. This was the life she wanted. Xavier secretly feared that he would lose her, not so much to his own weaknesses, as to her own independent spirit. At the United Nations, she was never fitted for a tourist guide uniform nor asked to give any public tours. To Xavier's discomfort, she became Patrick Kyenge's little soldier. The two men distrusted each other. Patrick called Xavi "The Whaler." Xavi called Patrick "The Pharaoh."

A year earlier, on a dark December afternoon, Patrick Kyenge had made himself a cup of tea and walked into his good friend Mary's office. She was busy with the selection process of the new interpreters that was scheduled for late February.

"Sit," she said to Patrick. "Talk to me. I'm going mad."

Patrick sat down, looked out the window, sighed, and sipped his tea. He didn't like winter. He was bored. He saw the pile of candidate files on her desk.

"Do you mind if I have a look at your candidates, Mary?" he said.

"Go ahead. I still have to narrow these down. We are seeing sixty. The logistics are horrendous and the best candidates are quite obvious. But…"

Patrick was curious. He went through the files methodically. He was stopped by Adrienne's picture. She looked like a schoolgirl. He checked the file. He read it twice. Twenty-four years old. European experience. A recommendation from the president of the Real Madrid, no less. This caught his attention, as he was an avid soccer fan. University instructor in Montréal. From New Brunswick, Canada. French mother tongue. She was one of those Acadians. Patrick had studied European colonialism and knew the story of the Acadian people. He looked at the picture carefully. He raised the file for Mary to see. She shook her head noncommittally.

"This one looks interesting," said Patrick. He raised his eyebrows showing curiosity.

"Do you think so?" Mary said. "She has the most perfect psychotechnical scores I have ever come across. Seriously. But that, you know, could be a fluke. She has no serious experience to speak of. Young. A bit of a shot in the dark, I think. Can't see her in the Security Council at three in the morning with You-Know-Who throwing a fit."

Patrick laughed but he had seen the numbers. He had read the five-hundred-word essay. Twice. He knew Mary had heard him. He put the file back on her desk on top of the pile. And then he winked.

When Adrienne appeared, she was much more mature and sophisticated than she looked in her picture. Patrick stayed close. He was a good judge of character. She was smart, she was clearheaded, she had nerve, and she was incorrigibly pleasant. Patrick had been playing with an idea that would be good for the UN and good for him. Maybe this girl could be the right person for the job. He was always looking for talent.

Patrick was not the child of extreme poverty. The Kyenge family inhabitated Kinshasa, the largest French-speaking city in the world after Paris. His father had been a French teacher in a Catholic elementary school. His mother had been a chambermaid in the best hotel in the city. He had grown up in a building with electricity and running water everyday from five to eight o'clock in the evening. There were books in the tiny apartment and a radio that Patrick's father took good care of hiding and protecting. They listened to France International and the BBC. The Kyenge boys attended the Catholic school where their father taught and Patrick became a choirboy. Of five boys, three survived. The oldest disappeared when he was twelve. The baby died of meningitis. Three out of five was a good average in those days.

Life was precarious in General Mobutu's Zaïre, the former name of the Democratic Republic of the Congo. Patrick managed to reach the age of thirteen without falling ill, being raped, or being abducted into an army. This was because his parents were vigilant but also because Patrick had balls the size of two large coconuts. He founded his own secret gang at age eight. He began by drawing a sophisticated map of the neighbourhood, which was a maze within a maze within a maze. In fact, there were no maps of greater Kinshasa. He mapped out escape routes and hiding places. He invited other boys to his secret hideouts, which he regularly changed.

He would blindfold them when they got near until he trusted them. Patrick was a survivor.

His parents were overjoyed when the principal of the school recommended Patrick for study in a Belgian seminary. At age thirteen in 1962, he was whisked away to Brussels with a group of fifty young Congolese boys. The Catholic church needed its own black army.

The day of Patrick's departure was imprinted in his memory. Early in the morning, they took him to the neighbourhood barber, who shaved his head while a group of neighbours looked on. His parents had borrowed money to prepare his student trousseau. He was dressed in a crisp white cotton shirt, impeccably ironed grey trousers, and a navy blue blazer. The new shiny black shoes were uncomfortable because they were too large. His parents had bought them big so that he could grow into them. They were breathlessly proud.

Patrick was ready more than an hour ahead of time. The family fidgeted around him. He sat on his suitcase. Would this be the last time they saw him? What would become of him? What would become of them? What did this mean? His brothers looked at him with a new respect. Suddenly, he had a sense of future and destiny.

The father's only thought was to teach his son how to shake hands properly.

"Firm, but not too tight. Not too long. Look into people's eyes," he said.

They practised so many times that Patrick's hand hurt. He felt embarrassed looking into his father's agitated eyes.

His mother's last act was to douse him in Old Spice cologne. She never took a thing from the hotel, but a departing client had forgotten a half-finished bottle of the cologne and she had guiltily slipped it into her bosom to take home. She would not permit any Europeans to say that this African boy had a funny smell.

He was placed in a seminary with Francophone boys from around the world. Patrick took to European comfort and civilization extremely well. He was excellent at languages and he loved history. Very early on, they saw that the personable young Patrick had no spirituality whatsoever but that he was a leader, was talented, and had a mind of his own.

He navigated the seminary boldly and with only the necessary respect. He was not malleable, but they permitted him to stay. The church took on all the expenses of his studies. He worked in the library and helped the younger boys with their Latin and English, but he was not prepared for the priesthood. The plans for Patrick were changed without his knowledge.

At eighteen, he was encouraged to study political science and history at the Université catholique de Louvain. Of course, he was drawn to European colonial history. He had become proficient in five languages and during the time he was in Louvain, he was chosen twice for summer internships at the United Nations in New York. Patrick became a worldly and sophisticated young man.

One day in his last year, a professor tapped him on the shoulder and invited him to his office to meet with an interesting gentleman. It was the CIA knocking at his door. After finishing at Louvain, he did his time in Langley, Virginia, and became an agent of the United States Government. Patrick performed well. He would be planted at the United Nations in a regular job with real responsibilities, yet work for the American Government. He would spend one year in four in the field in Africa on tasks related to the United Nations and perform other missions for the agency.

Thanks to the CIA, his aging parents lived in a very nice bungalow on Long Island and his two brothers drove New York City cabs. He had a vague title as Cultural and Employee Liaison, which loosely meant he had a finger in every pie. He had his eyes and ears on everyone and everything.

In the mid-eighties, the USSR was a teetering house of cards. The European Union was in its adolescence. Central America was in turmoil. China was a looming shadow. Africa was in pain. North America was in a vortex of wealth and growth. The Internet did not exist. In the political landscape of the eighties, the corridors of the United Nations were the superhighways of information, negotiation, and deceit.

Adrienne was given a desk outside Patrick's office and assigned her first task. She was to institutionalize and design private tours of the United Nations for prominent guests of the 159 ambassadors. It took almost three months to put her plan into practise. It involved meeting with all the ambassadors to explain the initiative, setting up a serious reservation system, and designing the tour. Adrienne would only be able to comfortably handle one visit per day.

True Identity

The tour consisted of an in-depth visit of the building and meeting rooms accompanied by a smiling, charming, and informative Adrienne. Ideally, the General Assembly would be in session. They would take a peek into an interpreter's booth, at the private art collection, and, yes, they would be shown the bomb shelter, which was not as impressive as Adrienne had fantasized. The tour would end with lunch in the executive dining room joined by the corresponding ambassador, who would foot the bill. Finally, an official photo of the group was taken by the UN photographer. A month later, Adrienne would send the guests the photograph along with a note from the secretary general and information on how to contribute to UN causes. It was quite brilliant.

By December 1, when she started the tours, she had forty-five reservations. The first was an American Supreme Court judge with his eight grandchildren coming to celebrate his eightieth birthday. The wife of the French president was coming on an unofficial visit to Manhattan with her girlfriends and thought it would be interesting. A scowling Russian ballet dancer who eventually defected two weeks later in Toronto also made a reservation. A Mexican beer magnate with his nineteen in-laws, a shy and introverted Arab prince who fell in love with Adrienne and demanded a private and personal tour every day for a week, and, on one occasion five African queens. Patrick was delighted. It was new access to powerful people outside the strictly political realm.

The search for new ventures took Xavier all over the United States. The traveling also meant solitude. Xavier's demons tended to stir whenever he left the city. What had to happen, eventually did. It was in Chicago only six months after Adrienne had moved to New York. It had been a long and disappointing trip. He needed a good workout.

It was very warm in the empty hotel gym. He decided to remove his jacket, although he wasn't wearing a tee-shirt. It was not considered proper etiquette in hotel gyms but he was alone. Besides, his coach in New York, an Iranian olympic weight-lifting champion always worked bare-chested, barefoot, and in running shorts. He was in the mood to train hard. Xavier was autonomous in the gym. His coach had taught him a routine that worked every muscle of his body and left him completely spent. He found the weights and organized a work area in front of the mirror. He took his stance, did his preliminary stretching, and then began to pump the weights.

Suddenly, the pop music on the speakers was turned up. He saw the gym attendant come out of a small office. He watched her in the mirror as she approached him. She locked on his eyes and he stared back. The insinuation was unmistakably clear. He had spoken to her briefly the day before. Her name was Marisa. She was a Latin girl with a Puerto Rican accent. She was pretty, dark, and solid. She had the body of a mature gymnast.

"*Señor Aramburu?*" she asked.

"*Si?*"

"*Holá.*"

"*Holá.*"[88]

He felt a tightness in his stomach. He knew instantly that he would fail Adrienne. Old habits die hard.

"Let me help you with your stance," she said.

"Go ahead," Xavier knew his stance was perfect.

"Careful not to overextend your knees," she said.

She squatted close to the floor and lightly passed her hands over the thin cotton of his workout pants, gently pulling down the waistband to just above his pubic hair. Her face was resting on his thigh, looking up at him. From above, he could see her breasts and small dark nipples in her low-cut, electric blue spandex body suit. Xavier smiled politely and waited for her next move. He would never be caught forcing anyone. He didn't have to. She stretched up to her full height, which was not very tall, and stood behind him.

"Square your hips," she said.

He let his hands fall to his sides. She was behind him, leaning suggestively on his back. She placed both her hands flat on each hip bone, pointing down to his groin. She pressed on his lower stomach, first left, then right, gently directing his pelvis. Her mound was pushing against the bottom curve of his buttocks.

He pursed his lips and swallowed hard. They could both see his erection in the mirror. Her hands and his penis formed a triangle.

"Inhale. Expand your rib cage. Now exhale."

---

88 Mr. Aramburu?. Yes. Hi. Hi.

Still leaning on his back, she put one hand on each breast. He humoured her and exagerrated the expansive movement of the air in his lungs. He couldn't help rolling his head and moving his shoulders sensuously. She lowered her hands to his waist, caressed his navel with the tips of her fingers, blew softly on the back of his neck, and covered his shoulder with tiny kisses as she looked at him from the mirror. He put the weights down carefully and turned to face her. He still hadn't touched her. He put his hands on his hips.

"The doors?" he asked.

"They're locked," she said.

"Are you going to finish what you started?" Xavier said.

"You're not very affectionate are you?"

"Not with people I don't know."

They went into the small massage room. He had seen cameras in the gym. He turned off the lights and asked her for a condom. The poor girl looked like she regretted her acts. She had only been fishing for a hot date with a gorgeous Spanish-speaking businessman, but she removed her tight jumpsuit rather ungainly and climbed onto the narrow shaky table. He stood at the far end of the table and used her with her permission.

He returned home a day later on a cold February evening. He climbed the stairs and saw a thin finger of light under their door. He knew that as he put the key in the lock, he would hear his name in her soft accent. It felt so good to be home and to see her; he was almost free of the burden of guilt. If anything, he felt more tenderness towards Adrienne than ever.

He walked in and left his suitcase on the floor. The noises were coming from the kitchen.

"Xavi?"

Home sounds. Radio music. The clatter of kitchen utensils. He leaned against the refrigerator. He couldn't have looked more dashing and masculine. She saw his smile, his pose, his eyes. She saw the man she had met at a party in Montréal a year before. She went to him, rested her head on his chest, and circled his waist with her arms.

"I missed you," he said.

"You're home now," she said.

"I know." He buried his face in her neck.

He thought that maybe it was a good thing to have it out of the way. He was sure he could handle it.

And Adrienne?

This was her choice.

Five African Queens

It was shortly after that when Adrienne found out exactly who Patrick Kyenge was. Her program was in full swing. They called her "Blanchard" and she moved around the UN like she had been born there. The secretary general called her personally to thank her for being so gracious and attentive with a group of his old school chums and their wives. Patrick was happy. The tours that had been his brainchild would become a permanent feature of the institution. Many substantial donations had come in. Patrick lobbied to deflect some of the funds to *"Puits D'Afrique,"*[89] a project he had created that provided money for wells in African villages.

It was all on account of five African queens. Grace, Violette, Fleurette, Marguerite, and Amandine. They were all married to the same king of a small Central African kingdom sitting on a world of oil. The five queens disembarked from their long, white limousine on a beautiful May morning wearing their voluminous headdresses and colourful traditional robes. Vibrant flowers contrasting against the blue sky and the long, white limousine. Adrienne looked at Patrick and commented jokingly, "Why do I have the feeling that this is going to be an interesting day?" It was Adrienne trying to make the boss laugh.

It was unusual for Patrick to receive guests with her at the entrance. Adrienne assumed that it was because they were important Africans and he wished to act as host. She was devoted to her boss even if Xavier made a point of suggesting that she keep her distance. There was no chemistry between Patrick and Xavier for obvious reasons. He saw the exotic and smooth African diplomat as a competitor for Adrienne's admiration and

---

89 African wells.

affection. Patrick's plans for Adrienne had not included a JP Morgan banker who was close to a US senator and had terrorist connections.

Queen Grace was sultry and sulky. She was young and beautiful but also nervous and irritated. She stood haughtily off to herself. Her robes were brilliant blue and yellow. Adrienne intercepted a dark look between Grace and Patrick.

Queens Violette and Fleurette were clearly identical twins. Adrienne calculated them to be about thirty years old. They were big, shiny, loud, and boisterous. They blew kisses and waved regally to the curious tourists in line for the paying tour. Violette was dressed in red and white, Fleurette in orange and purple. Adrienne immediately adored them. They played with her hair, squeezed her waist, and told her she was too thin. While being pinched and caressed, she tried to get her queens organized. Patrick directed the chauffeur to the diplomats' parking area.

The fourth queen, Marguerite, was the twins' mother. The King had wanted the twins and Marguerite had come in the kit. Marguerite was an older woman, of course. She was overweight and slow, but very straight and poised. She commanded respect. Marguerite was in beige and orange.

Then there was baby queen Amandine. She was a wide-eyed and shy teenager wrapped in gold and pistachio green. She had the tall narrow body of an African warrior. She couldn't have been more than sixteen, if that. The girl had the most intricately braided hair that Adrienne had ever seen. The braids criss-crossed her skull in a geometric pattern and culminated in a pointed rhinoceros-like cone at the top of her head. Poor little Amandine was trembling like a baby sparrow in January. Adrienne tried to make her feel safe.

"Amandine, je suis Adrienne. Restez avec moi. Je vais prendre soin de vous ce matin."[90]

Amandine reached for Adrienne's pale, smooth hair. They looked like two young trees of different species that had grown too close together.

Patrick had explained to Adrienne that the king had never managed to produce an heir and was continually marrying and divorcing women

---

90 Amandine, I am Adrienne. You stay with me. I am going to take care of you this morning.

from his native village. It had not entered His Supreme and Brilliantly Splendourous Majesty King Alfred the First's mind that he might be the one with the fertility problem.

In any case, the king was doing business with his private bankers on Wall Street that day and the ladies were to be shown the United Nations.

The adventure started early. The first stop on Adrienne's road show was an architect's scale model of the United Nations complex. Adrienne crowded her girls around the large table and began her explanation. Violette and Fleurette paid no attention at all.

"*C'est où Bloumi?*"[91] They interrupted several times.

"*Bloumi?*" Adrienne repeated, not comprehending.

"*Ouiii Bloumi!*" they insisted.

"Bloomingdale's?" Adrienne finally caught on. She called Patrick on her walkie-talkie.

"They want to go to Bloomingdale's, Patrick! They insist. Can I tell them they'll be taken there later. Shall I continue the tour?"

"Adrienne, would you mind taking them?"

"Where?"

"To Bloomingdale's if that's what they want. I'll get you a car."

"Of course."

"You'll need some money. Come down to the office."

Adrienne accepted but not without some preoccupation. She could see the difficulty in moving these five women around a crowded department store. What if she lost one? There were no security people available to accompany her, Patrick explained, but there shouldn't be any problem. Twenty minutes later, Adrienne was sitting in a black van with her queens, her walkie-talkie, and a thick wad of cash in her bag.

Bloomingdale's was a very sophisticated and trendy place, but nevertheless, five African queens in multi-coloured traditional dress waving and blowing kisses did get a lot of attention, to say the least. Amandine, the black willow in gold silk with a twelve-inch triangular cone resembling a miniature Christmas tree on the top of her head, was a sight to see. Customers, and

---

91 Where is Bloomy's?

even store personnel, thought it was a marketing event – an advertising campaign for a new exotic perfume.

Perfume is where they started. The Bloomingdale's sales girls were delighted. They competed to spray their most exquisite scent on all of the girls. This was the twins' moment. Violette and Fleurette were exuberant and charming. They joyfully threw out their wrists, arms, and necks to the salesgirls, and gushed over each perfume. They walked regally from stand to stand and invited curious onlookers to follow along.

Adrienne walked sideways with her arms stretched out in a wide, empty embrace, moving them along. She worried about Grace, who lagged behind and stopped to examine every pretty bottle and every pretty box in that shining fantasy world. One did not have to be from a dusty African village to be awed by the brilliance and luxury of the cosmetics department of Bloomingdale's. Adrienne looked at her watch. It was past eleven. *Shoes,* she thought. *Was there a woman in the world who didn't like shoes? Or maybe one of those cupcakes. Then back to headquarters.* But it was not to be a quiet morning eating cupcakes and trying on shoes with the girls.

"*Une robe de bal. Il faut s'acheter une robe de bal pour ce soir, Mademoiselle!*"[92] Violette demanded.

A ball gown. For tonight. They went up the escalators to Evening Wear, Prom Gowns, and Cocktail Dresses on the seventh floor. Adrienne's heart fell when she saw the multitude of racks packed with hundreds of dresses. It was a forest of pastel satin, lace, and sequins. All the queens except Amandine dispersed within seconds. Adrienne premonitorily stayed behind Grace and kept Amandine by her side. The sales ladies on this floor, were less enthusiastic with size fourteen Fleurette insisting loudly that she try on a size six.

A young, black sales girl came to Adrienne's rescue. She took care of the twins and helped them choose ten dresses of their size to try on. Despite the language barrier, she connected to Violette and Fleurette immediately. The giggling was contagious. The more extravagant the dress, the better. The sales girl approached Adrienne.

"Miss, I'll give you the dressing room in Bridal's. There's nobody there today. You'll be more comfortable and the older lady can sit down," she said.

---

92 a ball gown. We need to buy a ball gown for tonight, miss!

"That would be great. Thank you so much," Adrienne said.

"No problem. Queens of Africa. Wow!" she said, laughing. "Name's Angie, if you need anything."

At last, Adrienne reached the quiet serenity of the bridal dressing room with her queens. It was a small living room that had beige and white furniture, a large oval mirror on the wall, and a curtain divider for the brides' privacy. The twins went behind the curtain, and Grace, Marguerite, and Amandine sat on the French Provincial sofa. Adrienne relaxed and took a moment to count the money in the wad.

The twins, of course, needed help. It seemed Adrienne had been promoted to lady-in-waiting. She went behind the curtain where Violette and Fleurette were struggling to get into their Miss America dresses. She helped Fleurette into a fuchsia chiffon, Greek toga with a gold metallic belt. There was a long zipper hidden in a side seam and a complicated hanging veil at the back. The truth was that Fleurette looked absolutely wonderful. Adrienne looked at the price tag. It was five hundred and twenty-five dollars. It was expensive but there was more than enough money in the wad.

"Superb!" Adrienne nodded and smiled approvingly at Fleurette.

Meanwhile, Violette was sucking in her large tummy to get into a skintight, sequinned mermaid gown. The white dress was fastened by a long row of small satin buttons that fit into delicate textile loops all the way down the back. Adrienne got down on her knees to work more comfortably as she fastened the tiny buttons. She glanced under the curtain. Amandine scratched her right foot with her left big toe like a little kid. Adrienne smiled and went on buttoning.

She had a delayed reaction. Four feet, not six. Grace was gone. She jumped to her feet and ripped open the curtain in horror.

"Where is Grace?" she demanded.

Marguerite and Amandine shrugged guiltily.

"Don't move!" Adrienne shouted as severely as she could.

She ran out of the dressing room, closed the door, and galloped over to the evening wear section.

"Angie!" She called out from thirty feet away, waving her arms. "The one in blue! Where did she go?"

Angie stood on tiptoe to see over the racks and shouted back, "She left with a big guy in a navy blue suit and a red tie. Sunglasses."

"When?"

"Maybe ten minutes?"

The United Nations had trusted Adrienne Blanchard with five African queens and if it was the last thing she did, she would deliver five African queens back to the United Nations.

Fleurette and Violette, indifferent to Grace's disappearance, were standing on the white leather pedestal admiring themselves in the mirror. Adrienne marched up to Amandine, took her face between her hands, looked into her eyes, and said, "We must find Grace. She may be in danger. You must tell me where she is."

Adrienne was betting that there was a reason Amandine had been trembling that morning. She could have overheard something. She was right.

"The police," she said.

"What police?"

"The Harlem police," Amandine said.

"Harlem is a big place," Adrienne said.

"I think they said 125th street. Mademoiselle, I don't want to stay here. I want to go back home. My home."

Adrienne would have loved to take the African princess to her home far, far away but this was not a fairy tale.

"First we must find Grace and make sure she's well."

Maybe Grace was in love. Maybe she wanted asylum. But she was Adrienne's responsibility. Grace could do what she wanted but not on Adrienne's watch.

In the mid-eighties, the pendulum of world power was swinging like an incense burner in a Spanish cathedral. The line between East and West was getting fuzzy. Old alliances the blocks had made with oil-rich tribal kings and small dictators were less crucial. That was bad news for King Alfred, who had gotten greedy and delusional.

While Adrienne was at Bloomingdale's buttoning up Fleurette's sequinned gown, Our Splendourous Majesty, etcetera, etcetera, Alfred the First, was being deposed in favour of a cheaper, more sensible tribal leader who happened to be Grace's father. He had negotiated his daughter's safety and US citizenship with the Central Intelligence Agency. Grace's cousin, the chauffeur, was included in the deal. The coup was staged while the king was out of the country, and Grace's escape was carefully planned. By Patrick Kyenge.

An impassioned and unstoppable Adrienne held her walkie-talkie up high in her right hand and pulled Amandine, Marguerite, and the twins in single file through Bloomingdale's with her left. The gold Amandine, the elderly Marguerite, Fleurette in the shocking pink toga, and the curvaceous Violette waddling courageously in her white sequinned gown with a mermaid's tail made quite a scene. The curious procession plowed its way through the shoppers and down the escalators.

"Make way! Make way! United Nations! This is a medical emergency," Adrienne repeated with as much authority as she could muster. "Thank you. United Nations. Coming through! Medical emergency! Medical emergency! Thank you."

Progress was slow down the escalators. Marguerite stepped hesitantly onto the moving stairs and Violette moved along clumsily because her dress was extremely narrow at the knees. Angie managed to catch up with Adrienne at the second floor, furious that she had had two of her best dresses stolen from under her nose.

"The money is in the dressing room under the pedestal. Whatever's left over you give to charity," Adrienne shouted over her shoulder.

The information stopped Angie in her tracks. She ran back upstairs to recoup the money. There was over twelve hundred dollars extra, which eventually went towards her tuition at New York University. Angie's education was a charity as good as any.

At one point, Adrienne must have inadvertently touched the on button of her walkie-talkie. Patrick, who was commanding the operation from the three phones in his office at the UN, suddenly heard Adrienne's voice calling "medical emergency" through the heavy static of the walkie-talkie in his jacket pocket. He immediately deduced that Adrienne was on a rescue mission. Grace and the cousin were on their way to Harlem. In Africa, everything was in place. He raised his eyebrows and clicked his tongue. He knew he should have confided in her, but he had thought it was too early. Any other girl would have called for help and returned to headquarters. But not Adrienne. He grabbed his jacket and ran down to the waiting car. He had to limit the damage.

Adrienne finally made it down the seven floors to the exit on Lexington Avenue with her four remaining queens to join the race to 125th Street. It took three full turns of the revolving doors to get out of the store. Adrienne, Amandine, Marguerite, and Violette turned round and round in the glass merry-go-round, holding hands and taking small steps. Poor Fleurette, who was last in line, had let go of Violette's hand. She only had one second to jump in and hadn't made up her mind to do so. She was flustered by the speed of the doors. On the third pass, Adrienne desperately grabbed Fleurette by the waist. At last, they all spilled out onto Lexington Avenue.

At the taxi stand, Adrienne shouted to be heard over the traffic. She and the queens were all holding hands.

"We're going to 125th Street police station. It's an emergency. I'm with the United Nations," she said.

She showed the identification tag that was hanging around her neck. She made her intentions clear, knowing full well that not every cab driver would go to Harlem, and certainly not to a police station with an unexplained emergency. Finally, an older black man raised his hand.

"Okay. You'll have to hide one of these ladies. Only allowed four."

They had time to catch their breath. It was a long way and the gods were not on Adrienne's side that day. They hit almost every red light and moved up Manhattan slowly. The queens were quiet. They looked out the cab window and saw the face of Manhattan change from the Upper East Side to Harlem. Amandine approved.

"A very large village," she said.

Adrienne arrived too late to take Grace back to the United Nations. When she reached the reception desk at the police station, an amused policeman leaned forward on his elbows, watching the picturesque group arrive.

"You must be Blanchard," he said.

"Yes."

"I'll take you in. They're waiting for you."

He butted his cigarette and nudged his head towards a low-swinging door that lead to the large working area. Adrienne had to leave her beautiful queens in their lovely dresses huddled together on a hard metal bench. Africa was gone forever. Exile.

Patrick and Adrienne had a frank conversation in his office later that evening. By then, she had been briefed. Because of Adrienne and her presence at the police station, all the queens had to be processed. The afternoon had been spent at State Department offices making sworn declarations. Grace, the chauffeur, and Amandine were being granted the right of asylum. Their escape had to be recorded for a future hearing. Adrienne had involuntarily complicated events, forcing Patrick to stick his neck out. Fortunately, there had been no press, no pictures, which was what he had feared. It was just another obscure coup.

After two hours with Patrick and a French-speaking State Department psychologist, Amandine chose to stay in the United States rather than go to Switzerland with the deposed king, the twins, and Marguerite. Amandine, for all intents and purposes, was an abandoned alien child. She was alone and could neither speak nor understand the language of North America, let alone the culture. Her options were patiently explained to her, yet, she preferred to stay rather than follow the king, whom she feared. Perhaps young Amandine, through Adrienne, had sensed a different future. Patrick assured her she would be cared for and that she would receive an education. He made a personal commitment to sponsor Amandine until she was eighteen. She was fifteen years old.

It was difficult for Adrienne when they had taken Amandine away in the company car. She was being taken to a safe house somewhere in Virginia where papers would be processed and a feasible and suitable future would be planned for her. For the moment, Patrick told Adrienne, she would probably be sent to a Catholic residential girls' school. There would be French speakers and other African girls, he assured Adrienne. A good sum of money for an education and a start in life would be confiscated from the king's accounts.

It was cold in the dark parking lot when the car arrived. Adrienne knew she had been an insignificant actor in this rocambolesque story but she fretted that Amandine would probably have been boarding the private jet to Geneva had she not persevered in keeping Grace in her custody. She was responsible for drastically changing this girl's life. She draped her red blazer over Amandine's shoulders. The girl hugged the jacket around her narrow African warrior body. She leaned on Adrienne until the last possible second. It was Adrienne who opened the door of the car. Her heart felt heavier than the door. And then Amandine was gone.

Patrick gave her a short description of what becoming an international agent of the CIA implied. Adrienne had grown up in a small, quiet town but in a home where the line between a good man and a bad man, right and wrong, just and unjust, was opaque. The idea was not so terribly far-fetched. Philippe Blanchard had kept a gun and, to their mother's dismay, had shown the children where it was. Patrick's suggestion didn't even surprise her very much. She had expected the UN to be full of spies. That was what made her perfect.

"My answer is no," she said, "because I'm sure it would mean violence at some point, political ideas I might not agree with, and, well, even if I did, this is not my country. Why would I work for it?"

"I understand, Adrienne. But...be aware that your conception of the job is perhaps somewhat inaccurate. Believe me, it is exagerrated by films and fiction. It is very rarely so dramatic, glamourous, or dangerous," Patrick said.

"Have you ever killed anyone?" she asked. She held her chin up and looked into his eyes as if to prove a point. Patrick didn't pick up the glove. He didn't insist. He was moderately sure that she would bend eventually. Her answer was typical. Only bad agents said yes the first time they were approached.

"Now that you know, you must also understand that working for me, you are close to that. I need your loyalty and your silence."

"You have it. You can trust me."

"I will." Patrick nodded. He looked away for a moment and said, "I'll ask you two questions that I don't want you to answer right now. Whenever you're ready. One: Would you kill in self-defence or to protect an innocent? Two: Do you know whose side you're on?" Adrienne nodded. It seemed fair.

Patrick had said enough. He sighed. The African queens had made him nostalgic for home. He often wondered what would have become of him had he made his life in Kinshasa.

"You know, when I was a boy in the slums of Kinshasa, I had my own gang. Only children I trusted. You would have been in my gang." He nodded confidently like the vain little *Kinois*[93] he had once been.

"I don't think so, Patrick. I would have had my own gang. Just the girls. Me and Marguerite. The hell with you guys."

---

93 Native of Kinshasa.

Patrick laughed so hard he bent over at the waist. Adrienne laughed with him. He had been sitting on his desk, his feet firmly on the floor. He reached for her hand.

"Thank you for everything today. You did your job magnificently well. Too magnificently!" He laughed again.

He put his hand paternally on Adrienne's shoulder and said, *"Mon plus beau soldat. Allez. Rentre chez toi et repose toi bien."*[94]

---

94 My prettiest soldier. Go home and get some rest.

Oh Happy Day

The seduction of Adrienne by the CIA was not extraordinarily effective. Patrick occasionally dropped brochures on her desk. Martial arts, Arabic language courses, archery, and transcendental meditation of all things. She signed up for gym jazz, Arabic language, and evening courses in International Relations at Columbia University. Although the offer never completely slipped her mind, her life was full and she was not tempted. She did not feel connected to the idea no matter how well Patrick rationalized it into a flexible international instrument for order. It was an insurance policy against excess and anarchy, he said. An intelligent whip. Selective surgery.

Her eyes were open. She kept her silence. Patrick parachuted guests into her tour schedule. While she took them through the conference rooms and to lunch in the dining room, contents of pockets and briefcases were photographed, and tracking devices were planted into hems of coats. There were whispered insinuations and documents changing hands between toilet stalls. This was the order of the day at the UN. It was not a kindergarten although sometimes it seemed like it.

Then Patrick was gone for almost a year to supervise and consolidate the administration of new UN delegations in African countries. His administrative tasks and duties in New York would be shared by Mary and Adrienne. Adrienne looked forward to it. She was tiring of the tours and was told she could train two guides to replace her. The day before he left, Patrick walked by her desk, checked the time, and looked out the window. As he watched the activity on the East River, he said, "Adrienne Lise Blanchard. Have you thought about those two questions I asked you?"

"Yes, I have and I know the answers," she said.

Patrick came back in November of '89 with a slight limp and was disappointed to find Adrienne wearing a wedding ring.

Joaquín Múgica was responsible for Xavier and Adrienne's decision to marry. Their marriage would be his last act as a Catholic priest. The wedding took place on March 21, a year and a half after Xavier's meeting with Mentxu in Bilbao.

Joaquín's laicization took time. It was his American bishop who didn't want to let him go. The combative and personable Irish bishop adored him. "My partner in crime," he called Joaquín. They shared political views, liked a good whiskey, and a good joke. Joaquín's parish was well-run and active in the community. He had single-handedly refurbished the church basement, which was home to several local community organizations, from knitting clubs to Alcoholics Anonymous. His was one of the few parishes that had grown in the last ten years.

His Spanish ways had also made him popular. The powerfully built and gregarious young priest with the beret was a familiar figure in the neighbourhood. He went out for coffee every morning and had a drink many evenings between seven o'clock mass and his nine o'clock supper. There was not a waiter or a waitress in the diners and bars in those twenty square blocks of Queens Long Island who didn't recognize the Spanish Father (who was actually Basque). He stopped bothering to explain the difference. They called him Father Joe. Priests like that were few and far between.

As for his political vocation, for years he took the subway back and forth to St. John's University wearing his clergyman's collar and his *Elosegui* beret.[95] He had stitched a small Ikurriña, the Basque flag, onto his backpack in case any compatriots crossed his path, which they often did. They were told where to look for him. It was his point of contact. His office was a swaying subway car.

Joaquín himself presented the proof of the violation of his vows. He was asked to reconsider for six long months. He was asked to leave Evelyn and his adorable little girl. A passionate and lonely man who had not been allowed to attend his father's funeral nor see his aging mother in ten years, he had done what he could for God and for Euskadi. Joaquín's request for voluntary laicization was granted at last. As of March 22, 1989, Joaquín Múgica Izaguirre was stripped of the power to administer the Holy Sacraments.

When he received the news in early March, he called Xavier.

---

95 Authentic and traditional Basque berets made in Tolosa, Guipuzcoa, since 1858.

"If you want me to marry you to Adrienne," he said, "you have three weeks. Tell me tomorrow because we have to publish the banns."[96]

Xavier fiddled with his pen. He had been working at his desk in the living room when the phone rang. Adrienne was sitting cross-legged on the bed in the guest suite, reading *Time* magazine in her bathrobe, a towel rolled around her head. On Sunday nights, she liked to use the large guest bathroom for long baths and beauty treatments. He leaned in the doorway and looked at her.

"Hola!" Xavier said.

"Hola!"[97] she said.

Smiles. A pause.

"Yes?" Adrienne was puzzled.

"Adri. I think I would like to get married," he said.

Disbelief. Amusement.

"Why? Are you pregnant?" she giggled, pleased with her little joke.

"No. Don't laugh. I'm serious."

He jumped onto the bed, pushed her down, stretched out on top of her, and kissed the tip of her nose. He was suddenly absolutely sure it was the best idea he had ever had in his life.

"Joaquín is, well, retiring."

"You mean he's been defrocked," she said.

"It's not defrocked, Adrienne, it's laicized. He remains a priest."

"It doesn't matter. How is he?"

Adrienne was still not aware that this was a proposal of marriage.

"Torn. OK. So we have to decide now. For him to marry us. To publish the banns."

"To publish the *banns*?" She emphasized the ancient word. "That's medieval, Xavi. Are you serious?" Adrienne said, eyes widening.

"Hostia. Would I mention marriage if I wasn't serious?"

Her mind flew ahead.

"Xavi, let me think. Wouldn't a civil marriage be more realistic?"

"I want to get married Adri. I don't want to start a company."

"You want to get married. To me. In the church."

---

96 Notification of intention to marry for Catholic couples to be posted in church bulletin or vestibule at least 21 days before the ceremony.

97 Hi! Hi!

"Adri, I can't remember life before you. I can't imagine life without you. Will you marry me?"

He put his hands under her neck and held up her towelled head. His face was pure innocence.

"Well. Yes. I think so," she said.

"You think so? Yes or No. *Hostia. Mujer!*"[98]

"Yes."

"Good. Good. Good. Thank you."

"You're welcome." Adrienne was stunned.

Xavier kissed her with the wild happiness of a soccer fan whose team has just scored a championship goal in overtime. Adrienne was in shock. All she could think of was that she had just been proposed to and her hair was greasy with conditioner under the towel.

"Are we really getting married?" she asked.

"Saturday, March 21," he said.

"That's in three weeks!"

"Plenty of time. First day of spring. I like it."

"I need to rinse my hair. Oh my God."

Xavier grabbed her by the waist and dragged her into the bathroom. She knelt on the floor and hung her long hair over the tub while Xavier rinsed it with the shower head.

"Morning or evening? Adrienne?"

"Ummmm. Better morning. Evenings are still cold and dark in March. Don't you think?"

"Yes. You're right. So, morning. Your family. My family."

"Oh yes. Very intimate, Xavi. I hope everyone can come on such short notice. We need to organize a nice meal, Xavi."

"Lobster. Roast beef. The typical," said Xavier.

"Strawberries. Chocolate. Champagne," said Adrienne.

"The River Café? Windows of the World?" he suggested.

"Where else?" she said, unenthused.

"The Harvard Club?" he said doubtfully.

---

[98] Jesus Christ. Woman!

"No, please. I know: The Glass Pavilion in Central Park on that small lake. Eh? Charlie reserved it once for Pat's surprise party. It was wonderful," Adrienne said.

"Yes. Very good idea. Perfect."

"Music. Flowers. Rings. Dress. Suit. Shoes. Xavi," Adrienne wailed. "This is crazy!"

"No, it's not. This is good."

And so it was. For the next three weeks, Adrienne and Xavier organized their ceremony. They held hands in their sleep. Xavier was happy with his choice, but more importantly, he was sure of his choice. Adrienne felt elated and guiltily triumphant.

Xavier waited with Charles at the front of the church while guests and families sat in the three front pews. In the end, best friends, aunts, uncles, and cousins had joined the party. Judge Mackenzie Powell had come with wife number four. Koldo had come with a new girlfriend, and cousin Lillian had made it at the last minute. She walked down the aisle waving an oar that had the Canadian flag painted on it. It was her wedding gift to Xavier.

The group looked slightly puzzled to find themselves in this humble church, light-years away from Manhattan in every sense of the word. The Spanish family knew of the priest and tried to bury their qualms. Although silenced in the rest of the country, in Bilbao, the Múgica affair had been a cause célèbre. He was, besides that, the son of a long-time employee.

Koldo was standing near the altar to serve as choirboy. Jon, Iñaki, Catherine, and Valerie eyed each other suspiciously at the back of the church where they waited for their aunt Adrienne. They would accompany the bride down the aisle in a procession carefully choreographed by Claude. They each carried an armful of lilacs in honour of the first day of spring and the lilac bushes of Crane Road.

As the wedding party waited quietly, a gospel choir came through the door and walked in military formation down the aisle to form behind the altar. Joaquín had hired one of the best gospel choirs in Brooklyn. This was his gift. It was a surprise. Xavier smiled and nodded to the director. He looked down and grinned, looking forward to Adrienne's reaction. Charles looked at Xavier and nodded enthusiastically. The guests nudged each other and smiled in expectation. Claude signaled to the photographer she had hired to take some pictures and was angry at herself for not thinking of bringing recording equipment.

Xavier was not nervous at all about getting married. It fell into the natural order of things. He was worried about his friend, who was alone in the sacristy. At one minute before noon, Joaquín appeared carrying his missal in both hands over his chest. He preapred his altar for the last time, shining the silver candlesticks carefully with a linen cloth.

Noon. The angelus. As the bells rang out, Adrienne appeared in the entrance on her brother's arm. She was the swan of the ballet in a pure white top with very long sleeves and a knee-length skirt of layers upon layers of tulle. Her hair was in a soft chignon, resting on the back of her neck and adorned by the art deco hair ornament she had worn to Arantxa's wedding. She carried a bouquet of orange tulips to match her sexy orange high-heeled shoes.

Xavier was shocked. They had gone shopping together and chosen an elegant ivory silk dress with a matching coat from a Japanese designer who was all the rage in Manhattan. It was very pure, architectural, and minimal, they said. When she went to pick her wedding outfit up, Adrienne decided that "minimal" and "architectural" was not what she was feeling. She stopped at a dancewear store, then went to Bloomie's for the sexiest shoes she could find. She kept it a secret from Xavi.

The choir broke into a jazzy version of "Come Sing a Song of Joy" from Beethoven's Ninth. Adrienne's face broke into an expression of delight and surprise. She walked down the aisle smiling from ear to ear. Little Iñaki led the procession holding his large bunch of lilacs as if he were carrying the Olympic torch. The other children followed suit. Xavier reached for Adrienne's hand and kissed her palm. He was too moved to speak.

"Are you happy?" Adrienne asked. He nodded.

Joaquín took a deep breath, acknowledged the guests, and smiled with affection at Xavier and Adrienne who were sitting on two straight-back chairs in the middle of the centre aisle. Claude, maid of honour, and Charles, best man, were at their side. In English and Spanish he welcomed the families to his church.

There were noises at the back of the church. Heavy wooden pews scraped on the tile floor. Joaquín lost his train of thought. He looked off beyond the bride and groom to see a steady stream of parishioners filing quietly into the church. They had waited outside, let the bride enter, and then come in to attend Father Joe's last service. Xavier motioned to Joaquín to stop and wait for everyone to settle. The priest, for twelve more hours, watched the crowds of people coming to his side. He became so emotional, he put his elbows on the altar and his hands over his face. When he was ready and the church was full, he began again.

Xavier and Adrienne had an unforgettable wedding. It was standing room only. They exchanged their vows and kissed to a multidudinous "ahhhhhh," and a booming "Hallelujah" from the choir. The singers belted out gospel hymns, "All You Need Is Love," "Here Comes the Sun," and the old favourite, "Oh Happy Day." The nephews and nieces were joined by more children. Joaquín invited them to sit on the steps and on the communion railing around the altar. The children sang and clapped along with the powerful choir.

It was his last Mass. Joaquín took his microphone and sat with the children on the stairs to recite the The Lord's Prayer. He paused. The congregation was expectant. He closed his eyes to savour and cherish the moment. When he opened them, he saw Evelyn and Estíbaliz sitting in the last pew. Then, he looked at Xavi, smiled, and recited the prayer in Euskerra,[99] his mother tongue. He led, the children repeated.

---

99 The Basque language.

A Place Called π

They lived in privilege. True privilege when there is nothing that you need and everything is within your grasp. They were beautiful, strong, wealthy, and young. Sadly, there was a crack in the perfect vase, hairline thin, and invisible to the naked eye. Yet the vase remained beautiful.

Xavier made a small fortune for JP Morgan with his portfolio. He stood by his ventures. He was patient and loyal. Other firms and investment banks approached him about joining them, but he had chosen JP Morgan and that was where he would pursue his financial career. The old-timers on the street began to think that he was there to stay. They made bets about how far a Spaniard could make it up the JP Morgan ladder.

He was thirty-one years old when he became independently wealthy. A Japanese automotive giant paid an indecent sum of money for the patent, the technology, and the manufacturing processes of an inexpensive and long-lasting battery developed by a group of young MIT engineers working in a dreary industrial park outside Boston. They were dead broke and closing shop when Morgan, a.k.a. Xavier Aramburu, kept them alive with thirty million dollars for a 70 percent share of the business.

It was a revolution in the industry. The Japanese could not believe they had not invented it first, so they bought it for an astronomical amount and locked down the MIT boys for three years to keep it to themselves. The deal was signed in New York. The Japanese chief financial officer and his Morgan counterpart had a legendary dinner party at a private club on the Upper East Side. Not even Xavier was invited. It was said that the Japanese gentleman's tastes had been extremely peculiar and that JP Morgan had obliged.

Meanwhile, Xavier waited for his bonus. It was rumoured to be a big one. The story had made the front page of the *Wall Street Journal. The Financial Times* in London wanted an interview. Harvard Business School wanted him back. Charles wanted him in Washington. And Morgan didn't want him to leave. Xavier needed to think. His normally clear and well-balanced head was spinning. He was invited to a breakfast meeting with the president of the bank first thing on a Monday morning. The chief financial officer handed Xavier a cashier's cheque for five million dollars. It was an extraordinary amount and, in the eighties, a life changing sum.

It was a coincidence that just a week before, Begoña had called. She had come across a jewel. She landed an excellent contract decorating five homes for a group of architects on the sleepy, sparsely populated Balearic island of Formentera and had fallen in love with the place herself. The five unconventional architects had bought ninety isolated beachfront acres and built seven fabulous houses. They planned to finance some of the project with the sale of the two extra villas. Formentera was not fashionable; therefore the prices were very reasonable. The houses were modern and sleek but with a Mediterranean inspiration.

Begoña proposed they buy both; one for him, one for her. It was so beautiful, he could hardly imagine, and it was cheap for what it was. It would sell for triple in two years. They were building a marina. At last: his own boat! They would own twenty acres on a Mediterranean island beach. It was "only" a nine-hour flight followed by a one-hour flight followed by a two-hour ferry crossing followed by a fifty-minute car ride. Then Begoña fired the heavy artillery: "You've been gone too long; we need you."

He loved Cape Cod. He loved Crane Road. However, neither of those places was his. A place in Spain? It didn't seem feasible. His life was in New York. A boat in Formentera? On the other hand, he had been wanting to mark their marriage in some way. This might be it. So, when he saw the cheque, he gave in and let himself be happy. He called Begoña and told her that if she needed it, he could help with her share. They decided to have the architects build a dock on the beach in front of his house.

He took the rest of the day off and went to the park to skate while he waited for Adrienne. He skated with his hands in his pockets and a dizzy feeling of expectation and change. He bit at his bottom lip, trying not to laugh out loud like a wild man. His own boat. He was tempted to buy a medium-sized catamaran. It would be perfect for the Mediterranean and for Begoña's boys. Catherine and Valerie would come too. Xavier was feeling like a family man. Older. Better. Expanded. He imagined Adrienne sleeping on the tarp in the warm Spanish sun. He pushed away the uncomfortable feeling that everything was too good to be true.

They took four weeks holiday in July to discover their new house. The community had no name, just the mathematical symbol π which the Islanders chose to ignore. It became known as '*Los Arquitectos.*'[100] It was on the northeastern shore of Formentera, facing Ibiza. The winds and the sea were gentler on that side of the island. Theoretically, it was a working community. The architects had built their homes closer together so as to share two tennis courts, storage areas, wine cellars, and a serpentine glass building under a grouping of tall Mediterranean pines, which housed their state-of-the-art studios. The marina clubhouse was built high on stilts and on the dock. A pagoda equipped with a professional kitchen seemed to float on the perfect blue water.

On entering π off the main road, a simple, white villa housed the caretaker and his family. The Aramburu properties were down a road to the left in the opposite direction of the main compound. Xavier and Adrienne arrived on a very hot day in a rented Land Rover. They had flown out of New York almost twenty-four hours before. It was to be their first vacation alone. Just the two of them. Their honeymoon.

Xavier followed Begoña's careful instructions: *Around a bend, at an orange marker by the side of the road.*

"OK. I think our property starts here," he said.

He drove very slowly down the narrow country road, turning his head from side to side taking inventory of what they had bought - irresponsibly and sight unseen - for a good deal of money.

It was a classical Mediterranean landscape. As he drove, he counted approximately ninety century-old olive trees on their land. Knee-high stone walls divided the ancient farmland into square corrals empty of sheep and grain but laden with small white flowers, cacti, and fig trees heavy with

---

[100] The architects.

fruit. Begoña had kept one secret from them: a three-hundred-year-old Balearic windmill on their property, registered by the Spanish Ministry of Culture as a National Heritage monument. A conical structure twenty metres high, the blades formed a wheel of giant arrows. It was magical. Xavier stopped the car and rolled down the window.

"*La Hostia!* Adri! Look at that," he said. She put her hand over her mouth in disbelief.

They reached their villa, which was just as he had imagined: white blocks almost invisible under dark pink bougainvillea. They decided to save the house for last. They walked in the burning sun to the waterfront, their hands grasped tightly together. They shook their heads, not in disagreement but in admiration. It exceeded their expectations.

Not a human soul. Only the hum of nature and the soft lapping of the sea on the sand. It was a long, sandy beach limited to the north by a rocky, beige-and-blue cliff jutting into the Mediterranean. Ibiza was a low, blue shadow on the horizon. They saw Begoña's house which was about three hundred meters away and hidden like theirs under cascades of fuchsia flowers. It had a Moorish-style domed roof.

As they walked back to the house in the hot sun, Xavier squatted to feel the water in the pool while Adrienne struggled to open the antique door that Begoña had bought in Granada. The contrast of the medieval door with the modern house was perfect. They walked in, arms at each others' waists in a conspiratorial and happy silence, smiling in delight. The pictures they had seen had not done it justice.

They were inside and outside at once. They were protected from the heat by thick adobe walls and numerous narrow, recessed floor-to-ceiling windows placed to let in the soft wind but to limit the heat. Suddenly, they came upon a small courtyard shaded by white beams and hanging grapevines. Pure air and light flowed through it all. The floor was the colour of baked earth. The long, natural linen curtains fluttered. The air smelled of basil and lemon.

They wandered around the house and collapsed on a large, comfortable cream-coloured sofa in the living room. They were physically and emotionally drained.

"It's paradise, Xavi."

"Yes. It is."

Adrienne felt sticky after the long trip. She kicked off her sandals and pulled off all her clothes. Xavier misunderstood. He turned on his side and stretched out his arms. He was tired, but he liked to make her happy. But it was not sex she wanted in the midday heat, it was a swim.

"Let's go in for a swim! It will do us good before we unpack," she said.

She took his hand and walked out of the house. Xavier was in a trance behind her. Tired, he didn't bother to undress. They ignored the pool and headed for the beach. The sea floor was sandy and smooth. They held hands and took small, slow steps in the water. The heat of their bodies made the water feel cold. Xavier's clothes stuck to him like a second skin. When the water reached the top of their thighs, they submerged. Xavier removed his clothes and let them float away. When they came back up, they passed their hands over each other's faces and hooked their legs around each other's hips.

They began by baptizing the sea in this place that was no place and every place at once. Adrienne had found her Garden of Eden and her Adam.

A Fool in a Top Hat

Xavier's fall from grace wore the face of Carla Montenegro née Maria Concepción Alvarez Garcia, born in Tenerife, one of the Canary Islands. The Spanish Islands off the coast of Africa are known as the "The Fortunate Islands" for their permanent balmy spring weather, tropical gardens, Mardi Gras carnival, and pretty women who often happen to be outstanding beauty pageant contestants.

Xavier had two cell phones. One, for family, the other for everyone else. The family phone rang. He interrupted what he was doing to respond. He was expecting news from Adrienne.

"*Hola! Xavi! Que tal?*"[101]

He didn't recognize the voice. A young woman. Not Adrienne. Not Bego. Not Jocelyne, Clo, Lilly, or Pat.

"Who is this?" he asked gruffly.

"Carla. Begoña's friend. She didn't tell you I was coming?" she said.

His sister had a very good friend called Carla, but he had never met her. Begoña was in Southeast Asia, in Thailand or Burma or somewhere, buying antiques for the store. It must have slipped her mind. He was not happy. He had told her not to give out his personal number. Ever.

"Ah! OK. Begoña gave you my number? She forgot to tell me. Is there anything I can help you with?"

"Well, yes. Have lunch with a lonely Spanish girl all by herself in New York? I'm here representing emerging Spanish artists at a show at the LaPlante Gallery and no one has arrived yet. Poor little me."

He raised his eyebrows. He was an old fox and didn't buy into this woman's overly intimate and flirty attitude. This Carla must be a public

---

101 Xavi! Hi! How are you?

relations person of some sort. Maybe she wanted to sell him a painting or get a free lunch. He had no desire at all to meet her.

Xavier was being more and more careful about his extracurricular sex because he was committed to his marriage. The conditions had to perfect. He was exquisite and difficult. The girl, or girls, had to be hot. The scene had to be clean. The intentions had to be clear. The time had to be right. A friend of Begoña's was definitely off limits, however, by the same token, he had no choice but to take her out for lunch.

But when the devil stirs the pot, he makes sure no one is at home....

It was December 9. Adrienne had gone to Geneva where she was taking a two week seminar in International Law and NGOs, which was sponsored by the UN. She would fly directly to Madrid to meet Xavier on the 22nd. It was to be an Aramburu Christmas. They were spending Christmas Eve in Madrid, then on Christmas Day driving to Baqueira-Beret in the Catalonian Pyrennées for a ski vacation where they were to meet the Bilbao Aramburus.

Xavier was free and alone in New York for two weeks. He arranged to meet lonely Carla the next day for lunch at the 21 Club on 57th Street near Rockefeller Center. It was a very business, very masculine, very Manhattan place. He had a look at her as the maître d' helped him with his coat. She was a ravishing, leggy brunette in a tight, sleeveless red leather dress, legs primly leaning to one side. Her shiny, dark hair fell to her shoulders. She had the face of a doe with large, round brown eyes, plump, heart-shaped lips, high cheek-bones, a good chin, and healthy, rosy skin. In contrast with the exceptional softness and innocence of her facial features, she had two very sexy beauty spots. One just over her upper lip at the corner of her mouth and the other, high on her left cheekbone at the corner of her eye.

At the sight of this beautiful woman, Xavier forgave his sister and decided to enjoy lunch. The flirt on the phone turned out to be a very polite and sincere young woman who asked him about himself and told her life story with a pretty smile and a sense of humour. She ate slowly and very little, and never took her eyes off him. She talked about her simple childhood in the Canary Islands and her beginnings as a model in Madrid. She blushed and giggled in embarrassment.

"You know, I participated in the Miss Spain pageant when I was nineteen and I was First Runner Up!"

She made an amusing and silly face to show her embarrassment at such a minor and uncultivated accomplishment. And what does a man say to that?

"You should have won. You are very beautiful," he said.

"Oh, no," she said modestly. "How awful! But it did give me a start in Madrid. My real love is art."

Her modeling jobs had financed art history and marketing studies, she explained. She was now learning the art business as the assistant of an important gallery owner. Begoña worked in collaboration with her gallery and they had become friends. She admired his sister very much and his nephews were adorable. Xavier's ego was flying high over Rockefeller Center.

She was certainly very tempting, but some survival instinct told him to get out of there. Suddenly, he felt the compulsion to flee. He got up when they had not yet finished their coffee. He was terribly sorry, he explained, time had flown by and he was late for an appointment. He apologized, he had enjoyed meeting her, and he wished her luck. He was a regular at 21 and asked her to stay for a drink. Everything was arranged with the maître d'.

"And please," he said, "give my sister a kiss for me."

Carla seemed to panic. She grabbed her handbag and pulled at his arm. She gave him the invitation to the show opening for the next night, putting it firmly into his pocket.

"I'd love you to come, Xavi. Please come. I need some moral support from somebody from home. It's my first job in New York."

The pouting flirt was back.

"Thank you. I'll try. But it's Christmas and there's a lot going on. I'm so sorry to leave like this but I really have to go. Good luck with the show and have a good trip home."

He gave her a kiss on the cheek and shrugged his shoulders, attempting to show regret.

In fact, his department's Christmas party was that evening. It was always fun. The atmosphere at work was good. They had organized a Secret Santa gift exchange and this was hat year. Xavier's Santa got him a magician's top hat. They took pictures in their funny hats, drank too much, sang "Jingle Bells," and, just as it was getting noisy and fun, the party broke up because most of the people had trains to catch.

He headed home with the frustrated feeling of when a party is over early and you are still raring to go. He hailed a taxi. Two minutes later, as the cab was going up Broadway, the family phone rang. It was too late for a call from Europe.

"Sí?"

"Una copita?"[102]

Carla's paparazzi-manager boyfriend had been waiting outside the JP Morgan building's main door. He called Carla from a phone booth as soon as he saw Xavier walk out.

The Gilt Bar at the New York Plaza on Madison Avenue was crowded. It was a gold place full of golden people. All eyes were on a perfect man and a beautiful girl in a top hat seducing each other. They were standing face-to-face, caressing each other's cheeks. Xavier was hurting like a sixteen-year-old. Unaware of his surroundings, only conscious of the woman.

"Come to my room or I'll die," she said.

He wanted her so badly that, incredibly, he tried to stop the elevator but she didn't let him. His heart was beating in his mouth.

He had her for the first time on her hands and knees as they crawled on the floor in the direction of the bed. The second time, Mademoiselle Montenegro was on top in all her glory. Swinging hair, loud noises, expert moves. The third time was on the floor again. The fourth time, they were standing in the window, curtains open and lights on, giving the city a show. A sexy black corset mysteriously appeared. The fifth time, she was bending over the armchair, head down. The curtains were still open, the lights were still on. Then, he passed out.

Some hours later, Xavier woke up with a headache and a very dry mouth. She was sitting on the edge of the bed holding a glass of water in her hand. It all came back to him. He knew his own sexuality and realized he had been drugged. He refused the glass of water and remained silent.

First rules of disaster: Don't panic. Protect yourself. Control the consequences.

"Good morning!" she said, giggling.

In the morning light, he could see that the beauty spots were tattoos. Her breasts were also false, her lips were artificially inflated, her nose had been shortened, her chin was an implant, and her ears had been surgically

---

102 A little drink?

glued to her head. The surgeon, or surgeons, had done a good job on her face but she had thick, ugly scars behind her ears.

"I was just thinking. What is Begoña going to say when she finds out about us? I think she'll be glad. Don't you?"

It was clearly a threat. She pushed away the sheets, lowered her head to his penis and started to lick delicately around the base as she looked up at him.

"Let's keep it a secret just a little longer, OK? Let me enjoy you," he said, pushing her head down firmly.

She liked the answer and persevered in her task. Xavier had a wily rival. At that point of the match, he was losing. He had to play to the end in order to have any chance at all to win.

Carla Montenegro's curriculum was a mile long. She had never studied art or marketing or anything of the sort, but she had been runner up for the Miss Spain title. She had accused the winner of sleeping with the president of the jury, who was a renowned female journalist. It had provoked such a scandal that she became more famous than the girl who wore the crown. This was the premonitory beginning of her career. Ruthless and driven, Carla was a prostitute of fame.

She worked briefly as a model but soon gave it up to fulfill her dream to be an actress. She managed to land a role in a film by an excellent director. She thought she had made it. However, her performance was so absolutely deficient that most of her scenes had been cut and she had had to be dubbed in her own language. She was the joke of the Spanish cinema world. Any disastrous performance in the Spanish Cinema after that had been coined a "Montenegro."

Her fame resided in her beauty. Her doe-like face, her dark hair and eyes, her tall and lithe body was all she had. She was voted the most beautiful Spanish girl alive. There were rumours that the king of Spain fancied her. She frequented high society and eventually married an Austrian aristocrat who, to her great surprise, was penniless. Soon after, she appeared on the cover of gossip magazines exhibiting a black eye and accusing the count of abuse. She cultivated the image of a beautiful, humble girl out in the cold, cruel world of the rich. The magazines loved her. She rivalled Princess Caroline of Monaco for monthly covers.

She was never taken seriously as an actress or a model, but she did manage to be a permanent character of the society tabloid world. She was rumoured to be part of an escort service network for Saudi princes and millionaires, and apparently was instrumental in the break up of a respected business man's marriage. The exclusive clique of high-class women of Madrid whom she wanted to be a part of, drew a cross on Carla Montenegro forever. She was approaching thirty. Her star was beginning to fade.

Xavier Aramburu had been gone for years and had absolutely no idea who she was. The crux of the whole affair was her name. He knew his sister had a friend named Carla who worked in the same business and that Begoña liked her very much. The name and profession fit, but the girl did not. He couldn't imagine a friend of Begoña's spiking his drink and performing a blow job worthy of the best pro in Bangkok.

But how had the mix-up happened? The devil again. Begoña's friend was Carla Arespacochaga, a fellow decorator from Bilbao, not Carla Montenegro. The coincidence was that Begoña knew the famous Carla well and detested her intensely. The starlet had ordered an antique French Provence dining room from the store. It was Begoña's showpiece. Carla had it delivered, complete with eight chairs, a chandelier, and a rug and had never paid a *peseta*.[103] She had posed in her new dining room for the cover of a society magazine and had the nerve to tell Begoña that she should pay her for the free publicity.

She had continued to frequent the store as it was a very chic place to be seen. Carla's pretty cheeks were as hard as wood. That fall, she had pushed her way into Begoña's office to ask for a living room set for a photo shoot for a magazine. Begoña could have it all back after the session. Xavier's sister could not believe the gall. On her desk, Begoña had a very nice, framed picture of Xavier in a wetsuit zipped down to his waist. Xavier, Iñaki, and Jon were carrying kiteboards on the beach in Formentera. Xavier's hair was long and wet. He was tanned. He looked more like a fabulous model than a banker.

"Your husband and kids?" Carla asked.

"My brother, Xavi, with my sons. I'm divorced."

---

[103] Spanish currency before the Euro.

"What a beautiful family!"

"Thank you. Excuse me for a moment. I have to attend to one of my clients who, by the way, pays her bills," Begoña said.

Begoña left her office to go onto the sales floor to say hello to a good client. She left Carla sitting at her desk alone in her office. Carla slid her hand over the table and reached for Begoña's agenda. She flipped it open. Inside the cover, Begoña had jotted down her most important telephone numbers.

School

Hairdresser

Customs

Iberia

Xavi New York (personal)

Xavi New York (other)

Carla Montenegro smiled wickedly. A little research and the hunt was on.

She was too dangerous an enemy to alienate. Either it was blackmail she intended or she was applying to be his mistress and future wife. Both options made his skin crawl. He needed time to think about how to stop it.

"*Carlita*.[104] We have to talk," he said.

He smoothed her hair. He smiled affectionately. She had the dramatic expression of a very bad actress playing the star-crossed lover separated by cruel destiny.

"Listen, sweetheart. I have to run home, change, and go to work. What time is the opening tonight?"

"Eight. Will you come, my love?" she said, triumphantly.

He hoped he wasn't sinking deeper.

"Yes. I'll pick you up. How's a quarter to eight?"

"Oh, yes. Wonderful. I'll reserve a car. I'm so, so, so happy." She was gushing.

He picked up his jacket and saw it on the floor. He saw himself the night before: a fool in a top hat.

---

104 Diminutive of Carla.

He calmed down somewhat during the day. It was not the first time an overly enthusiastic woman had crossed his path, yet the Begoña connection troubled him. He hated to implicate her, but he was in deep water and she was the only person who could help him sort things out. He located her in Hong Kong. She was surprised at his call.

"Xavi, you're not canceling Christmas are you? I hope not," she said. "It's the first time I have the boys for Christmas Eve in three years! I want the whole family together."

"No. Don't worry. You know Adri's arriving two days before me. You'll have to pick her up at the airport," he said.

"Of course, give me her arrival time as soon as you can. The *aita* will come too. He's very excited about this vacation. Paloma is very well these days and the *ama* is keen."

"Good. Thank you. Begoña?"

"Yes?"

"Your friend Carla?"

"My friend Carla? What about my friend Carla?"

"How is she?"

"At home, happy with her new baby. Born last week. Four kilos, two hundred grams! Why? Xavi, you don't know Carla."

"Another Carla, I think."

"Carla Arespacochaga is the only Carla I know."

"A brunette? Very pretty? Miss Spain or something like that," Xavier said. There was a short pause.

"Oh my god. Carla Montenegro. What's going on?" she said.

"Did you give her my phone number?"

"Of course not! Has she called you? Stay away, Xavi. Do you hear me?"

"I had lunch with her yesterday. She said she was a good friend of yours so I took her to 21. You like it there."

"Achh! The little witch got a free lunch at my expense? Oh, I despise her! Pay attention to me. Have nothing to do with her!"

"How did she get my personal number?"

"I can't imagine."

"Think."

Begoña remembered Montenegro's last visit to the store.

"Wait. She was alone in my office for five minutes a couple of months ago. She could have looked in my agenda that I keep on my desk. Xavi, she is - how could I explain Carla Montenegro to you? Run, *hermano*,[105] in the other direction."

"It's too late, Begoña."

Begoña absorbed the information. She said in a low and horrified tone.

"Oh, Xavi. No. Please don't tell me that. For the love of God, tell me it's not true," she said.

"I have no excuse."

Xavier left out the details but described the situation accurately. Begoña worked for many celebrities and had practised law. She would know what to do. She listened carefully. She knew about the Spanish art show at the LaPlante Gallery and thought he had no choice but to go. Carla's first objective was always photos and visibility. She was a narcissist and addicted to fame. It might be dangerous to cross her so soon.

The best hypothesis was that she wanted a couple of free lunches and a date for the opening. She needed somebody to foot the bill for her New York expenses. Begoña didn't think that Xavier was a candidate for Carla's tabloid existence. He was Basque, he lived in New York, and had nothing to do with the social circles she moved in. He was very good looking but that wouldn't sell many magazines. A conservative, middle-aged Spanish banker with a paunch, for example, was a much better bet.

"Let her have a man on her arm for the pictures tonight," she said. "Spain is in fashion. They're trying to push our contemporary art in the States, but the event won't be too important. Queen Sofía was supposed to attend but her sister is having an operation or something and she has cancelled. I guess Irene LaPlante was quite upset. So the party pictures will be in the back pages of the magazines, the society pages, and that's innocent enough. Play it down and be careful. Go to the opening. Feed her stomach and her ego. She's an expert at not paying her bills so she'll appreciate that type of thing. And for the love of God, don't go to bed with her again! I'll be in Madrid in two days, so keep me informed. If it gets nasty, which I doubt because she's too afraid to be unmasked, we'll decide what to do. And Xavi, you have to do something about this problem of yours. Really. You're

---

105 brother

married now to a wonderful girl. You've been sleeping around since you were eleven! God almighty."

"Thirteen," he said in a weak attempt at self-defence.

Begoña didn't go on. He had called and asked for help. She knew he had to be suffering. A lot.

It was freezing. Carla appeared in a flimsy shawl and a thin, quasi-transparent white gown that resembled a negligée. Her nipples saluted high and hard against the material of the dress. She didn't need a bra as her breasts were two stiff, round sponges.

Carla wore her shoulder length hair in a wavy fifties style. She was so beautiful that even the daring gown seemed adolescent and pure. He tried to avoid pictures but to no avail. Her hand was a claw on his forearm. They stood for twenty seconds, which seemed like a century, in the blinding flashes of the cameras. He forcefully removed her hand and said, "This is your moment." He turned his back and climbed the stairs alone.

Of course, Carla Montenegro had no responsibility at all in the affair nor was she expected by the gallery owners. She was received with a measure of surprise, amusement, and condescension. She floated around the gallery, keeping a few steps ahead of the photographers, staring into space, pointing at paintings, and nodding daintily into the distance. Xavier spent a good deal of time in the corridor leading to the restrooms looking down at the floor.

The rest of the week was a battle to keep Carla neutralized. She called several times a day. He had opera tickets delivered to the hotel accompanied by a note saying that he would meet her at Lincoln Center. He never showed up but apologized profusely the next day pleading an emergency at work. He invited her to lunch again. He arrived late and left early. He was relieved, and a little surprised, that she didn't insist on any additional intimate encounters. She did swoon and sigh as she passed her fingers through his hair. Could he imagine what his life would be like if she were waiting for him at home every night? What were they to do about these strong feelings they had for each other?

At long last, Carla left on December 18. Xavier received a bill for thirty-five thousand dollars from the LaPlante Gallery for a painting by one of the emerging Spanish artists. The painting had been delivered to the New York Palace Hotel. To avoid any problems with the Art Gallery and to contain the disaster, he paid the bill. Begoña laughed and said that she thought that that was probably the the end of it.

"I like that artist. The painting should look nice with my dining room," she said, chuckling ironically.

An Aramburu Christmas

Xavier hardly slept on the flight to Madrid. He spent the last hour of the journey looking down at the patchwork countryside of Central Spain. He had heard nothing from Carla. The Christmas editions of the tabloids and the society magazines had come out on December 22. As Begoña had predicted, there were pictures of Carla at the gallery, but Xavier was not mentioned and was nowhere to be seen. Despite the reprieve, he felt tired and heavy. His sister was optimistic. It saddened him as he relived the events in his mind that, drugged or not, he would probably have slept with Carla Montenegro. He had answered the call and rushed to the hotel. To insist on justifying these things to himself as a harmless gratification of his pronounced sexual appetite was no longer possible. This was self-destructive. He had too much to lose.

It was six o'clock in the morning Madrid time when he arrived at his parents' apartment. He could hardly believe it when he crawled into bed with Adrienne. She wanted to get up and get breakfast, but he begged her just to lay on top of him and not move.

Christmas Eve was the traditional day that Begoña had wanted. They went to City Hall to visit the traditional *creche*.[106] The boys bought camels for their own *creche* at the Christmas market in Plaza Mayor.[107] They spent an infernal hour in the toy section of the Corte Inglés, Madrid's most popular department store, where Xavier bought the boys an enormous black automated spider. They skipped lunch in favour of a good *aperitivo*[108] at a seafood place where customers were six-deep at the bar. In the afternoon,

---

106 Nativity scene. Popular Spanish Christmas tradition.

107 Madrid's oldest square.

108 Light snacks before a meal.

Xavier and Adrienne took the boys skating to Retiro Park where groups of teenagers wandered about singing Christmas songs and playing the tambourine. To end the day, they sat down to a traditional Chrismas dinner around a beautifully decorated table. Abundant food, wine, and good cheer. And family. And love. Xavier was in a daze that everyone except Begoña attributed to jet lag.

Early on Christmas Day, they set out for Baqueira-Beret by car. They arrived just minutes after the exuberant and noisy Bilbao Aramburus. The two families greeted each other with loud enthusiasm in the hotel lobby.

As for Xavier, with every passing hour, the coffee tasted better, the sky was bluer, the snow was whiter, the air was sweeter. With every passing minute, he loved her more. The shadow of guilt and the fear of loss lifted like fog burning in the midday sun. By December 29, Xavier was a happy man, in love with his life, his family, and the present moment.

On December 30, Adrienne's birthday, the January issues appeared at the newstands. Carla had cashed in on the pictures. She had made the covers: *Carla Montenegro Finds Love Again in the Arms of Basque Millionaire*.

The picture is fuzzy and taken through a window. They are sleeping, spoonlike in the large bed. Carla is behind him and holding him in her arms. Their faces are perfect and serene. They are both so lovely you don't know which one to look at. The sheets are pulled up to show only naked shoulders. On the upper corner of the magazine cover, there is a darker photo of Carla in the Gilt Bar wearing the top hat, body to body with Xavier. There is a third, smaller picture of Carla in her jeans, chic bomber jacket, and sunglasses buying flowers at the Korean Grocery below Xavier and Adrienne's apartment. In smaller letters, the caption reads: *The couple will reside in Manhattan as millionaire Aramburu and heir to the Quiroga fortune is an objective of ETA terrorists.*

The pièce de résistance is in the cheaper adult magazines. Carla and Xavier are at the window. She is wearing a black corset as nipples are not suitable for a magazine cover. Her head is thrown back in ecstasy. He is crouching behind her about to bite her neck. His mouth is open. He is in the throes of passion.

Xavier was having coffee with his mother, Paloma, and his aunt and uncle in the hotel dining room. Adrienne and Begoña headed out early every day for ski school with Jon and Iñaki. Koldo's sister, Arantxa, and her husband, Anton, went their own way while Xavier and Koldo hit the more difficult slopes at around ten. The ski vacation was turning out to be a great success and Begoña had already reserved for the next year.

On the fateful December 30, Koldo waved from the door of the dining room to his cousin. Koldo preferred to go into town for breakfast. It was a quarter to ten.

"Xavi, come!" he said.

"Give me two minutes!" Xavier said, sipping at his coffee. He enjoyed these moments with the family. There were only two days left.

"Now," said Koldo very impatiently.

"What's your hurry?" Xavier said.

"Now. Come outside to the car. I need to show you something."

Xavier thought that there might be a problem with the car. Koldo was to drive them to the airport in Barcelona on January 2. They walked to the hotel parking lot. Xavier didn't notice the set of Koldo's jaw or see his fists in his pockets.

Koldo opened the trunk of the car abruptly. It was full of magazines. He had tried to buy all the copies in town but had run out of cash.

"What the fuck is this? What the fuck is this?" he repeated angrily, pointing to the pile of sleeping Xaviers and Carlas.

Xavier looked down into the trunk and saw Xavier the fool. He swallowed the bitter pill. He had contemplated the possibility and was prepared.

"You can beat me up later. *Primo*,[109] I need you now. Go get Adrienne and Begoña, and tell them to come down. You stay with the boys for the day and come back at four as usual. Don't alarm Adrienne. I need to tell her myself. Make something up. Tell her the *aitas* would like to have her join them for lunch in France."

Xavier picked up several copies and said, "Go, please."

Koldo violently closed the trunk of the car, took an angry step in Xavier's direction but changed his mind and got into the driver's seat. He rolled down the car window and said, "Xavi, how do you look at yourself in the

---

109 Cousin.

mirror, man? You're married. *Hostia*, you have Adrienne and you sleep with that slut? There has to be something wrong with you! *Hijo de puta!*"[110]

The families gathered in the hotel lounge every night at eight o'clock to go out for dinner. That night they came down early, nervous and eager to be together. Their lives were far from the subworld of Madrid's sleezy tabloids. All of a sudden and without pursuing it, the Aramburu name was on the cover of the country's best selling magazines. And worse yet, related to ETA. It was a public humiliation for Xavier. The gossip in Bilbao would be terrible. The older generation had not even heard of Carla. Xavier's father shook his head remembering the thirteen-year-old boy who had said, "I had the best fucking time of my life." He was resigned to the fact that his son would never be able to control his instincts.

Xavier's mother stayed with Paloma in her room. Xavier and Adrienne went to see her first before going downstairs to talk to the family. Everyone heaved a sigh of relief when they walked into the hotel lounge hand in hand. Begoña relaxed, assuming that they had decided to weather the storm. Xavier's face was serious. Adrienne kissed all of them one by one and received comforting hugs and kisses in return. It was her birthday. Begoña gave the boys some coins to play pinball in the recreation room.

And then silence. It was cousin Arantxa who broke the ice. She had always been a bright and straightforward girl. In her deep, husky voice, she spoke while wagging her finger at her cousin. Xavier couldn't help smiling.

"*Primo*,[111] Begoña told us what happened. OK. You put your foot in it. Really deep. You really did, but it was a trap! It could have happened to anybody."

Her husband Anton, who was a modern and sophisticated young man, a publicist for Bilbao's most important advertising agency, was dying to say something. His foot shook nervously. He was still in awe of his wife's powerful family. The conversation was serious and personal, but he decided his opinion was important and spoke.

"Xavi, I've had to deal with these people and they're very good at what they do. You were manipulated. I've been analyzing the pictures. I wouldn't

---

110 Son of a bitch.
111 Cousin.

be surprised at all if you had been drugged. As a matter of fact, I'm sure of it. If you like, I'll show you exactly how they organized it. The angles of the pictures. Everything. That photographer is well-known. They call him 'The Vulture.' Every professional knows what happened here. Really."

Xavier twitched slightly, surprised and thankful for the small vindication of Anton's correct supposition. Anton noticed Xavier's involuntary reaction and said proudly to his young wife, "Look, I told you! I was sure of it!"

Begoña was furious with the detestable Carla.

"This doesn't end here. I'm quite sure that we can take her to court for, at the very least, invasion of privacy. I may sue her for my dining room and Xavi can sue for the painting she made him pay for. I heard the gallery received her hotel bill. It won't do anything for Xavier's reputation but at least it will expose her for what she is. She will probably sell their sad break-up in the next issue and that will be it. She needs to feed her legend. You would be surprised to know how much they pay her for this trash. It sells magazines."

While not defending her brother, Begoña had spent the day trying to put things into perspective. The circumstances were extenuating. She had told her own story with the infamous Carla. Xavier had to speak. He and Adrienne had discussed what they would do.

"Arantxa, *cariño*,[112] and Anton, thank you," he said. "But the truth is that it happened and there's nothing I can do except live with it. I am very upset and I apologize for any consequences this might have for you. Drugged or not, I will tell you that I was a fool and that I knew it right away. So, let's come to now. There's already papparazzi outside the hotel. Adrienne and I will have dinner here in the dining room and leave tomorrow morning early. And..." Xavier paused and put his hand on his forehead. "Adrienne has decided to leave me, which I surely deserve. So that's it. We leave early tomorrow. We came down to say goodbye. I'm so sorry to upset you."

The group's respectful countenance up to that point broke into a loud exclamatory presence. They did not expect or want to accept such a drastic and final outcome. Begoña felt responsible and was heartbroken. Her hand over her mouth, she looked down at the floor. Iñaki took Adrienne's hand

---

112 Sweetheart. Colloquial and frequent term of endearment.

and said, "Take some time, Adrienne. I hope you can forgive him. He loves you very much. And you know how we love you. What can we do?"

Adrienne stood up to give her father-in-law a hug. It only occurred to her to say, "I'm so sorry we've ruined this wonderful vacation." She had not yet shed a tear. She let out a single hiccup of sorrow. Xavier tried to grab her hand but Koldo reached her first and put his arms around her.

"You're sorry?" he said. "It's Xavi who should be sorry, Adrienne. You do what you have to do. I am here for you."

They hardly spoke between Baqueira and New York but stayed close to each other like a couple in a multitude who fear being separated.

At the apartment, he helped her pack. He got her suitcases from the storage room. He found a large box for her shoes and boots. He sat on the bed while she emptied her drawers. When the red shoes she was wearing the first time they made love came out of the closet, he grabbed her wrist.

"You still have them?"

"Yes. I love them. Every time I see them, well, you know what I think about."

He let himself fall back onto the bed. He reached for a pillow and hugged it to his chest. As she folded her things, Xavier looked up at the ceiling.

"I should have left you alone. I wanted to. I tried," he said.

"That's true, Xavi. But I didn't let you. You didn't blindfold me. You warned me. I knew what I was getting into. And Xavi, I accepted it. Did you think I didn't know? The first time was in Chicago wasn't it?" she asked.

Adrienne smiled as she remembered her own determination and stubbornness. She folded another blouse carefully.

"And I was happy. That was you. My beautiful Xavier. I was being so modern and progressive. True love doesn't have rules, I told myself."

Xavier let out an unhappy moan. Adrienne stopped packing, sat down on the bed, and stared at the wall as she spoke. Xavier deserved to know the simple truth.

"The pictures have pushed me over a cliff. I'm letting myself fall because I know it is irreversible. This is not good for me, for us. Maybe my love is not as unconditional as I thought it was. I can't ask you to change. I refuse to ask you to change. That wouldn't work either. We are a broken thing. Can we put the pieces back together? Maybe. But I don't want us to live with such an ugly scar. So now? I had you. We had each other. And it's over. I have no regrets and I swear to you that I would do it again. I don't think I will ever love anyone the way I have loved you. I will miss you. That is all there is."

Xavier knew Adrienne was not weighing her words. She was not playing for time or trying to punish him. This was definite. It was over. He had destroyed the most important thing he had ever had. He had what he deserved: a broken thing. He screamed into his hands in rage. Then he left the room. In one month, it would have been four years since they had met in Montréal.

Adrienne checked into the Wesley Hotel while she considered where she would live.

When she returned to work on January 3, she waited impatiently for Patrick to come into the office. He was late as usual.

"Happy New Year! I see Blanchard is back!" he said cheerfully as he took off his hat and coat.

"Happy New Year! Patrick?" Patrick looked up expectantly. "Could we have lunch today?"

Part Five

The Red Saddlebag Man

Adrienne confided in Patrick, who showed no surprise at all at the events. However, he was surprised by Adrienne's reaction. No depression, no apathy, no insecurity, no anger. He sensed only a sadness or disappointment that she had translated into a strange mental hyperactivity. She was not looking for consolation or sympathy. Ideas and plans tumbled out of her mouth. Was there a possibility of being transferred to Europe? Or maybe she should go back to school? What did he think? How did one go about requesting a leave of absence? Maybe she could go to Africa to work for his wells foundation? She had lots of good ideas. She had always loved that project. Adrienne was charging blindly into the future like a runaway locomotive. Obviously, Patrick observed, she had closed a door that Xavier Aramburu might never be able to reopen.

Patrick needed to slow her down. He didn't want to lose her. She was an asset to the United Nations: a well balanced individual, a persevering worker, a good linguist, a creative mind, an excellent communicator. He did see her as his successor, at least in an official manner. He told her to be patient while she made a positive transition to this new stage in her life. Her separation had nothing to do with her career, he insisted. They would think of something if she really thought that she needed a change professionally.

Patrick shook his head. The Whaler had just made the worst mistake of his life. He would tell him so if he ever had the opportunity. Indeed, Patrick thought it was for the best.

Soon after, he proposed something to Adrienne that appealed to her. Under the auspices of the UN, she would be sent to the American University of Beirut for a three-month intensive Arabic language and civilization course.

True Identity

This would reinforce the Arabic-speaking presence in the department which was sorely needed. For Adrienne, it would be language number five. Professionally, she was looking forward to pushing through in Arabic. She had two years of the language at the UN Institute under her belt and knew that a good immersion would bring her close to fluency. It would be a great advantage for work regardless of the direction she chose, and a fascinating experience. Adrienne packed her bags.

And she did fall in love again, with the city of Beirut. She hadn't expected it to be so beautiful. After a long and terrible civil war, it was a mutilated and dangerous place but at sunset it was covered with a golden veil. Cradled between the mountains and the Mediterranean, its past glory shone through the ruins. It was a crossroads of East and West, of religions, of races, of customs, architecture, and even cuisine. She loved its contradictions and its chaos, its smells, its electricity. More than New York, to Adrienne, Beirut felt like the centre of the world.

Patrick kept an eye on Adrienne through a colleague. Khalil Haddad was a pilot in the Lebanese Air Force but in reality, he was number fourteen of the CIA in the region. Initially irritated about the "babysitting job," his face changed when he saw the winsome Adrienne walk out of the university gates. He became her friend and her guide beyond the call of duty. He took her out for dinner, to bookstores, on picnics, and to outdoor concerts. He showed her extraordinarily beautiful Roman ruins but also the refugee camps on the outskirts of the city. He introduced her to his French grandmother. He loved his city and his country and introduced Adrienne to it with grace, humour, and generosity.

The American University was a sophisticated and brilliant place to study. She never missed a class and took advantage of all the cultural events. She studied hard and made great progress. She made interesting friends and was sorry to leave. Thus, a more serene Adrienne returned to her desk at the UN and to a new life without Xavier.

To keep her restlessness at bay, Patrick frequently sent her to interpret on confidential assignments abroad. As far as he was concerned, she had a high security clearance.

Adrienne was fine. Time, relentless but healing, passed.

It was June 1992 in Amsterdam. She sat at the same table every day. She was in the beautiful breakfast room of the Pulitzer Hotel in Amsterdam's Jordaan neighbourhood. The Pulitzer was on the picturesque Prinzengracht Canal but the dining room looked out on the narrow, cobblestone Reestraat. The street was so narrow and the café so close to the street, she could see the rings on the fingers of the Amsterdamians as they rode by on their bicycles.

She could make out the objects through the dusty shop windows across the street. Directly opposite her table, there was a quaint old haberdashery. She would buy a hat before she left. They had a natural straw Panama hat with a red ribbon in the window. She might give it to Clo for her birthday. If she could manage it, she'd stop in London on the way home to spend a night with her sister. Beside the hat shop, there was an antique and second-hand watch dealer. She stopped by the watch dealer every day to look at one watch in particular. It was a 1960s Rolex Daytona like the one Paul Newman wore. She knew he would love it. He had shown her a picture of it once in a magazine.

Adrienne daydreamed about giving Xavier exquisite gifts in odd places where she would bump into him by chance. A restaurant, the subway, a museum, a party, a store. "Oh Xavier, I thought you would like this," she would say nonchalantly. She would give him the gift, he would love it and demand she have sex with him then and there. They would make dirty, passionate love hiding in corners, alleys, stairways, and tunnels. He would tear at her blouse and suck at her breasts. She would hold his head while she watched his girlfriend in the distance.

Adrienne sighed and shook her head, scolding herself for her adolescent sexual fantasies. Xavier was surely not fantasizing about her. It had been a year and a half since they separated. She had signed the divorce papers and they were waiting for the final decree.

On this occasion in Amsterdam, she was to interpret in discreet negotiations between Salvadorans, Russians, Cubans, and Americans to find a way to split the pie in Central America. She was amused that the location of the negotiations happened to be the home of the Canadian ambassador. So far, the ambassador had told her with a smile when she had gone to visit the venue, the delegations seemed to be negotiating in the red-light district and smoking the peace pipe in the coffee shops. The negotiation table was set but the Cubans had not arrived. Adrienne wore an electronic bracelet controlled by the American delegate. When it vibrated at any moment of the day or night, she would make her way immediately to the neutral location of the negotiations. The delegations waited impatiently for the Cubans to show up.

Adrienne was in a beautiful hotel in a great city and she was fine with that. She had a routine that began with a leisurely breakfast from eight to nine. She looked out from her favourite window to the spectacle on the street. The Dutch rode bicycles with no regard for safety or caution. They drove too fast. They rode with no hands. They carried their helmetless babies in bicycle baskets and pulled their pets behind them in wooden carts. They held their coffee cup in one hand. They spread the newspaper out on the handlebars. Sometimes, they did this all at the same time. It did not seem to fit such a civilized nation.

She amused herself by practising her memory and observation skills. A beautiful young black woman wearing a pale blue turban caught her attention. Adrienne checked her watch. It was 8:19. She saw her twice. The next day, she was a bit later: 8:21. A lady in a hopelessly old-fashioned tie-dye dress who had decorated her bicycle and hat with plastic daisies was close behind on both days. Obviously, the same people at approximately the same time every day. The Reestraat was on their way to work.

Another distinguishing element of the bicycles of Amsterdam was the saddlebags. While the bicycles were all very similar, the saddlebags showed personal preferences. The European flag. Bob Marley's effigy. Snoopy. One man who followed close behind the daisy woman at 8:45 had very nice red patent leather bags with a black-and-white checkered flag in the centre, Formula 1 Grand-Prix style. She liked those.

The Blue Turban 8:19.

The Daisy Lady 8:45.

The Red Saddlebag Man 8:46.

On day four at 8:48, the red saddlebag man pulled over on the narrow curb. He took out a pack of cigarettes and a lighter from his shirt pocket. He was so close that, had there not been a window, she could have touched him. As he raised his Zippo to light the cigarette, the long sleeve of his shirt fell away to expose his left arm. He had burn scars from wrist to elbow. Adrienne, incredulous, looked up at his face.

Clear as day. No doubt about it. Michel Bourgeois.

Adrienne's Pursuit

It was Michel. Out of the blue. Her father's face flashed inside her head.

She showed no surprise. As an interpreter she had learned to keep a neutral tone and expression at all times, no matter what the obscenity or the barbarity of the threat. The sun was shining on the window. He would see only his own reflection. She had the privilege of the voyeur. She could see him, but he could not see her.

He took four long drags on his cigarette before making up his mind to continue on his way. She accumulated all the information she could in that short minute. It had been nineteen years since she had seen him. He was a pleasant-looking young man with light brown hair, a narrow face, a small mouth, a classical nose, and brown eyes. She didn't understand how she had not recognized him the day before and the day before that. He hadn't changed very much. She observed him carefully and came to her own Sherlock Holmes-esque conclusions.

He smoked Dutch cigarettes. He was dressed very casually. Nothing was ironed. His hair was growing out of a good cut. He didn't have a nice mustache. It was too pale and sparse. He was thin but out of shape. He had narrow shoulders and a flat, concave chest. He was pale and hadn't shaved for a couple of days. His hands looked rough. He wore an expensive brand of glasses and running shoes. His eyes were dull. Perhaps they showed his age more than anything else. A pack of Bulldog rolling papers stuck out of his back pocket. He rubbed his neck and sat back on his bicycle seat. He stretched one leg and then the other. He was not in a hurry. He leaned back and exhaled his last drag very slowly. He filled his lungs with the smoke and exhaled it with gusto. Michel Bourgeois really enjoyed that cigarette, but he didn't know that it would change his life.

From all of that, Adrienne presumed that he lived in Amsterdam. He probably worked indoors but not in an office. Maybe he wore a uniform over his clothes. He followed a poor diet. He lived alone and worked hard. He was not poor. He did not take very good care of himself. He frequented Amsterdam's coffee shops. He was apathetic as to his circumstances but felt secure. She was right on every count.

When he flicked his cigarette to the ground and raised his foot to the pedal, Adrienne got to her feet. There was a door to the street on her left. She judged the time lapse so as not to run into him. She wasn't ready to confront him. She would follow him by sight as long as she could. Through the window she saw him turn left. She hurried out of the café. She was so close that if she had shouted "Michel" he might have turned around. She could have but she didn't. She half ran, half skipped down the narrow sidewalk and watched him turn right at the next bridge over the Keizergracht Canal. He continued on straight ahead.

He was riding in the direction of Central Amsterdam when she lost him. There was no mistake. It was Michel. Adrienne had a dark premonition. She put her hand on her stomach. It would not be the happy end to a curious local mystery as in a television show with an amusing amateur detective. It would be a painful catharsis for several innocent people.

She did not rush to her room and set out to find Michel immediately. Instead, she went back to her table and stared out the window. She was not seeing the watch or the hat or the colourful inhabitants of Amsterdam. She examined her possible courses of action and reflected on her own responsibility. Should she leave well enough alone, or do what had to be done? All options were debatable. One thing could be foreseen: it was not in Adrienne's nature to look away.

She retraced Michel's route to the spot where she had lost him. It was a busy artery that converged on Dam Square four blocks up. He could have taken a side street from there, but it was logical to think that he had been going straight to the central square where, from the route he had taken, he would be headed west. *What was west of Dam Platz?* The red-light district, the coffee shops. She recalled the pack of Bulldogs and sighed. Unfortunately, it fit.

She had a capuccino at a café on the square and thought it out. Nobody goes to coffee shops at nine in the morning. For one thing, they are not open. He was going to work just like everybody else. He had worked at Bright's. He was a cook. It made sense. He had been hiding in kitchens for twenty years. A good place to hide if you thought about it. She decided against roaming around central Amsterdam searching for a needle in a haystack. She needed a day to think. At least, his whereabouts were now known. Perhaps unconsciously, she wanted to give Michel one more day to run away and disappear. She now knew what René, who ignored the letters, may have felt. However, it was her father's unfinished business. She felt she had no choice.

Adrienne had lunch at the flower market. She visited the Widows' Garden and the bookstores near the old law faculty of the University of Amsterdam. On the way back to the hotel, she stopped at the haberdashery to buy the hat and ask the watch dealer for a business card. When the sun was setting on Amsterdam's rooftops, she put on the simple black dress that she wore when interpreting at gala dinners. She broke the rule never to drink alcohol while on call. She nursed a gin and tonic in the bar before dinner and then sat alone at a table for two in the elegant hotel restaurant.

She treated herself to an expensive bordeaux. Adrienne wondered if Xavier kept some bottles of Rioja at his new girlfriend's house. He was dating an Asian American political journalist who lived in Washington. He met her at a dinner at the Perry's. Pat Perry had apologized profusely to Adrienne, explaining that the woman had been extremely forward and insistent. She had literally begged for an invitation. Nicole Polk was very well-known, classy, and brilliant. She had a reputation for being blunt and conservative. She appeared weekly on a television political affairs program. Adrienne couldn't help watching the show. She detested the woman's nasal accent.

Nicole was short, delicate, and flat-chested. Her face was exquisite. She had very fine and perfect Asian features. She was Adrienne's opposite. She had posed beside him on the steps of the White House for the Press Corps dinner like a triumphant athlete with her trophy. Her artificial and condescending smile irritated Adrienne so much that she had come very close to getting the keys to the apartment and showing up on his doorstep. Their doorstep. Nicole infuriated her whereas Carla just made her sad.

Adrienne didn't know that Nicole had been relentless in her pursuit and had seduced him with sexual games.

Adrienne had given Xavier up like an addict gives up drugs or alcohol: painfully. Needing to but not wanting to. She saw him often. They had lunch every two weeks under the pretense that they were not yet divorced and had financial affairs in common. She was entitled to half of all he had earned during their marriage, but she wanted nothing. Xavier insisted on buying her an apartment in Manhattan in exchange for half the house in Formentera. She accepted. It would have been an act of foolishness to refuse. He never begged for sympathy but as they said goodbye, he would hold her in his arms one second too long, brush his lips over her ear, and say, "Please forgive me."

A reconciliation might still be in her hands, but Adrienne was sure that it would be doomed to fail. He was, she was sure, the love of her life, but the pictures with Carla had simply broken her heart. It was also true that as time passed, Adrienne had found a place without him. Life without Xavier had other objectives, other goals, and even other pleasures. And she was still very young. Life was pulling at her.

In the meantime, Xavier did not let the Blanchard family go. He went kayaking in Colorado with Lilly. In Boston, he bought a junior sailboat for Catherine and Valerie and drove it all the way up to Crane Road in July, precariously attached to the roof of Judge Powell's old Oldsmobile. Claude used the house on Formentera with Jean Pierre and gave Adrienne speeches on the virtues of sexual freedom and open marriages. René, Jocelyne, and the girls visited New York and stayed at Xavier's, as Adrienne was still living in a small studio while waiting for the new apartment to be finished. All of the Blanchards, including her mother and feminist Lilly, considered the circumstances of Xavier's infidelity a sleazy trap.

"When are you and Uncle Xavi going to get back together?" little Valerie pouted. "He says we're all going to go to Formentera to celebrate. Can it be soon please?"

The Aramburus were less willing to forgive. Begoña and Koldo were Adrienne's avenging angels. Begoña would have nothing to do with *"La*

China"[113] and Koldo broke off all contact with Xavier. Koldo wined and dined Adrienne for a full week when he came to New York. He ranted over the call girl, the oversexed banker, and the fascist journalist. Xavier was furious. The cousins had always had a territorial issue over Adrienne and now it had finally surfaced.

The last time she saw Xavier, he was serious and severe. He could have been angry because he learned Adrienne had a lover. Adrienne was sleeping with Khalil Haddad.

Khalil had been waiting for her outside her building with a huge intricately wrapped box of chocolates one night the previous November. His teeth were chattering in the awful cold. It was totally unexpected. She had been delighted to see him.

"You're freezing, *Habibi*.[114] Come inside!" she said.

He smiled widely and rushed boyishly to her side, carefully balancing his extravagant gift. He had an Arab face. Fierce in repose, tender and beguiling in laughter. He didn't come often and he made no demands. She never knew where he was. His life's mission was another.

After her gin and tonic, solitary dinner, and bottle of wine, Adrienne walked as steadily as she could to the lobby and asked the concierge to organize a bicycle rental for the following morning at 8:00 a.m. She thanked God the Cubans were such pains in the neck. Her bracelet hadn't vibrated. She went to bed and slept uneasily.

The next day was a Saturday. At ten past eight, she was waiting on a street corner slightly off the Raadhuisstraat, two blocks from Dam Platz. It would be a warm day but at 8.00 a.m., it was cool. She wore sunglasses, blue jeans, sandals, a white tee-shirt, and a white blazer. She had a blue knapsack on her back and she wore a white baseball hat with her ponytail sticking out of the back opening. This was Adrienne at thirty. She had been eleven years old the last time he had seen her. She doubted he would recognize her inmediately. She kept her eyes on the bicycles filing by. There would be no blue turban or daisy lady today; she had to concentrate. He caught

---

113 The Chinese woman.

114 Arabic (affectionate term): Friend, Buddy, chum.

her off guard. She almost missed him while sipping casually on her cup of coffee. He was early: 8:26.

She turned into Raadhuisstraat and followed at a cautious distance. Michel beat a streetcar into Dam Platz but Adrienne had to wait for it to pass. He was now all the way across the square. She pumped the pedals and managed to stay with him. He was zigzagging through old Amsterdam. Some streets were barely six feet wide. There were fewer bicycles in the area. She had to be much more careful. At one point, she had to risk losing him. The pursuit would have been too obvious. He was riding more slowly now and reaching into his breast pocket for his cigarettes. He was probably approaching his destination. She slowed down to keep a safe distance.

The bracelet vibrated twice. "Damn!" she exclaimed.

She memorized where she was, made a full turn, and headed directly for the Canadian ambassador's residence. She didn't need to go back to the hotel to change. She had carefully folded a blouse and a skirt into her backpack, just in case. She reached the meeting place in twenty-one minutes. She had met the delegate before. He was a mature and handsome, high-ranking marine. He was in uniform, leaning on his official car, waiting on the street in front of the residence. She got off her bicycle and stood beside it holding the handlebars. They shook hands. It was a short, informal message. There was no meeting that day.

"So, enjoying Amsterdam are you ma'am? Adrienne is it? Nice name," he said.

"Yes, Adrienne Blanchard. And yes, I am enjoying Amsterdam. Beautiful city," she said.

The colonel wanted to chat. He was flirting with the interpreter. This was unfortunately common and one of the downsides of the business for Adrienne. It took a good twenty minutes to get away. She tried to be nice but distant. Fortunately, the marine was also a gentleman and understood the signals. The good news was she didn't have to work. They were giving "these Cuban clowns" four more days – until the following Wednesday. If they didn't sit down, the negotiations would be aborted. Adrienne was relieved. Four days. She could concentrate on Michel. The next day was Sunday and she worried about that. He might not go to work. She headed back to the red-light district with the determination to find Michel

Bourgeois and to confront him that very day. She told herself that things might even turn out fine.

She left her bicycle where she had lost him and walked the streets, keeping a geometrical order. Amsterdamians park their bicycles anywhere and everywhere. They chain them to trees, lampposts, monuments, trash cans, or any other inanimate object. Adrienne combed the streets looking for the bicycle with the red saddlebags. This was a waste of time because Michel had bought himself an expensive bike, which meant he stored it carefully in the alley behind his small takeout food outlet. He used it only to go to and from his place of work. The prostitute, coffee shop, and bar he frequented were close by. He picked it up in the evening when he was ready to go back to his apartment in a working-class neighbourhood of Amsterdam. Around noon, Adrienne started to get impatient. She had walked up and down the same streets several times and had found no trace of the bicycle or Michel. Convinced that he was close by, she was reluctant to take her search to the contiguous neighbourhood, which was dull and industrial.

The sex trade was not as obvious on the main streets but on the side streets where Adrienne searched, there were rows and rows of full-length windows on each side of the street and on every floor of the buildings. Each window was occupied by a semi-nude woman of every shape, race, and age. Some sat in boredom, others preened and gesticulated. Adrienne was reminded of a zoo. For the ladies in the windows of Amsterdam, a pretty girl was a welcome change from the traditional customer: a foul-smelling, unattractive male. They wagged their tongues at Adrienne, carressed their own breasts, and blew her kisses. Adrienne avoided looking into the windows as she tried to find a piece of the puzzle to her family's past.

What was Michel Bourgeois doing in such a place? If his mother had imagined her son living a middle-class suburban life somewhere in the United States, she was very mistaken. The truth was, that despite the unsavoury neighbourhood, he was doing well. He owned his own business called Stowaway's Fish and Chips, and it was quite popular. He had two employees and a regular clientele. As Adrienne had deduced, he lived alone, worked hard, and was not poor.

Everything had gone according to the Dutch captain's plan. He had returned to a comfortable and profitable European route for three years and then retired to a small villa in Mallorca. He bought a yacht that he chartered for day trips to rich German tourists. Before he left, he had felt the obligation to help his loyal and discreet employee, Cook, who had been with him for ten years. Cook, a.k.a. Brian, a.k.a. Michel, did not wish to re-embark with another captain and needed some kind of livelihood. The captain sensed Michel's difficult circumstances. He was a seaman with no past, no family, and no plans.

He took Michel in hand and helped him start fresh in Holland. Working under the Dutch flag, Michel had been paying into the Netherlands Seafarer's Union and was eligible for an assisted rental housing unit in Amsterdam. It was a very comfortable and cheerful place in an experimental housing development designed by a famous architect on the outskirts of Amsterdam. The captain had negotiated it all. It was Michel's first home since the apartment he had shared with his mother as a young boy. The captain gave him a framed picture of the ship as a souvenir. Michel carefully nailed it to the wall. He also hung a calendar. It was June 1992 but the calendar was on the September 1990 page. It was a picture of the Iguazú waterfalls.

Brian Gordon Ogilvy was also a legal resident of the Netherlands. On arriving in Europe five years before, the captain had sponsored Brian's permanent residency papers. Technically, the man with no home had three nationalities.

But by far the most important thing that the captain did for Cook was to invest in a small, street-level commercial property in old Amsterdam. It was perfect for a fast-food takeout in a neighbourhood that the millions of tourists who came to Amsterdam each year never failed to visit. He rented it to Michel for three years for a symbolic amount to cover municipal taxes and co-op fees. As the ship was to be refurbished by the buyer, he arranged to have Cook's professional galley kitchen moved to its new home in Amsterdam. Michel was set. He had saved about 50 percent of his salary over the years and could afford to open his own business.

The Dutch captain weighed 250 pounds. He was bald, jowly, and suffered from gout, but he was the closest to a fairy godmother Michel had ever had.

She had noticed Stowaway's Fish and Chips on one of the quieter side streets. It looked like a good place for street food. Michel had worked at Bright's in Moncton but fish and chips with different sauces were also popular in

True Identity

Amsterdam. She didn't automatically assume he worked there. She checked anyway. There was a sandwich board on the street with the day's specials nicely printed in chalk:

Soup of the day: Spanish Gazpacho

Salad of the day: Moroccan Tabbouleh

Cookie of the day: White Chocolate and Macadamia

She peered inside. The kitchen was in plain sight. A dark-haired man was serving the soup into transparent plastic bowls and fitting the bowls with a lid. It was probably run by Arabs, she thought. Adrienne didn't peer inside long enough. Michel was in the tiny supply room unpacking soup containers. The second time she walked by at half past twelve, there was a line-up outside. Some tourists, mostly locals. She decided that Amsterdam was probably not the best place to have gazpacho or tabbouleh and settled on a greasy pizza slice from down the street.

Michel specialized in five things: breaded, deep fried cod, crispy French fries, soups, salads and cookies. The fish and chips were always available but he varied the soups, salads, and cookies daily. His supplies were delivered early, he did his cooking and baking, and then opened shop from eleven to six. Joao, a retired Brazilian seaman who lived in the neighbourhood, came in to help at rush hour from twelve to two. Joao's wife came in from five to seven to help Michel close and clean up while he did his ordering and administrative work. He was doing fine. He had a good reputation, good clients, money in the bank, and no problems. At night, there were lots of places to get stoned and listen to music. Amsterdam was a city of dark cafés filled with foggy-minded loners who didn't ask questions.

He had noticed Adrienne that morning but he had not recognized her. He saw her as she had seen him, through the window. She was looking around like a curious tourist wearing a baseball hat and sunglasses. Michel chuckled when Margie, the prostitute who occupied the window across the street, blew her a kiss. The exasperated girl had looked away impatiently. He liked Margie. She called him Soup Man. She bought two bowls of soup every night before she went home. One for her and one for her mother. At three or so, he always made sure to put two portions aside in case he ran out.

At half past two, Adrienne was retracing her route for the fourth and last time. She was ready to give up. She could always flag him down in the street the next morning. Although she did not like the idea, it might be necessary.

The pompous balloon of her desire to be a saviour had deflated. Maybe the best thing to do was to keep it to herself. He would have returned if he had wanted to. Was it so unacceptable to respect an innocent man who had chosen to flee? Her father had. The alternative was to call Interpol or the Dutch Police. She didn't like either idea. It felt too violent, too cold. A letter or a call to the Moncton Police might be the safest. But for Michel, it might backfire into a long and painful process. She was sure of his innocence. Adrienne wanted him to return to Moncton and turn himself in. That was where it had happened. That was where it mattered. And that's what her father would have wanted as well. She had to take him home.

She looked up the street where Stowaway's was. She saw the sign, remembered the cookie, and felt the urge for a sweet. She hoped they might serve coffee as well. Momentarily, she forgot Michel.

She saw him as she was about to walk in. He had his back to the door. He was squatting down to refill the drinks cooler, which was in the customer space on the street side of the counter. He was stacking the water bottles, the juices, and the soft drinks.

She backed up and got out of sight. This was it. She took off her hat and her sunglasses, pulled the elastic band from her ponytail, and let her hair hang long. She looked at her reflection in a window. He would know who she was when she told him.

The Language of Memory

His back was turned. The voice was soft. It couldn't be real.

"Michel," Adrienne said.

It was more than a name. It was a place and a time. He was afraid to move. The voice came again.

"Michel Bourgeois," she spoke again.

He got up slowly and turned to the voice. His eyes looked up from behind his glasses. He didn't speak.

"Adrienne Blanchard. Moncton," Adrienne introduced herself.

"Ah."

No thunderclap, no burst of gunfire, no pack of dogs. He picked up the box off the floor. It was heavy. He walked around the counter and set it down on his work area. He shook his head but the ghost was still there. It hadn't moved. It was not a momentary hallucination. It was the little sister. He wiped his face with his hands and adjusted his glasses.

"Je t'ai trouvé,"[115] she said.

"C'est ça que ça ressemble,"[116] he responded.

It came automatically but speaking French sounded strange even to his own ears. It was as if he had been given the gift of an ancient tongue. Michel stepped into a new place in his life. The after. The arrival. It had been nineteen years in transit from then to now.

"Nobody is sending me, Michel. I'm in Amsterdam for work. I saw you by chance through a café window. Driving by on your bicycle. I followed you," Adrienne said.

"Yeah. I saw that. You've been roaming around all morning," he said.

---

115 I found you.

116 That's what it looks like.

Adrienne grasped the moment. He had accepted her presence and he had admitted his identity. She had thought about what she would like to hear if she were in his position.

"Your mother's very well. So is Ron. Still running the taxis," she said. "Gary's a mechanic, a good one they say. Mary Ann's doing her master's at the University. In education, I think, but I'm not sure. Maybe psychology. I don't know if you know all this stuff, but I'm telling you anyway."

Michel rocked back and forth on his heels. He was behind his counter. He looked over her head to the street. The sun was shining but he was standing in the soft, nourishing rain of news of his family and the sound of his language. A customer came in.

"One gazpacho and two pieces of fish, please."

Adrienne stepped aside. Michel robotically dispatched the order. The customer gave him twenty gilders. It came to $f8.50$. Michel stared at the amount on the cash register. His dislocated brain was unable to make the mathematical calculation. The customer finally said, "Excuse me? I get $f11.50$ back, I think."

"Sorry, sorry," Michel said.

He struggled to come back to the immediate reality of the simple arithmetic. He gave the man his change. Adrienne closed the door behind the customer as he left and turned the open sign over to closed.

"Your father?" Michel asked.

"He died not long after you left. Heart attack, shoveling the snow one morning."

"I didn't know. Sorry."

"It's okay. A long time ago now. We all left Moncton. My mother's in Québec. René's in Ottawa."

The doctor was dead. The empty house. That's what had happened. That explained a lot of things. He wasn't sure if it would have changed anything, but he wished he had known. Then he reached for a cigarette.

"Smoke?"

"No thank you."

To Adrienne, suddenly, things were clear.

Xavier would say: "Leave the man alone."

Khalil would say: "Turn him in."

Patrick would say: "Do what is good for you and your family."
Philippe would say: "Give him a choice and then help him."
That's what she decided to do.
"What are we going to do, Michel?"
He exhaled a long column of smoke. He pushed his tongue into his top lip and said, "What are we going to do? What do I know? Isn't it always the Blanchards who decide?"

A low blow. She ignored it. She put the backpack on a stool and took out her white blazer and bottle of water. She took a long gulp of the water, screwed the plastic cap back on tightly, and then put on the jacket very deliberately. She put on her hat, arranged her hair behind her ears, put on her sunglasses, and adjusted the backpack carefully. All the while, she was searching the place for information. She read his false name and memorized his business identification number on a food manipulation licence on the wall. She had been looking for it.

"We have to talk. You close at six. I'll come back to pick you up. We can have a beer somewhere," she said.

"Whatever," he said in English as if it were of no importance.

She switched the sign back to "open," pushed on the door, and looked back at him. As she walked out, she also switched to English and said in a defiant tone, "Michel? Sorry, Brian, right? Whatever. I have proof of your innocence if you're interested." She walked out of the place and didn't look back.

She intentionally was not punctual. She arrived at 6:20. If he had not been there, she might have halted her pursuit. Michel had not run away. He had closed early and was leaning on the door having a cigarette. For the rest of the afternoon, he had been a pack of nerves. He both dreaded and waited impatiently for the meeting with Adrienne. He had had a taste of home and it wasn't enough. He needed more.

Michel believed her. They had their faults, but you could trust the Blanchards. No one had sent her. René knew his false name, but René would not look for him, he was sure. She had found him by chance. He felt dizzy with probable change, but he didn't sense an imminent threat to his freedom. This didn't stop his heart from pounding.

It was very smart of her to arrive late. As the minutes passed and Adrienne didn't show up, he felt cheated. Abandoned by the Blanchards again. She came up the narrow street on foot and waved to him. Michel acknowledged the wave with a lateral lean of his head and a raised chin as he exhaled the smoke of his thirtieth cigarette of the day through his nose. The prey was thankful to see the trapper.

"Hi Michel! Bet you really need a good drink right now!" she said.

She greeted him in a light tone to lessen the drama. She needed to rewind, to start again. He exhaled the smoke through his nose and managed an ironic smile.

"You could be right," he said.

He was relieved that she chose to speak English. French no longer came naturally to him. His vocabulary failed him. His tongue felt thick and heavy pronouncing the delicate words. Adrienne had sensed that. She juggled the languages in her own interest. French made him remember. English made him talk.

"Which way?" she said.

He pointed south. "Not bad places down there but food's not great in Amsterdam," he said, shrugging.

"That's fine," said Adrienne.

They walked slowly down the street, uncomfortable with each other.

"So you're not too crazy about the food here?" Adrienne attempted small talk.

"No. Well, I've been around so you know…"

"Hmmm, Michel," she took a darkly humourous tone. "Now that's really, really good. You won't mind my asking: Where around? Just curiosity, mind you!"

He pursed his lips and blew into the air. "All over."

Adrienne prodded him gently. She said "Michel" and looked into his eyes every time she addressed him. On that evening with Adrienne, Michel was unchained from Brian. He experienced the liberation and peace of his true identity. After a beer and a joint, he fell into a gentle euphoria. He needed to tell his story. His life spilled out like a sudden cloudburst. He talked and talked and talked, as he had never talked in his life. He talked about the good things, the years in Asia, the years on the ocean. He told her how he ended up in Amsterdam and how he came to own Stowaway's.

He retraced his steps all the way back to the Boston boarding house. His was a lonely and solitary life. Not always easy and not always hard. It was a life of effort, apprenticeship, and unforgettable landscapes. *Papa would be relieved*, thought Adrienne.

They could very well have been two people from the same town who had met by chance and shared a nice evening in a foreign place, but sadly, it was not the case. They reached the narrow dock in front of the Pulitzer Hotel entrance. There was a bench facing the canal. It was a warm night. He leaned his bicycle on the bench, sat down beside Adrienne, lit a cigarette, and forced a smile. She asked the same question again.

"So, what are we going to do, Michel?"

"You can turn me in!" He held up his hands in sign of surrender.

Adrienne ignored his weak attempt at humour.

"I can do that. And I can do nothing. I want to know something: Do you want to go home?"

The answer was swift and sure.

"That depends. I don't want to spend the rest of my life in jail. But yes, I have thought about going back."

"There's no statute of limitations on murder in Canada. You'll have to stand trial even it it's been twenty years."

"Nineteen years. I know. I looked it up."

"Really?"

"Vancouver Public Library."

Adrienne was surprised and glad that he had not always been passive about his reality.

"You're innocent. I know that. But you could be found guilty," she said.

"Probably. That was the whole point, wasn't it?"

"Yes." Adrienne was not apologetic."Or you can stay where you are."

"That's the plan."

"I can come to see you once a year. Give you news." She shrugged. She had contemplated that possibility if that was what he wanted.

"Yeah. That would be okay."

"It would be hard not to tell your mother," Adrienne said with a sigh. "She is so nice and sweet. She still comes to see us in the summer at the beach, you know?"

"She knows I'm okay."

Adrienne supposed that somehow he had managed to send Pauline a message. He leaned forward and stared into the canal. It had been six years since he had dropped the card with his picture in her mailbox.

Picturesque houseboats sailed by. Elegant Amsterdamians were enjoying a nightcap on their decks. It was a beautiful June night. The storybook city seemed unreal. It was in direct opposition to the tragic and difficult decision they were trying to make.

"You know you're not perfectly safe, Michel. Anybody could just walk into Stowaway's like I did. This is not exactly the middle of nowhere."

"I stopped thinking about that a long time ago." Michel shrugged.

Adrienne wouldn't give up. "You're young, Michel. René's age. Thirty-seven? Thirty-eight? You could have another life. Are you going to live this life forever? You're going to be Brian forever? Are you Brian or are you Michel?"

It was painful. Adrienne didn't realize the brutality of her question but perhaps Michel needed to hear it. He closed his eyes and took the blow.

"If someone turned you in here, extradition would probably be complicated. You're an American citizen, a Dutch resident. You could be detained here in Europe for months or even years before you stepped into a courtroom in Moncton."

Michel winced and shook his head. "Jesus," he mumbled. He passed his right hand through his hair.

"I'm just pointing out your options, Michel. Now, listen to me. I'm not finished. I have good news, believe it or not."

"Good news? You're kidding, right?"

"No, I'm not. Listen."

Adrienne told him what she had learned from the letters in the *Merck Manual*. Soon after the Bourgeois–Landry affair, the forensic pathologist who had ruled in the case had his licence to practise medicine revoked by the Royal College of Physicians and Surgeons of Canada. Not because of the Moncton case, which had not been contested, but for three cases of gross negligence that had occurred in Québec prior to his post in Moncton. He was an incompetent drunk or he was incompetent when drunk. Therefore, all of his autopsies must be put into question.

The day after Yvette was found, Dr. Bouchard had extended to Dr. Blanchard the professional courtesy of seeing the body. Philippe Blanchard's examination of Yvette Landry's cadaver totally contradicted the pathologist's findings. He saw the physical clues of long term abuse: years of slapping, pinching, crushing, and pushing always left marks. Yvette had sparse hair and worn teeth due to stress. She had old hairline rib fractures, an atrophied ear drum, crushed nose cartilage, an enlarged right ear pavilion, uneven skin tone on her arms, neck and legs, and crushed, deformed toes. These were injuries she had sustained through life, not from a single beating. The physical signs of the week by the creek and the moving of the body were simply scratches from the brush. The girl had a full stomach and evidence of marijuana in her blood. There were remains of semen in her vagina but no sign of forced intercourse. She was not a virgin. The victim had a lump in the suboccipital triangle and a large amount of blood between the skull and the brain due to a ruptured blood clot. The cause of death: a massive ischemic stroke which was probably the consequence of a fall that the girl could have suffered earlier. The location of the lump was inconsistent with a blow from above or from the side applied by an exterior force. The blow necessarily had an upward trajectory. It was the result of falling back with her full weight and hitting her head on a hard object, thus seriously injuring an artery. She hit a sharp corner of some kind. It was a head injury that was common in household falls. The inhalation of the marijuana, the horizontal position, and the effort of intercourse had accelerated her death. The girl could have been saved had she been taken to the hospital for observation after the fall. The pathologist had ruled that Yvette Landry's death was a result of injuries sustained in a violent beating aggravated by rape. The autopsy was a hasty and shabby job performed by a drunk. Philippe Blanchard testified as to the pathologist's alcohol consumption during the examination. There was a bottle of gin on his instrument tray in the morgue.

"Michel, my father wrote out an official report. The document is in a safe place. It is waiting for you," she said.

An impetuous Adrienne, suddenly sure that all was so very simple, tried to convince him.

"You need a good lawyer, Michel. You could win your case! They'll throw out the original pathologist's conclusions and use my father's. It should be easy to demonstrate the abuse. You explain your reasons for not going to the police: panic and disorientation. You were young and scared. Maybe it's worth it. You just said that you think about going home. I think you would if you could. Am I right?"

She was right. Michel's lips were pressed tightly together. He rubbed his eyes. Adrienne put her arm around his shoulders. Michel turned his head away from her. He was trying not to break down. He looked the other way as he explained, for the first time, in a trembling voice why he had hid and abandoned Yvette's body.

"I thought I had killed her, that I had hurt her. I thought that the joint was laced with some bad stuff. There were always rumours about that. But I was okay. I didn't understand anything. And then it was too late."

"Michel, listen to me. It wasn't your fault. She died of natural causes as a result of a head injury from a fall at home."

"That's what your father said. And she did fall, she told me, down the stairs. Hit her head on the radiator."

He sat back and looked up at the sky, then covered his face with his hands. Adrienne had one more thing to say.

"I'll go back with you because that's what my father would want me to do. Tomorrow, next week, in a year, in twenty years. You decide. I have to give you the letters. There are two: the affidavit and a personal message for you from my father. I'm leaving for New York very early on Wednesday. I will not turn you in. I'll come back in September, okay? We'll talk again. That's three months for you to think about it and prepare yourself. I work at the United Nations headquarters in New York City if you ever want to get in touch with me. It's easy to find me."

"No, Adrienne, I'll come and see you before Wednesday whatever I decide. I might give you something for my mother." Poor Michel did not want the ghost of his past to go away.

"OK, that's fair. You have until Wednesday morning. I'll be leaving the hotel at around seven for the airport."

He sat on his sofa bed and looked around his silent apartment. The expired calendar on the wall, the row of cookbooks on the cheap bookshelf, the picture of the ship. His hands were shaking. He couldn't sleep. He felt invigorated and excited, not afraid. He felt encouraged by the information Adrienne had given him. Dr. Blanchard thought he should go back. The decision was surprisingly easy. He had stepped back into his own body and he wanted to stay inside it. Michel was ready.

Rough Landing

Lilly had a soft drink as she waited for her cousin at Moncton Airport. She was curious as to why Adrienne was arriving almost three weeks early for her holidays. Adrienne had called her from Europe at five in the morning to say she was arriving that evening. It was only June 28. No one had arrived yet. She supposed that Adrienne had had to change her holidays.

Since Lilly had moved to Moncton, she'd used her aunt's cottage a lot. She kept her kayak in the shed and spent weekends training on the bay. Crane Road was a blessing. It was a break from her small, rented apartment in the city. She chose not to spend very much on housing because she had other priorities. She ran the New York Marathon every November, took a week every year to go white-water kayaking out west, and loved to visit Claude for theatre and restaurant binges in London. She was satisfied and happy with her life and her job.

The plane was landing. Lilly threw the empty can into the trash and checked her watch. She was in a good mood. The weather was nice, the summer was on the road. She and Adrienne would have some fun. Maybe they'd hit the town bars a couple of nights. Her cousin was quirky and fun, and now that she worked at the UN, she always had interesting stories to tell.

It was a small airport with only one gate. The planes taxied right up to the doors and Lilly could see the disembarking passengers through the large windows. Adrienne was among the last to come down the stairs. She looked back and waited for someone who was coming behind her. They walked side by side on the tarmac. Lilly frowned. Who was the guy? He was thin. He was wearing a bush jacket, worn jeans, and a baseball cap. He had a mustache, long hair, and glasses. He was very ordinary, seventies looking, a little scruffy, maybe. He was difficult to categorize even for Lilly, who was very good at character analysis. She waited several yards away from the

True Identity

arrivals area inside the airport and decided to let this play out Adrienne's way. Maybe it was a new boyfriend? It didn't seem so.

They came through the doors. Adrienne looked straight at Lilly but did not smile or wave. The companion was close behind. The cousins kissed each other on the cheek very formally. It was definitely not a typical family greeting. Something was wrong.

"So. You're early for your holidays aren't you?" Lilly said.

"Yeah, I'll tell you about it. Lilly, this is Brian. He's from Moncton. Would you mind if we drop him off downtown before we go on to the cottage?"

"Sure."

Lilly wasn't given much choice. The drive into the city was uncomfortable and Adrienne made unnatural small talk. The Brian guy sat immobile in the back seat. In only a few minutes they were driving into the city. Adrienne directed Lilly to Main Street and asked Brian a curious question: "Are you sure?"

"Yes," said Brian.

Wierd, thought Lilly.

As they drove by the courthouse and the police station, Adrienne said, "Pull up here, Lilly. Thank you."

"You're coming here?" Lilly was taken aback.

"Yes."

They all got out of the car. Brian took his backpack, suitcase, and a garment bag out of the trunk, and thanked Lilly politely.

"We'll see you," he said to Adrienne.

"Yes. Tomorrow morning. Good luck," she said.

Lilly looked on in amazement as Michel struggled up the staircase with his three pieces of luggage. She had had enough mystery.

"Who, may I ask, is that?" she said.

When he had gone through the doors, Adrienne turned to her cousin and said, "Michel Bourgeois."

Lilly's face dropped.

"I'm sorry to put you in this position Lilly, but I need you on our side."

"Our side? What the hell? Jesus, Mary and Joseph. What?"

"I found him and convinced him to come home," Adrienne said.

261

"Just like that? You found him? Playing Blackjack in Monaco? Adrienne!" Lilly was incredulous.

"In Amsterdam. Long story. Let's go home. I have to show you something."

Adrienne told the story on the way to the cottage. Astonishment was not the word. Lilly tried to concentrate on the road. This was not good. Not good at all. They walked into the cottage and went straight to the bookshelf. Adrienne was relieved to find the letters in their place. She handed them to Lilly, who read them silently as she paced between the living room and the porch. She got a glass of water, drank it down, and then read both letters again sitting at the dining room table.

"Destroy it. Now," said Lilly harshly.

"I can't," Adrienne said, taking the letter. "It's Michel's property."

"Do you really believe your father was saving a life, Adrienne?"

"Yes, of course."

"You call it saving a life. I call it accesory to murder as defined by the Canadian Criminal Code. Your brother faces prison and you're lucky your mother is not mentioned in the letter. This is a confession. Destroy it."

Lilly was furious. She was horrified at the possible consequences for René. She had to think.

"I'm going into town. I'll call your brother from my place. Come to my office tomorrow morning." Lilly shook her head as she grabbed her bag and her car keys. "René has been living with this hanging over his head for twenty years. Why didn't he tell me years ago? I could have helped. Adrienne, you are going to be questioned. You recognized him. You know the family. Seeing you made him decide to come home. You accompanied him. Say. No. More."

"I am going to see Michel tomorrow, Lilly."

"Do you want my help or not?"

"Yes."

"Do as I say. Destroy the letter. Say nothing. Stay away from Michel Bourgeois." She put the unofficial autopsy report away in her handbag and said, "I'm taking this to try to get it into the right hands. It's only hearsay for the moment. Did you think you had the winning number in your hand?"

"I believed it would replace the other one. And it will. It has too," Adrienne said.

"You're right. It had better but I doubt it. Unfortunately for us, we depend on Michel Bourgeois being found innocent."

"He is."

"I'm not so sure. You know, I can't believe this. An innocent sixteen-year-old girl dies of a blow to the head and everybody breaks their asses to save the stupid pothead who abandoned her in the creek. Hasn't anybody wondered if she was alive when he left her there? That's the value of a female life in this society," said Lilly.

She turned in the doorway and slammed the screen door. She looked back at Adrienne and said: "Adrienne Blanchard, you live by your own rules, don't you? You and your father. Both alike. Jesus Christ."

She stormed down the stairs to her car. From the window, Adrienne watched her cousin drive too fast up the dirt road. Lilly's reaction had been logical but more vehement than Adrienne had expected. She was a public prosecutor. Her place was on the other side.

Despite the conviction that she had done the right thing the right way, Adrienne could not sleep. Lilly's lack of sympathy had jolted her confidence that there would be a civilized and proper end to the story. Her brother had been just a boy at the time, a minor. How could he be accused of anything other than bending to paternal authority? For the first time, Adrienne calculated her brother's age at the time. His birthday was April 4. He had been eighteen, legal age. Not old enough to drink a glass of wine, but old enough to go to jail. Nevertheless, she felt regret but not guilt. She hung on to the notion that she was doing what her father would have wanted her to do. She disregarded Lilly's warnings and went to the police station the following morning.

"Good morning. My name is Adrienne Blanchard. This is my passport and my driver's licence. I believe Michel Bourgeois is being held here. I arranged with Mr. Bourgeois to contact him today. I'm a close friend."

"Yes. Bourgeois. Everybody in town wants to see this guy. It's like the prime minister's in town or something. Let me check," she said. "Blanchard. No, you're not on the list for Bourgeois. But there's a note here that the captain wants to speak to you. Okay? He's busy right now with the family. Take a seat over there. It won't be long."

Without blinking an eye, Adrienne saw the writing on the wall. She had lost control of the situation but not her cold blood.

"Great!" Adrienne exclaimed as if she had just been invited to a very good party. "Fine. Listen: could I use the washroom please?" Adrienne winced at the policewoman insinuating a female problem.

"Yeah, sure. Down that corridor to your left. Second door to your right. Here's the key. You got what you need? There's a machine in there."

"Oh good. Thanks a lot," she said, heaving a false sigh of relief and smiling.

It was an individual female employee bathroom. She locked the door behind her. Her years at the UN had taught her a thing or two. She checked for cameras. Then, she reached into her bag and expertly disposed of the letter.

Canadian judicial procedures kicked in. It was time to let justice take its course and to hope that compassionate and objective justice would be done. That was all that Philippe Blanchard had ever intended.

Part Six

Keep Walking

Adrienne waited quietly in the reception area for her interrogation. The police station in Moncton was not at all a threatening place. It looked like an insurance company office or a motor vehicles examination branch. She didn't feel sorry for Michel. He was where he was supposed to be and was setting things straight. Adrienne would do what Lilly had said: keep her mouth shut until they spoke to a lawyer. The family needed a single voice. It was clear to Adrienne now that this was Lilly's territory.

It was the summer of 1992. It had been nineteen years since Michel fled justice with Phillipe Blanchard's help. The babies born in 1973 were driving cars, delivering pizzas, and voting. Modest and sleepy Moncton was becoming a busy urban community with large shopping malls, a cultural centre, a half-dozen exotic restaurants, a jazz club, and a wine bar. The Université de Moncton was flourishing and a small international population of professors and entrepreneurial immigrants was slowly invading the old Anglo-Franco landscape. People moved away to Alberta, Ontario, and Québec less frequently. Many baby boomers were staying at home. René, in fact, was considering coming back to open an international bookstore.

Adrienne was worried about her own situation as well. She had called Patrick from Amsterdam Airport to delay her return to the office because of a family emergency. Patrick had sounded puzzled. Perhaps, she thought, it was time to ask for the leave of absence she had been considering since her separation. This would take time. She needed to be with her family and near Michel. In a way, this turn of events had made the decision for her.

She looked at the clock. It was almost noon. Lilly would be worried, wondering where she was. Two opaque glass doors led to the office area. They opened with a sudden muted thud. Busy office noises came from inside. The McKay family walked out the doors into the reception area on their way to the exit. Their faces were set with indignation and purpose. Adrienne was eleven years old again. She forgot herself and jumped up in expectation. She had done something good. She had brought him home. Their son. Their brother.

"Mummy. Don't look at her. Just don't look at her. Keep walking, Mummy," said Mary Ann McKay.

Son, Gary, and daughter, Mary Ann, walked very close behind their mother and father. They carried themselves with the self-importance and determination of two young adults who have decided they are now their parents' guardians. The family had just been reunited with Michel. As he had self-consciously entered the small conference room, they had spontaneously circled him in a family huddle. His knees had weakened. The first thing he did was ask Ron to forgive him. Ron was so moved that he only managed to shake his head violently in a gesture meaning that it did not matter anymore. His brother and sister, now young adults, searched for his eyes.

"Hey, do you remember us?" Gary asked with an enormous smile.

His mother put her head on his chest and said,

"*Enfin. Mon Michel. Dieu merci.*"[117]

As he walked through the police station reception area, Ron McKay held his wife's hand and carried Michel's large suitcase in the other. He limped as the heavy suitcase bounced on his leg. He was carrying his load with pride. He was a big fellow with a red face and a large stomach who walked straight and proud like a young man.

"It sure took you guys quite a while to bring him home, eh?" he shouted bitterly at Adrienne. "So what were you guys worried about?"

"Shut up, Dad. Please. Keep walking," said Gary.

Gary McKay looked at Adrienne in disgust. The children herded their parents away from Adrienne and out the door. She was left standing in the waiting area hoping this would end better than it had started.

Ron McKay took over where Philippe Blanchard had left off. His way.

At the arraignment only days later, Michel was accused of murder in the first degree. He pleaded innocent and chose to be tried by jury in the English language. The McKay family hired Simon Hanley, an eccentric

---

[117] At last. My Michel. Thank God.

young lawyer from Saint John. It was an odd choice. Hanley was high-class and expensive.

There was little connection between Saint John, the province's largest city, and Moncton. It had a busy international port, a thriving beer industry, and a generally healthy business climate. New Brunswick's handful of large fortunes called Saint John their home away from the Bahamas. Founded at the time of the American Revolution by American colonists loyal to King George, they were monarchists, staunch conservatives, and very proud of their history. Needless to say, anything involving the Acadian population of New Brunswick did not impress, interest, or worry the people of Saint John very much at all. In all fairness, however, it would be correct to say that the opposite was also true.

Thanks to shoptalk at the office, Lilly learned how it had come about. Ron McKay had a regular client from Saint John every second Tuesday. He was a businessman who flew his own twin motor plane. He owned two buildings and a veterinary clinic in Moncton. For years, Ron had picked him up at the airport and chauffeured him around town to his business appointments. Jeffrey Brooks was very fond of Ron McKay and it was he who suggested Hanley.

"This is about murder, Ron. Don't waste your time with local yahoos. He's the son of a friend of mine. He's not cheap but I'll talk to him. If he likes the case, he'll take it. This kid is the best. Your boy will walk."

Lilly had been ruled out as prosecutor because of her family relationship to the Blanchards. Her only female colleague, Kathy Crossman, was assigned to the case. Kathy was a Monctonian and a feminist. Lilly thought she was a good choice. Lilly would have attacked the case from a feminist view point as well. Kathy wanted a conviction. Rough sex or drugged frenzy, she didn't care. She was disgusted by the shameful plague of male violence towards women. It was her personal crusade. She would go after René Blanchard later. There would be no more boys covering for the boys. To the pen.

Very soon, Michel's return was public knowledge and subject of gossip and speculation. General opinion was favourable to Michel and unfavourable to the Blanchard family. The headline in the *Moncton Times & Transcript* read:

True Identity

WAR VETERAN RETURNS TO FACE MURDER CHARGES: PLEADS INNOCENT. LOCAL DOCTOR IMPLICATED

Michel spent the summer in a temporary prison cell of a medium security facility. It was bearable and he had known what to expect. However, he wasn't sure how, at age eighteen, he would have resisted years behind bars. He was fortunate that no one had looked for him. Nevertheless, he did not regret coming back. He dared to hope that if he was found guilty, he might receive a lenient sentence. He felt strong. He felt at peace. His family held him up.

It was not in his interest to stay close to the Blanchards. His defence would involve blaming them for his wrong decisions. The Blanchards had therefore become collateral damage just as Lilly predicted.

Meanwhile, Adrienne took important decisions. She went to New York to officially request an indefinite leave of absence from the UN and to see Xavier. She needed to tell him what was happening. Like Claude, he had no inkling that the murder he had heard about almost six years before had anything to do with the Blanchard family.

It had been more than a month since they had seen each other. The invisible rope that tied them together was tugging. Xavier was patiently waiting or, better said, hopefully expecting, the day they would fall into each others' arms like naughty strangers or frenetic teenagers. If and when that happened, he would not let her go. He would kiss every female on the planet goodbye forever. But he could not tell Adrienne this. He had no choice but to wait for it to happen. He was aware that he had condemned himself. A loss of trust was a life sentence.

While he waited for Adrienne, his phone buzzed. It was Nicole so he didn't answer. He had to do something about her. She was a sophisticated companion for social events, and exotic and complacent in bed – a mini Alexa without the heart or the humour. He had met her at the Perrys' in Washington and she had been aggressive in her seduction. She appeared at his door in high heels and naked under her trenchcoat one night. He thought he had seen the same scene in a movie but after six months of celibacy and without any encouragement from Adrienne, he had taken the bait. But now, she was organizing day trips with her children and hinting about the summer in Formentera. Just the thought depressed him. Formentera was so difficult without Adrienne. The problem was that after Nicole, there would be another Nicole and then another and another. He was waiting for Adrienne and very unhappy about her Lebanese friend.

He nursed a martini at the bar of a trendy restaurant in Soho and waited for his wife. He thought of Adrienne as his wife because he still felt married to her. To the tiny Jesuit hiding inside him, marriage was an indelible sacrament.

As she walked towards him in a little black dress, he immediately noticed a beautiful amber pendant on an ornate gold chain around her neck. He recognized the authentic amber and the Arab taste for excess in the chain. After their greeting, he smiled teasingly and touched the golden stone with his fingers.

"How is your friend?" he said.

"Fine. How is yours?"

"Fine."

"Adri, Adri, Adri," he said, teasing her.

Adrienne was embarrassed. The pendant was perfect for the dress and, preoccupied with other things, it had not crossed her mind that Xavier might notice this obviously expensive and romantic gift. She had not seen nor heard from Khalil for weeks - well before Amsterdam. She suspected he had gone undercover in Pakistan. She was beginning to think that the amber pendant had been a gift of farewell. *Amber is the stone of memory*, he had said as he helped her with the clasp. He had smiled at her so very fondly.

"Xavi, something very complicated is happening to my family. We all want you to know," she said.

He was surprised and intrigued but didn't take it too seriously. He wrinkled his nose and smiled lopsidedly.

"Almost exactly nineteen years ago," she began, and told the whole story from beginning to end. His facial expression changed to disbelief, then shock, then worry.

"When is this idiot's trial?"

"August 20. You share Lilly's opinion, I see."

"Well, of course. She has a head on her shoulders. How can I help? Do you mind if I go? I can stay at Lilly's."

"Come. René will appreciate it. Lilly's staying with us at the cottage for the summer. We've convinced my mother to stay with Aunt Madeleine at her house in Sainte-Irénée. We haven't told her about René's possible criminal responsibility so as not to worry her more than she already is. We hope we won't have to. They say it should last five or six days at most. You can stay with us, Xavi."

She had said "stay with us," not "stay with me." They exchanged a long and weary look, remembering Saturday night dinners, cycling trails, and UPicks. The life before television journalists and electronic bracelets.

"Are we still married, Xavi? I have been so involved in this, I haven't paid attention. Do I have to sign anything else?"

"Yes, we are still married and no, you don't have to sign anything else. It's a bureaucratic thing. Not final for a couple of months they said. But it's done."

"Oh, okay."

"What the hell were you doing in Amsterdam?"

He could not get the Lebanese guy out of his mind.

René was a wall. He refused to participate in any conversation on the subject or reveal any information. To Lilly's dismay, he refused to get a lawyer.

Claude asked for a leave of absence as well. She descended on Crane Road on July 12 with five huge suitcases, her organizational skills, and her self-appointed authority as head of family. She whispered to Adrienne in a scolding tone that she had come prepared to take charge of her brother's business if need be. She could hardly believe she was the only member of the family who had absolutely no knowledge of the affair and of the two incriminating letters that had sat in the bookcase for twenty years.

Lilly, Adrienne, and Claude spent the summer together at the cottage. Lilly protected the family the best she could. She managed to have any case against René postponed pending Michel's sentencing. Kathy Crossman also accepted not to prosecute the sixty-five-year-old Charlotte Blanchard. Philippe had protected Charlotte. Although she had knowledge of the events, she had not seen Michel or acted in any way. René had cooperated in Michel's escape. He would come forth and take responsibility.

Claude and Adrienne were first in line to attend the three days of jury selection. Claude observed in extreme concentration, glaring at Simon

Hanley every time he selected a candidate she did not like. Only three of the eleven were Francophones. She worried that the Anglophone jurors would not consider him one of their own, even if Lilly disagreed. The girls had a bottle of wine at dinner every night as they discussed the jurors and the strengths and weaknesses of their case.

Xavier had dark dreams. The Blanchard family disappeared and he could not find Adrienne. He ran everywhere. From the beach in Getxo to the streets of Montréal, up Koldo's stairs and down to the mine, Adrienne was nowhere to be found.

The Blanchards had the certainty that Michel was innocent and this encouraged them while they waited for the trial and the jury's decision. If truth prevailed, which it should, everything would be alright. In the end, the family accepted the situation with a certain pragmatism and sense of inevitability. It was a reminder of who and where they came from.

The Nervous Viking

Simon Hanley loved the case so much he would have done it for free. Of course, he loved murder cases in general and felt guilty at times because he wished there were more murders in New Brunswick. Simon's real dream was to be a detective or a crime novelist, but family tradition had made him a lawyer.

Things had moved fast. By July 3, he was on the job. Simon was doing his homework. He was studying the human geography of the case very carefully. With a map and comfortable shoes, he had paced the city. He followed the road from Michel and Pauline's first apartment in the East End to the path Michel must have followed to the Blanchard's garage the night he heard two policemen waiting in line at Bright's say that a body had just been found near Hall's Creek. Simon sat on the play structure that had replaced the swings at the playground and located the living room window of the witness who had seen the two young people chatting on that Friday afternoon nineteen years before. The ruins of the old rink were still standing. He knew the exact spot where Yvette had died. He had asked Michel to draw a sketch. Simon laid down and looked up at the sky. While he laid there, he pulled a picture of Yvette from his briefcase. She looked sweet. She had dimples and round cheeks. Her hair was shoulder length, dark, and teased into an old-fashioned bouffant flip-up style with very short bangs. He looked for the enlarged ear Blanchard had described, but Yvette's hair was carefully combed to conceal it. Simon talked to her out loud.

"You had a lot of little tricks to hide it all, didn't you, Yvette?" She didn't answer. He sighed and sat up.

He traced Michel's steps to the creek where he had half carried and half dragged the body, and then up the tracks to the railroad bridge. He stood outside the abandoned candy factory where two little girls had seen the boy from Bright's walking up the tracks. Simon visited the penitentiary to talk to the guards, inmates, and administrative workers who still remembered Dr. Blanchard. The Landry family refused to speak to him, but he did talk to a chatty and curious neighbour who revealed more than he could have hoped for. He had long talks with Michel who was exceptionally cooperative. Simon was pleased. He was expensive but worth every penny.

It was on July 12 that he met the Blanchards for the first time. He was not at all finished with his preparation. There was still a long way to go before August 20 but Simon liked to acquaint himself with the physical facts – the silent witnesses, the houses, the streets, and the windows. He liked to visualize the scenery, like a film director with a storyboard. In the hotel lounge, he waited impatiently to meet the three Blanchards. He had permission to visit the family house on Temple Street that evening. He would take the Blanchards with him. He was looking forward to it. It didn't occur to him that for René, Claude, and Adrienne, it would be a difficult and emotional journey.

His legs were crossed, his foot was shaking. As a child, Simon had been diagnosed with higher than average hyperactivity. Had he been born in the eighties he would have been drugged into passivity, but he was born in the fifties and was just given a lot of stuff to do. Thus, he played the piano like a wild man, had read thousands of mystery and crime novels, was an expert sprint canoeist, watched television as he pedaled on his stationary bicycle, and spent hours jumping on his trampoline in the back of his rented house. He had to move often because neighbours invariably complained to the city about the wild man who pirouetted into the sky above their backyards every three seconds. It was distracting – to say the least – to host a barbecue while your neighbour is flying through the air stretching out his arms like a crazy bird. He was thirty-four then. He had been married once briefly. She had cheated on him, but it had actually been a relief. No harm done.

Time was slowly but surely tempering his personal hyperelectrical wiring. He had auburn hair and hazel eyes. He was a handsome, square-jawed young man with a perky, almost feminine, nose. He was as thin as a rake because of his physical activity but also because he didn't eat very much; mostly apples, sardines, and nuts. Simon found eating made him sluggish and muddled his thought processes. He was not particularly tall, but at five feet, nine inches and so very thin, he looked extremely good in the fashionable clothes his mother ordered for him from New England. His classical, preppy style was disturbed by a full red beard. His hair was thinning at the temples and his thinness deepened the expression lines on his face. Perhaps, more than the cute boy next door, Simon Hanley looked like a nervous Viking.

At exactly half past six, three attractive young people walked into the lounge. He saw a beautiful blonde wearing sunglasses, an elegant, sleeveless navy blue dress, and smart, navy blue and beige pumps. A long-haired girl in Roman sandals and a large man's shirt caught at the waist by a large leather belt, walked beside her. A young man about Simon's age with enviably thick, white hair, and wire-framed glasses dressed in jeans and a blazer came up behind them. It had to be them. They shook his hand and greeted him formally.

"Monsieur Hanley?"

"Bonsoir, monsieur."

"Monsieur."[118]

Greeting in French was Blanchard family politics. A Monctonian would have just said "Hi!" but unilingual Simon of unilingual Saint John momentarily hesitated, unfamiliar with the protocol of bilingualism.

"Ummm…is it okay with you if we speak English or should I get a translator?" Simon said. He was attempting to be exquisitely correct.

"Oh! That's silly. Of course we'll speak English!" replied Claude who, by personal twist of fate, was an Acadian with a posh British accent.

Simon put his foot in his mouth again when he looked at René and said "Claude?" Claude sighed with a hint of exasperation.

"I am Claude. This is my brother René and my sister Adrienne. If you must know, my mother liked boys' names for girls and girls' names for boys. It's quite simple really," she said.

"Oh? That's interesting!" said Simon very seriously. He sincerely liked the idea.

Simon was looking for clues as to why, if he were innocent, Michel had chosen to run away. Those Blanchards were imposing, he thought. As a matter of fact, if that blonde told him to jump off a bridge right then, he just might consider it.

---

118 Mister Hanley. Good evening, sir. Sir.

The Blanchard children had been instructed by Lilly to cooperate fully with Hanley. In effect, he was their lawyer. René had flown in from Ottawa that morning for the meeting and Claude had arrived from London barely two hours earlier. They hadn't had a chance to talk very much. Claude had taken a shower and changed into a fresh outfit.

"Where does this strange man come from?" she asked Adrienne as they were walking to Simon's car for the drive to the house on Temple Street. Simon walked ahead with René. The sisters stayed close together.

"The McKays. He's from Saint John," said Adrienne.

"I don't know if I would have chosen him." said Claude.

"We have no choice," said Adrienne.

"I don't like his nose," said Claude in a whisper.

It was Simon Hanley of Saint John who took the Blanchards home.

They fell naturally into their sibling order as they walked down the long, roofed porch. Simon was holding the keys. It felt strange to the children as there was one thing that they could always count on: the door was never locked. They walked into the house which smelled of antiseptic. The smell of tobacco and pie was gone. Simon headed straight upstairs. He asked the sisters what they had seen from their window. Nothing, they said. They only remembered the commotion when Yvette's body had been found and then the funeral which had been on TV.

The basement hadn't been touched. It was still dark, unfinished, and dusty with the exception of one room. That room, however, had always been locked. The children seldom went inside unless they hurt themselves. It had held a stretcher, a sink, a glass cabinet with a handful of instruments, and a small refrigerator. Philippe kept boxes of Valium, various vaccinations, unguents, and vials of antidotes in the fridge. He also kept a gun in the freezer. The Blanchards' eyes met, knowing not to mention the gun. When they were small, they had sworn to their father together in this very spot, that they would never touch it and never tell. Never. Simon asked how many days Michel had come for his arm.

"Every day during the first month and then off and on, the second month," René said. He was the only one who remembered. René could still hear their laughter. He had been jealous of it and still was.

They went out the kitchen door to the backyard, where they had practised cartwheels in the fall and played Four Corner tag in the snow in the winter. It was where poor Claude had found her father on the morning of his heart attack. He was on his back in the deep snow clutching at his shirt, reaching for his pills. She wailed and screamed but there was nothing to be done. The snowflakes just fell softly on his face. Within minutes, the neighbourhood became a howling metropolis of ambulance sirens and flashing police car lights, frantic friends wanting to help and only getting in the way, neighbours carrying trays of sandwiches, women shielding the new widow and the fatherless daughters. Death in a small town.

He was taken away in a green plastic bag with a long zipper. Adrienne wasn't permitted to see the body until later. He was in a shiny wooden box with a white satin lining. Adrienne looked away. The ruffles around his head made it look like he was wearing a silly bonnet. The guards from the prison came in a chartered bus to serve as pallbearers and to form a corridor of honour. His friend Roger came from Rome to officiate at the funeral. It was said there were some ex-cons at the back of the Cathedral.

Simon saved the garage for last. He let René talk.

"The entrance was here. That tree has grown wider," René said.

"Was he hiding inside?"

"No. I came out for a smoke and he was crouching right there in the back, by the fence. There used to be a house there, so you couldn't see him. He was waiting for me I guess. He knew I used to sneak a smoke out here."

"What did you think?"

"Well, I didn't even know he was in trouble. His face was grey and he was holding his head in his hands. I thought he had been hit by a car and needed my father again. He asked me to get my father, so I did."

"How long was he here?"

"Three nights. On the fourth night, we left."

"Down to Nova Scotia. In your father's car?"

"It was a black Comet. I don't know whose car it was. My father gave me the keys. I picked it up in the parking lot at the liquor store on Mountain Road. Then I dropped it at a parking lot downtown and walked home."

"Late at night?"

"More or less. I don't remember what time I left. I was back by half past one."

"Was Michel nervous?"
"Yes, but..."
"But what?"
"He looked excited."
"And your dad?"
"It was his life. He was used to that stuff."
"So you and your dad were the only ones who knew anything?"
"Officially, yeah."
"Unofficially?" asked Simon.

René looked at Adrienne. "How do you say '*évêque*' in English?" he asked.

"Bishop," answered Adrienne.

"A priest?" Simon was surprised and very interested. "The bishop at that time?"

"Yes. A friend of my father's. My father wanted to confess. Said it was a higher law or something."

"OK! Thank you, René. This is good for now," Simon said.

Simon was very very happy. The house had talked. He had known it would. René took a deep breath. He had been choking for nineteen years.

A Question of Faith

The trial began on a bright blue morning when August feels and smells like September. The air was new, clean, and crisp like the first day of school. Before leaving for court, Adrienne went down to the beach for a moment of solitude. The sky was the same deep blue as the water. It was windy. The white caps curled and snarled. There was not a single cloud in the sky, yet it seemed to be moving. She had come for strength but was reminded only of her smallness. She heard Claude impatiently beeping the horn of the car and hurried back to the cottage.

Claude and Adrienne sat in the fourth and last row, on the aisle. They would sit there-behind the defence - for the six days the trial lasted. The sisters' view would be partly blocked by Ron, Pauline, Gary, and Mary Ann McKay. On the first day, the first row was left empty until the last minute. The McKays had waited in the parking lot of the courthouse to see Michel arrive and give him a victory sign. He was handcuffed to a police officer. He was wearing Gary's navy blue graduation blazer, a pale blue shirt and beige trousers. Simon had said no tie. His hair was nicely cut and he was clean shaven. He looked very nice.

Simon Hanley and Kathy Crossman were perfect rivals. They were in complete equilibrium. They were the same age. They were both brilliant professionals. Where Kathy was passionate and driven, Simon was pragmatic, soft spoken, sensible, and relaxed.

The jury members wore the self-important expression of those who are secretly proud to be there although they have told everyone that they have much more important things to do. Throughout their lives, they would never lose the opportunity to say, "I was on a jury once. Murder trial. The Landry case?"

Judge Samuel Harris was, according to script, dishevelled, disorganized, and shrewd. He was just three months from retirement and had just gotten back from his holidays. He was slightly put out about being there; he wanted to get back to writing his memoirs and to the purchase of a condo in Florida.

Everyone stands, everyone sits. The vocabulary of justice is repeated. No one needs a booklet. The trial with its liturgy is similar to a Mass.

Every day as they sat down following the judge's arrival, Michel turned his head very slightly to the left and looked over his shoulder. He saw her in the corner of his eye. She would wait for the turned head and nod just once. She was representing someone else. Michel knew that. It had turned out the way it had turned out. It was out of their hands.

Simon turned too. He looked at the girls and smiled a smile that looked more like a wince. Then he greeted the McKays. He exuded confidence.

Lilly was in her office two floors up. René was at the cottage, painting the garden furniture bright yellow with his girls. Catherine chose the colour. It was like the sun and it would bring them luck, she said. Xavier arrived on a Thursday night. He would begin to attend trial on the third day.

Like a black-and-white photograph slowly developing in a darkroom, the story came to life. As each witness testified, the contrasts in the photograph became sharper. 1973 floated to the surface. First, only grey shadows, and then it seemed like yesterday. The Monctonians in the courtroom all recognized themselves somewhere in that photograph. Most of them were between the ages of thirty and fifty. They remembered Brights' Fish and Chips and Friday night dances. They knew exactly how the red earth around Hall's creek was soft and muddy. The story was a mirror of the dignity, the conflicts, and the tenacity of the people of the stubborn and peculiar little city of Moncton.

The first witness was the Vanier High School student who had seen Yvette and Michel at the playground swings from her living room window. She was the last person to see her alive. She remembered Yvette losing her balance when she got off the swing and the boy putting his arm around her shoulders to hold her up. Kathy asked her very bluntly if she was absolutely sure about that. The woman, who was seventeen at the time, said she had been hurrying to finish sewing a satin blouse to go to the dance, but that, yes, she thought so.

"You think so but you're not sure?" Kathy asked.

Simon wanted to know why Yvette wasn't going to the dance that night.

"She was babysitting a lot to save money to run away," answered her schoolmate.

"Why do you think Yvette would run away?" asked Simon.

"Strict father," the witness answered, very sure of herself. "Very strict father." The girl, who was now a woman, smiled and remembered something else. "Yvette always had to go home before last dance anyway."

"Last dance? Sorry, I went to an all-boys school," said Simon. He pleaded ignorance and took advantage to play to the crowd.

"Yes," the witness said, smiling indulgently. "That's when you get asked to be walked home."

The jury allowed itself some gentle, nostalgic laughter. The judge scolded.

It was time for Kathy's cross-examination; she made a statement as well as asking a question.

"She wasn't the only one who had to go home early was she?" Kathy said. "I mean, I went to Trimble High, I had to be home by eleven, too."

The witness felt intimidated and embarrassed. She hoped she had not done anyone any harm. "No. Yvette wasn't the only one. Lots of girls had to go home early," she said. Yvette's classmate left the stand, wanting to cry.

The character witnesses, such as Michel's boss at Bright's and his teachers, spoke of Michel well. He was described as polite, artistic, solitary. There was some absenteeism but no trouble. Lovely mother. But at every turn Kathy introduced doubt and an element of inadaptation. Simon would not let this bother him. Kathy produced no witness that spoke of Michel as threatening or violent in any way.

Michel's honourable discharge papers from the US military and a glowing recommendation from the Dutch captain were read aloud. Kathy fought to have the documents declared inadmissible on the grounds that they had been obtained under a false and illegal name. The judge ruled for the defence, who argued very cleverly on the true sense of identity. Years before, Michel's sergeant in Okinawa had described Brian Ogilvy as a success story of the Foreign Combatant Program. Ogilvy had given seven years of service and obtained a superior professional certification. They had made a fine American citizen out of this foreign boy. The Dutch captain wrote a very touching tribute to the solitary men who work on the sea. They are men who are running from pain, from mistakes, from misery, and even from memory.

Of the eleven jurors, eight were men. To an Eastern Canadian postal worker and a retired insurance salesman, it was high adventure. They listened with interest. Simon was satisfied. The jury saw a responsible man and a veteran, certainly not a delinquent or a danger to society.

Then things started going wrong, starting with the pot. Michel had smoked his first joint at the tender age of twelve. This was shocking even in 1992. Kathy called a medical expert who testified as to the as yet unknown long-term effects of child drug use. An RCMP officer of the narcotics squad warned of drugs laced with chemicals that could produce bouts of extreme violence in an otherwise well-balanced person. The Moncton Police Officer could not bring up Michel's juvenile conviction but did testify that, according to their records, the defendant was known to the police at the time as a habitual drug user and heavy consumer.

Fortunately, the Court-appointed psychiatrist saved the day, at least in part. Simon realized they had been lucky. She was a progressive, young Torontonian who had married a Moncton orthopedist. She gave Michel a clean bill of health. He was the child of a single teenage mother of the fifties. The mother and son had born the stigma of the disgrace in a rural Catholic society. Michel's love for his mother combined with Pauline's courage and devotion had shaped his personality and provided a small but solid family base for the young man.

Simon had purposely chosen a single mother for the jury and she suddenly sat up very straight. This fact had escaped Kathy. Only Simon knew who she was. She was an Anglophone and a born-again Christian. Claude had protested his choice. The juror stole a look at Pauline and for the rest of the trial, it was her son sitting there.

Michel Bourgeois had an important sense of responsibility, a strong protection instinct, a certain tendency to self-effacement, and the logical desire for a male role model. His return had been voluntary with full knowledge of the possible consequences, which showed an exceptional degree of maturity.

The doctor did not give much importance to this drug use and pointed out the increasing therapeutic use of marijuana.

"What could have prompted the unacceptable act of abandoning the girl in the marsh?" Simon asked the psychiatrist.

"An unadulterated panic attack, pure and simple. Then, as the hours passed, the realization of an incorrigeable mistake. He believed that his socio-economic profile would mean a conviction and a life sentence for murder. Not catatonic, but almost, he mechanically went on with his daily life."

The more the eloquent and knowledgeable doctor spoke, the more she made sense - the more everything made sense. It was obvious that the psychiatrist did not doubt Michel's innocence. Simon began to transfer responsibility to Philippe.

According to the psychiatrist, Dr. Philippe Blanchard's decisions and behaviour demonstrated a clear case of abuse of authority. The doctor had admininistered Valium, which dulled Michel's own judgement. He had hesitated in taking him to the police and then offered him a relatively easy way out. This stepped beyond the boundaries of a medical doctor and, indeed, of any law-abiding citizen. At that moment in time, Michel had been too fragile to make his own decisions. He should never have been given that choice. It was too powerful a cocktail from a man he idolized.

Simon probed into the relationship between Michel and the doctor. The psychiatrist believed that the months that Dr. Blanchard had cared for Michel's burns had cemented an already strong relationship. The doctor was a role model, a caregiver, a friend. Michel saw a man he could trust in Philippe. In the comfortable and warm Blanchard home, he saw a safe haven. It was the place that had welcomed him and his mother.

Kathy had kept one question for her cross-examination.

"Is it your opinion that Dr. Blanchard helped Michel Bourgeois to escape because he was very fond of him and believed in his innocence? Because if he believed in his innocence, the logical thing would have been to turn him in."

The psychiatrist paused and spoke slowly, like a teacher who wants to make sure she is understood by everyone.

"Having examined Michel and studied Dr. Blanchard's professional file, in this case, I believe that the defendant's guilt or innocence was of no consequence to the doctor. Either way, he would have helped. This is my professional opinion."

"Either way, then. Innocent or guilty. Thank you, doctor," concluded Kathy.

It was late Friday afternoon, the court adjourned for the weekend, and the Blanchards retreated to Crane Road in Lilly's old car. René, Jocelyne, and the girls stood by the car in the driveway as Lilly, Xavier, Adrienne, and Claude wearily got out of the old Land Rover.

"Good. Very good," said Lilly as optimistically as she could while she opened the trunk to get the grocery bags. She handed them to the girls. And that was it. Since the trial had begun and René had arrived, they had stopped talking about it. Valerie and Catherine were having a difficult time. This was a complication added to their natural adolescent growing pains.

René and Xavier became emotional and kept their embrace for longer than usual. Both brothers of sisters, the male empathy was comforting. Then, the barbecue was started and the beer put on ice.

Xavier had arrived late the night before and spent the night at an airport hotel. In the morning he met Claude and Adrienne at the courthouse, still horrified at what was happening. Although he accepted that Michel was innocent, he was glad to see him standing trial. Xavier considered him a coward who had never taken responsibility for his actions. He had been infuriated when he learned that Michel had barred Adrienne from the visitors' list. He was worried that the McKays would sue René. He had consulted a lawyer in New York who warned it would be a definite possibility were the events to have occurred in the United States. René could be left without his house and without his business.

He also needed to be near Adrienne and her family for a last time. Their marriage was almost over. It was a question of weeks. However civilized the relationships were, once the divorce was final, he could not stay attached neither to Adrienne nor the family. He was drinking in the North Atlantic air and memorizing the faces of these people and children he adored. It looked like they were getting back together but they were really saying goodbye.

Bad weather forced everyone to stay inside for the rest of the weekend. Xavier and Adrienne enjoyed a physical closeness that was dangerously comforting. He ruffled her hair. She patted his back. The family looked on in encouragement.

By Sunday evening, Lilly could no longer stand being cooped up and went out into the drizzle and unseasonable cold. She carried her kayak over her head down to the beach like an old French Canadian trapper. Xavier joined her with an old kayak that a neighbour let them use. As they paddled on the choppy bay, he asked Lilly what to expect. They still had three or four days of trial ahead, and then the jury's deliberation. The most important witnessses had yet to testify.

"OK. First thing is to discredit Dr. Bouchard, which is going to be very important. Then René's testimony. You realize that their father is taking a beating?"

"Yes. They don't talk about it, do they?"

"No, they don't. He would probably get a kick out of it all. He wasn't your ordinary Joe, my Uncle Phil. Look at the career he chose. His children aren't ordinary either."

"Or his niece!" Xavier added fondly.

She smiled wryly and continued, "Kathy has managed to seriously suggest that Philippe was not acting on the assumption of innocence."

"Yes. I thought she was quite brilliant."

"Yup. Who said Kathy Crossman wasn't good? Hanley is clever and dedicated but Kathy can and should win this. Then, cause of death. All we have is Michel's word that she had hit her head and that she died of some kind of hemorrhage. It might come down to whether the jury believes him or not. We're hoping Adrienne can bring up her father's examination of the body. And I don't think much is going to come from the bishop. He's coming you know. Big deal." Lilly the atheist huffed.

"He is? I thought he was in Rome," Xavier said.

"Yeah, he's decided to come. He's up north right now apparently."

"If they prove the abuse, then the cause of death should be credible. Can't they exhume the body?"

Lilly explained Simon's strategy, pausing at times to execute a difficult manoeuver. Xavier, who was less an expert than Lilly in the kayak, imitated her moves.

"It's not that easy. The family opposes exhumation. Should we fight for that? Before we even start, it's been twenty years. The decomposition might be insurmountable," Lilly said. "The only really expert team for that is in Montréal and they have a two year backlog. Even without that, it would mean a legal battle that could take months. The judge is on the verge of retiring, so he doesn't want to hear of it. Simon doesn't want to lose our positive momentum and, to a certain extent, I agree with him. But we are not out of the woods. We have our medical experts tomorrow. Maybe it's just my personal involvement but I'm nervous. I know Kathy will go for René. She was clear to me on that. Six to eight years for accessory to murder. If we're lucky, he could be released after two."

"I know. I can't even imagine." Xavier shook his head.

It was getting dark. He struggled with the current. Not used to kayaking in the darkness, he had to concentrate. Lilly seemed relieved to have somebody other than her cousins to talk to. She moved closer to Xavi so that he could hear her without effort.

"I thought Robert, the brother, would talk. I'm still hoping but I don't think it'll happen. He's told his friends he wants ten years for every hour his sister spent under the rain in the marsh."

"*Hostia.*"

"Yeah. *Hostia* is right! The thing is, Xavi, that he's such a nice guy. I thought he would come out with it. His father was violent. Growing up in that house couldn't have been too pretty. Simon will have to get it out of him. Then, there's Michel."

"The idiot," said Xavier.

"Two months ago, I would have agreed with you. I know it looks like that but, you know, I'm not worried about him. He will be fine. I can tell. He emanates acceptance and responsibility. He seems to be glad he's where he is. It's like he needs to be exonerated for his own peace and if he's not, he'll accept. Deep down, he's a hippie and a hometown boy. The jury will like that. I think he's suffered a lot."

"Oh right! Between Tahiti and Puerto Vallarta. Poor guy."

"You might have a point there!" she said, laughing. She shook her head at Xavier's stubborness and pointed towards home.

They started back at dusk. The shore was an irregular dark green wall under a charcoal dome. Small, pale lights like flickering candles shone at intervals between the trees. Crane Road was at sea level; it seemed to float on a hard metal sheet. It had a stark, lonely beauty, like the faraway place of a Danish folk tale.

"I know Robert personally, you know? He's a runner," said Lilly. "We workout at the same gym. He volunteers for everything. Takes little kids out on the fire truck at Christmas time. He's adorable. Everybody in town loves him."

"What did his father do to him?"

"Probably nothing. He was a strong boy and a superb hockey player. Played pro in Alberta for a while. Robert was his father's pride and joy. The old man has Alzheimer's now. Incapacitated. The mother died a few years ago. Young. Lung cancer, I think."

"Robert's still a fireman? I remember him on the beach the first summer I came. Do you remember?"

"Yes, perfectly. A fireman, runner, vegetarian. I see him at the health food store all the time."

"A fireman and a vegetarian?"

"Yeah. Weird, isn't it?"

"Not really. His father probably tortured his dog or something."

Xavier didn't realize the effect his words would have on Lilly. ETA intimidated families by poisoning family pets or kidnapping them and dropping them on the highway. It was the type of thing Ander's cousins did. Anesthesized by terrorism, it had occurred to Xavier quite naturally as a perfectly plausible explanation for Robert's vegetarianism. He remembered a friend from school who had been seriously traumatized by the same situation.

Lilly froze, paddle in mid air. *Was that it? Was it possible? Why had she not thought of it?* She barely avoided capsizing as her mind raced. She paddled to shore, digging into the water at gold medal speed. Xavier was left gasping behind her wondering what had happened. By the time he had carried the two kayaks back up from the beach to the back yard, Lilly had left for Moncton and Adrienne had been notified she was testifying the next morning.

Adrienne was the first witness to be called at 10:00 a.m. Lilly came down from her office to the courtroom and stood near the door, her back to the wall. She acknowledged Xavier and Claude, who were sitting in their usual place, with a confident nod of the head. Eager to tell the story but aware of their weaknesses, they were all conscious of a turning point.

Kathy had changed the order of the witnesses with Simon's consent. The jury had retired for the weekend with a favourable opinion of Michel. Too favourable. She needed to start the week by changing that perspective. As for Simon, he was secretly happy to have Adrienne testify before the medical experts to plant the seeds of doubt. If she could refer to her father's unofficial autopsy, it could be an advantage.

Adrienne walked confidently - even enthusisastically - to the witness stand. She asked to take the oath in French, which pushed things back several minutes. These linguistic demands would not endear her to the jury. Claude held back a disapproving tsk and Xavier held back a frown. It was not the moment to make a point. But then, it never is. The judge sighed and took advantage of the lull to clean his glasses. Luckily, the bailiff was francophone. He quickly put his hand on the French version and Adrienne took her oath. She would declare, however, in the English language, so there was no need for a translator.

After situating Adrienne in Amsterdam and establishing her reasons for being there, Kathy followed with a bang. Her words dripped with sarcasm.

"You know what is so so curious about this case?" she asked rhetorically. "That of all the Monctonians who have gone to Amsterdam in the last few years, it would be Adrienne Blanchard who would come across Michel Bourgeois. What a coincidence! Now, how did that ever happen?"

She insinuated that Adrienne and René had had knowledge of Michel's whereabouts for years, that the brother and sister had been waiting for the ideal moment to bring him home. She aroused Adrienne's astonishment when she asked if the Blanchards had been financing Michel since his departure. It was an exercise in provocation. Finally, Kathy had Adrienne in a corner, defensive and angry. It was just where she wanted her.

She gave Adrienne no opportunity to explain anything. Quickly realizing that her position was one of inferiority, Adrienne stopped trying to win the verbal battle. She waited for a weakness and hoped she would win the war.

Kathy showed Adrienne a photo of Stowaway's on the small but busy side street of Amsterdam.

"Is this a picture of Mr. Bourgeois' takeout restaurant?" she asked.
"Yes."
"Where is this restaurant, please?"
"In central Amsterdam."

"Any particular part of Amsterdam?"

"In central Amsterdam. Near Dam Platz. The old section."

"Is that the section they call the 'the red-light district'?"

"Yes."

"Therefore, the restaurant was frequented by prostitutes?"

"I suppose so. And tourists, office workers, shop attendants from local businesses. It's not a dangerous neighbourhood and it's very popular."

"But prostitutes mostly, am I right?"

"No. Not really. I didn't see a majority of prostitutes in the line-up at rush hour. No."

"But there were prostitutes?"

"Yes."

"Will you look at this picture please?"

Kathy showed Adrienne a shot of Margie in her window. She was wearing mesh stockings and a black bikini. She was leaning forward, pushing her breasts together with her fists, and sticking out her tongue. You could clearly see a skull tattooed around her navel. Kathy walked over to the jury and distastefully held the large photograph out for them to see. The jury members leaned forward in their chairs to get a better view. Their expressions were varied: discomfort, disapproval, and even amusement.

"This photograph was taken from Mr. Bourgeois' restaurant. Do you recognize it?"

"Those are the women in the windows. They're all over the district, not just on that street. That's how it's organized," Adrienne said.

"What is organized?"

"The sex trade."

"The sex trade? Oh, you mean the brothels and the prostitutes and the pimps? Where women stand in shop windows with a price tag? So they can feed their families?" Kathy's tone dripped with sarcasm and moral authority.

"I understand they've legalized it. There are no pimps and the women get social security."

Adrienne disliked Kathy so much that she couldn't help contradicting her. Michel looked down at his hands. Here was Adrienne Blanchard defending his friend Margie.

"Oh, I see. Social security makes it alright then?"

"I wouldn't know. But it is one of the most important social experiments happening in the world right now."

"Oh, is it?'" Kathy rolled her eyes. "Hope this 'social experiment' doesn't come to Moncton any time soon. Frankly, it's not the ideal place to take the family to brunch. Nice view, eh kids?"

There was loud and sympathetic laughter. Kathy was enjoying herself. The judge scowled, however. He disliked theatrics and exaggeration. Simon objected and the judge sustained. Kathy bowed apologetically but she knew where she was going. She was destroying the saintly myth that had been created around Michel. Her objective was to put him in a different light. He was a drug user and a man who had always been on the fence between delinquency and all that was good, simple, and honest in their community. He had come home voluntarily but hedging his bets on some kind of promise. He was a man who was perfectly capable of a fit of fury; an unstable drug user, easily influenced by others and fond of prostitutes.

"You and Mr. Bourgeois went out a couple of times. To discuss his return?"

"Yes. We went out four times."

"You weren't apprehensive about having a drink with a suspected murderer?"

"No. I don't believe he is a murderer."

"That's not your decision nor was it your father's, Miss Blanchard."

"I know that. You asked me a question. I answered it."

Kathy reconfirmed her personal opinion that Adrienne Blanchard was a smartass.

"Yes. Right. Did you go to any of those coffee houses?"

"Yes."

"Where people take drugs?"

"Where people smoke cannabis, yes."

"Miss Blanchard…" Kathy paused, and then spoke in a condescending tone, "The sex trade, smoking cannabis…Maybe at the United Nations or in The Hague or wherever, people talk like that…but it's still called prostitution and taking drugs around here, OK?"

Adrienne felt the sting of Kathy's subliminal slap in the face. She realized she had been called a snob of the worst kind. She was one of those people who leave and then, come back home to show off. She wouldn't have cared except that she knew the jury probably shared the same opinion.

290

"Mr. Bourgeois smoked 'cannabis' then?"

"He smoked more cigarettes than joints, but, yes, he smoked. It's legal there."

"And you?"

"I don't smoke. Anything. We had a beer and a pizza at an Italian restaurant in downtown Amsterdam."

"So two old friends in a drug joint by a brothel?"

"We had a beer and a pizza at an Italian restaurant in downtown Amsterdam. One night we went to an Indonesian restaurant. Another night, we had Chinese."

Kathy shrugged and smiled with smug superiority. Happy with herself, even her language became colloquial and youthful. She pushed too hard and she would pay for it.

"So, do you think Michel Bourgeois would have come home if you hadn't showed up in Amsterdam and encouraged him? I mean, coming back a war hero, and voluntarily at that, is a whole lot better than coming home cuffed to a European Interpol officer, right? Was that your argument? What did you promise this guy, Adrienne Blanchard?"

The judge glared at Simon, who let it pass without objection. Kathy had made a bad mistake and Simon fervently hoped that Adrienne would see the open door. She did. She grabbed the opportunity, turned to face the jury, and very deliberately said, "I told him I knew he hadn't killed her. I told him that I had medical proof of his innocence."

Kathy shouted over Adrienne's last words, "That will be all! Your witness, counsellor."

The judge pounded his gavel, dismissed the court until one o'clock, and demanded to see Simon and Kathy inmediately in his chambers. If they wanted to move to Hollywood and appear on Courtroom TV, they could go right ahead, but there would be no more theatre in his courtroom. He could give a damn about their crusades or reputations.

When the court resumed, both lawyers seemed to have come to some kind of a non-belligerency agreement. In fact, Simon's cross-examination of Adrienne in the afternoon was quite beautiful, in so far as a courtroom testimony about murder can be beautiful. Kathy objected to only one technicality and Simon bowed like a gentleman.

He was masterful in his cross-examination of Adrienne. In a soft voice, he began: "Adrienne, I want you to remember Michel. I want you to remember Michel, when he was hurt, when he came to your house everyday to see your father."

Simon, gently guiding Adrienne with his questions, drew a scene from her childhood. Everyone in the courtroom was transported to 1971. A nine-year-old girl sat in her house after school. A sixteen-year-old boy waited every day across the street for her father to come home. Every day, the girl's mother would look out the window, see the boy waiting there and send her son to invite him in. He would always be offered milk or tea with cookies, but never asked for more than a glass of water. They would all watch television in the den until Papa came home. The boys loved the Road Runner cartoons. They would burst into hysterical laughter every time the poor coyote was foiled by the road runner. Adrienne couldn't understand it, she always felt sorry for the coyote. As soon as her father arrived, Michel would spring up and go down directly to the basement. A short time later, the door was closed so quietly that no one knew he had gone. From the window, Adrienne would see him walk away, protecting his arm now wrapped in pristine white bandages.

Simon took Adrienne back to the day she read a poem at school for Yvette's memorial. All the little girls whispered about Michel Bourgeois and called him a monster. She had also called him a monster, but little Adrienne had known it wasn't true.

Simon had Adrienne explain how in Amsterdam, she had told Michel how to find her if he decided to go home. How she had arranged to meet him at the airport at the Air Canada desk if he chose to return home and give himself up. She had made two reservations for Moncton and one for New York in case he didn't show up. But he had arrived before her. Afraid to miss the flight, he had not slept.

And that was Adrienne Blanchard's day in court.

Hubris

Michel's guilt or innocence did not rest on Adrienne's testimony but on the hard facts of Dr. Bouchard's autopsy. Simon's defence had to demonstrate Bouchard's incompetence, or at the very least, suggest that his autopsy could not be considered trustworthy. Dr. Bouchard's licence to practise medicine had been revoked in the fall of 1974, following a legal battle in the province of Québec that had lasted several years. All of these events had occurred long before. Dr. Stephen Fowler, the representative of the New Brunswick Medical Association, had to base his testimony on smudged and badly typed reports found in rusty file cabinets in the basement at the Association's headquarters.

He was predictably lukewarm in his condemnation of Dr. Bouchard. He had only third-hand knowledge of the case and the self-preservation instinct of those of the same profession. He related the facts. The Québec Medical Association had alerted the New Brunswick Association of the decision. Dr. Bouchard and the Hotel Dieu Hospital had been notified by registered mail and Dr. Bouchard had quietly disappeared. The sentence had been firm, and Bouchard had not contested.

"Does this mean that all of Bouchard's work was invalid? Those were thousands of cases," said Kathy.

"Not by any means," stated the doctor. He was adamant that if a case was not contested there was no basis for doubt.

Dr. Fowler went on to explain that Dr. Bouchard had been one of the most brilliant students of the *Ecole de Médecine*[119] of the Université de Montréal of the class of 1955. The French Hospital of Moncton had been extremely lucky to have him, as good pathologists were few and far between

---

[119] Faculty of Medicine.

and could choose their postings. In fact, during the four years Bouchard had been in Moncton, he had been an asset to the medical community of the Atlantic provinces. He had been called several times for consultation in difficult cases in Saint John, Halifax, and St. John's, Newfoundland.

"There's absolutely no reason at all to doubt his findings?" asked Kathy.

"No reason at all," the doctor responded.

Simon focused on the negligence. Doctor Fowler had no details of the actual cases. It had been long ago. The Québec Medical Association had not answered his requests for information.

"Doesn't it seem to you, doctor, that three counts of gross negligence - three - are particularly significant?" Simon asked. "These could not be isolated occurences due to accidental circumstance. It had to be a pattern."

Kathy objected but the judge allowed Simon to continue.

"Yes, I must say that this is true and, in fact, he was excluded from the profession. These actions are not taken lightly. They affect a colleague's livelihood and reputation, and reflect badly on our profession. As a matter of fact, these sentences are quite rare. There are warnings, there are suspensions ..."

"Dr. Bouchard, in effect, was stopped from doing any further harm?"

"In a manner of speaking," the doctor admitted.

"Was alcohol a factor in any of these cases?" Simon asked.

"Yes. All of them."

"Thank you. No more questions, your Honour."

Kathy's cross-examination was brief.

"Was there ever any evidence of malpractice or negligence during the four years he worked in New Brunswick?"

"Not a single case."

"He was guest speaker at the 1972 New Brunswick Medical Doctors convention in Saint Andrew's, was he not? There was a dinner given in his honour, was there not?"

"Yes, that is true," the doctor said.

"Thank you, sir."

Simon called Dora LeBlanc, the doctor's secretary.

"You worked for Dr. Bouchard at the Hotel Dieu Hospital in the early seventies, Mrs. LeBlanc?"

"That's Ms. LeBlanc. Yes, and I still work there. It's called Dr. Georges L. Dumont University Hospital Centre now. Got the day off to come here!"

"What were your responsibilities?"

"Bilingual secretary," she said proudly.

"Did you think Dr. Bouchard was a good doctor?"

Kathy objected. How could a secretary judge if a doctor was good or not? Simon rephrased the question.

"Did the doctor ever show any behaviour that you thought might not be appropriate for a doctor?"

"Yes, he did."

"What kind of behaviour?"

"Well, he always had a bottle of liquor under his desk. It went down fast, let me tell you!" Dora spoke in a low voice as if she were sharing a terrible secret. "Once, he sent me out to buy a bottle of vodka! I'll always remember that: Smirnoff, 40 ounces!"

Kathy had to object again. How many professionals keep a bottle of liquor in their offices for an occasional after-hours drink?

"You didn't work for the doctor very long?" Simon inquired.

"No. I asked for a transfer."

"Why?"

"Well, I didn't like him. He had a temper and he treated me like I was second-class, you know?"

"How do you mean?"

"Well, he was from Montréal. He used to laugh at how I spoke French. You know, we talk a little different here."

"How? I don't understand."

"Because I use English words a lot. It's the way we talk here, a lot of us."

"Wow…Nice guy, this Bouchard."

"Objection," said Kathy.

"Sustained," said the judge.

"So you got the transfer?" asked Simon.

"Yes, into the accounting department. I am retiring in two more years!" said Dora.

"Congratulations Dora. Thank you for your time."

Dora sat very straight with a big smile on her face, proud of her shiny auburn hair fresh from the beauty shop. Kathy walked up to the witness box.

"How long did you work for Dr. Bouchard, Dora?" asked Kathy.

"Hi Kathy, remember me? I used to babysit you when I was a teenager and you were just little."

"Yes, I do. Hi Dora! Answer my questions, OK?" said Kathy. Kathy couldn't help a friendly and amused smile. The people in the courtroom giggled. The exasperated judge sighed again. "So, how long did you work for the doctor?"

"Not long. Not a whole year, I don't think."

"Do you remember the dates?"

"Yes, he arrived in the summer of 1971, I was his first secretary. I didn't make it to the next summer."

"That was before the Landry murder. So, during that time did you ever see him take a drink? I mean: did he fill a glass from a bottle and drink it in front of you?"

"No. I didn't see that."

"You saw his mail. You knew his affairs. Was he ever criticized or did he run into any professional troubles from what you could see?"

"No. Not that I know of."

"Thank you, Dora," Kathy said.

"Is that all? Can I leave?"

"Yes."

"Oh, that was quick. Say 'Hi' to your mom!" Dora said.

"Sure will!"

Dora LeBlanc won everybody's heart but Simon Hanley still hadn't won the case. It was difficult to say which way the scale was tipping. However, Simon was reasonably content. Dr. Bouchard had not come out smelling of roses. It was clearer and clearer every day that this was going to be a question of faith.

The medical experts, two retired professors from Dalhousie University Medical School in Halifax, did not help Michel's case at all. They both declared that the autopsy was in order and that a sixteen-year-old girl found abandoned on a riverbank with bruises, scratches, semen in her vagina, and a lump on her head had a 95 percent chance of having died a violent death. The alternate theory of a massive hemorrhage due to a ruptured artery from a previous fall was possible of course, although rare. The horizontal position, the increase of blood circulation during intercourse and the smoking of cannabis could have contributed to that scenario. Without the body, one would never know. Both experts were equally cautious as to the hemorrhage theory but did say that it was a possibility.

Kathy did not go much further than that. She concluded: "The autopsy is in order?"

"Yes," said the medical expert.

"A 95 percent chance of violent death?"

"Oh yes, absolutely."

Simon had the privilege to go last.

"Is it possible that a pathologist could have jumped to conclusions?" he asked.

"Yes, very easily. All of the arrows pointed the same way. But a good pathologist would understand that this was a child. This was murder. You can make a mistake but you don't jump to conclusions at a time like that unless…"

"Unless what?"

"Unless you're incompetent, you're drunk, or you don't care."

Sadly, it would have been the perfect time to introduce Philippe's written testimony of his examination of the body. All of the arrows pointing in the same direction was exactly what he had worried about.

The bishop was next. He wore his robes to court. He had a small, wood crucifix on a string around his neck, which he held in both hands as he took the oath. He sat down slowly and carefully, spreading his cassock like a Spanish queen about to receive her court. It was not typical of Roger who, the night before, had stopped by Crane Road to see the children in his Bermuda shorts and Adidas sneakers. Perhaps he just wanted to impress the court with the information that he knew his best friend would want him to share. He put his chin up and raised his eyebrows regally as he waited for Simon's questions.

"Your Grace, do you recall the events that transpired on the night of May 30, 1973?"

"Please call me Father Losier, if you don't mind." The Bishop corrected Simon nicely.

"Of course. Father Losier, do you recall that night in May nineteen years ago?"

"Yes, I remember it very well and in every detail because it was out of the ordinary. Also, I lost my dear friend Philippe shortly after that. I took a position at the Canadian delegation to the Vatican in October of 1973 and that was one of the last times that I saw him. As a matter of fact, it was Philippe who encouraged me to apply for the position."

"Could you relate the events, please?"

"Yes. Philippe called me at the presbitary around two in the morning. He told me that he needed the sacrament of confession. I was surprised and worried at the urgency. I assumed that something terrible had happened at the penitentiary. However, when I arrived at the house on Temple Street, he was calm and serene. He closed the curtains and knelt in the living room with his son. I told him that this was not appropriate but he insisted. His son needed to hear his confession. He was my best friend so I - how do you say that? - I humoured him. Yes. I always did. You could say that Philippe had designed his own religion, and I respected that."

"Will you violate the secret of confession, Father?"

"Well, usually, you have to ask your bishop for permission, but as my bishop is the Holy Father, I will take the decision myself. He's a little busy, you know?"

Roger spoke excellent English but with a familiar and heavy Acadian accent. He made the Pope seem like the guy next door. Even the judge permitted himself a chuckle. Roger waited for silence before he spoke. He knew it would come. It was not everyday one could hear the confession of another's sins. The priest chose his moment and carefully and deliberately pronounced only one word in the quiet and expectant courtroom.

"Hubris."

The judge sat back in his chair and resisted an urge to smile. He knew exactly the definition of hubris. He was a judge. He had to fight with it every day.

"Hubris?" said Simon.

"Yes, he accused himself of the greatest sin of all: the sin of pride. The sin of Satan, the fallen angel, who thought he was greater than God."

The only noise heard in the courtroom was the distant rumble of light city traffic.

"Hubris," he continued. "When one sees oneself as omnipotent, but only God is omnipotent, of course. One can not put oneself in God's place. The confusion comes because we are created in God's image and we are beautiful, but we are not divine. That is what happened to Lucifer, the most magnificent of God's angels. And the most favoured. The Archangel. He dared to compare himself to God. He forced other angels to worship him and he was condemned for eternity. Now, you can say, and I will agree with you, that these are myths created in the imagination of medieval monks."

Roger paused like a Shakesperian actor, pointed his finger to heaven and shouted:

"BUT!"

Startled, Simon looked up. He was totally absorbed in the story. Simon Hanley was a subdued and non-practising Episcopalian, unused to Catholic myths and lore.

"The sin of pride is one of the most common sins," the bishop said. "It happens when one has such an inflated perception of their own intelligence, goodness, wisdom, or righteousness that one no longer perceives their own frailties or limitations. It's a disregard for the welfare of others. For example, world leaders who have so much power that they feel infallible. But we don't have to go so far. No. Not so far at all. Pride is the seed of selfishness, the opposite of humility. It is putting one's own wants and desires above those of others and above the common good. Who has not committed the sin of pride?"

Simon's question came naturally. It was not planned, weighed, or calculated.

"Would you say then, that this was Dr. Blanchard's state of mind that night? That somehow - how could I say this? He had taken God's place in choosing Michel's future? And that he was asking for forgiveness?"

"Yes, I do. But I don't think Phil wanted God's forgiveness. He was too rational for that and he had seen too much in his life. I think he wanted the boys' forgiveness. Michel and René."

It was a small triumph for Michel's case. Even the judge had what looked like an approving look on his face. Simon was very pleased. He had taken a risk in calling the bishop to the stand. Roger Losier had not taken his phone calls and refused a preparatory interview.

Xavier sat with his arms crossed over his chest wondering if Philippe had planned it. He had come back from the dead to take at least part of the blame. Michel looked out the window and resisted looking back at Adrienne.

It was Tuesday afternoon. The trial had begun almost a full week before. The weather had turned from cold and windy to hot and balmy. The jury was beginning to tire. They had been sequestered since the previous Friday at a Motor Hotel on a boring highway outside town. Only testimonies remaining were from the three boys: René, Robert, and Michel. That evening, the headline of the Moncton *Times & Transcript* read:

LANDRY MURDER CASE

EXPERTS SAY 95% PROBABILITY OF VIOLENT DEATH

Les Trois Garçons[120]

René sat in the witness box waiting to relive those four days again. He also took his oath in his mother tongue.

It seemed an eternity had passed since he had been an unwilling participant in Michel's nightmare. His father's death. His literary studies at l'Université de Moncton. Meeting his soulmate Jocelyne one summer on the beach. Being awarded a France-Acadie bursary and living in Paris for a year. Writing poetry. Then starting out, getting married, working two jobs. Finally, he opened his own business and now had three employees. White hair. Allergy problems. Two daughters. Ballet classes and soccer practises. He was thirty-eight years old, the same age as Michel. And now what? Simon had said "trust me."

René realized that he hadn't seen Michel since the night he watched him walk down a deserted street to a bus stop where no one was waiting. He looked over to Michel, who met his eyes. René's feelings were undetermined, abstract. What was certain was that they were now two men. Those two boys were past selves that existed in some forgotten loop in time, reliving the same event again and again.

Lilly had insisted that René be publicly advised of his rights.

"Mr. Blanchard, you are testifying today in the case of the Crown versus Michel Bourgeois. Do you understand that you are obliged to answer all questions fully and truthfully even if you must confess to actions that could incriminate you?"

"Yes, I do. I understand."

---

[120] The Three Boys.

"Do you understand that this testimony will not be used against you if, in the future, you stand trial for any illegal or criminal act to which you may admit today."

"I understand. I will answer to the best of my recollection and with the truth."

René repeated what he had told Simon. He found Michel sitting on the ground in a quasi-fetal position. His first impression was that Michel was sick, that he was dying, that he had been hit by a car. René could see his heart beating in his throat. "Please, go get your father," Michel had croaked. Philippe had crouched down beside Michel in the tiny space and recognized an acute anxiety attack.

"Listen to me. Calm down. Whatever it is, it's not the end of the world."

"*Oui, Docteur. C'est la fin du monde. C'est vraiment la fin du monde.*"[121]

Philippe sent René inside to get Valium from the refrigerator in the basement. Fortunately, his mother was not at home. She had gone shopping with his sisters. They moved carefully into the small tool room in the garage. Michel sat on a stool. René watched the door. Philippe listened to Michel's agitated account of the previous days and pieced the story together. The Valium calmed Michel down. Philippe spoke quietly, his hand on Michel's burned arm at all times. Michel was relieved and grateful. His breathing became easier. Philippe would take Michel to the police personally and help his family find a good lawyer. It would be difficult but Michel was not alone and Yvette's death surely had a logical explanation.

But first the doctor asked Michel for permission to check something out. It would mean hiding in the garage until the next afternoon. But it could be important. At that point, another twenty-four hours would not make much difference. Michel, in his confusion, said yes. René agreed obediently. Michel was given another pill.

"This is the first time we've heard that, in the beginning, your father intended to take Michel to the police. What changed his mind?"

"He changed his mind the next day when he came home from the hospital. He had examined the body. With Dr. Bouchard."

"Your father examined Yvette Landry's body with Dr. Bouchard?"

---

121 Yes, Doctor. It is the end of the world. It is really the end of the world.

"Yes. He knew Bouchard well. My father performed autopsies at the hospital with Dr. Bouchard's help. Deaths or occasional suicides from the prison."

"What did he say to you when he came home?"

"They're going to lock him up."

"They're going to lock him up," Simon repeated. "Did you hear what he said to Michel?"

Kathy objected but the judge overruled.

He said, "It wasn't the pot, Michel. But it doesn't look good. Tell me exactly how, when, and where she hit her head."

René wasn't sure when the decision to escape had been taken. He had suffered from anxiety as well but he wasn't given any pills. The police were combing the city. The funeral had been on the national news. René was told to stay out of the garage and to go to class as usual. On the fourth day, his father asked him to drive Michel to a bus stop an hour and a half away. A car would be parked in the neighbourhood and Michel would be inside. For that hour and a half, René would be vulnerable. He accepted but he didn't feel that he had a choice.

The questions became more and more technical. René was on the stand for two hours. The truth was extraordinary and banal. He answered each question conscientiously. René was determined to leave no strings hanging.

> He left at five to ten. As he walked down the porch, he saw his father through the living room window. One hand was over his eyes, the other over his heart. He had a medical journal open on his lap. His father was in turmoil. Somehow that made René feel better. Proud. Strong. Loved. The black Comet was in the parking lot of a liquor store four blocks away.
>
> "Es tu là? Are you there?" he whispered into the darkness of the empty car as he put the keys into the ignition. Michel was under a blanket, squeezed into the space behind the front seat.
>
> "Fuck off." He heard Michel's voice from under the blanket.
>
> It struck René funny. He laughed and drove off. They had barely reached the Trans-Canada Highway when Michel climbed into the

front seat and they looked for a good rock music station on the radio. They were only eighteen years old.

Michel pulled out the brown wallet with his new identification. Cigarette hanging from the corner of his mouth, he said, "I didn't do it, you know. So you'll feel better about this."

"Jesus. Of course you didn't do it. You're afraid of mosquitoes."

"Spiders. Not mosquitoes."

"Jesus Christ." René shook his head.

"Yeah, I know. Fucking bastard."

"Her father, right?"

"Pushed her down the stairs. She smashed her head against the corner of the radiator."

"Fuck."

Michel used the glove compartment light to study his new ID. He went through the thick pile of wallet-size cards.

"Jesus. Birth certificate. Driver's licence. Everything. Even Red Cross blood type card."

"Throw out the blood card. What if you're in an accident and they give you the wrong type?"

"Right. Hey, same birthday as me. But different year."

"That's cool. Maybe it's lucky."

"Maybe. And maybe I'll be back tomorrow night."

"So, what's your name?"

"Brian."

"Hi there, Brian!"

"Brian Gordon Ogilvy. Ha! Hey, I'm an English dude all of a sudden."

They laughed because they knew that was impossible.

René Blanchard's testimony was not all it had been cracked up to be. It was just more of Dr. Blanchard's involvement. There was a reference to his examination of the body but no hint as to the abuse. They had mentioned the blow to the head, but it was not enough information to counteract the experts and establish a reasonable doubt.

There was only one moment that might have shed some positive light on Michel's case. But again, it was faith. It was Simon's last question.

"Do you believe Michel Bourgeois beat Yvette Landry to death? That he smashed her head with a rock, punched her repeatedly, cracked her ribs, and used a sharp instrument to scratch and mutilate her skin?"

"No."

"Why?"

René didn't answer right away. It was a good question. *Why did he believe? He hadn't been there.* René looked for the truth and he found it.

"Because he told my father he didn't. And Michel would never lie to my father."

Robert Landry was Kathy's star witness. The vegetarian-cum-runner-cum-fireman was a clean cut, well-built young man in his early thirties. He was a volunteer hockey referee and was studying psychology at the university. As a fireman he was able to juggle his timetable to attend most of his classes. Not surprisingly, he was specializing in trauma studies to help victims of violence, conflicts, and accidents.

Robert came to testify with a very clear purpose: to remind everyone of the true victim. Yvette had not had the privilege of travelling the world. She had not been received as a romantic and tragic Ulysses. She had been left to rot by the creek. Robert had a recurrent nightmare: he was lying on his back, soaked to the bone, unable to move.

He was dressed casually that day but there was something military about Robert. He was perfectly groomed, he shook hands too firmly, and he was polite to the point of exaggeration. As he took his seat, he glanced briefly at Michel but remained impassive. He looked for Adrienne and located where she was. When Kathy approached the stand to begin questioning, he gave her a sad, circumstantial smile. They had met to discuss the testimony he wished to give. Kathy would work her closing arguments around it.

"It's been a long time since your sister died."

"Yes, I was twelve years old. I was in grade eight at Aberdeen School."

"She was a good sister? Did you get along?"

"The best. Everybody will tell you that. She was the sweetest thing you ever met. She was only four years older than me, but I was her baby. She used to comb my hair and pick out my clothes. She bought me penny candy with her babysitting money."

Robert had held up well up to that point, but his voice cracked with emotion. He took a sip of water.

"Are you okay, Robert?" Kathy asked.

"I'm fine. Happy, well, not happy to be here but happy to be here. I don't know if you understand what I mean."

"I think everybody understands what you mean."

"Thank you. I'm fine. Really. We can continue."

"Do you recognize the man sitting at the end of this table?" Kathy pointed to Michel.

"Yes. Michel Bourgeois. He was going out with my sister at the time."

"What did you think about that?"

"I was twelve. I didn't think about it too much. But my parents detested him. They thought that he was a bad influence."

"A bad influence. Why did they worry? What was it about Michel Bourgeois they didn't like?"

"They hated everything. His hair, his clothes, his life."

"His life?"

"Well, I don't like to say this, but he was what you'd call a loser, I suppose."

"How so?"

"He was a dropout. He lived in a trailer. He had been in trouble."

"Not Prince Charming," Kathy said.

"Not exactly."

"Did she talk to you about him?"

"Yes, she did. She told me not to pay attention to my dad's ranting and raving, that Michel was a very nice guy. You know, 'big sister in love' talk."

Robert shrugged self-consciously and then bit his lip. He was reaching into some treasured but painful memories. His fairness towards Michel, in spite of everything, was admirable.

"You say your father shouted at her a lot. Was he a strict father?"

"Yes. I guess so. He was. He wanted the best for us. For me, it was hockey. For Yvette, probably a good job, marriage, kids, a pretty house. He was afraid that she'd get pregnant and end up on welfare. My dad was old fashioned. He brought us up the way he was brought up. Yelled a little too much maybe, but he cared."

"Do you remember the last time you saw your sister?"

"You never forget something like that."

"When was it exactly?"

"We lost her on a Friday. On the Tuesday before, at lunch, she came by my school to say 'Hi.' She was at Vanier High. I was eating my lunch in the school-yard. She was on her way to Bright's to have her lunch with Michel while he was on his break."

"What happened the day Yvette disappeared? Did Michel come and pick her up at home?"

"Well, I wasn't home that week. But he never came to the house. He always waited for her on the corner in front of a small confectionary store that's gone now. Smoking. It used to make my father really mad. I hadn't seen her for four days. I was staying at my cousin Paul's."

"You were at your cousin's?"

"Yes. Both my parents worked shifts. My dad at CN, my mom at the Arlington Street Bakery. My cousin and I were on the same hockey team. It was my aunt who drove us to the practises and the games. That year, I think we had ice time at six in the morning. I kept my gear in Aunt Annette's station wagon, so I ended up staying overnight sometimes, that's all. They had bunk beds. It was easier that way."

"Yvette talked about running away to Montréal. Did you know about that?"

"Yes. We kept it a secret from my parents. My father would have gone nuts."

"Why was she so obsessed with Montréal?"

"That came from a long way back. We went to the World's Fair, Expo '67, with my dad when we were kids. I don't remember the trip too much - only La Ronde[122]- and that mini train that went through the big globe,

---

122 Amusement park of the Montréal World's Fair.

but Yvette loved it. She stood in line with my dad at all the pavilions with that Expo passport and got a bunch of stamps. Thirty-two stamps, I think. I still have the passport. We went to the top of Mount Royal at night to see the city lights. She begged my father to stay one more day but we couldn't afford it, we had to come home. And, well, there's more but it's probably not important."

"Tell us about her. We don't know anything about her, Robert."

Kathy prodded him for more details about his sister. It was important for the jury to visualize the pretty young teenager who had lost her life. All of the attention was on Michel and the Blanchard boy. Yvette deserved her place.

"My sister loved clothes and make-up and music. She was dying to live in a big city. She wanted to be a single girl - a 'bachelorette'- she called it. Work in a fancy store, eat in big Chinese restaurants. She had this plan: I would be drafted by the Montréal Canadiens[123] and we would rent a big house on the mountain. With a pool!"

He chuckled wryly. Almost everyone in Moncton knew that Robert Landry's hockey career had been promising but that he had not made it to the big league. He had had a good shot. Everyone respected that. Robert didn't seem to have any pretenses or regrets. As Lilly had said, he was adorable. He had the jury in the palm of his hand.

"Strict dad. Tired of school. Money in her pocket. She had just turned sixteen, working age. Did you think she had gone to Montréal?"

"Yes, I did! Actually, my aunt told me she was gone but that she'd be back. So, I was almost glad for her. For days, I calculated where she was. I wondered if she had found a job. I checked the mailbox every day. I even thought of going to Bright's on my lunch hour and asking Michel what he could tell me, but we weren't allowed to leave the school yard."

He looked to the back of the courtroom where Adrienne was sitting and she nodded in agreement.

"And then they found her," Kathy said quietly.

Robert made a small grimace and nodded.

"Please say 'yes' or 'no,' Mr. Landry. For the records."

---

123 NHL ice hockey team based in Montréal.

"Yes. They found her. He had left her there. All alone. Half buried in the mud."

Kathy let the abominable truth hang in the air. Robert Landry did not make a fuss when he said it. His poise was extraordinary. Vengeance would be a false relief, but he wanted the solace of justice and the comfort of closure.

The courtroom was quiet. Michel remembered the fear that had paralyzed his mind. He remembered trying to breathe with the desperation of a fish struggling on a hook. He knew what he had done wrong. He had wanted to survive.

Then Simon's cross-examination began. He was confident. He used his first trump card.

"Mr. Landry. Several times during your testimony, when you refer to your father, you use curious vocabulary." Simon read from a note pad he held in his hand. "I quote: *detested, screamed, really mad, ranting and raving, hated, yelled, go nuts, strict, angry*. Would you say that your father was a violent man?"

Robert was upset. He felt he had given the wrong impression. The violence he had lived at home was forgiven, a thing of the past. Somehow it had seeped into his language. Alzheimer's had slowly erased his father's rage. Antoine Landry had become a sweet and affable old man who lived in a home and remembered Robert on many days. He would ask him how many goals he had scored. "Two!" Robert would answer every time. Assists? "One!" Robert would answer. Antoine would exclaim, "That's my boy! You know, your sister came to see me yesterday."

Robert was honest and decent. He answered the question.

"He had a temper. We tried to avoid getting him upset."

"Did he ever use physical violence?" asked Simon. He knew everyone was expecting this question. Robert was ready for it. Kathy had warned him. They had discussed his answer.

"Like I said, he brought us up the way he was brought up. With discipline. To be obedient and respectful."

"Right."

Kathy was taken aback when Simon did not follow the line of questioning. He changed the subject.

"In September of 1979, you were interviewed on CBC Radio. Is that correct?"

"I've been on a lot of radio shows for one reason or another. Can you be more specific?"

"A teen program called *Reaching Out*?"

"Yes." Robert realized he had been caught off guard yet again.

"You were representing the Moncton chapter of Alateen, were you not?"

"Yes."

"What is Alateen?"

"It's a support group for teenagers who are affected by someone else's drinking. It's a spin-off of Alcoholics Anonymous."

"Was it a family member in your case?"

"Yes. My father."

Simon ran his hands over his face and back around his head. He pushed his hair back, held up his own head by the neck, looked up at the ceiling, and took a deep breath in preparation for an important revelation. The judge scowled, lowered his head, and looked up over his glasses. Simon got the message. He resumed.

"OK, Robert. You said you were staying at your cousin Paul's?"

"Yes, I was."

"Because of hockey."

"Right."

Simon paused for effect. Very softly, very diplomatically, he said, "Robert. It was the end of May. There's no hockey in May. The season was finished."

A dog barked in the distance. A truck outside the building backed up. Everyone waited for the explanation. Robert was ashamed to have been caught in a half-truth.

"Oh, maybe. But, I stayed there a lot. Paul was my best friend. Still is."

"Maybe. OK."

Simon paused and once again changed his line of questioning. He was careful and considerate in his tone.

"Robert, who was Casper?"

Robert froze. Casper was his other nightmare. He didn't know if he would be able to bear it. He looked at Michel, who appeared to be both surprised and apologetic. Late Sunday night, Simon had called the detention centre to ask Michel if Robert had ever had a dog. The night guard had let him answer the phone only because he was on trial. A sleepy Michel vaguely remembered Yvette mentioning something about a dog and that Robert had been heartbroken when it had died. Nobody really knew what had happened but Yvette suspected that her father had been rough. On Monday at lunch, Simon had visited the Landry's chatty neighbour. She remembered the puppy's name and shared an ugly rumour.

Robert's answer was not much more than a worried whisper. "My dog. When I was little."

"Named after Casper the friendly ghost? Of the comic books? I liked Casper."

"Yes."

"What kind of dog? White I bet!"

"Just a mutt. Small, white, fluffy, friendly. He was half-poodle so he was very smart."

"How long did you have him?"

"About six months."

Simon paused again and pressed his lips together as if he really did not want to ask this question. He dipped his head and asked in a quiet voice, "What happened to Casper, Robert?"

Kathy voiced a strong objection. The defence was going nowhere and wasting time. The judge ordered both lawyers to approach the bench. The tension that had been missing from the trial surfaced. The McKays, the Blanchards, the jury, the journalists, and the public shifted in their seats, unsure, not grasping what was happening. Xavier put his hand over his mouth and waited uncomfortably. He had immediately understood that this was the result of his brief comment to Lilly and of her race to shore.

Robert had been a child star. The best in his league. The best in town. At age ten, he had already been scouted. But hockey wasn't fun anymore. Getting up at five everyday. The obligation to score, not to disappoint. Everyone was more worried about his getting injured than if he passed his exams at school. The dog had helped him have fun again. Casper had been a ray of sunshine. All through that summer, Robert had taken him everywhere. Casper gave Robert unconditional love. Simply, a boy and his dog.

Even as a young boy, Robert Landry had had the guts and the heart of a champion. He had always known what he wanted. He was tired of hockey. He had decided to tell his father.

Simon asked again, "What happened to Casper?"

Robert braced himself and looked at Simon straight in the eye. Simon nodded and put his hand on his heart. Robert acknowledged the gesture with an imperceptible nod. Robert was a good and honest man. He had come to testify, understanding the consequences.

"He died."

"How?"

"My father killed him."

"Did he put him down because he was sick?"

"No. He killed him to punish me."

"What had you done?"

"I asked to give up hockey and try basketball or swimming instead."

"So he killed your dog."

Robert took a deep breath and told the story, determined to keep his emotions under control.

"He beat him to death with the shovel. He smashed him against the house two or three times. Smashed his paws. Casper tried to run away but my father hit him real hard over his lower back with the spade. His hind legs gave up. He was dragging himself to me on his tummy, whimpering, looking up at me. It was my fault. I couldn't stand to see him suffer because of me. I screamed at my father, 'Hurry up! Kill him! Kill him now!' And then he smashed Casper on the head."

Robert wasn't crying but his breathing was fast, and his voice was high pitched. The last sentences had tumbled out of a frightened little boy. Simon kept his eyes locked on Robert's. He had taken him this far, he couldn't stop before the end. They were in it together.

"And then what?"

"October. We were burning leaves in the back yard. He threw him on the fire."

"Was he dead?"

"I don't know. He twitched and made a noise."

Someone in the room could not contain a horrified gasp.

"And now you're a firefighter and a vegetarian."

In the silence, the young fireman nodded, made an acquiescing noise in his throat, and tried not to cry. The courtroom was still. The judge covered his eyes and scribbled frantically on a legal pad. He had three prize Labradors.

Robert controlled himself quickly and looked up at the ceiling, opening his eyes wide to contain the tears. Simon gave him a moment.

"Do you need a glass of water?"

"No."

"I'm not finished."

"I know. Shoot."

"Thank you. That Tuesday, that last time you saw Yvette, she was wearing long sleeves, wasn't she?"

"Yes."

"It was hot that day. I looked it up. It's in the province's records as one of the warmest May days ever, 82 degrees. Why was she wearing long sleeves and pants?"

"To hide the bruises."

"Your father beat her up?"

"He didn't really beat her up. He used to pinch her and then twist really hard. It made big, dark bruises that lasted a long time. On her arms and legs. He did it so she wouldn't wear miniskirts or sleeveless tops. Sometimes she tried to resist but it was useless. He was stronger than her. He would just push her hard against a wall or shake her like a rag doll."

"She didn't come by your school just to say 'Hi' that day, did she?"

"No."

"What did she come to tell you?"

"She told me that dad was on a binge and to go to my aunt's. She'd let me know when he was better."

"Did she have a lot of marks and signs of violence on her body?"

"Too many. She wore hers and mine."

"I have no further questions. Thank you."

Kathy had planned a dramatic cross-examination but now she wasn't sure. She remained seated at first. Her right elbow was on the table, her chin in her hand. She was going over what had just happened and decided it would be conterproductive to fight it or deny it. She slowly got up. She smiled gently at Robert. She really didn't want to make him suffer again.

"You had some sister my friend, didn't you?"

"She was more than a sister. She was my angel. She still is."

"She's there, in your heart, I'm sure."

"Oh. She's watching for me from heaven. I know that. Two years ago, she saved my life."

Kathy widened her eyes and raised her shoulders up to her ears in a delicately humorous gesture. It would be good to lighten the atmosphere a bit.

"How is that possible?" she asked.

Robert was also more relaxed. At last, it was off his chest. He had decompressed. And his sister was having her moment. He was glad.

"Oh yeah. We were fighting a barn fire out on Salisbury Road. Routine. But barn fires can be tricky, eh? I was inside, doing my job. Not worried. It looked like it was under control. And then I heard her voice. It was clear but far away at the same time. The voice was floating around me in the smoke. I know it sounds weird but it was Yvette. I swear to God. It was her. She said…" Robert frowned, he needed to say it the way he had felt it, inside him. "Can I say it in French?"

"Of course."

"*Sauve-toi Robert! Cours!*"

Kathy could understand and speak French reasonably well. In fact, she was in the process of preparing her bilingualism certification. She looked at the jury and translated.

"'Save yourself, Robert Run!'. And what happened?" She turned again to Robert.

"I dropped the hose and ran out of there like I had the devil on my tail. Not two seconds later, the roof collapsed. I wouldn't be here today."

Kathy crossed her arms over her chest, pulled in her shoulders, leaned forward, and said sadly, "Yvette. Let's not forget that this is about her. She was sixteen years old. No more questions Mr. Landry. All of us thank you very much. For everything."

Robert swallowed hard and squared his shoulders. He nodded first to the judge, and then to Michel. He was escorted from the silent courtroom by the bailiff, who opened the door for him.

True Identity

Although it was only eleven o'clock, the judge decided to give the jury time to absorb Robert's dramatic testimony before listening to Michel. He adjourned until one and drove to his home outside town for lunch. He needed to be with his dogs. He walked down to the stream at the back of his property with Groucho, Harpo, and Chico, who competed for his attention. He played Three Ball, their favourite game. It consisted of throwing three tennis balls in opposite directions and studying their reactions and decisions. He cheered them on, patted them vigorously, let them kiss him, and - to their unbridled ecstasy - threw the balls again. As luck would have it, Chico was the smartest and Groucho the dumbest. Sam sometimes took Groucho out alone so he could fetch his own ball. Poor Groucho seemed to know this and nudged at the judge when the other two were asleep. Almost all judges have a phobia, a personal red line. For Sam Harris, it was cruelty to animals. He had been absolutely horrified by Casper's story and impressed by Robert Landry's spirit.

He had kept it to himself, but as a young public defender thirty years before, he had known Philippe Blanchard. He had worked for the parole board and visited the penitentiary often. Blanchard was already a legend at that time. He was a perfectly bilingual, attractive blond fellow who looked more like he belonged in a big city clinic than in a maximum security correctional institution. Blanchard had been taken hostage once and had successfully negotiated his own release, which had only added to his notoriety. Sam Harris sighed. It was obvious the doctor had seen the outcome clearly and decided to give the kid a chance. The temptation was always there. Hubris. It was too bad, but there was no way he could have admitted Philippe's medical report as evidence. The son of a gun had managed to wangle himself into Bouchard's morgue and examine the body. Such a shame that the man had died young.

The judge made himself a sandwich and prepared to return to court. As he was leaving the house, he looked into the mirror of the foyer. He stopped to adjust his tie. His cherished marble figure of Lady Justice was on the console table. A voluptuous, blindfolded maiden holding her scale and her sword. The scale was to weigh the facts, the blindfold to show impartiality, the sword to show strength and determination. He swept his fingers carefully over the scale. It had been a difficult morning. It had been a long career. He was surprised to feel his eyes fill with tears. His body had finally divorced his brain. It was the last day of his last trial.

The hour of reckoning was on Wednesday, August 26, 1992 at 1:15 p.m. When they called his name, Michel sprung from his chair without hesitation. Adrienne held her breath. Would the quiet and introspective Michel be able to defend himself?

For the first three or four minutes, his voice trembled. Except for a slightly familiar French intonation that perhaps only a Monctonian would grasp, his accent had completely disappeared. The jury saw him up close for the first time. His glasses were too big for his face. They made him look bookish and younger than he was. His profile was attractive.

The men and women of the jury had filed into their pre-assigned rows long-faced and looking tired. Robert Landry's tragic testimony had erased the glamorous whodunit atmosphere of the trial. Michel was the prodigal son who had returned to answer for his acts - undeniable acts. Which were real? Which were false? Did one act necessarily imply the other? The jury were good people who were unsure. They were suddenly conscious of their responsibility and they worried about making a mistake. Robert's testimony had put things in their place.

He told his story, first to Simon and then to Kathy.

Simon's first question was easy.

"Michel, last June 23, when Adrienne Blanchard walked into your place, you were running your business just like any other day. Could you imagine that, just two months later, you would be sitting in a Canadian courthouse, here in Moncton, facing a long prison sentence?"

Michel cleared his throat and then answered,

"I think that, subconsciously, I knew right away when Adrienne Blanchard came into my shop in Amsterdam, that I would be coming home."

"What did she say to you? It must have been quite a shock."

Simon's tone was friendly.

"She said 'Michel, do you remember me? or something like that. I was stunned. Just stunned. It was like I was being rescued but I wasn't sure if I felt like being rescued. Like I might rather stay where I was, on my comfortable lifeboat. It was as if I had forgotten that I was lost."

"You forgot you were lost? You forgot who you were?" said Simon.

"It was a defence mechanism, I guess. If I didn't think about it, I didn't feel nervous or in danger. But when I'd see a Canadian flag, when it snowed, or when I'd hear people speaking French, it would come back."

Michel tried very hard to describe what he felt.

"So, what did she tell you?"

"She gave me news of my family right away. It shook me up."

"What hit you the hardest?" Simon asked.

"The most? Probably that my little sister was at university getting a master's degree. I don't know why. For some reason, that hit me. It was really good, actually, to know everybody was okay. Doing fine."

"Did she tell you her father had died?"

"Yes. She told me that first afternoon."

"That was not good news for you, was it?" said Simon

"Well, I was upset. He was my friend," Michel sighed and went on. "It explained a lot of things. I always thought he would look for me - that it would be him who would show up one day. Not his daughter."

"You weren't expecting the Blanchards to look for you? Not even René? He knew your name."

"No. I knew René wouldn't look for me. It was kind of understood between him and me. Adrienne found me by accident. I don't have any doubts about that."

"So, for four days in Amsterdam, you saw Adrienne Blanchard every day. What did you talk about? How did she convince you to come home?"

"Well, She picked me up after work for those four or five days and we went out for dinner. Then I'd walk her to her hotel. I got used to her, to speaking French, to talking about home. I got used to being Michel again. The feeling sort of grew that it was time. I had to face the mess I had made."

"You were conscious you would face murder charges?" Simon was blunt.

"I did understand that. But I decided it would be worth it. To see my mother. To talk to my father. I wanted them to know what had happened. I never knew what they believed and that affected me. It bothered me that I had made myself look guilty by running away."

Simon flirted with the Blanchards' secondary guilt.

"What about Adrienne Blanchard? Did she encourage you to come home? Did she seem worried about your coming home?"

317

"You could say that she encouraged me. You could say I needed to be encouraged. She told me about the doctor who did the autopsy losing his licence for drinking. I thought I might have a chance. At least I could try. And if I went to jail, if that happened, I would make the best of it. I was hoping I could work in the kitchens."

"It was a huge decision. You were okay in Amsterdam. Didn't you have doubts about being found innocent?" Simon asked.

"I just wanted to wake up in my own skin. Whatever that meant. Wherever that was."

Michel's reasons were simple. There was no indication of any dark purpose or manipulation. It was a gut decision with an understanding and an acceptance of the risks. He might have been apologetic about taking so long but he spoke in a quiet voice with no trace of anger or self-pity. It was an honest, intelligent, and respectable declaration.

It was obvious, too, that Adrienne Blanchard had been the catalyst of his return. But this fact favoured Simon's theory that the Blanchards, father and daughter, were responsible for Michel's most important decisions. Simon would have liked Michel to have been more melodramatic and to have insisted on the nostalgia, the homesickness, the anguish. The jury was going to need a lot of sympathy and a lot of faith.

It was not Simon's intention to dwell on the circumstantial events of Michel's life, of his escape, or of his traumas. He needed to convince the jury that Yvette had died of natural causes brought on by a terrible blow to the head. All else was a chain of unfortunate decisions with disastrous consequences.

Sadly, Robert's testimony had prepared everyone for what Michel would tell. Mr. Landry was a binge drinker. He'd be fine for a week or two or three and then very bad for several days. Young Yvette recognized the warnings. At the first sign, which might just be an empty beer can in the trash, she would send her brother to her Aunt Annette's. She'd spend most of the day out of the house, claiming she was babysitting. Yvette hated her mother more than she hated her father. Michel knew this sounded strange, but he thought that deep down, Yvette forgave her father but never forgave her mother for not defending her. Her father, paradoxically, was very loving when he was sober which was about half the time. Her mother hid in her room, chain-smoked, heated up frozen dinners, and watched soap operas on television. Yvette had sworn she would never be like her.

Yvette's father would squeeze her hand so tightly that her bones would crack. Her father often pulled her by the ear to drag her to her room. He once ripped out her earring and she had to go to the hospital for stitches. Her mother told the doctor she had been wrestling with her little brother.

The pinching was very painful but Yvette hated the shaking worst of all. Resisting her father only provoked him so she would let herself go limp. Michel thought she had probably suffered from whiplash because she often had bad headaches and always had a sore neck. And the day she died, he said, he was sure this had happened. She was dizzy and her knees gave out a couple of times. She told him that her father had pushed her down the stairs, but Michel wasn't so sure now. She might have lost her balance or passed out for a minute and tumbled down the stairs helplessly. She had hit her head very hard on the radiator pipe. She had a lump the size of an egg behind her ear, but she didn't complain. She never complained. Her speech was fuzzy that day. She repeated herself. She lost her balance. She was very pale. She had taken only one drag on the joint. When they were making out, she had acted strange. She pointed at the sky with her finger and hummed.

When they finished, he turned to her. He touched a big bruise on her arm to see if it was swollen. He leaned over to give it a kiss. The left side of her face was black and blue. Her eyes were open. She was dead.

His heart exploded and he heard howling in his ears. There was no air in his lungs. He felt a great thirst. He knelt beside her and rocked like a lunatic. He had a complete breakdown. He dragged her body about fifty yards to the creek and ran away. He thought he had done it. He thought the joint was bad. He wanted to dig a hole, crawl into it, and die. Despair and panic.

Michel dropped his head and stared at his hands. Then, with a neutral expression, he looked back up at Simon and waited for more questions. He was prepared for more.

Simon nodded paternally. He looked at Michel and took a spontaneous decision based on his instincts. No more Blanchards, no more excuses, no more shit. The jury was not stupid. *They believe it or they don't.*

"No more questions, your Honour," he said.

The judge seemed to agree. Kathy approached the stand.

She did not meet an enemy. On the contrary, Michel met her face-to-face and with respect, like the soldier that he had learned to be. It was "Yes ma'am" and "No ma'am." Seven years in the military and almost ten years on a ship had left their mark. They were hierarchical societies where the sensitive and solitary Michel had found refuge. He had welcomed the discipline and the order. Michel, as Brian, had survived. It was time now to survive the next part of his life. He answered again for his acts.

"Let's start with the drugs, Mr. Bourgeois. At what age did you start to smoke pot?"

"I think I was about twelve years old," Michel answered truthfully.

"Uh-huh. Ever had any bad experiences? Ever used anything stronger than pot?" Kathy asked, and pursed her lips in an expression of distaste.

"I might have had one or two bad experiences when I was young. I experimented a little, but it was expensive, and I didn't want to end up like a vegetable."

"But marijuana was okay?" Her tone was sarcastic.

The judge frowned.

"It made me feel better, I don't know, less worried. It was natural to me after a while. I functioned on it."

"Functioned?" Kathy did not let go of her belligerent attitude.

"Yes, I worked. Kids' jobs. Raked lawns. Shovelled snow. Packed groceries. Then the restaurant."

"So, how was high school, Mr. Bourgeois? Did you have lots of friends, do any sports, participate in student council?"

Kathy's tone was close to ridicule.

Simon protested loudly. "A little more respect for my client, please, Your Honour!"

The Judge agreed. Kathy rephrased.

"You quit school in grade 10. Didn't you have any friends? Was it so hard? Why did you quit?"

Kathy's first question had confused and upset Michel. His answer was vague. Only the loneliness he had felt as a boy came back to him.

"I didn't do any sports and I didn't have any friends, really. I changed schools and neighbourhoods when I was nine. My mother got married and had two kids. I had a job. I had a little money and I wanted to be on my own."

True Identity

"Define 'on my own,' please. Mr. Bourgeois," Kathy said.

Simon protested again. The judge overruled.

"My father gave me an old trailer he had, and I lived there. It was in a trailer park near the Moncton Stadium. When the winters got bad, I moved to the basement at my mother's house. I liked music, I worked, and I had a girlfriend. That was my life."

"I still don't understand how you would leave home, so young! Didn't you get along with your family?"

"I got along okay with the family but I grew up alone with my mom. So, the new life was a little hard."

Kathy drew a picture of the young Michel. It was a flat, one-dimensional view of a multi-dimensional human being. While it was factually accurate, it was out of context, unfair, and prejudiced. It was a picture in black and white of an uneducated, substance-abusing, unadapted teenager, totally subjugated by Dr. Philippe Blanchard. He was all of those things, but he was also a devoted and loving son, a good worker, a dreamer. He was a polite boy who packed grocery bags conscientiously, who raked leaves into neat piles, who fried a piece of cod to its perfect colour and consistency. Kathy tried to take away his dignity. The dignity of small things, of a modest life.

But Kathy Crossman was not a monster. How could she let a man with a 95 percent probability of being guilty of murdering a young girl walk away?

She also visited the death scene but from a very different angle. If he was stoned, if his ears were howling, if his heart was in his mouth, then he was out of his head, wasn't he?

"Were you or were you not, out of your head, Mr. Bourgeois? You have said you were beside yourself. You have said you were stoned and frantic and panicked. How can you even remember what happened? You might have killed her and you just don't remember!" she said while gesticulating theatrically.

Kathy's tone held alarm and urgency; it rang of a very possible truth. She was unforgivingly brutal.

Michel held on but Adrienne saw his face change. He lost hope. He felt guilty, which is what she had been afraid of. She struggled with her responsibility in bringing him home. Xavier felt her stiffen and squeezed her hand.

"You did the right thing, Adri," he whispered. "But this is necessary. He has to go through this. It wouldn't be right if he didn't."

She couldn't help thinking that twenty years before, her father had predicted that they would lock Michel up. He had been right. He knew more than any of them. René had been smarter than her. He had left it alone.

Kathy Crossman was not finished. She attacked with an unexpected weapon: photographs. Simon couldn't believe it. First the Amsterdam pictures and now these? They must have put a private detective on the case. It must have cost a pretty penny. He unsuccessfully objected to the photos.

> 1975: Michel is standing with a pretty girl, Judy, behind a giant cheque for $1,000. They are wearing happy and delighted smiles. The cheque was made out to the winners of the East Sector Recreation Centre Bridge tournament at Okinawa Naval Base.
>
> 1976: Fifty people in a group photo. Michel is sitting in the second row. He is in uniform, holding his diploma. It is the official photo of the graduation of US military sous-chefs, at the Military Culinary Institute in Oakland, California.
>
> 1978: Only three people in the photo. Michel is holding a second place trophy in a culinary competition for the desserts category. The photo was taken in Okinawa as well.
>
> 1984: The delighted sea captain is seated at a table. The white serviette folded into his collar does not even begin to cover his large chest and stomach. Michel is smiling. He is standing beside the captain, leaning forward to present him with a cake in the shape of a rum bottle. There is one candle on the cake and the words Happy Birthday are written in white icing in a circle to look like a label. When Michel was shown the picture, he nodded. It was him. He remembered making that cake. It had been complicated to get the neck just right. It was rum chocolate torte, the captain's favourite. It was truly delicious when made with and accompanied by dark Puerto Rican Rum.

1986: Istanbul. On a cruise boat restaurant on the Bosphorus, Michel is seated at a table with the rest of the crew watching a belly dancing performance. To baptize every new port of call, the captain liked to organize a typical dinner and a group photo. The Captain had wrapped a pale blue veil around his large hips and danced with the girls. The crew had died laughing.

This is what the jury heard. Michel had had the luck of the century. He had saved a lot of money. At age thirty-seven, he had two pension plans. One as a US veteran and the other from the Dutch Seafarers union. He had seen the world. He was trained in his profession by world-class professionals. He had lived in Europe and smoked pot to his heart's content. He owned his own business. He had had the Blanchards at his beck and call because they knew that if he returned they would also have to pay. But mostly, he had not died young. He had not been abandoned in a marsh. He was alive. She was dead. He had paid no penance.

The defence had the last word.
Simon got to his feet slowly. He realized he had met his equal in Kathy Crossman. He had put up a very good fight but Kathy had fought with all her skill and all her passion as well. All he could do was ask the question that needed to be asked.
"Michel, that day at the rink…Why didn't you immediately run for help and explain what happened when you realized she was dead?"
Michel's head fell back. Dejected and demoralized, he sighed and shrugged. The jury was close enough to hear the hopelessness in his breath.
"I knew nobody would believe me."

Closing Arguments

Only Claude and Lilly stayed for the closing arguments. Adrienne didn't want to hear Simon and Kathy persuading the jury of what she already knew. She and Xavier waited in Lilly's office. They served themselves a cup of coffee and looked out the window at the Petitcodiac River in silence. The Petitcodiac is the deep, narrow river that flows through the marshes of the city of Moncton. It is muddy and unattractive, but it is extraordinary. Only one other river in the world is like the Petitcodiac and the citizens of Moncton hold a humble pride for their river.

It was low tide. It was empty. There was only a thin ripple of murky brown water on the river bottom. First, there came a gust of wind. Then the birds. And at exactly 3:28, the tidal bore came in. They watched the lone wave roll down the river and follow its course without break, without pause, without care. The river swelled and in a matter of minutes it was full again, its current racing. One single unbroken wave that travelled for miles caused an instant tide. Every day, twice a day. No matter who was watching. No matter what was in the balance. Xavier liked to see the bore. It was an example of nature's greatness and God's indifference.

Kathy began her closing arguments: "He left her there, in the red mud."
Simon began: "Run, Robert. Save yourself."

At four o'clock, it was done. They met in the parking lot for the drive home.
"If they're fast," Lilly warned, "we might just have to turn around and come back. I left a message to call the cottage. I hope René or Jocelyne are near the phone."

It would have been good news if the jury had been fast. But there was no news when they reached the cottage. An hour wasn't enough for the jury to freshen up, eat something, and officially begin their deliberations. Just in case they did receive the call, nobody changed into more comfortable cottage things. They sat around the table in their city clothes eating a lasagna Jocelyne had prepared. They ate silently, looking down at their plates. They avoided each other's eyes, afraid that the lack of faith would show.

Later that night, they made tentative plans for the return to everyday life. It was part an act of necessity and part an act of affirmation. Claude couldn't stay any longer. Jean Pierre was getting hysterical. Adrienne had started taking his calls on the pretext that Claude had laryngitis and couldn't speak. He had landed a contract with an important golf championship and he needed Claude yesterday. René and Jocelyne needed to get the girls home. The school year had started that same day in Ottawa. They would drive back on Saturday morning and stop over in Québec City to see their mother. René would fly back if there was a need. Lilly asked Claude if she'd mind a roomate for a couple of weeks. They made tentative plans to spend a weekend in Barcelona. Xavier also had to return. He'd fly to Montréal on Saturday morning on the same flight as Claude and Lilly, and then transfer to New York.

Adrienne announced she had decided to stay for another month on her own. She was in no hurry to leave. Everyone disagreed. It would be too cold, and she would be lonely and bored, they warned. Come to Ottawa, go to Québec, come to London. The truth was that she preferred not to assume a favourable verdict would be reached. In that case, she wanted to be there.

Thursday was a difficult day. Every minute that passed made a guilty verdict more probable. Every time the phone rang, it was Lilly saying there was nothing yet. Everyone occupied themselves as best they could. Xavier and René prepared firewood for Adrienne, stored the garden furniture in the shed, replaced a broken window, and repaired a ten-by-four plank on the deck.

Friday was Thursday all over again. It hardly seemed possible that after all that time, everyone would be leaving with the issue unresolved. The phone rang once early in the morning. A leak. The jury had asked for more photocopies of Bouchard's autopsy. Claude made an effort not to cry as she informed the others. They were all deeply troubled.

The waiting was difficult. The verdict could come at any moment, like a rock thrown through a window. It was not a verdict but the future they were waiting for.

Xavier needed to be alone. He went down to the beach, gathered some flat, grey stones, and pitched them expertly into the water one by one. He watched them skip and then sink. It was a silly boyish thing that he liked to do.

He sat down on an old log and wrapped his arms around himself in a lonely act of self-consolation. Whatever happened, he had to leave. Life would have to go on one way or another. He had to face the future without Adrienne and without this family. His own choices and the winds of chance had taken him to where he was. Choices and Chance. These were the forces that moved lives.

Michel's time had come. At that very moment, he was preparing for the consequences of his actions. He was not an idiot but an example of dignity. Robert Landry had become a better man. Robert had turned all the bad into good. René had been a fine son - Philippe Blanchard's son. He was accepting the consequences in his father's name. He had kept the secrets and suffered in silence.

Ander had followed his heart and his passions and died for them. Joaquín, still in exile, had become a social worker in the Dominican Republic. He was always helping others. Koldo, only twenty-eight years old, had been elected just the week before to the Basque assembly. He and Adrienne had called to congratulate him together. Koldo's voice had been thick with emotion.

And Francisco Xavier Aramburu Quiroga? The privileged, brilliant, and gifted boy from Bilbao. What had he done? Satisfied his appetites with superficial sex. He found the perfect girl, convinced her to marry him, and then lost her to an empty lust. He used his gifts to create his own wealth and buy bigger and better boats to feel the wind on his face. To sail away into the horizon, never looking back. He closed his eyes and massaged his forehead.

He heard the distant noise of Lilly's car driving down the road and then Adrienne calling everyone to lunch. The thirty-four-year-old man got to his feet wearily and walked over the dune back to the old cottage. He carried a heavy conscience but also the clarity and peace of one who has come to a decision. Something had to change. But, at that moment, it was René who mattered. And Michel. He went to lunch and tried to act as if everything was going to be fine.

Lilly had come to speak to René. She took him to the porch and closed the doors. For a half hour, she talked and René nodded. Lilly wouldn't leave Moncton until a verdict was reached. It was one-thirty when she left. The next two hours were unbearable. At three-thirty, Claude announced, "Listen everybody! To the shower. We're going out for dinner! It's our last night! This funeral is over!"

They were magic words. The Blanchard family came back to life. There was a noisy line-up for the single rudimentary shower. An hour later when the family was ready and congregated in the kitchen and as René was reaching for the car keys on the kitchen nail, the phone rang. They all froze. It was Lilly.

"It's in. Come fast. We're waiting for the judge," she said.

It was a stroke of luck that they were ready. Xavier took the wheel of the van. It took twenty-four minutes for a trip that usually took thirty-five. "Fuck the fine," he said. Everyone giggled nervously. For the first time, they were made to line-up to enter the courtroom. Jocelyne, René, and the girls took the back stairs to Lilly's office to stay close together and avoid the prying eyes of onlookers. Once the judge was inside the building, the doors of the courtroom were opened.

It was amazing how word had gotten around. There were reporters from Halifax and Montréal, courthouse employees, the usual public, relatives of jury members, the McKay family, and the Blanchards. If tension, excitement, and unhealthy curiosity could be considered physical entities, then they were there in great force as well. The room was electric.

The judge took his time. Adrienne's eyes wandered. Was it possible that her father was there in some metaphysical form? In that plant in a pot on the judge's desk? In that breeze that came in through the open window? In that peach-coloured sphere of light reflecting off the lampshade? Maybe. Once the others left, she would go to the cemetery. What would she whisper to the tombstone? What note would she leave with the flowers? "You were right. They locked him up." Or: "I brought him back Papa, like you wanted. Everything's fine. We're all fine."

The exhiliration of the verdict had already worn off. It was Friday. It was hot. The jury wanted to go home. The facts were the facts. "Guilty" was the buzz-word in the courtroom. Would the facts prevail or would the jury trust in faith?

As Adrienne mused, as the journalists shuffled, as the onlookers pointed to Simon and Kathy, Pauline McKay got to her feet and made her way to the back of the courtroom. She was clasping her hands waist high and looking down at the floor. The Blanchard girls didn't pay much attention; they had become indifferent to the McKays' misplaced hostility. Then Pauline stopped beside Claude, who was seated on the aisle beside Adrienne and Xavier. The two sisters looked at her cautiously. What did she want?

"Adrienne. I wanted to thank you for bringing him home. Even if things don't work out…"

But she never finished her sentence. Someone shouted "Please rise." Pauline panicked and rushed back to her place. Claude grabbed Adrienne's hand. Xavier reached over and put his arm over her shoulder.

The jury was seated. Some looked at their watches, impatient to return home. Judge Harris made himself comfortable. He took out his fountain pen and scribbled on a piece of paper to make sure it was working properly. Then he sat up straight, took a drink of water, gave himself a very good and satisfying twirl on his judge's chair, and swept his eyes over the courtroom. Everything seemed to be in order. He waited for the quiet, his eyes rested on Michel for a moment, and then he ceremoniously pounded his gavel.

"Have you reached a verdict?"

"Yes, your Honour," said the foreman.

Simon and Michel were asked to rise. And then Ron McKay stood up.

"Sir. Please sit down," said the judge.

"I would like to stand with my son, if I may, Your Honour."

"You are not accused of any crime here, sir. But your son is. Please sit down or we will have to forcefully remove you from the room."

"I stand with my son," Ron said.

"Please. Sit down," said the judge.

The judge's tone was not aggressive. He was touched by the father's gesture towards his son and smiled kindly. His expression seemed to plead with the man to take his seat and let everyone get down to business. He couldn't believe this was happening on his last day in court. Michel was standing directly in front of Ron. He twisted his upper body in his father's direction. With a concerned look on his face, he said very quietly, "It's okay Ron. Whatever it is, it's going to be okay. Really. Sit down." He waved his hand behind him in a downward motion urging his father to sit. Ron accepted his son's instructions. Pauline reached for his hand and pulled him down gently.

In the meantime, Claude hadn't taken her eyes off the jury. When Michel turned and urged Ron to sit down, she saw one of the three female jurors stifle a smile. That stifled smile exploded like a cannon in Claude's head. She pressed her face to her sister's cheek and, in a whisper that was a kiss, and a wish, and a victory, she breathed, "Innocent!"

"We find the defendant, Michel Joseph Bourgeois, not guilty of the charges held against him."

The verdict was accompanied by one single stunned second of silence. It was a frozen moment followed by a frenetic flutter of human activity. Of life pushing forward. Kathy's head dropped. Simon put his hand on Michel's shoulder but otherwise did not flinch.

Michel put his face in his hands, uncomfortable with his joy. He knew who he had to thank but when he turned to find her, the verdict still ringing in his ears, she had gone.

The nesting doves were still cooing at five in the morning when Adrienne got up and tiptoed through the living room to the porch. Her brother was sound asleep and didn't stir. Xavier was lying on his back, sleeping only lightly. He raised his head as she opened the doors.

"Hi," she whispered.

"Hi. You can't sleep?" he said.

"No."

She sat on the edge of the convertible couch. She held her hands together and smiled at him. She looked worried.

"It's over now. Relax," Xavier said softly so as not to wake René. He crossed his arms behind his head and smiled. It had been a strange but happy night. Deep sleep had not come.

Xavier was leaving in six hours. He knew he would not be back. He was touched that she had come to give him a private goodbye. It was almost dawn. How beautiful and young she looked in her cotton night dress here in her family home. She was like the romantic heroine of an old-fashioned book. How lucky he had been to meet her, to come to this place, and that she had loved him despite everything. She had made his life so much better. He sat up and kissed her shoulder. He lifted her hair lovingly and rested his head in the crook of her neck.

"Thank you, Adri. Thank you for everything," he said and passed his thumb over her cheek. They leaned against each other.

"Xavi, could you stay an extra day?"

He sat up and put his hand on her forehead. She was shivering with cold, but her body temperature was high.

"You're very warm. Are you alright?"

"I'm not feeling well. But it's not because of that. Xavi, I need you for a day. If you can."

"For a day? Only a day?"

"Yes."

"OK."

She took his face in her hands, gave him a kiss on the cheek, and then got up carefully so as not to wake René.

"Does your throat hurt?" Xavier whispered.

"No. I'm just feeling funny. I don't know why," she said.

"It's been hard. Your body is reacting to all the tension. Go to bed. I'll drive Clo to the airport and change my ticket while I'm there."

"No. I'll be okay. We'll go together. Don't tell her I'm not feeling well. She'll worry. I'm going to take an aspirin."

From the next couch, René emitted a loud multi-level snore, mumbled something unintelligible, and rolled over. His pyjamas slipped down allowing his thin, naked bottom to stick out from under the covers. Xavi and Adri both giggled silently.

"See you in three hours," she said.

"Yes. Don't worry. If you need me longer I'll stay longer," Xavier said.

"I know."

True Identity

Shortly after, there was noise and activity around the Blanchard cottage. Early bird neighbours wandered nearby, coffee mugs in hand, observing from a distance but not wanting to interfere in the preparations. They waved and nodded their heads, expressing their satisfaction at the outcome of the trial. They had all learned the verdict almost as soon as the Blanchards. There had been a news bulletin on the radio directly from the courthouse. Everyone had waved in welcome from their yards when René's van came down the road. The neighbours smiled as the happy voices carried into the night air from the Blanchard's deck.

René repacked the car three times. The girls argued over something silly. Jocelyne made sandwiches for the trip. The family set out at eight. René beeped his horn all the way down the road to tease his girls. They had to leave to come back again.

Claude was next. At ten past ten she felt sufficiently prepared to leave the cottage. She looked into the open trunk of the small car Adrienne had rented and asked Xavier where his suitcase was.

"I'm flying out later," he said.

"Oh," said Claude. Then she checked her bag for tickets, passport, and Jean Pierre's new cell phone number. She was gone already. Oblivious to yesterday.

Lilly almost missed the flight. Adrienne and Xavier waited for her at the security entrance. At the very last second, she came running down the airport hall shouting, "Where's Clo?"

"She's inside," said Xavi.

"Last call," Adrienne called out. "No kisses. Go!"

"You?" Lilly said breathlessly to Xavier as she zigzagged furiously through the empty line-up grid. He was standing beside Adrienne in his tee-shirt, jeans, and old sneakers, car keys in hand.

"I'm staying for a couple of days," he said.

"*La hostia!*" exclaimed Lilly with a huge smile. She disappeared through the sliding doors.

Back at the cottage, Xavier took Adrienne into the bathroom, sat her down, and looked for a thermometer in the medicine cabinet. The domesticity of the moment was not how he had imagined a passionate reconciliation, probably because it was not meant to be a reconciliation. Xavier was unsure of Adrienne's pretensions that day, but he knew he was where he was supposed to be.

As for Adrienne, keeping Xavi for a day was simply a physical desire that she did not wish to repress. She wanted to be with him for a last time. It made her sad that she could not remember their last night, the night before the magazines. Paradoxically, she felt that making love with him would give her strength to go on without him. The closeness of the past eight days had played tricks with her resistance.

Adrienne was not completely at peace. The innocent verdict had not chased the dark cloud over her head. She could not help but feel responsible for the upheaval and the emotional anguish she had caused by bringing Michel home in such an abrupt and foolish way. Only Xavi had said she had done the right thing. Only Pauline had said thank you.

She had decided to take two years off. She could live on her savings and on the high rent she could get from her Manhattan apartment. No plan. No itinerary. A beach somewhere for a while. Time with her mother. Brush up her languages. She had always wanted to join Begoña on one of her long, exotic shopping trips to Asia. Another course in Beirut would probably be a good idea. She would think about Patrick's offer. She was not uncomfortable with the idea anymore. She was not naive and she knew she was almost there. Patrick had said he would wait. The Mapa Mundi danced in her head.

But she was sick. Adrienne was burning up with fever, not desire. Xavier put cool towels on her forehead, elbows, knees, and ankles. She started to shiver with cold, so he covered her with a blanket and gave her a warm drink. He knew what to do because he had often helped with Paloma's fevers. The fever abated in mid-afternoon. Adrienne was quiet and disciplined, but her temperature shot up again at sunset. It was going to be a long night.

Sleep finally came. Xavier made himself as small as he could on the edge of Madame Blanchard's small double bed in order to give Adrienne room. She had asked him to stay by her side.

At six in the morning, her temperature was normal. She woke up peacefully while Xavier was still sleeping. She watched him in the pale light of sunrise. He was beautiful. There was no other way to describe him. He was lying on his side, arms crossed over his upper chest, one hand on each shoulder. His legs were squeezed together and perfectly straight in order to occupy a minimum of space. She could see his navel and the soft fuzz of his pubic hair that reached into his jeans. His chest expanded with every long, deep breath. Her Xavi.

"Xavi?" she said softly.

His eyes opened instantly. He reached over to touch her forehead with a sleepy frown.

"Oh, Adri. You look better. How are you feeling?"

"Much better. Will you help me with my shower? Wash my hair?" She passed her thumb over his open mouth, let it play inside his lip, and laughed softly.

That was all he was waiting for.

This was the day.

Wild horses stampeded in his chest.

Not forty-eight hours after the verdict was read, life had resumed its course as on any given Monday morning. However, Simon Hanley stayed on the job for several weeks. He helped Michel unravel the knots of his American citizenship and his Dutch residency with their corresponding benefits and pension plans, as well as his partnership in the restaurant in Amsterdam. He did a good job. Michel didn't lose it all.

Simon had trouble letting it go. He felt lonely, as if all of his best friends had moved away. He drove up to Moncton several times. He was interviewed by the local newspaper. He visited with Adrienne at Crane Road for a full day. He had lunch with Kathy Crossman. He stopped by the Firehouse to shake Robert Landry's hand. Simon couldn't get the beautiful and obstinate Claude Blanchard out of his head. He bounced and bounced on his trampoline, trying to think of a good excuse to go to London and see her again.

Finally, around October 15, the legalities had fallen into place and the case was officially closed. Simon had one last thing to do. Adrienne Blanchard had asked him to personally deliver a letter to Michel once all was over.

"Adrienne Blanchard asked me to give you this," he said.

Michel turned it over in his hands and nodded. He knew what it was.

"Thanks for everything, Simon. Without you, I really don't know…"

They shook hands. Simon nodded and confided to Michel something he felt was true.

"Now that it's over, I can tell you it was a close call. I don't know if we could have won this in 1973."

Simon had always felt respect for Philippe Blanchard's actions.

"You know, I told René I might have done the same as his father. I can understand," said Simon.

"René's a good guy. So was his father. But they were different," Michel said.

"I would have liked to meet Phillipe," said Simon.

"Well, you know the daughter." Michel shrugged and smiled.

"Right. OK. I'm on my way! Good luck, Michel. You know, you've got a lot going for you! And you know where I am."

Simon grabbed Michel's hand again, gave it a vigorous shake, and off he went. Michel watched him from the window. When Simon's car pulled out of the driveway, Michel sat on the sofa, not sure his legs would hold him up. He opened the envelope with mixed feelings. He was reluctant and expectant at once. There were two letters inside.

August 30th, 1992

Dear Michel,

This letter has been transcribed from memory, as the original letter was destroyed. It was accompanied by a medical journal clipping reporting the revocation of Dr. Bouchard's licence to practise medicine, which we have not been able to reproduce.

We are proud of our father and understand the respect and love he had for you. It was his wish that you should read this if he should die before your return.

René

Marie-Claude

Adrienne

True Identity

October 10th, 1974

For Michel Bourgeois in the event of my death.

Please deliver with attached medical report.

Dear Michel,

You have been gone now for more than a year. I would not be surprised to find that you are doing well. You are sensitive and intelligent. You have a mind of your own, but you are discreet and quiet. These qualities must be helping you now. They are a result of your childhood. It was your way of caring for your mother. Not to add to the heavy burden of her struggle to give you a good home. A little boy trying to be a man. You found your own solutions.

When I think of you, I don't think of the terrified young man hiding in my garage. I remember a small boy sleeping in his young mother's arms in the hospital reception. Your mother took a taxi for the first time in her life that day. You were groggy and unsteady after the tonsillectomy. It was too cold and dark to walk to the bus stop with a sick child. That's the day she met Ron McKay. He carried you up the four floors to your apartment.

I remember sixteen-year-old Michel on my doorstep in unbearable pain, holding his arm that was wrapped in dishrags. Again, Ron came to the hospital to pick you up. He was angry. If you had called him, he would have driven you to the hospital like a bat out of hell. You know that. He fell in love with both of you that night he carried you upstairs. He's a good man. I think he suspects that I have something to do with your disappearance, but he keeps it to himself.

I remember you with tears of laughter rolling down your cheeks at those jailhouse jokes I told you as I tended to your burns. I always timed the best one for the moment we removed your bandages. Your arm was a horrible mess. Perhaps the laughter helped it heal so well. We did a good job. I was proud of that and proud of you.

How do I explain my actions to you, to your parents, to my son, to society? I work inside prison walls. I see them come in, young and proud of themselves. Even proud of their crimes. They say, "Hi Doc!" They show me their muscles and their tattoos. I tell them to eat properly and exercise, to buy time with a job, to read, and to stay out of trouble. To work on their parole. But they smile, ask me for a smoke, and walk into the yard like young cocks to measure themselves against the others. Twenty years later, they walk out, old beyond their years, hoping someone is waiting behind the gate. I do what I can to keep them healthy and strong for the day they leave. I fix what can be fixed but the system slowly breaks their spirit. I could not let that happen to you. You were innocent and I cared for you very much.

You see, despite your innocence, I was sure you would be convicted. To me, the choice was clear and I made that choice possible for you. I urged you to escape the law and I used René to help me. My son stood by me. My eldest. My poet. God help me, but I would probably do it again. I exercised my own justice and put both your lives into the balance.

And now I wonder if God will forgive me for stealing his role as the Great Puppeteer. I wandered into his territory. I interfered with his plans for you. I interfered with your life. I didn't have the right to do that. We can only wait for your return. I can only hope that I will see your return.

My dear Michel,

I beg you to forgive me,

Philippe Louis Blanchard

Alone in his mother's house, Michel folded the letter carefully then sat back on the sofa. There was nothing to forgive. He would do it again. It had been his choice. He had desperately and passionately run for his life. Philippe Blanchard had been the wind at his back.

The pink canopy of the cherry trees of Kyoto. The whales swimming along with the ship in the Pacific Ocean. The taste of a freshly picked guayaba in Colombia. Sunrise in Peru. The fish market of Marseilles. The blue and white islands of Greece. His captain's stories. The line-up at half past twelve at the door of his restaurant.

His run for freedom had been a voyage of discovery and growth. His return, an emotional need.

He had lived with a stolen identity, which in reality had only been a name. The language and the memories of the past had never died. Like Adrienne, like Xavier, he carried his history inside him.